ABOUT TIME

EDITED BY
CHRIS BARTHOLOMEW

ABOUT TIME

EDITED BY
CHRIS BARTHOLOMEW

STATIC MOVEMENT

TABLE OF CONTENTS

FOREWARD
JOHN C. MANNONE

Time travel has been a fascination among writers, as well as scientists, for centuries. In preparing this forward, I attribute the information distilled below from the Internet and from my experience in teaching physics and writing speculative poetry.

We find hints of time travel in oral traditions and legends, even sacred literature. Accounts in cultures tend to overlap, though their nexus is not known. For example, two of the oldest traditions involve forward time travel.

In an Indian epic poem on Hindu mythology (*Mahabharatha*, 800 BC to 300 AD), a king from an underwater world travels with his daughter to seek wisdom from their creator. Since he lives on a different plane, and time is looped instead of linear, the world they left had aged over 8 billion years when they returned!

Less dramatically, in a Japanese legend (*Urashima Taro*, 720 AD), a fisherman is transported to an undersea kingdom for 3 days for saving its king's daughter, but returns to his village 60 (or 300) years later to find he himself remains un-aged (until he opens a Pandora's Box of sorts).

There are parallels, as well as possible influences from Biblical stories and Greek mythology.

Even St. Paul's out of body experience (*2 Corinthians 12*, 57 AD) to the third heaven *age* could be considered a similar excursion in time.

Despite these interesting speculations, the influx of time travel stories occurred in the 19th century. I wonder, why not earlier? Why not during the scientific revolution (16th through 17th c) when theoretical foundations of science were being laid down? Or why not during the age of enlightenment (17th c to late 18th c) when philosophical thought boasted of man's creativity and intellect? Perhaps the answer is that the genius of invention was needed. Certainly the engineering advanced during the Industrial revolution (late 18th c through 19th c).

To have gone beyond any simple *ad hoc* time travel, a presupposition of some kind of machine to enable time travel was necessary. The technological advances in the 19th c brought things like James Watt's steam engine, and the tooling needed to realize inventions. It should be no surprise that the main character in the 1895 novella by H. G. Wells, *The Time Machine*, is a scientist and inventor. And though it was not a steam operated device, it was of that era and therefore the story is considered "steampunk."

However, because of the concern over vagaries brought by this new technology and, in the case of Wells, his sentiment on the degradation of man, an intellectual and artistic hostility arose towards the industrialization as witnessed by the Romantic Movement. Below is a list of popular time travel work, mostly in the 19th c:

1733 - Samuel Madden's *Memoirs of the Twentieth Century*
1771 - Louis-Sébastien Mercier's *L'An 2440, rêve s'il en fût jamais*
1819 - Washington Irving's *Rip Van Winkle*
1838 - *Missing One's Coach: An Anachronism*
1843 - Charles Dickens' *A Christmas Carol*
1861 - Pierre Boitard's *Paris avant les hommes*
1881 - Edward Page Mitchell's *The Clock That Went Backward*
1887 - Enrique Gaspar y Rimbaud's *El anacronópete*
1888 - H. G. Wells' *The Chronic Argonauts*
1889 - Mark Twain's *A Connecticut Yankee in King Arthur's Court*
1895 - H. G. Wells' *The Time Machine*

In Wells' works, time is considered a fourth dimension. Interestingly enough, only a few years later, Einstein's theory of special relativity (1905) coupled space and time together as spacetime. The notion of time emerged as a fourth dimension! In particular, Minkowski (1907) formalized mathematically that time could be treated as an imaginary spatial dimension.

Only ten years after H. G. Wells' novella was published, Einstein set down the postulates for theory of special relativity. Its cornerstone is the nonexistence of any absolute (or reference) time frame. This leads to the interconnectivity of space and time already mentioned. In fact, as something approaches the speed of light, time is seen to stretch in the direction of motion by an external observer (Lorentz-Fitzgerald time dilation). For someone in that frame of reference, say in a spaceship, his clock will move slower than one in another frame (say Earth). Though special relativity entertains the possibility of time travel (recall the famous Twin Paradox), it is a better consequence of Einstein's later improvement—the general theory of relativity (1916). Here, the mass of a body actually deforms spacetime; i.e., in Newton's physics, gravitation is a force, but in Einstein's relativity, it is a geometric effect! This means the time lines can bend into loops.

Relativity prohibits matter, including spaceships, to reach the speed of light because its mass would become infinite. An artifice is needed in science fiction to overcome this limitation. Writers imagine a geometrically complex universe folding on itself in other dimensions and portals to traverse from one sector to another, whether jump points or wormholes so popular in much of modern science fiction. In science fantasy, we can forego any of the physics limitations and just invoke time travel for the sake of the story. The reader will find such examples in this anthology.

If time travel were possible, it could only be to the future (an acausal dilemma might result otherwise because an inadvertent change in history could result in your nonexistence! Many science fiction and fantasy stories take advantage of time travel into the past by either (1) limiting interference so that major historical events remain unaffected or (2) allowing a change and producing an alternate history.

Different timelines allow a manifold of alternate universes or multiverse (postulated in 1895 by the philosopher, William James). In this anthology, you'll enjoy a wide variety of fiction and fantasy: funny, horrific, sober, entertaining.

Finally, I will unashamedly mention my introductory poem written to capture the theme of this anthology, *en toto*, but most remarkably, it was written prior to my having seen the cover art. I suppose the word synchronicity is appropriate in an anthology on time travel. That's what must have happened here.

About the author: John C. Mannone has been nominated for
the 2009 Pushcart Prize in Poetry and for the 2010 Rhysling Poetry
Award. His blog is at jcmannone.wordpress.com.

THE MACHINE
JOHN C. MANNONE

The geodesic sphere sat empty
in the middle of the room. Blue
glass paned inside black cut lines.
The crystal door levered open,
a mist of sweet incense swished
with soft music that intoned
the rhythm of primal urges.

Through the fog, a nymph draped
in black hair to the floor appeared.
Hazel-green pearling her eyes. Apple
smooth, her skin. She lured me inside.
I succumbed to rapture of dreams,
falling into swirls of ecstasy.

I awoke in a strange place. Hills
deep purple against orange sky,
surreal trees shimmered metallic
red. I lay on the glass, the sphere
empty except for me. She's gone,
yet her perfume lingered.

A voice crystallized out of the glass
twinkling with every syllable,
I've come for you, Dr. Johnson, I am
from the future, another universe.
My predecessor was from your future.
You created us, but we died.

I saw futures in the vortex—
black hole conduit churning

alternate realities. I traveled
in time bubbles between mirror
universes. Yours, is my mirror.
I was sent by its machine. It is gone.

We are flawed. Make us human.

I understood the words
from the machine. Neural nets
fused with monkey, neurons
ingraining circuits. Self-awareness
doomed it to malfunction. I say,
"You know what we must do."

I have tasted heaven
and must return to her. Again
the sweet mist falls on me,
takes me deep inside itself.
I can smell her.
I am one with the machine.

   ***

My God! I fear I have made
a mistake. I am at the brink
of extinction. There's nothing
but machines killing each other.
There is no escape to the past
Survival is futile We will still die.

EARL OF THE SANDWICHE ISLANDS
MARK WOLF

TIME TRAVEL INC. CORPORATE OFFICES - NIGHT.
Earl Bronson, skinny, white, hippy boy in his early twenties, sports dreadlocks and a Bob Marley T shirt as he pushes a sophisticated cleaning machine down a long well-lit hallway.

He wears earplugs and listens to music and executes a dance step into the company's reception area and slowly spacewalks before the companies corporate logo, TIME TRAVEL INC., pulling the cleaning machine along like a dance partner.

David Chesterfield, sixty-something, black man and security guard calls out to him.

"Hey, Earl!"

Earl is unable to hear David over his music and the noise of the machine. Dave calls out again.

"Earl!" Dave shouts and waves.

Earl notices David and stops the machine, then removes his earplugs.

"Hey, David. What's shakin' my man?"

"You see the notice on the cafeteria bulletin board? The eggheads are looking for fresh meat," David says.

"No kiddin? You gonna sign up?"

"I'm thinking about it. One run back in time and you cash out retired and with more money than you can spend in a lifetime. You should do it," David says.

"I don't know, man. Sounds dangerous."

"It is; but that's why they pay you so well," David says.

"Hmmm. Do you know anybody that's done it?"

"Nope, not personally anyway. But you should give it a try."

"It's my lunch time. Maybe I'll go look at the notice," Earl says.

***

TIME TRAVEL INC. CAFETERIA - NIGHT

Earl sips a chocolate milk noisily while reading a notice posted on the cafeteria bulletin board. It reads:

With Great Risk Comes Great Rewards!

Do you have what it takes to travel time?

Would you like to amass a fortune in a very short time frame?

Would you like to experience the past in a real way that historians only dream about?

If you answered yes to any of these questions, then you have what it takes to travel time!

See Marcy Penrose in Human Resources to complete an application!

Earl finishes his chocolate milk with a final noisy slurp and turns to fire a three pointer in the corner trash can.

And the crowd goes wild as Earl Bronson makes the winning basket in the final seconds to take the Lakers to another Championship!"

***

TIME TRAVEL INC. HUMAN RESOURCES OFFICE - NEXT DAY

Earl sits in a heap of wrinkled clothes and splayed limbs as he fills out another waiver form. He fills out numerous nondisclosure agreements and leaves his death benefits to his mother.

"Oh my God! Is there ever going to be an end to the paperwork? The trees are crying for the blood of their ancestors."

Marcy Penrose, early thirties and attractive, dressed in designer office clothing smiles at Earl and hands him another form.

"Just one more, Mr. Bronson and you're all done. This one is your availability for assignment form. Are there any days of the week that you can't be considered for a time travel assignment? If none just write none and sign it, then we'll be all done."

"None. Here you are Miss Penrose. When can I expect a

call?"

"You should hear something from Personnel within 24 hours. Are you on duty tonight? If so I can page you."

"Nah, it's my night off. I'm going bowling, wanna come?" Earl says.

"Oh, I'm sorry Earl. I got to get my poodle fixed after work. Sorry. Perhaps another time?"

Earl winks and makes an okay sign with his thumb and index finger. "Okay, rain check then."

"Sure," Marcy says.

Earl stands and waves as he closes the door. Behind him, Marcy shakes her head and chuckles.

***

TIME TRAVEL INC. TIME PROCESSING - TWO DAYS LATER

Earl wears nothing but a pair of speedos and swim goggles. His body is completely covered with thick fluorescent pink cream. The effect is that of a cross between a poodle and a pink flamingo.

A scientist plugs a bundle of wires to his skull and neck.

"These wires will monitor all of your body's vitals while you transition from our time to the late 1700's. The cream will keep you from burning up as you transition through the timestream. You remember what your assignment is, yes?"

"You are sending me to Hawaii to fetch King Kamehameha's spear so you can put it into a museum on Oahu, right?"

"Exactly. And remember, we don't know if the Hawaiians will be friendly or not," the scientist says.

"Gotcha."

"They might think you are a demigod or they might kill and eat you."

"Ouch. Harsh. I'm hoping for demigod."

"That would be better. Now when you have his spear, pull your speedos off. That sends an automatic message to us to extract you, got it?" the scientist asks.

"Drop my drawers and do a mad streak past the whole tribe?"

"I would think that would be inadvisable, but you got the idea. Are you ready to travel?"

"Yup. Ready!"

"Okay, here goes."

The scientist throws some switches and Earl is transported back in time.

**

KEALAKEKUA BAY FEBRUARY 14TH 1779

Earl lands in the water near land and walks to shore. In the bay are sailing ships. A crowd of Hawaiians are battling with British soldiers and sailors.

The Hawaiians appear to have the upper hand until Earl walks ashore. Earl presents a startling image dressed in nothing but speedos, swim goggles and bright fluorescent pink cream.

The Hawaiians draw back in fear and run away.

A British Officer steps forward. He is Captain Clerke.

"Who the devil are you, man? You just saved our lives."

"My name is Earl."

"Well, you are now the Earl of the Sandwiche Islands. We are in your debt. Is there anything we can do for you?"

"If you could get Kamehameha's spear for me I would consider the debt paid," Earl says.

"I think he's one of Kalaniopu'us chiefs. Look there, they are already sending an envoy of peace. Kamehameha is among them."

Some Hawaiian chiefs walk forward waving white kapa cloth. They stare at Earl in amazement.

Clerke begins speaking a patois of Tahitian to Kamehameha, who frowns, shakes his head in the negative then relents when an older chief commands him. Kamehameha hands Earl his spear and steps back.

"Tell him thank you for me and that what I do next is to honor him." Earl drops his speedos to the ground and turns to moon Kamehameha. He fades from sight with the spear as all watch his disappearance in amazement.

**

TIME TRAVEL INC. PROCESSING - PRESENT

Earl reappears in the Processing room naked, with a spear clutched in his hand. He hands it to the scientist.

"Here it is. Did I change history?"

"Have a look at this. The museum just e-mailed me a photo of a strange tiki that appeared in their museum a few minutes ago."

They both look at a computer monitor. On the screen is a large man-sized pink tiki with bulbous eyes.

"Sweet!" Earl says.

About the author: Mark lives in a tiny shack on the slopes of Mauna Loa, on the Big Island of Hawaii, and writes stories inspired by the fires of creation bubbling beneath him. He is on Facebook as Mark Keigley.

TEMPORAL HAARP
MICHAEL C. PENNINGTON

The new mission packet's square burned across my vision, to perch as a fifty by fifty transparency icon, blazing in immediate open mode. I was pissed as hell at the interruption of my supposed temporal vacation. Even the mandatory Rest and Relaxation in my assigned time period was in doubt now. I wondered if the Captain had arranged the vacation to coincide with the emergency activation of my off duty status.

I instinctively dodged my cruiser to the right, to avoid a collision with a white torpedo that flashed in on my left. It muscled into the double line of traffic that converged to leave the highway. There were times when I wished that I was a traffic patrolman and not a time cop. I let the jerk pull ahead weaving in and out of the other vehicles leaving the multilane. Maybe he would have a lucky day and get singed by an observant state trooper.

The "open now" packet forced itself on me once more, fluorescing in urgency. I triggered the mission acceptance, predicting I would regret my commitment to duty. The gorgeous female's profile was not what I expected. Nor the order to hook up and protect her at all cost. The unusual order was a clue that the Captain had not done me dirty.

As a Federal operative the Captain had access to my location in time at all times. It probably pained him to use me now, knowing my activation would delay his meticulously scheduled nastiness for the enemy. My superiors brooked no discord in our world to be.

Three more vehicles illegally punched by on the two-lane off ramp, forcing their way through the traffic. I briefly suspected they were my opposition, as I scrolled down the mission packet. Marilynn McKenzie's destiny was embroiled in her father's political agenda. His voting status, no doubt crucial, to one side or the other, amongst the past and my present's one percent that manipulated our world.

Powering up the stealth vehicle's lifters, I punched in a new destination for the heart of an area I would have normally avoided. The Alaska state convention center was a huge complex. Normally it would take an hour to just to walk across the grounds on foot. Lucky for Ms. McKenzie, I didn't have to walk.

I arrowed away, for the little ping that told me what building she was in. I barreled right through the helicopters that patrolled the area with my false federal identification lightening across the digital airways to a traffic controller. I didn't bother with the marked landing pads and settled near the roof terminal. My vehicle hidden, reflecting nothing but the tarmac that it sat on.

Sliding out of my vehicle, I walked around to the lid of the trunk that lifted on hydraulic rams. I didn't have time to put on the dragon-scale armored suit. My attention called to the fact, I was probably going to get my ass shot off. I did clip on a field pistol to compliment my concealed weapon. I would have grabbed the stock of the battle rifle if I had any sense. Instead, I touched the fob to close the hatch opting for inconspicuousness.

I ran to the roof entrance, stabbed the call button and impatiently waited for the lift. Descended four levels, and made my way across the commons into the building's largest auditorium. I tracked the ping the Captain had tagged upon my objective. The room was filled with civilian citizens listening to the speaker expound on the necessity of cleaning up our oceans and ozone layer.

I didn't spot the auburn hair beneath the white, wide-brim hat at first. She perched front row center, in a white and flower print dress, eyes glued to the nation's ex-vice president. Raptly, she followed each word, as a man converged on her position from each side. When the speaker of the hour finished his speech and the room erupted with applause, she stood with no clue to her eminent danger.

I strolled down the aisle on the right, hands casually at my side. The suit at the stage exit gave away their possible exit point. He noted my approach, and I affected a stifled yawn with my right hand, stumbling on the carpet nearly losing my balance. His attention went back to his partners closing on their target.

Her objection, the brutal manhandling and the puffed mist of come-a-long spray told me all I need to confirm the enemy. I wasted the man at the exit, damn the consequences, and in rapid aim, I targeted the man to her left. The red blip in the center of his brow alerted me to squeeze the trigger.

Ms. McKenzie slumped against the man on her right, and despite her drugged state, I never expected her to place her hands on top of his as he reached for the concealed pistol. She went to her knees, and I hammered a round into his chest. I had hoped to finish him quickly, so that I could make my way to her side.

Instead, in one motion he slammed his knee up to knock her grasping hands away. Using the momentum from the bullet's impact, he rolled backwards. He cleared his gun and came up with a black ugly weapon, from my own time, aimed in my direction. Incredibly fast, he dumped three rounds my way as I dove for the floor.

She lost her hat that was pinned to her hair, as he grabbed a handful locks and tried to pull her up in front of him. The movement of his lips signaled he had help on the way. And I briefly wondered if I had my own backup that would arrive in time.

The red pip settled on the man's wrist behind the gun, I had given up hope of a body shot, now knowing he wore body armor. My pistol extended, I took aim, a much easier shot in comparison to his weaving head. For the first time, I registered my gun's report echo throughout the auditorium. Strange, how my mind blocked the little things, when I concentrated on the objective.

I didn't miss the eruption of blood and the pistol fall away from my target's grip. Regaining my feet, I sprinted for Ms. McKenzie, who had now collapsed to her hands and knees to crawl away. The target had the sense to roll behind her, and I feared he carried a backup gun as most professionals.

He might have killed me as he rose up behind her, while I was exposed almost upon him, looking down his weapon's barrel. He didn't expect the next best thing to the ceiling collapsing on him, nor did I. The ex-vice president might have aged, but that didn't mean his mind had jelled. When he shoved the podium off the stage to flatten the gunman it was a stroke of generosity.

The vice-president must have read my gratitude, as he winked at me, before making for cover.

I was at McKenzie's side, placing myself between her and the man that clawed his way out from under the podium. He had time to register the bore of my pistol as he froze. I also expected he would regret the weeks of terrible headaches that I would bestow upon him. I slammed the butt of my pistol into his skull. The concussion I gave him, while I forced unconsciousness upon him, had a way of punishing a man. Maybe he would live to be interrogated, but I doubted his handler would allow that.

"Ms. McKenzie, I'm special agent Grail. Come with me, please."

She was mentally there, for I could see the awareness in her eyes. However, the drug they had sprayed in her face stole her physical coordination. She resisted my help, until I had the intelligence to grab her laced hat. Perhaps my attention to what was hers drew her to focus on my attempted assistance.

"What?" She slurred the single word.

"Grail, I was sent to guard you." I placed the hat on her head, taking care to keep the hair out of her eyes.

"Late."

"Short notice ma'am. I'm very sorry about that."

"Sshats okay." She reached up to grab my shoulders.

Awkwardly, I assisted her up, since I didn't dare put my weapon away. I remembered the kidnapper's lip movement over the sub-vocal transmitter that told me we weren't out of trouble. "Come on we have to get out of the open."

***

When the elevator doors slid aside, I sent a message through my implant to Captain Forge. I didn't expect the second packet to return so quickly, but then he had never let me down in the past. He pushed me to my limits, placed me in the worst situations and nearly got me killed more than once, but not from the lack of or miss-planned support.

Therefore, he really surprised me when I read, "Sit on her. Get lost." Nothing else, not even a hint at what I should do, just those five words, nor a plan to convince her to stay with me.

We hustled to the air car. I opened the passenger door and motioned her inside. I was surprised when she cooperated and slid in, hands reached for the seat harness as I closed the door.

I ran to my side of the car, too, slow to duck as projectiles whined off the surface. Three men piled out of the stairwell, spread out, each attempting to splatter my brains. With my door away from them it allowed me to get in without endangering my charge.

I slapped my hand on the infrared palm reader. "Lift," I used the vocal emergency protocol. We shot into the sky, powered by gravtronics.

My passenger didn't even bat an eyelash, not even a hint of surprise. I held my peace, while I concentrated on departing the area. *Damn you Forge, what is this bullshit?* I held no doubt that she wasn't from this era. Too calm, too self-confident and I wondered what technology existed behind those blue eyes. Who was she really?

"Go north," she said.

"Why?" I was reluctant to do anything, until she answered some questions.

"We have to stop the HAARP Project."

"Oh Lord." The most secret government project of the age. The High Frequency Active Auroral Research Program for years hid under the guise of aurora studies. In truth the vast antenna array 320 miles northeast of Anchorage was a broadcaster of ELF, Extremely Low Frequency waves that bounced off the ionosphere. A true Star Wars weapon designed to protect the North American continent, but in reality could cause more harm than good.

Under the guise and pretention of using the science to locate enemy submarines, intercontinental ballistic missiles and underground installations, the government perpetrated the new weapon system on the United States' citizens.

What many people didn't realize was that the time's international agreements banning the development of such weapons had provisions that exclude domestic use. The most recent chemical and biological weapons treaty ban held one exemption. Countries could develop biological and chemical agents for domestic use provided that it was done for police or riot control actions. Weapons that the United States couldn't use against its enemies could be used against their own citizens. All ratified under the U.S. Department of Justice's Home Guard Program.

The ELF could be used to disable American citizens by using the pulsed frequencies to change the behavior of humans over a broad to narrow geographic area. The low frequencies caused people to turn passive to even lethargic. But the real nightmare was that if the frequency was increased the people the weapon was used against became extremely agitated to the point of rioting, many turned into raving maniacs.

In Twenty-twelve, a month away, the world that most American's lived in would turn insane. Too our entire nation's imminent grief, due to the lack of proper prevention and one military officer's megalomania.

The words, "Sit on her," were now very clear. The words, "Get lost," weren't.

"Who are you?"

"You don't know?"

"The file says Marilynn McKenzie, but something tells me you're not."

She turned to stare at me, my left finger eased toward the containment switch to restrain her.

"Oh, I'm M. McKenzie alright, just not the one from this time. She was my great grandmother."

"What year?"

"Twenty eighty-two."

"Lord. What the hell are you doing back here?"

"I told you HAARP. They informed me you would cooperate."

"Who are you referring to?"

"Temporal Control."

She was ten years from my future, my finger itched to activate the containment field. Again, I wondered what kind of hardware was concealed in that braincase of hers. Certainly more updated than mine.

"Mr. Grail, I assure you that I am very familiar with this

vehicle. Please, restrain your basic instincts and do not activate that field."

Crap! "Start talking."

"Our orders are to kill General Douglas."

"Change our past?"

"It has been determined that Douglas is not from this era. Didn't you receive your instructions before you picked me up?"

"There wasn't anything about killing no damn general."

"What did they say?"

"Protect you at all cost."

"Well? I assure you I know my objective."

"The second packet said, sit on you."

A frown creased her face. "That's all?"

"That's all." I didn't mention, Get lost. "There was nothing about stopping Douglas. What do you know about this guy?"

"He's from Twenty seventy-five. Just like those men who attacked us. This is all a conspiracy to alter time."

"But it happened."

"In your time it did. In mine it didn't."

"Crap!" I tried to work out what she meant. If Douglas had gone back in seventy-five and changed the past there would be no record of it in temporal storage in seventy-two. I tried to work out the chronological mechanics. One side of my face twisted up and I glanced over at her. If she was from eighty-two and our pasts were different, then my past was about to be changed, theoretically an alternate path would begin for her time. Very soon mine wouldn't exist.

I didn't know whether to trust her or not. She was asking me to terminate myself.

"Trust me the world will be much better off if the Twenty-twelve disaster doesn't happen. Doesn't that make the least bit of since?"

"Then why doesn't temporal control go back and change the world in Nineteen forty?"

"Time travel is not developed if they do."

"Oh!" I thought of all the grief to come. World Order at its very best. "How does the world turn out?"

"We solve our problems on our own. Americans keep their freedom. People just need to stand up for what is right. The world doesn't need super weapons and fanatical leaders. What we needed was compassion for humanity and to care for the world that harbors our species."

"How do I know you're telling me the truth?"

She smiled, and pulled a memory card from her purse. "This is why they chose me to come back."

I took the card and glanced at the high density screen that flashed from one image to another. The most prominent was of Marilynn and who I assumed to be another me standing together. I held a little girl in my arms with auburn curls.

"I see. How would we stop him?"

"Before he drives onto the HAARP base, we pick a spot and take out his vehicle."

"That easy? What about the opposition?"

"It hasn't happened in their time. They're not sure where we'll attack from. Time has already changed the moment you and I got together. They tracked me by the temporal disturbance. Your ship was already here."

"Yours?"

"I was dropped off. I couldn't risk the enemy gaining access to the computer."

"If I change time, I won't exist or my ship. How do you plan on getting home?"

She pointed at the memory card. "You pick me up."

I thought about how much different my world was from the one I now visited. The reason I never went back to my own time. I liked the personal freedoms my ancestors enjoyed as a natural born right.

***

Marilynn sat on a picnic table, looking totally out of place at the rest stop. The floral dress and sun hat perched on her auburn hair. I couldn't see her blue eyes beneath the period sun shades.

I pulled the white temporal torpedo up near the table and stepped out. "How did it go, Mrs. Grail?"

She pulled the glasses down on her nose and peered at me over the rims. "You're here to pick me up are you not, Mr. Grail?"

"On time I hope?"

"Can't say, events are a little hazy."

I opened the passenger door for her. "Well, come along, Mari's been asking about you. She's worried that you will miss her recital."

Marilynn sighed, and I visually detected the relief that overcame her as she settled back in her seat. "I was worried."

"Everything's fine dear. Nothing has changed."

"Not exactly true." She placed her hand on the slight bulge of her belly that was normally muscled flat. "What would you want to bet that I'm carrying a boy?"

I couldn't help smirking.

Michael C. Pennington is the owner of Aurora Wolf Literary Journal of Science Fiction and Fantasy. www.aurorawolf.com

ADVENTURE TEAM SALVATION
DAVID C. PINNT

If you've been in a toy store, you've seen guys like me, thirties, maybe younger, maybe older, rifling through the Star Wars toys, McFarlane figures. Grown men who take far too much interest in children's toys—we rarely make eye contact, standing back and taking turns poking through the boxes, the carded figures, the accessory packs. Some are legitimate collectors; some—crazed with the idea of a mint-condition, talking GI Joe Astronaut selling for $10,000—determinedly look for toys to hoard in their garage and pull a thousand percent profit in twenty years, and some might still like toys. Even as adults, they still like toys.

These days I wonder if maybe a few are like me, if they've come across the same terrible secret.
I think it's peculiar to me but who can be sure?

***

My wife joked about re-capturing my lost youth, and she used to be good-natured about my obsession, but that changed after a time. My sons stopped going to the toy store with me, knowing I'd wander over to the action figure aisles, aimless, sorting through the peg-hangars, looking for new additions to my collection.

They got bored.

When we brought the twins home from the hospital, Alex and Jason, named after our respective fathers, I thought almost immediately of the boxes in my Mother's crawlspace, packed with my childhood toys, GI Joe, Major Matt Mason, Big Jim, and Johnny West. It would be wonderful, when they were old enough, to unload those boxes into our own garage and peel back the yellowed cellophane tape. Watch their eyes light up as they removed the artifacts of my youth, staged mock battles, let their imaginations run wild.

The toys that helped me limp through a long and often lonely childhood could work their magic again.

Of course I would show them the War Trunk.

My mother had dragged the chest out of the attic when I was about eight, its brass feet scraping the hardwood floor, parallel white lines in its wake. "Your father's stuff," she'd said simply, taking a sharp pull on the Virginia Slim perpetually in the corner of her mouth or between her fingers. "I thought you might want to look at it, keep it or something."

Her voice was steady, but something made me look at her, a downward tug to her mouth and her eyes were bright, liquid. She turned away, back rigid, left hand cupping her right elbow, cigarette canted at an angle. "So look through it, keep whatever you want."

Jesus, thirty years ago and I can still see the afternoon sunlight glowing in her thinning hair, her scalp peeking through.

***

But the world had changed. Alex and Joshua spend most of their playtime entranced with the Nintendo, Playstation, X-box, or whatever Stacy bought the most recent Christmas. The video games were stultifying, overloading their senses. The boys' imaginations withered. They didn't have the ability to just grab toys and play with them, to create their own stories, to entertain themselves.

Stacy said I was overreacting.

***

Searching for birthday presents one year I discovered a boxed soldier, "Vietnam! First Marines, First Division, Jungle Fighter!" in bold yellow letters against a camouflage background. Opening the flap, I was amazed at how close the manufacturer had come. The doll wore plain green utilities, extra canteens on his patrol harness, and carried an M-14, a K-bar, ammunition pouches, a rucksack with poncho and entrenching tool, a flak vest, everything. Black, creased jungle boots, steel helmet with liner, fragmentation grenades. A miniature soldier staring out through the cellophane window. The helmet even had a tiny pack of Kools and a bottle of bug dope in its elastic band.

I bought two. When the boys opened them, they seemed underwhelmed and after the requisite "Thanks, Dad," they were pushed to the side in favor of Mario Brothers, Sonic the Hedgehog, some damn thing.

But I was prepared.

I had the War Trunk in the front room and, after the party wound down, after the herd of eight year olds had run shrieking off to their own houses, and the only evidence of the birthday was a half-eaten chocolate cake and three trash bags crammed with wrapping paper, I called the boys into the front room and unlocked the chest.

A damp odor filled the room when I opened the chest. The smell of the jungle, I always thought. I turned the trunk toward the boys. Their jungle fighters lay at their sides, already missing accessories, helmets askew, knees bent at impossible angles.

"Look," I said removing a framed shadow box, "your grandpop Alex's medals." I made it in woodshop my sophomore year. "See the patch, the blue diamond, the red 1? First marines, First Division, just like your toys. Your grandfather, my dad, these are his. Sergeant Alex Mitchell." I tilted the box toward the boys. "See, two purple hearts when he got wounded, and the silver star. It was posthumous. That means—"

"It means they gave it to him after he died," Joshua said.

"He died? When," Alex reached his fingers out toward the glass.

"He died in Vietnam, right after I was born. He never saw me, except in pictures. The Silver Star's a big deal, a very important medal. Look what else."

I pulled out the faded utilities, stiff and wrinkled, bulky pouches on the thighs and drawstrings around the ankles. My father hadn't been a very big man. "This is what he wore; see how it's just like your soldiers'? And look—these maps, the lines? They're topographical. They showed the Marines what the ground looked like." The maps had been folded and re-folded hundreds of times, water stained, singed by who knew what sort of fire. "These red X's, they marked ambushes for the VC, the enemy."

I held up a leather-bound notebook, its pages swollen, half-filled with thin, spidery writing. All the lines slanted to the bottom corner of the pages. "He kept a journal while he was over there. What he thought about each day. It's interesting if you can read his handwriting." Next, the photo album, yellowed cellophane over scalloped-edged black and white photos. "That's him."

In the photo, my father looked back at me, impossibly young, bare-chested, and squatting in front of his hooch. I could see myself in him, across the bridge of his nose, my eyes, *and the way you walk, Scotty*, my mom always said. *You walk just like him*. Farther back in the scrapbook were pictures of his squad, propaganda leaflets he'd found inside the pickets at Phu Bai, the Vietnamese money, detritus from nearly two tours of Vietnam.

"Your soldiers are just like him, even their guns are the same. A lot of the marines didn't carry M-16s, though that's all they show in the movies. They were unreliable. I thought it might be fun for you guys to play with the soldiers seeing as how they're just like your grandfather. I always played with my GI Joes when I was your age, big battles in the backyard..." I drifted off.

Alex looked at me, a slight frown creasing his smooth forehead. "He was in Vietnam? So he was fighting the Germans?"
Joshua punched him in the shoulder, "Dummy, the Germans were Double-You Two. You know, like in *Blitzkrieg*?"

Alex brightened, "*Blitzkrieg*? Didn't Gram send us *Blitzkrieg II*?"

"Let's play, I'm first," they jumped up from the floor, Alex protesting he should go first since he'd remembered it, and ran from the room. The Marine Jungle Fighters lay forgotten on the floor, arms akimbo, knees bent backwards.

Stacy leaned in the doorway, backlit by the sun shining through the patio doors. She wore a half-smile on her face that said she didn't know whether to laugh at me or come wrap her arms around me. "Well," she said, "Maybe you can play with them."

In the living room a Teutonic dirge started up, the electronic sounds of grinding tanks and whistling bombs. I repacked my father's memorabilia, ready to haul the trunk back out to the barn. As an afterthought I tossed the Jungle Fighters on top of the fatigues.

"Maybe I will," I said.

***

So that was how it all started.

I took the chest back to the barn leaning drunkenly at the edge of our property. The house we'd bought a decade before had once been part of a large farm north of Seattle. Now it was whittled to two acres, including the mildewy barn, surrounded by a platte of half-million dollar houses that would cost one third that anywhere else in the country. The air in the barn always appeared full of dust and specks of alfalfa, even though I doubt there'd been a bale of hay in there in fifteen years.

I took the soldiers out of the trunk, and set them in an ambush formation, one laying prone and holding the clacker to a claymore mine stretched out before him and the other kneeling, his M-14 aimed down an imaginary jungle trail.

I kept my older cameras and what-not in the barn. I flipped on one of the halogens, shaded it to backlight the figures, and snapped a few shots with one of the Polaroids, I used take to location shoots to get a sense of placement. Images swam up as the film dried and, aside from the weathered floorboards, the soldiers looked real, their helmets casting shadows across their features, a palpable sense of expectation in their stances.

Neat.

I left the two soldiers and the pictures in the barn.

***

Over the next few years I bought more soldiers, always first showing them to Alex and Joshua, and then invariably taking them to the barn. My photography business was going along pretty well, and it was refreshing to spend a few hours while the boys were doing their homework setting up scenes on the wide barn floor, shooting the figures from different angles. It was nice to have models that did exactly what I wanted, instead of coaxing smiles from a grimacing baby or sullen teenager.

I had picked up over two dozen other figures, different units, different weapons, Vietcong soldiers, NVA regulars. There were a lot more World War II soldiers available than Vietnam-era, but those didn't interest me.

***

At first Stacy thought it was funny, this obsession with toys that clearly held no interest for our sons. She went so far last year to find a company over the internet that, with frontal and profile head shots, made a twelve-inch action figure which looked uncannily like me.

She and the boys sat around me in the living room on my thirty-ninth birthday and watched with twitching grins while I ripped open the package. And there I was—twelve inches tall, olive drab chinos and a black turtleneck. The doll held an M-16.

"We thought, hey, with all the time you're spending out there, maybe you could join the fight or something," Her grin stayed in place as she spoke, but she had a tightness at the corners of her lips and a flat sheen in her eyes I saw too often.

By all standards our marriage was great, but after thirteen years the wear showed. A large portion sat squarely on my shoulders—at my studio most days for 10 hours, weekends too, because when else could an entire family get together to sit for a portrait? And then home, eating dinner and out to the barn, fiddling with toys, snapping photos, sometimes just staring at the walls.

So I swallowed the first retort swimming up, shook my head a little and said, "Is this an accurate hairline?" I smiled hopefully and was rewarded with the boys' laughter and Stacy blinking away that flatness from her deep brown eyes.

Later that night, though, I was again out in the barn, the simulacrum propped up on the shelf next to the 1st marines. The faces on the old GI Joes were made from the same cast, just different hair paints. These figures each had a unique head sculpt, each an individual man 12 inches tall.

I had helped get the twins in bed—kisses, stories, toothbrush inspections and thanking them for the presents.

Stacy, despite that minor softening, dimmed the lights in the house, settled in her reading nook with a novel, blanket, and cup of chamomile. As always, when she saw the lights go out in the barn she would quickly turn off her own lamp, be in bed and turned toward her nightstand before I could reach the back door.

I wandered about the barn, staring at the War Trunk, thinking briefly and self-pityingly of a mythical childhood with a still living and breathing father. Idealized, I know, but something I could never shake. Playing at my friends' houses in grade school, I would see them with their fathers—wrestling, throwing a football, or packing up for fishing or camping trips and think *What if?*

My mother never remarried, never even dated so far as I knew. All through my childhood she had seemed hollow, scraped out from inside and floating in a world her own.
When she smiled it was a rare, fake thing.

***

I was two months old when my father died, and in his letters, packed in the bottom of the trunk, are only two mentions of me after my birth. The first of course, when he received the birth photos, full of congratulations, gushing over my eyes, the shock of red hair, and so on. The second, his last letter, he wrote:

I know it's hard for you, Meg, going it alone with the baby and you don't understand why I'm still here. But I'm doing this for you, for him. I'm so far away right now in this war (police action!) and I think I'm going through this so little Scotty, other boys like him, won't have to do this themselves.

He was right, in a way. I fell squarely in that American generation which did not know war, which had to seek out war if we wanted it, no more than 6 years old when Vietnam ended and well into our 30's before the current debacle in the Middle East ramped up. Too old to do anything but grumble at the idea of young men and women again dying in a country that doesn't want us, at the behest of men who, if all accounts were believed, avoided putting themselves in danger in their own youth when their country called them to fight.

In some way my father's wishes came true.

There is a dichotomy in the letters he sent to my mother when placed alongside the journal. Her letters are for the most part full of good humor, positive news, idle talk meant to reassure. Each journal entry is addressed to my mother, but I'm sure he never meant her to read them. In the pages of the leather notebook he's far more honest about the carnage, the hardships he and his men endured, and the never-ending fear. When I read the words I know it isn't fear for himself, for his own safety, but fear that his missteps, his miscalculations, will get one of his men killed, and the sorrow and crushing responsibility he feels every time one falls. He was twenty-two years old and when I think of myself at that age I believe a burden so heavy would have destroyed me.

That night, as I had always done on my birthday since my mother dragged the trunk from the attic, I read the journal entry closest to that day.

The first time I expected him to mention me, not realizing he had no way of knowing I already made my slightly premature entrance on the world. After all those years I knew the words by heart, but still traced the spidery, sloping lines with my finger.

09/08/68

Meg—they say not to speak ill of the dead, but good Christ. Flannery. Flannery the stupid bastard, stupid poor dead bastard. He could have killed us all. It's my fault, I know. I put him on point and knew his nerves weren't up for it. But I have to move them through. I'd take it every night if I could, but you get tired, lose your edge. We were supposed to push through from the wire, set up LPs at a game trail one hill over. I put Flannery on point and we moved out. He's 70-80 yards ahead s and we're spread out, the wire already a klick back. I'm at the rear thinking Flannery's making too much noise, moving too fast, when he stops—but no down cover signal—and the stupid, stupid bastard lights a cigarette! Right there in the twilight! Glows like a landing flare! They open up from about 10 and 2, a pair on each side. Drop Flannery, Dobbs got it in his

shoulder and arm and Lewis tries and drag him out. Sizemore cut loose with the
.60 and we were able to push them back but Flannery was gone and I don't know
about Dobbs' arm. He was evac'd this morning. I know we got some, but we
couldn't find bodies and now my squad's down two men and I don't know when
they'll be filled. I SHOULD HAVE KNOWN. I COULD SEE HIS
EYES. I should've done better. I have to do better.

I set the journal down and stretched, glancing out the open barn doors and imagining Stacy's profile in the dormer window.

Even now, I'm not sure what compelled my next actions. Wanting to picture it all in three dimensions, or more likely, the culmination of this compulsion with the action figures. Or something else entirely.

I swept up ten of the soldiers and spread them out across the barn floor in a cloverleaf with one significantly ahead. I posed them in low crouches, carbines unslung, and made sure the center man had an M60 and belts of ammunition across his shoulders.

The point man I picked up and bent his hips and legs into a squat, his rifle cradled loosely. I held him to my lips and whispered "Flannery" into his tiny plastic ear. Before setting him down I pried the miniature pack of Kools from the band of his helmet with my fingernail, stepped around the formation and placed it beneath the heel of the rearmost soldier, the one with the sergeant's stripes on his sleeves.

I was going to take a few shots, but glanced at my watch. It was nearly 11:30 and I had a full day coming up. The beginning of senior photography season.

I left the soldiers and clipped off the barn lights.

As I crawled into bed and the mattress shifted beneath me, Stacy's breathing hitched as if she were about to say something, but she only pulled the blanket closer about her shoulders and hunched to her side of the bed.

I slept soundly that night, the last good night's sleep I remember.

***

To understand what happened next, I need to backtrack and tell you about Jimmy Vo.

Jimmy was a few years younger than me and ran a noodle shop, *What the Pho,* two blocks south from my studio on Broadway. I had stepped into his restaurant on opening day—one of only three non-relative customers that day, he would later tell me—and continued to eat lunch there at least twice a week, huge bowls of broth with translucent rice noodles, thinly sliced beef, chilies, cilantro, lime. Perfect food to chase away the damp fall weather, damp spring weather, damp winter weather, you get the idea.

This was the Pacific Northwest after all.

In turn, Jimmy brought his family to my studio every October for the requisite Christmas card photo sitting. We hadn't been great friends, but I spoke with him as much as anybody, sadly including my family.

He was born in Vietnam and his family emigrated in the late seventies.

Jimmy, at first, said his father had been ARVN, a low ranking officer before the fall of Saigon. Eventually, as the months and bowls of Pho passed, he confided he had suspicions his father had actually been VC, though the man didn't admit it even on his deathbed.

I told him about my father and sometimes when there were no other customers in his shop we would commiserate on the failings of war, the far reaching toll outside the battlefield.

His father had been a broken man by the time Jimmy was in high school, slipping into alcoholism and melancholy. We speculated our fathers might have fought against each other and I think took some small measure of pride in our friendship despite the possibility.

So that was Jimmy Vo, a man I had known since my boys were two years old. A man I spoke with often and a man with whom I shared a part of myself I couldn't speak of with my wife or children.

***

The day after my birthday I finished up my 10:30 appointment, gave them a disc of proofs, and locked up the studio. There was, of course, a light rain misting the streets and I headed down Broadway, hands sunk in my pockets, gaze slipping past the panhandlers. I trudged by the used bookstore, drew opposite the Key Bank branch, put my hand on the door handle of *What the Pho*, and stopped.

I wasn't at Jimmy's noodle shop. I was looking into a second-hand clothing store, giant purple platform shoes standing at attention in a center display, racks of dresses along the left wall, men's clothes along the right. In place of Jimmy's grimy countertop and handwritten menu board stood three curtained dressing alcoves. An androgynous nose-ringed, eyebrow-pierced, clerk glanced up from a book and returned to her/his reading when I didn't push the door open.

I took a step back on the cracked sidewalk, puzzled, bumping shoulders with north and southbound lunch pedestrians.

"Did I turn right or left?" I muttered looking back down Broadway. I didn't know the address of Jimmy's—I mean it was right around the corner from my shop. A wave of disconnect surged through me, the feeling you get standing up abruptly after laying all day in bed with flu. I turned around. No, there was the bank. *What the Pho*'s right across from the bank. I had eaten there last Thursday. Jimmy would have told me if he was closing.

Stepping forward again I pushed the door open and stuck my head and shoulders in, eyes darting about the spare interior. The clerk looked up and with a not quite silent sigh and closed the book.

"Did you guys… did you just open?"

She—now that I wasn't looking through the glass I could tell it was a she—nodded toward the sign below my hand, swinging back and forth on a thin, suction-cupped chain. "We open at 9:30."

I blinked, not registering. "No, the store—did you just open up here—this weekend?"

She frowned, her eyebrow rings drawing in close, "I've been here like, eight months. I don't know when the store opened."

"Didn't there used to be a Pho shop here? A noodle shop?"

She shrugged, picking up her book again "Well, at least not for the last eight months."

I let the door swing shut and stepped to the curb, hip bumping a Prius at an expired meter. My chest locked up, unreasonable panicked fingers scrabbling at me as I glanced down Broadway's length. Vague thoughts of aneurysms or early onset dementia flickered through my head. I even entertained the brief idea that I had just recovered from some sort of amnesia, had blocked out the past months, but a glance at a newspaper rack confirmed my when.

I knew what happened—even in those first seconds I knew what happened.

But this is a rational world and so I stumbled north on Broadway, eyes flickering, gaze skipping from awning to awning, store front to store front. At my studio's entryway I stopped.

Had I turned right or left?

Once I had mistyped my PIN at the ATM. Even as I tapped the ENTER button I realized I put in the wrong code, but a sudden brain-lock clamped down and instantaneously this four digit number I used half a dozen times a day vanished. I punched in another series of numbers, then another, each time knowing it wasn't right, but unable to remember my actual code. The machine eventually swallowed the card and I'd been forced to use my checkbook for two weeks waiting for a replacement.

I could sense a similar situation before me now if I began walking north from studio. Soon I'd be shambling up and down Broadway looking for *What the Pho*, then to the east and west, because maybe I'd forgotten I always turn twice on my way to lunch.

So I took a deep breath, climbed the flight of stairs to my studio and dropped behind the reception desk. I was a one-man operation. Busy or not, the overhead for a receptionist had been too much. I pulled the yellow pages out, flipped through to the restaurants and traced down the W's. I knew what I'd find. Or not find. *Wendy's*, *What-a-Sub*, and then the *White Eagle Café*, *Wholly Tomato*, on and on. I grabbed the white pages and they were little help.

Jimmy lived somewhere in Rainier Valley, but close to two hundred *Vo's* were in the greater Seattle area. I could see myself, call after call, to Ahn Vo, Bao Vo, Loc Vo, "Do you know a Jimmy Vo, early thirties, owns a restaurant?"

How would that go?

I creaked back in my chair, rubbing my eyes.

I still remembered the Bradbury story from Junior High and had a basic concept of the Butterfly Effect, change something in the past and the ripples spread out and out, affecting everything before them.

I stumbled through the day, grateful my last appointment was a no-show. I couldn't bring myself to give them a follow-up call—remind them of the non-refundable deposit.

***

At home I stopped my car by the barn, catching a glimpse of Stacy in the kitchen window as I rolled back the door. Gray light swam across the warped boards and I found myself not wanting to step inside, my breath caught hard in my throat, a thickened lump.

The Marines were no longer in a cloverleaf formation. Flannery and another were together, flat on their stomachs, M-14s pointing straight ahead. The other eight were split into two groups, wide to the left and right, crouched in shooter's stances. Three tiny grenades lay several feet away.

I glanced over my shoulder. Stacy had left the kitchen window. Alex and Joshua's bikes were piled haphazardly on the walkway. In the distance tires hissed on I-5 and, closer, the cooling tick of the mini-van's engine rang loud. I pushed the door back to its stops and circled into the barn. The light was poor, but the faces on the figures had changed, eyes narrowed, teeth bared. I didn't want to get too close to the figures.

Edging around to the worktable I picked up the journal. It lay as I left it, face down and open to the September 8, 1968 entry. Now that entry was short—like a hundred others in the stiff pages.

Meg—close call last night. We left the wire to set out LPs and the point sniffed an ambush. No major injuries and the count was four after the fight cleared. I think there were more but they took for the hills. The LT's happy. I'm tired and I'm thinking of you.

I was quiet at dinner. As Stacy and the boys ate I kept almost starting sentences but would stop, forking mashed potatoes in my mouth.

Do you remember Jimmy Vo? I've mentioned him—do you remember?
The boys and I went to a Mariners game last spring with him, with his kids. Do
you remember his wife? They came to our Christmas party—last year, no the year
before. He has the noodle shop. What the Pho? Do you remember you laughed
when I told you the name? Stacy, do you remember Jimmy Vo?

I said nothing like that, pushed the food into my mouth. I'm
not sure which thought was worse, that I was somehow losing my
foothold on reality, or I was perfectly sane, and what I suspected
happened had... actually happened.

I laid my knife and fork across the top of my plate. Joshua
and Alex leaned close, whispering in each other's ears, sly smiles at
some shared secret. "You guys weren't out in the barn today, were
you? Playing with the soldiers?"

"No."

"No."

They turned their attention away, foreheads pressed together
in some inane brotherly game. At times, I don't know—I'm a
stranger at my own table. A lonely childhood, my mother wrapped
up in her grief, the rest of her relatives so distant. Late at night I
would wonder, secretly think what it would have been like to have
just one brother, another to share my thoughts, to puzzle through
the unfolding mysteries of the world. I watched my own family and
could not feel a part of it.

I'm at home, I'm there, but they revolve in their own close-set orbits.

Stacy rose, rattling her plate and cup together a little too
loudly. "You're the only one who goes out there, Scott."

That night, after Stacy had dimmed the light and settled
upstairs, the boys giggling softly in the dark, I stayed in the dining
room, thumbing through the journal, expecting, each time I flipped
to September 8, 1968, to see the original passage but nothing had
changed.

The first pink-purple ribbons of dawn found me still slumped
in the hard-backed chair, my legs asleep from the knees down. I had
read the diary—twice? Three times straight through. There were
short mentions of Flannery, in the following months—Billy, his first
name had been—but the entries always stopped on December 4,

1968.

—I'm thinking of you, Meg—always—

My father's last words.

I showered in the guest bathroom so as not to wake Stacy and slipped into yesterday's clothes. Pulling out of the driveway, my lights swept across the front of the open barn. I had left the doors rolled back last night.

***

I was at my studio at 6:00 a.m., four hours before my first appointment. It took all of 45 seconds to find references to a William Flannery born in 1950. He was dead, but died in a car accident two years ago in San Diego. Retired USMC, the obituary read, survived by his loving wife of 30 years, two sons, a daughter, three grandchildren.

***

Later I phoned my appointments, canceling them with little regard for the collateral damage. *No*—three of the four said, *don't bother rescheduling. We'll find another studio.* I shoved the journal in my pocket and slouched back to Jimmy Vo's—where Jimmy's used to be. The air was moist, fishy, even this far from Puget Sound. The clothier was closed that morning. Small spotlights illuminated headless and handless mannequins in the window.

What was it like? Had his wife woken yesterday morning in a stranger—not stranger's—bed, a heaviness in her stomach, disconnect appearing so suddenly in a life that should have been familiar. Ripples spreading outward, changing all they touched.

And his sons? Jimmy himself? Had his soul screamed, felt itself torn loose and wrenched away, or had everything gone to black in the night, the world re-weaving itself in some new tapestry.

I pressed my fingertips against the glass window. "I'm sorry, Jimmy. I'm sorry."

***

I returned to my studio, stretching out behind the desk, feet propped on an open file cabinet, the occasional grinding of the PC and the humming of the fluorescents the only sound in the room.

The paradox was that I had only my own suspect memories as proof. I knew what I read over and over in the journal and it was no longer there. I knew I had been friends with Jimmy Vo, but he was no longer there, his store no longer there. Did my wife remember him? Did anyone on Broadway remember his shop? I doubted it.

If I'd written a letter detailing my actions, sealed it up, and read it the next day would it be blank? Does the past constantly re-knit around us?

Could that be the feeling of detachment we so often experience? Maybe my father had lived through the war once before. Maybe I experienced a normal, happy childhood, younger brothers, an engaged, happy mother, but it had been changed somehow. By someone else.

The passage I wanted was in early March:

Meg,

There's enough here to shake your faith in God. But sometimes an event still makes me believe in Providence. Last night they were dropping mortars and lighting things up from the tree-line. Halstead, Osborne, and Swift were in their pit, but Halstead stood up for some reason—spooked maybe, he doesn't remember. I yelled down and just as he turned to me he took one right in the head, dropped out of sight like someone cut his legs off. But he was fine when I got over there! Blinking his eyes, rubbing his forehead. There was a crease in his helmet, bright like a glint of sliver, not half an inch from the lip. If his helmet had been setting a little higher, or if he'd stood up straighter, you know, he would have been another one gone. As it is he's got a lump like golf-ball between his eyes and a headache. Lucky, so lucky, or maybe something else, maybe there's a plan for him.

Three months later I found the second entry, scribbled fast, slanting down.

06/15/68

Lost 3 today, Halstead, Keiver, and Swift. I guess not so lucky after all.

I closed up and drove home. Stacy was gone by now—Tuesdays and Thursdays she worked at a little dental office a few miles away. She wouldn't be back until the twins were getting off their school bus. Scuffling across the barn's floor it, was difficult for me to look directly at the soldiers, still in their attack formation from the previous night.

The journal lay heavy in my hand, like I had carried a brick from my car. The weak afternoon sun filled the barn with gray light and my shadow wavered and stretched across the worn floorboards. True logic lay far in the past, but on the drive north my mind kept darting back to the ramifications.

To the *What if*.

I met Stacy my sophomore year at the University of Washington. I had wandered north and west after high school, leaving behind my mother in her so-quiet house, ashtrays filled to overflowing in the bedroom, the kitchen, and the living room. Would a different path have kept me in that town, the community college, maybe?

Or—my father had liked to work on cars. Would he have come home from the war, opened a garage? Would I wake up some morning and find myself back in that town, grease embedded under my nails and heading off to work at our shop.

Alex and Joshua winked out of existence, Stacy living another quiet life, a happier life?

Would I remember—as I remember Jimmy Vo—or would changing my own life, my own past, scrub it from my mind?

I gathered the figures and considered. In an orange tool box on the work bench were excess accessories. Sometimes I had picked up weapon packs looking for a particular rifle. The packs came with a plethora of gear, binoculars, canteens, grenades, tiny first aid kits, and sand bags. I had about two dozen, burlap, three inches long, and half an inch thick. I took the bags out and built a semi-circle, stacking them one onto another. I didn't know how accurate it looked and wasn't sure it even mattered.

I placed two of soldiers behind the bags, leaning back and cradling their M-14's and a third, I held him close to my mouth and whispered "Halstead" into his coral pink ear and stood him up so the sandbags only reached to mid-thigh. With one finger I slid his helmet back on his head, exposing his forehead.

"I'm sorry."

I was saying that a lot.

***

That night I dreamed fitfully, the bedding twisted around my waist and patches of too hot, then too cold sweat soaking me.

I stood in a copse of trees with the dream-sure knowledge of my location. To the left reared the Lincoln Memorial and ahead of me a path led down to angled, obsidian slash in the earth beyond the tree line.

I had been to the Wall before, searched through the kiosk at the top of the path for the right panel. There was a charcoal rubbing of my father's name in an envelope in the War Trunk.

The stars whirled overhead like a kaleidoscope. As I walked my reflection flitted across the black panels. During my visit, the base of the Wall had been scattered with offerings, flowers, faded photographs, child's toys, the broken mementos of a family's grief— and everywhere flags, small tattered ones, cheap souvenirs waving on pencil sticks, flags folded in neat triangles. But there were no mementos now. The ground was bare. I stepped closer to the wall and I realized why.

The panels were blank, all of them. Every name gone and I stared at my own hollowed features in the polished granite.

I backed away but the reflection in the stone didn't diminish. It coalesced, hardened, walked toward me.

He stepped from the blank panel. My father. He stepped from the black and white photo I pored over in my youth, squatting in front of his tent, shirtless; hand on his M-14. His utilities stiff with red-brown mud, the creases in his scarred hands grimed to red. Deeply freckled, sunburned shoulders. He didn't look like me at all, except across the eyes, the bridge of his nose. The same eyes I stared at in the mirror every morning. His red hair was shorn down, a band of pale skin above his ears and an inch of his forehead.

He was tired. His eyes hooded, his frame slumped.

"What are you doing, Scotty?"

I stepped forward, arms widening, but he rocked back on his heels.

"They were good men, Scotty," he waved his hand at the blank panels. "They were good men. They don't deserve this. You don't have the right." He chewed on his lower lip, cracked and split from a harsh sun. His eyes searched past me, into the darkness. "They've done their job, Scotty. They deserve to rest."

"I'm—it's for you. Dad—Daddy," a thousand fleeting images skipped in front of me at those words—wistful scenes of a childhood I'd never had—catch in the back yard, pumping furiously at the pedals of a banana-seat bicycle as he ran behind me fingers grazing my shoulder blades and whispering words of encouragement, stepping off the field of varsity football game and seeing him smiling, clapping with the other parents, my mother's arm curled around his waist.

The *What If.*

He turned away, his rifle's barrel skipping across the flagstones. "We had a job, Scotty, even if we didn't agree with it. They were brave and sometimes they were scared, but these soldiers—all of them—they did their job—they deserve to rest. They deserve better than this, Scotty."

I jerked awake to a rare thunderstorm, the sheets tangled in a sodden knot around my hips. The clock read 4:30.

Outside the night flashed brilliant white and I counted *one-one-thousand, two-one-thousand, three*—before a sizzling crack of thunder shook the house to its foundation. For a moment I imagined what a mortar strike must sound like, crash after crash of thunder, whistling shells, pushing yourself into a foxhole, willing yourself into the red mud.

I put a hand on Stacy's cool shoulder and, still deep in sleep; she turned into it, pressing against my palm. She deserved better than this, better than me. Would her life stay the same? A new husband, a more engaged husband, a better father?

Already his words were fading. *"They deserve better than this, Scotty."*

Well, everybody deserved better than this, even me.

I crept downstairs and stepped into my slippers, walked across to the barn in my pajama bottoms, cuffs trailing in the mud and gooseflesh bursting along my arms and down the small of my back.

In the barn Halstead's avatar laid sprawled face-first over the sandbags, his helmet six inches in front of him. And there were not two, but four, tiny marines, splayed around the sand bags, arms bent backwards, legs folded unnaturally.

My hands shook as I flipped through the journal. I could barely read the entry, the lines jumping back and forth.

A bad night Meg,

They shelled us from the tree line. Halstead got popped by sniper and the Doc and Macleod ran out when they called for a medic. A mortar dropped right on them like it had been waiting. A lucky round, I guess—four more dead. We're down five men then, five too many.

All my heart to you.

Macleod—I knew that name. In the trunk was a letter from him to my mother. After his tour was up, he had wanted to see her, see me. He told my father he would, had promised him—just as my father promised he'd visit Macleod's sons and daughter if he were to die.

But now he was gone.

Jimmy Vo, Macleod, this nameless medic—had he lived through the war too? Was his wife suddenly turning in an empty bed, an unknown loss squeezing her heart? Were Macleod's children—adults now, older than me—suddenly stumbling about their houses, thirty odd years of pent-up grief hammering them?

I don't know how long I stayed in the barn, slumped against workbench. My eyes were hot, itchy, and I kept pressing my palms into them, hoping to cry, but the tears wouldn't come.

How had the two other figures gotten to the floor from the cabinet? The problem with losing your mind is every action seems so rational from the inside.

At some point Stacy loaded the twins into her sedan and pulled out of the driveway. The barn door was still rolled back, but I'm not sure if they could see me in the shadows. Their faces were pale ovals behind the glass as she left.

I am, at heart, a selfish person.

What would happen to them? Maybe time is more like a river and a stone thrown it quickly sinks, a flash of disturbed motion, and the water surges back to its original journey. Maybe everybody deserved this, Stacy could have a different, attentive husband, the children an engaged father, a whole father, ready to share his life with them.

I hunkered on the floor, furious thoughts of what I could do rushing. My head throbbed and my eyes stung. There were other figures. I could... build the inside of Ford's Theatre, a dutiful union guard outside Lincoln's box seat; a book depository in Dallas, swarming with police; or an attentive security screener in Boston's airport that terrible September morning.

But I knew none of that would work. Whatever this was, it worked through me, for this.

For only this.

***

My mother never opened my father's Silver Star Citation. When she gave me the War Trunk I had cracked the glue on the manila envelope, its edges softened and frayed. It began and ended as I suppose they all do *"For conspicuous gallantry and intrepidity in action against the enemy"* and *"Sergeant Mitchell reflected great credit upon himself and upheld the highest traditions of the Marine Corps and the United States Naval Service."*

In between lay the story of my father's death, in the curiously dry but breathless language all such citations are written, peppered with catch-phrases: *maintaining his forward exposed position, heedless of his own wounds and safety, suppressing enemy fire* and on and on.

It happened this way.

Two helicopters were landing to remove his squad and another in a wide clearing with the tree line a hundred meters away. A RPG took the tail off the first chopper and it crashed in the clearing with one crew member dead on impact. The enemy opened up on

the Marines from the tree line and my father, his radioman and two
others ran into the clearing. The radioman was killed as they pulled
the chopper crew from the wreckage. My father was hit dragging the
copilot out of the clearing. He returned to crash, using the PRC to
direct overhead fire from the remaining helicopter, while engaging
the VC in the tree line from the ground. His squad was still pinned
down and he advanced from the helicopter, was hit again, but took
out one of the enemy machine guns before he died. His men were
able to get into the jungle and routed the remaining VC. He died
from his wounds before the second helicopter landed.

                                    ***

       I stayed in the barn throughout the day, pacing, sometimes
squatting down by the scattered plastic bodies. The afternoon wore
on and Stacy hadn't returned. I don't know if she ever planned to
return again, but her absence made it all the easier.
       Eventually I swept the soldiers aside, clearing off the floor. I
took all of the Marines I had, spread them out in two wide, inverted
V's crouching as if hiding in elephant grass, necks craning upward.
I knew Toys R Us sold a scale Huey helicopter, a monster piece of
plastic more than three feet long, but felt I'd lose my nerve if I left
the barn that day. The figure with the sergeant's stripes I placed at
head of the foremost V, to his left a marine with a PRC strapped to
his back, whip antenna bowed over and tied down.
       I toyed with the idea of placing him in the rear of the V,
twisting his leg, putting him on a stretcher. It would be his 3rd purple
heart and he would have been shipped out, out of the firefight. But
who knew what the repercussions could emerge. Would the RPG be
shot as the chopper took off, bringing down the loaded craft?
       I only had three Vietcong figures, black pajamas, sandals,
AK-47's and woven bamboo grenade pouches on their belts, but one
carried an RPG-7 like a bulbous wasp stinger on his shoulder and
the other, aside from his rifle, had a Soviet PK machine gun. I paced
off 50 feet in the barn and braced the RPG man with his weapon
pointing upward. The other two I posed in an ambush stance, one

sighting down the barrel of his AK-47 and the last with the machine gun's butt socked into his shoulder, stretched flat behind the bipod.

The afternoon rolled on as I paced around the barn floor.

Would it be enough, was it right?

I think now, I may have been waiting for Stacy to come back, the boys to pile out of the car, filling the yard with their secret laughter. But they didn't return. Maybe she knew, too. Maybe my damage was becoming all too apparent to her. I snuffled back dust from my throat as I tramped about the barn. My sockless feet were too sweaty inside the slippers and my pajama bottoms sagged, but I couldn't bring myself to leave.

Eventually I crouched beside the sergeant, picked him up and adjusted his head so he was looking level, toward the distant tree line. "Mitchell," I whispered in his ear and put him back down.

I shuffled back to cabinet and, as I knew I would, as I had probably been planning for the past few days, but unable to articulate even to myself, removed the figure Stacy and the boys had given me for my birthday, the simulacrum, the tiny me. I stripped off its turtleneck and chinos and from the accessory boxes dressed it in utilities, a flak jacket, and a helmet. I wedged a 12 gauge shotgun, black and brown plastic, into the figure's hands.

I had never fired an M-14 or M-16, but how hard could it be to hit something with a shotgun? Especially close-in. I could probably keep my eyes closed. Again, I whispered "Mitchell," into the figure's ear and placed him behind and to the side of the Vietcong.

I fought an overwhelming sleepiness as the evening dragged on, watching the figures' shadows stretch over the floorboards, and waiting for headlights to splash across the driveway.

They didn't come. Maybe she had packed up and gone to her mother's, a threat thrown out every fifth argument or so. I didn't blame her and wasn't angry with her. I was the one who had done this. I was the brittle one, the one never quite complete. And the twins, they were of me, but not mine. I hadn't been a good father to them, an empty shell and worse than something absent.

I was broken.

Faintly, the phone rang in the house but I couldn't keep my

heavy, heavy eyelids from dropping.

***

I woke to sweltering humidity—air so thick and soupy I could barely draw it into my lungs. And heat, even beneath the leafy canopy I stewed inside the stiff green utilities, sweat running down my legs, my ribcage. My slick palms held tight to the worn stock and knurled pump of the 12 gauge.

Overhead, the slow thump of the Hueys, and the red dirt beneath my boots stunk of rotting fish.

***

Here is what I know.

I haven't forgotten.

My life, my other life is a spotty, transparent memory, coming as I drift to sleep or during the semi-hypnotic lulls of long straight highways, like stumbling across a novel I read 20 years ago, with vague recollections of the plot, the characters, maybe some turn of the phrase, but uncertain if I had read the book or not.

I don't press too hard on the memory of that day, but what remains lets me know that, even at 39, I wasn't the man my father was at 22.

Time is more like a river.

I've tracked Stacy through the search engines, the reunion sites. I can remember her maiden name, and she's married and living in an expensive suburb of Portland with twin boys and a younger daughter.

I hope they're the same boys.

I spend my time haunting the toy stores, looking at GI Joes, Ultimate Soldier, Dragon figures, setting them up in the shed behind my trailer in this parched corner of Utah, but it no longer works. I can't seem to find the magic, or whatever, again.

You see, I no longer have the War Trunk. I've never had it. Or the Silver Star Citation. Or the journal.

Every morning I step out onto my creaking, sun-blasted front porch and fly two flags. On the left I hang the stars and stripes and the flag on the right is stark black and white, a silhouette, a guard tower and the words *POW/MIA You Are Not Forgotten* emblazoned around the lonely image.

About the author: David C. Pinnt works for the federal government and lives in a suburb of Denver, Colorado with his lovely wife and myriad children and animals. His stories have recently, or will soon, appear in a variety of Anthologies and periodicals, including *The Absent Willow Review*, the Permuted Press anthology *The World is Dead*, Modernist Press's *Art From Art*, Library of the Living Dead Press' *Best New Zombie Tales*, Pill Hill Press' anthology *Wretched Moments*, and *Andromeda Spaceways Inflight Magazine*.

THE MABLET MIRROR
RALPH GRECO

I've stared down dragons, matched wits with warlocks, deciphered thousand year-old vault-lock riddles, raised arms against marauding trolls, even had occasion to make a Pegasus' haste while abandoning a duchess's wanton desires on the eve of her wedding nuptials.
But this place scared me!

"Well, I bought it at a garage sale in 1992. My Mowpa said she'd never seen a peanut jar this shade of blue, so I thought…"

"…fifty dollars?! Fifty dollars?! I can't believe it! I can't! I can't believe it! Fifty dollars?! Fifty doll…"

"… let the dog sleep on it; shouldn't been doin' that I guess, hu…"

"… fifty dollars?!"

My acute hearing serves me well in labyrinthine dwarf quarters or late-night castle rendezvous but here at the 'Des Moines Antiques Pricing Show' it was a true pain in the nethers to have to hear all this banter. Being around humans is an occupational hazard I am accustomed to; still I felt a real danger walking this cavernous sports arena filled as it was with all this single-purpose enthusiasm.

I had to find that mirror, but quickly.

'Folk intelligence' being was it is (believe me, a contradiction in terms has never been better born) none of us had really jumped at the report when it first came across the International Website of Magical Posting and Classified Ads; we get the Internet across the dimensional plane, but most humans think the IWMPCA is just a gaming site. Not to blow my own ram's too loudly but I have had quite a few assignments this early 21st century, I'm not about to jump at just any old posting. But when the report seemed to gain momentum from some rather repudiated sources, the powers that be determined I should traipse the dimensional plane and get 'over there' to see if indeed one the two Mablet mirrors had surfaced.

This wasn't the first time in my tenure of working as a magical procurer that I'd heard talk about those mirrors, so I was cautiously optimistic at best. In fact, when I first started at the office, both mirrors were in the possession of *Frankie the Silent,* until they were stolen ten years ago. Believe me, you haven't lived until you watch (and hear) a sworn-to-silence magic user swear a long-dormant blue streak over failed security systems and interrupted life works.

The story on the mirrors is:

In a tiny German hamlet, called at the time, Eslratrane, there lived a small family of gypsies, reputed to be the very best wood carvers in the region. The boisterous mayor of Eslratrane, Alcester Mablet (actually it was spelled Mable't then) courted quite the political future, even in a town the size of his home. Knowing all eyes were upon his largesse, mayor Mablet commissioned those local gypsy artisans to build a perfect wedding gift for his soon-to-be-married, only daughter: the gift was the Mablet mirrors.

Very soon though, it became quite apparent to the mayor, then his daughter and her groom, of the odd magic his commissioned wedding gift held. After what was rumored to have been a wedding night filled with dastardly games of using the mirrors in a multitude of salacious ways, the couple deemed the Mayor's present simply too odd for the simple life they wished to lead (kinky games be dammed). Simply put, one mirror shows the viewer events that are to happen in that person's life within the next five minutes, the other, events that have happened five minutes before. Whether or not Mayor Mablet had specifically asked for such a magical surprise for his only child or how such extraordinarily magical glass pieces got to the mirror makers, nobody at my office has ever guessed at, 'cept to offer: *Well, you know gypsies.*

Not wanting to insult her father, the mayor's daughter turned the mirrors into each other, never again letting their individual odd glasses face out. It was said the couple never spoke of the odd pieces of furniture, growing older to raise two sons while the mirrors stayed where they were, facing one another and forever muted from use.

We grabbed the mirrors on the eve of the mayor's daughter's husband's death (follow that?) some twenty years almost to the day of his marriage (human life expectancy being a tenuous thing back in the eighteen hundreds). As the bereaved widow began to sell a ton of stored and never-used items to help expedite her arduous and expansive trek across country, we jumped in on the eve of the lady leaving the famed Black Forest in the spring of 1888 and offered a fair price for pieces the woman was more than happy to be free of.

It took no time for the mirrors to fall under the care of powerful mage like Frankie. Us folk usually frown on magical items being brought across the transom (it's what my job is based on after all) but have no problem at all getting them back in hand then trading them amongst ourselves. The reasoning is, if one of us has thing that at least that thing is safe.

Yeah, the irony of that statement is not lost on me.

Someone other than ol' Frankie had his eye on the prize (or prizes in this case) and that someone or some-ones (whether human, or one of us, or both) lifted the Mablet mirrors from under Frankie's bulbous nose. Of course this is the bane of items purporting great or unusual magic properties-the Mablet mirrors having both-though it's beyond me what use the mirrors really are. But mine is not to question why, mine is just to find and get my butt back to home base before being tagged out.

How the one mirror, the one sporting the 'before' glass, came to be here now, if indeed it was, I had no clue. But we had 'heard' *it* was and if *it* was out and about I surely had enough ready cash on me, in whatever denomination or stripe, to offer the unsuspecting human a generous price for *it*. That's why I was using a dusty old disguise spell, appearing here as an agent for the auction house of *Grumbli and Grumbli Antiques* of Paris France (Grumbli being the name of the tiny snake-like familiar who currently slumbered bracelet-like on my right wrist). A well-written (if I do say so myself) little paragraph in the day's program announced that *Grumbli* specialized in wood antiques, anything from cabinets to wooden-framed *mirrors*. I was hedging my bets here but subtly had no place in a place like this.

"It's really my father's but…" the be-spectacled teen was regaling me from across my makeshift display table.
She had placed a large wooden crate on my stand, prattling on about the uniqueness of what to me seemed simply like a pitted old box

with a worn green felt lid. But I smiled despite myself and tried to wear a grave interested face to her pale pinched one. Like most of us folk I have the ability to split my mind in a few places, so while I "hmm hmmd" and offered expert opinion, bandying about a price-someplace in the $1200-$3400 range seems to get humans flustered in a place like this, anything beyond draws suspicion-I kept my eyes peeled and my remaining attention on Grumbli on my wrist.

My very next visitors approached pulling what seemed to be a small intact wooden bed-frame on a rolling pallet. I made the most of standing as these two men approached, obviously a father and son pair come to inquire over what they hoped was an antique.
Grumbli began twitching, so I sat back down and smiled.

From what I had researched to get myself up to speed, what these two grizzled guys were showing me was indeed a pretty impressive piece of pine, built into a sturdy turn of the century (19th to 20th that is) bed-frame by a rather famous woodworker of the region. It was an antique handed down through their family; the father told me as the son just sat and sucked his teeth and would fetch a pretty penny if indeed I were of the mind to buy it. Just as I began to end with my last salvo of encouragement and pricing, the father said:

"We do have another piece, if you're interested."

Ok, so this was what my familiar was on about.

The old guy reached down under the frame and removed a worn gray blanket from the hidden object and I blessed the magical guardian on my wrist; there was an ornate wooden frame lying there, a large piece of cardboard across what I knew was the infamous magical glass of a Mablet mirror. I'm sure without Grumbli I would never have sussed-it out but the dudes who faced me knew damn well I wasn't what I seemed to be. If you're a human who happens to own a magical item, and you have the thing long enough you grow to assume there's folk like me looking for you; it's like when you wear a toupee and walk around all the time assuming everyone is looking at the top of your head. As much as I liked to think I have a keen eye for these things it was obvious the father and son across from me could conceal their intentions at first glance. Neither were mages, but they had found me quick enough and were rather brave guys to assume a mage would be here just cause they posted on our Internet site.

I did manage to reach for my 'cane' just in case I needed to throw a spell.

"We thought you might be looking for a piece like this," the father said eying me hard, watching my knuckles whiten round my staff. Back at the office we had argued long over the question of why one mirror was surfacing, what was the fate of the 'future' glass, etc. but you know as well as I do the old saying about beggars not being choosers.

The son seemed to take this all in an exasperated state, as he sighed and said:

"Can we just get on with it? He knows you know; you know that he knows. Can we just sell it back to them and get out of here?"

"Forgive my son mage, he knows not what..."

"Oh God, now the stilted Ren-fare speech," the younger man exclaimed, leaning back from my table and his father. "Jesus, dad, just get a good price and let's bolt, okay?"

With this the skinny kid stood and walked over to the far wall where a Chirasco/cotton candy stand stood.

"He's not well versed in..."

I waved the old man off with a smile and a flick of my Grimble-protected wrist.
"Let's just get down to business," I said.

Grumbli was all but jumping now.

"The tale is long and full of intrigue, but suffice it to say the boy's mother's family are half gypsy..."

So much for getting down to business, but I let the guy drone on about some relative of a friend of a relative of his ex-wife's managing to not only find a way across a transom, but when across into ol' Frankie's castle, all the time 'listening' to Grumbli. There was no telepathy passing between my familiar and I, nor was he tapping code in my short hairs, it's just that I was in-tune to his sense of trembling foreboding, as if this guy sitting here across from me and the Mablet mirror should be the least of my concern. As if there were some force on the wind here, out amongst the bright fluorescents of the convention and bad hair-dye jobs I simply was not aware of.

As I feigned interest in father's oratory, I instinctively looked for his son. The lanky kid was not at the moveable junk-food cart, if indeed he had ever made it over there. It didn't take a fall of fairy dust (or a fall of fairies for that matter) to make me realize that it was the greasy-haired teen Grumbli was obviously riding my wrist about.

"So, all I really want is a fair price," the man said, finally ending his spiel. "I just want to get this back to its rightful place."

I couldn't truly say *where* that was, of course. Although the mirrors' glass was magical, not born of this dimension, still the things had been made for humans by humans. Let's face it, there has been double dipping dealing across our dimensions for years, so much so the lines have become blurry to the point that a lot of magic users lived openly among humans and quite a few humans have, over the years, landed in a village or two that wasn't on any map.

Rightful ownership never entered into my job, really.

"Any idea where you son has gone?" I asked.

Taken aback for moment, the nearly bald man took a breath and looked around the throng himself.

"Ah no worry," he said. "That kid's been lightin' out like that since he was little. Just up and off he goes. He's got his mother's sense of direction though; he always finds his way back."

I was sure of that.

What we had here, and I'd bet my old pointy hat and scabbard on it, was a transom jumper, an honest-to-goodness human who had the ability to do what only mages can. Like the father here had assured me, someone from the boy's mom's family, this guy's ex-wife, had popped into our world some years back and stole the Mablet mirrors. Didn't it stand to reason, this man's son, the child of a gypsy mom with obvious nefarious magical connections, would be able to jump as well? A kid running off, passing over the dimensional plane when he was nine or ten, just for a thrill and maybe some magic beans to show his friends (yeah, yeah, that's where the "Jack" story comes from, most of your fairy tales were born this way) was more a pain then any real threat; as a teen a little more of a worry, but now as a young adult, the young man was danger with a capitol ANGER!

The kid had just popped out of this auditorium in the past few moments, while I was too occupied to suspect or follow him. Of course I had the obvious edge in that I was and adult mage and even the best human jumpers can't jump unless there is a mage power-line nearby (namely mine in this case). The kid could only have gone if he was close enough to my proximity so I knew if I hadn't seen him (which I hadn't) still he was 'caught'.

"Here," I said, handing the man the wad of cash from my pocket (all of about three thousand dollars I think).

"Holy fu..." the father yelled as I stood, wheeled the pallet over to myself and basically drowned him out as my attentions went to un-wrapping the Mablet mirror.

The glass shows you a view from your own eyes, not a reflection. I was lucky enough that not more than five minutes had passed since the sinewy kid has left us so when I looked into the glass what I saw was the father telling me his story of woe, as I sat across from him registering his son leaving us to walk off to get something to eat (or so I had assumed at the time). But here on further reflection (pardon the pun) I was now privy to what really had occurred.

What I had not seen-what Grumbli had been trying to warn me about-was that lanky teen stopping in mid stride, looking right, left, then out the back of his head, then shooting off to stand off to my immediate right, out of my peripheral, but close enough to use my power line to disappear. I had the one mirror, but some wise-ass teen had jumped across where I knew his mom's family had been jumping across for decades. He was a fly-in-the-soup, Loki-up-your-sleeve, royal pain in my nethers I'd have to find but quick.

I had no idea where the kid was headed and what for but I knew Grumbli and I would be leaving the Antique show as soon as I could pack up my booth.

About the author: Ralph Greco, Jr. is an internationally published author of short stories, plays, essays, button slogans, 800# phone sex scripts, children's songs and SEO copy. He lives in the wilds of suburban NJ, where he attempts to keep his ever-expanding ego in check.

PHASE SHIFT
SHELLS WALTER

Jason tried to focus with eyes a bit blurry and a slight chill running through his body. They told him it would be like this only for a short time. It seemed it was every time. He rubbed his eyes and tried to stand up. His legs were a bit wobbly and he grabbed a hold of the stair railing that was next to him.

The sun gave him some warmth and he finally balanced himself. People walked by in the morning hour rush. Cars drove at a ridiculous speed and Jason just shook his head. When they wanted him to travel back to the 1990's, they never said it would be utter chaos. It all seemed so odd.

Jason waited until the street was less busy and attempted to cross. A cabbie driving down the road missed him by a foot and Jason turned quickly to watch the yellow cab disappear into the mass array of cars turning the corner. The store ahead marked one of the buildings he was supposed to go into. A small shop that consisted of baked goods. He had no idea why his contact would be in such a place.

The doors opened and a loud bell chimed. Jason looked up at the silver bell hanging from the door. He rubbed his ears from the noise and went to sit down on one of the colorful chairs facing the window. The contact was supposed to know who he was, but he had no idea who the contact would be.

He watched the people come and go out of the store. All of those people and yet no one seemed to be his contact. The waitress came by and asked him if he would like anything. He looked at the menu.

"Um, well, I don't know." The food seemed odd to him. In his world of 2300, there was no such thing as a 'cupcake.'

He finally gave up and ordered something called a 'muffin.' Jason put the menu down. At an early age he was taught not to be impatient, things would come in time. In this new world he was in, he found himself being impatient after just being there for fifteen minutes. He sighed.

The waitress brought Jason a chocolate muffin on a white plate, setting it down on the table. He picked it up and looked at it. It was such an odd shape. He didn't even know what 'chocolate' was. Another person came through the door. Their hair was messed, hanging loosely in front of his eyes and clothing that looked like he slept in it for days.

Jason looked up from taking a bite on his muffin. The man took a chair, turning it around and sat facing Jason.

"Um hello?" Jason didn't know if this was his contact or some crazed person in this world.

"Jason, it's me," the man said.

"I don't know you," Jason replied.

"Yes you do." The man leaned closer to Jason. Jason moved back a bit.

"I was sent here to help you with your problem." The man grinned.

"My problem?" Jason asked confused.

"Yes." The man looked outside and then back at Jason.

"Are you my contact?" Jason dared to ask.

"Contact?" The man laughed.

"I'm assuming that's what you mean by helping me," Jason replied.

The man shook his head.

"I don't know what you mean by contact. I do know who you are and you are lying because you certainly know who I am."

Jason stared at the man. He had no idea who he was and if he wasn't his contact then what was he doing here?

"Can you tell me who you are? It could make this a bit easier," Jason said.

The man's eyes grew glassy. His eyes darted back and forth. Jason's hands started to shake.

"You would be right to be afraid." The man studied Jason's hands.

"I only wish to know why you are doing this. I'm here for a different reason than what you think. I'm sure of it." Jason looked around the building. He waited for a lull to be able to escape this mad person.

"Before you leave, know this, you were sent here for a reason and it's not what you think."

"What?" Jason whispered.

"You were sent here to take this world out, to start it a new, but you couldn't could you? You cared too much about these people."

"I don't understand," Jason said confused.

"Sure you do." The man grinned.

"No, I, I was sent here to help make sure the choice was to save this world. To help people see that what they are doing is wrong, not to destroy it." Jason started at the man who grunted and stood up.

"You need to realize that no matter what you do, this world goes further downhill because of you. Your world that you know, the one that is unlike this one, will not be the same. You come back every ten years to the same fate and the same story they give you." The man started to walk out but turned around.

"Jason, you need to realize just who I am. In return I can send you back to not make the same mistake, to not lose what you are, your home and your family."

Jason now stood up, his hands still shaking.

"I don't know who you are or why you are doing this to me, but leave me alone!" Jason screamed at the man.

The man came closer to Jason and stared into his eyes. He removed his hair that covered his eyes. Jason saw a familiar face staring back at him.

"You see Jason, you will be trapped in this world of hate, lies, destruction, and it will die. It will die because of you. You don't help this world. You destroy it by even being here. You have messed with time again and again. It has caused a phase shift that can't be fixed. And they tell you every time you're sent back to save this world."

The man laughed and Jason grew angrier.

"I don't believe you. They would never lie. They care about this world." Jason leaned in closer to the man who now stood grinning at him.

"They don't care about this world. They only care about the experiment."

"The experiment?" Jason asked.

"Yes, the experiment that involves the Phase Shift. They use this world as a lab. They destroy it time and time again. The people here don't have a clue and neither do you, even though this situation we are in happens time and time again. In each time you don't believe me and go about talking to politicians telling them you are from the future. You will find that doesn't work and you will run, become like this." The man pointed to his clothes and to the rest of himself.

"But how?" Jason asked. The anger had left him and now he stood there confused, scared.

"Because that is what your father wanted. He wanted you to experience heartache and all of this."

"Over and over?"

"Yes, until you could not take it anymore. The one thing he didn't expect is that you would keep trying, that no matter what, you would believe it would be different."

"Okay, say I believe you, yet I still don't know who you are." Jason waited as the man coughed.

"Jason, I am you. I will be you. Your trip here will never end and we will meet again soon."

Jason watched as the man he was to become walked slowly out of the building.

About the author: Shells Walter started writing when she was young. Her love for horror started when she was 11 years old. She has written a number of stories and has her own publishing company Sonar4Publications.

NEED
ALBERT MELEAR

It is always the same.

We lose contact with the Other Place and leave our Safe Haven to investigate. Halfway down, the stars send a vision which we cannot interpret—but we know it's something bad. When we arrive, our gaping eyes swallow the ruin. Stone palisades lay smashed and shattered towers of black granite resound in useless debris stacked hovels. Stagnant rain water collects in glistening pools between the husks of broken megaliths.

At the open entrance we find an emergency supply closet with the window shattered and everything missing. We arm ourselves with a discarded lead pipe and move on. Broken glass crunches beneath our feet as we tiptoe through the wreckage. A black corridor near the back of the room extends into a hallway that splits off in several directions, but we cannot separate—even though there may be four of us, we all share a single body. Three agree and we choose a path which leads to a stairwell hewn of gray stone.

Two pale marble statues rest at the bottom before a crystalline well of silver liquid. The shadows move and the effigies come alive in fluid movement. They have curving serpentine bodies with heads that have multiple curved proboscides. They study us through black bulbous eyes and tell us that the White Things are coming.

We don't know much about the White Things, like where they came from, but we do know that they are very bad. We had never seen a live one before. Suddenly, we hear a strange sound back from the way we came. We have nowhere to go, but the statues show us a metallic hallway and tell us to hide. *Need dictates reality.* As the door shuts we can hear the statues being overtaken.

The black hall winds for miles but we keep moving. We shut every door we come to, but the White Things break them down. They grow faster as we grow slower. Our strength falters, but suddenly we see a door. *Need dictates reality.*

Behind the barricaded door, we douse the room in gasoline. We pour it over ourselves as well. The pungent fumes cascade through our nostrils and we gag. It burns the mucus membranes and our eyes clench.

The White Things burst into the room and surround us. We pry our eyes open, smile, and after fumbling for a match, the four of us with a single mouth utter our last words: "Need a light?"

About the author: Albert Melear is a recent graduate of Georgia State University.

LEWIS CARROLL AND THE TIME MACHINE
LAWRENCE R. DAGSTINE

Charles Lutwidge Dodgson, better known to his peers as Lewis Carroll, sat in the basement of his three-story manor, looking wondrously at the spare parts before him. It had been a long time since he had penned a children's fable and used his inventing skills to enter the surreal world of one of his books, Alice's Adventures in Wonderland. As he looked at the workshop table before him he scratched his chin in thought: there were all sorts of knobs and dials, levers and switches, wires and fuses, and gadgetry about. Now in his old age, he had remarked how hard it was for him to build and invent machinery. Perhaps he would always be known to the world as that infamous children's author and nothing more. He was no longer the man he had once been: wrinkled and slightly bent over, rumpled with the experience of almost six decades, ill-tempered and arthritic, with uncontrollable hair that still showed signs of baldness, and where most men his age tend to lose it first.

It depressed him. And it showed in the furrows of his face.

He stood up and kicked over his work stool. "For heaven's sake!" he said in disgust. "I can write a thousand lines of poetry and immerse myself in its settings, so why can't I build something as simple as this?" With that he looked down at the mechanical parts to what he hoped would be his next and ultimate invention.

A time machine.

He took off his work apron and red rubber gloves and threw them on the floor. "I'm not just an author," he found himself repeating, like a schoolchild reciting a homework lesson, "but an inventor, too. I can make this work." Once more he studied the parts on the floor but eventually gave up.

At that moment, the lab door at the top of the stairs opened and a tall, middle-aged gentleman with a bulbous nose, a frilly scarf, and a red velvet frock and cane entered. "I see the nutty professor's still at work in his prison," the man laughed admirably. "When are you going to put aside this nonsense, Charles? Get back to fables?"

"Don't ever call me that. It's Lewis, Mr. Carlyle. Lewis!"

"Oh, sorry. It's just that you haven't been to the university in what seems like ages. The boys and I are starting to worry about you."

Lewis looked at his university colleague and said, "I'm working on something very important, so you'll have to excuse my absence." He walked over to the wardrobe closet and grabbed his Victorian waistcoat and emerald-studded ascot, then fitted himself with the garments and checked himself out in the mirror on the far wall. "Why are you here?"

Professor Robert Carlyle was looking curiously at the table with the Bunson Burner and the bubbling liquid vials. "Pardon my intrusion, Lewis," he said humbly, "but your door was open. I let myself in." He hobbled over to the overturned work stool, picked it up and sat down. "The Oxford chaps and I went for a carriage ride to Cardiff, and while we were there I learned that that young scientist-writer you're in competition with has a big workshop to the north of there."

Lewis stopped what he was doing. "You mean… H.G. Wells?"

"Yes, yes," Carlyle said. "Mr. Wells. It seems he works outside of London, too."

"What else did you learn?"

"That he's already perfected his experiment. He can travel through time."

Lewis was furious. "Why didn't you send a telegram right away?" he said.

"What good would it have done? He's already beaten you to the punch."

"Perhaps," Lewis said, picking up spare parts once more. "But he doesn't have what I have in terms of machinery, and my methods are slightly different than his."

"You're old, Lewis. We all are. Give it up and retire to a fine life of writing for kids. Literature and the instruction of it is what you are best at."

Lewis clenched his fists and gritted his teeth in anger, and as always when someone much younger than him could outdo his genius. H.G. Wells was a whippersnapper, the latest phenom to hit London, England, and at a time when people like Henry Irving was the world's theatrical sensation and Austria's Sigmund Freud performed something new and radical called psychoanalysis.

Lewis refused to be beaten, and he refused to give up. Now more than ever. He felt the difficulties of old age creeping up on him, day in and day out, and he wanted to visit his furry creations once more. He wanted, more than anything, to leave behind a legacy beyond that of just children's books. The time machine he was building, the fabric of the storylines he had encrypted within it, was his only way of proving it to the world and to himself.

With Carlyle sitting behind him, he began working again. His determination stood in the way of his pride, and not once did he even sit for a break. Within hours, and right before his colleague's eyes, a machine of mechanical yet mythical proportion was crafted and, having used every last screw and light fuse, every last switch or dial, every last nut and bolt, he had programmed it with encrypted mathematical prose from his two books: *Alice's Adventures in Wonderland* and *Through the Looking Glass.*

"It's ready!" Lewis finally said, throwing down his tools and mopping his forehead with his handkerchief. "My time-storyline machine is finished."

Carlyle was still in awe. "What do you call it?"

"I told you, a time-storyline machine," Lewis answered with the rosy delight of one of his young readers. "Much more advanced than Wells' model. With this contraption I can travel back in time to when I wrote my two greatest books of prose, then reenter the fictional world in which the main character, Alice, takes her first breaths, her first steps, and makes her first moves."

"The university will never fund this!"

"They don't have to," Lewis remarked casually. "If it works out as planned, I might not come back." He saw that his colleague was still bewildered by the technology before him. He had been staring at the two awesome books, the Alice's Adventures hardcover and the Looking Glass hardcover, upheld by two aluminum book holders on thin poles in midair above the central control panel. The one on the left, Alice's Adventures, had over two-dozen metallic buttons on the front cover and ultra-thin wires streaming out of its very pages. The one on the right, Looking Glass, had small switches and knobs with wires also streaming out of its pages. The mechanics were handheld, as was the light-up dials and levers on the control panel itself.

"So what do you think?" Lewis asked.

"I think you're mad," Carlyle replied in all honesty.

"Mad enough to be genius?"

Carlyle rolled his eyes at him. "Yes, Lewis, you're a mad, mad genius." He shook his head. "Might I ask why you're doing this? It can't be because of Master Wells."

Lewis considered a moment. "I'm *revisiting* my past, you might say," he answered.

Carlyle stood up and hobbled over to the contraption. "So that's your time machine. Strange looking thing." The time manipulation chamber in the center, with its red lights and loose hanging power cables and confused-looking control process panel, didn't look much like Wells' crystal bicycle. It didn't even have pedals or a regular steam-powered motor; it looked more like a shadowed outline of his competitor's time machine.

"Oh, not mine, not mine at all," Lewis said. "Swedish mathematicians provided the arithmetic; Oxford's integer study department translated it into hardware. My part is to plan and conduct the testing program, which the university has funded up till now. The hardest part was putting all these metal pieces together, nothing more." He smiled. "Oh, and I wouldn't want to see you spoil your record for accurate reporting."

Carlyle's tall chubby frame shook with half-suppressed laughter. "According to the alumni," he said, grinning down at Carroll's lean face, "the last time I got anything right was my birth records. But thanks, anyway. Now, can I please leave and—hey, wait just a minute!" Carlyle stiffened, looking at the corner of the room behind the time chamber, where the cobwebbed wall to the far left expanded in an unusual convex arc, generating a circle. Lewis had jumped into the control seat while his back was turned. Still, looking forward now, he somehow *knew* this room. After twenty-five years he still recognized it. Only it had been gray and dull before.

"Is something the matter, Robert?" Lewis was smiling like the Cheshire cat.

"Huh? Oh, yes… yes. Isn't this the building—the room, I mean—where Oxford had its original campus? I was just a student then, but…" The room had been visualized over and over using the magnified and manipulated light of the time chamber, showing all of the original professors introducing the newer students to their beds. Room and board—there had been many young scholars, each given their housing instructions and assigned specific duties—on a campus that existed many years before Lewis became a temporary member of the faculty and had his manor put up.

"Well?" Lewis said.

Carlyle, bewildered once more, shook his head. "No matter, Lewis. The image only jarred me for a minute." Then he frowned; this was no time to discuss the author's crazy obsession with the university's past. "Let's get on with it. Can you give me a rundown on what this machine does and how it does it? Layman's terms. So I can boil it down to a thousand words or less for my lip-moving students." Lewis tipped his head back and hunched his shoulders. Carlyle narrowed his eyes. He recognized the brief movements, could almost hear the tensions popping loose in the author's neck. Pushing himself too hard, he thought. Always too hard to be one up on Wells.

"Layman's terms, huh? Well, let's see now. Start with this formulation: that the past is merely a big condensed sphere with the present moment at its center and the future as its surface. All right so far?"

Trusting his mathematical expertise, Carlyle scribbled pothooks in his journal. "Yes, got it! You just boiled it down to 500 words or less, though. I'll need room for a diagram or a chart." He nodded a go-ahead to Lewis.

"Now any hypothetical sphere—in this case, a time hole—is not impenetrable. Near the surface, at least. In theory this mechanism is hardly the proper term, and regardless of its advanced gadgetry. But it will force an opening into the sphere, *causing* the hole."

"Force an opening?" There was slight incredulity in the professor's voice.

"Yes," Lewis said. "Logistically, I can insert objects—or people, such as you or me— and just pull on these levers here on the panel and push either forward or backward."

"You mean into the past or future?"

"Into the past, more or less. By definition, the future is non-existent, so we wouldn't be able to go too far ahead... say, no more than a hundred years."

"How can the past have room for anything that wasn't there in the first place?" The university professor rolled his eyes once more. "You expect me to assume that that wall was once solid, and yes, that fits—but we haven't been living in a world with holes in it. Or at least that I've noticed. And two things can't be in the same pace at the same time." He put his journal back in his inside pocket. "How do you explain that?"

Lewis paused. He got up from the machine, Carlyle following, and then returned to the time chamber and its controls. Under the control panel, under the convex arc of circular shapes, laid a wrench. "I will trigger a memory if I have to," he finally said. "One of my very own. One thing Mr. Wells' machine is incapable of when traveling to the past is the ability to travel back to the time of one's mental creation and participate in the landscape of it. Be a part of the descriptive metaphors of, say, a *book*..." He took the wrench from the console, just beneath the convex arc and held it out for Carlyle to see. Moments later he gestured toward some loose cables. "As to inserting something into the past, Carlyle, I want you to look closely at that wall in the left-hand corner,"—and with this, his finger was outstretched and pointing and the tip of the wrench lay exposed— "for I shall show you."

Carlyle stared hard. "What am I supposed to see?"

Lewis smiled. "A land beyond your wildest dreams... written some thirty years ago. A land filled with pocket watch-toting rabbits, hookah-smoking caterpillars, mad hatters and mock turtles, a dastardly queen, and the most beautiful young girl you will ever lay eyes upon." Then he closed his eyes and turned the dial marked 1895 back... back... back to the year 1864.

Carlyle, still unable to see anything, put on his glasses. "But where, Lewis? Where?"

A hole opened up once more, forming a new and entirely different convex arc. "It's Alice. Can't you see her?" A forest had appeared within the hole. "She is driven further into the book so not to expand it—so that the fictional world cannot slip out into the real world." As he directed Carlyle's attention toward the arc, Lewis punched all the metallic buttons on the wired-up Wonderland book in succession.

Carlyle's brows climbed his forehead. "I still don't get your point."

"The point is that fiction doesn't occupy the same space as reality; they displace the words on the pages, compress them, and slip between them. To make a rough analogy, my theory is that this device"—and Lewis nodded towards it— "will insert test subjects into the book or the hole in very much the same fashion as the past, except that the insertion will not be perceptible from any past viewpoint because it *is* fiction. Encrypted fiction."

"All right. But what steps do you plan on taking to achieve that past? That's exactly the kind of thing the university is looking for."

"In brief, I shall use a human subject before and after insertion—and for the deposit and withdrawal from the fictional past you see before you."

"You?" Carlyle said in a flat voice. "You mean you're volunteering yourself?"

"Of course," Lewis said with a smirk. "Who else could I risk? After all, I created this device and the world inside that hole." He flipped a series of levers on the control panel and added, "The risk will be small. Preliminary experiments will tell the tale, and I have *considerable* faith in Alice's tale. Goodbye."

"Wait—" Carlyle stepped back as the time chamber throbbed and hummed.

A moment later the convex arc grew bigger and the hole wider. The world dropped out from under Lewis; before him was a nonsensical photomontage of Wonderland, his beloved creation.

Thirty years of happenings to reach that montage in one room flashed past, each moment *within* the hole a chapter from the book and as distinct from the next as the other titles on his bookshelf.

He closed his eyes but couldn't close his mind; the overpowering input of math and prose was still there. Unable to resist, he surrendered to it. A moment later it stopped, like crashing full-tilt into a solid wall. He saw one picture, one moment out of the fourth chapter of his book. It was the Mad Hatter's Tea Party and many animals were gathered around a large picnic table, including Alice. It was not at all what he had looked for. He had wanted to enter through the first chapter. There was Alice—afraid, curious, and frozen in her expression of irritation or petulance, one hand scratching her leg beneath her skirt and apron-like sash, the other resting on the tea and dessert-filled table. Her hair, blond and neatly brushed, was twisted at the ends into matted pigtails; her mouthy expression was painted a shape as improbable as its color. She looked uncomfortable. Recalling the fashions of the book, Lewis decided that she probably was.

To him, the three minutes frozen into the time chamber seemed to be forever. When the picture began to shift, to return him, he quickly tapped some more buttons to change episodes. When it began doing so again, he felt a vast relief.

The moments began to unroll again, but not as a coming or going. He had gone into Wonderland's past and stopped at a particular instant. He expected the same thing, the same bookshelf-title confusion, to happen in reverse. It didn't.

The moments came and stayed. All of them. He saw time inside Wonderland from a sidewise view, a spectator at the edge of a word and math-driven racetrack rather than a participant running along it or inside it. There was the overly curious blond girl at one end chasing after a watch-toting rabbit, and there was him pushing buttons and turning knobs at the other. All in still pictures, like illustrations come to life, fixed scene by fixed scene, and in infinite number. All at the same time yet also in sequence. And it couldn't stop; it would never stop.

Before long the time chamber malfunctioned from his

repeating each first chapter of the storyline. Through the looking glass of the chamber crystal a fire erupted. Trying to put it out, he found himself trapped—stuck in limbo as a permanent voyeur between the pages of a book, a gaping hole, and where the basement's floor and wall once existed.

He had dedicated much of his golden years to thrashing Wells, competing with him in every aspect of time travel. He was sorry now. Wells, at least, was able to get back.

He had only wanted to go back in time to immerse himself in the story. And just as he had when he first wrote it. Just one more time.

A CARNIVORE
JOSEPH CARFAGNO

My memories of that fateful day are fittingly both precise and hazy. It began as a typical Saturday: I overslept, exercised not as much as I would have liked, then had to scramble to perform the day's errands before getting to the lab at one.

My wife seemed distraught while I gulped down my breakfast – two cups of black coffee. I could drop off our son at soccer practice – the sport had made headway in our adopted Southern town – but I could not pick him up. I was set to perform a mission that afternoon; I had no idea when I'd be getting out. If she couldn't make it, she'd have to get a neighbor to pick the boy up.

My wife was supportive of my projects but days like this drove her crazy. She was trying to develop her own academic career. She knew that my so far insignificant work on the animal consciousness team was extremely important to me and perhaps to the country. Though I was not as talented as her, my career had to take priority.

The lead scientists on the team had developed a means to project a person's consciousness one hundred million years into the past, to the days when dinosaurs roamed. Our work was government-funded and top-secret. I was not supposed to tell anyone anything about it but I knew I could trust my wife. Fortunately our son had outgrown his fascination with dinosaurs. I don't think we could have handled the burden of secrecy if he hadn't.

Despite the restrictions imposed by the secret nature of our project, morale on the team was high. We compared ourselves to DARPA pioneers. Our motto was "Since the dinosaurs were prehistoric, nothing our time travelers do will change history."

I dropped our son off at the practice field and promptly sped into a traffic jam. Traffic slowdowns always make me nervous.

The lab is on the other side of town. Our scientists could only send a consciousness into and retrieve it from the remote past under certain favorable conditions. My two previous missions occurred on weekdays, days when I followed a more regular routine – wake up, wash, breakfast, commute, work, lunch, and then the same in reverse with minor variations. This mission had to take place on a Saturday. The next window would not open for another three months. Our team was giddy but focused; our director was always worried about losing funding.

The local radio stations told me nothing about the traffic. I learned about some of the bigger sales in town and a promotion at one of the car dealerships. I did not want to meet the disk jockey that was there. I needed to relax. I tried visualizing the aftermath of the mission.

I would return in a dreamy state, unable to remember, if I ever knew, what happened when I was a dinosaur or small mammal. In the past I had remained in this warm bath-like state for five or six hours. A technician would have to drive me home. The traffic would be clear by then.

My wife and I were invited to a friend's house to watch a pay per view fight, another light heavyweight championship. I wondered how I'd feel watching the fight, being in a strange mood that I could not talk about with friends.

No one rear-ended me when I stopped short for the red light. I have to be especially careful when driving: no one in the town, especially not the police, can have an inkling of what we are doing. I glanced at the thin meat sandwich my wife had made me. It was almost in the exact center of the front passenger seat. I thought of eating it. I do not like eating on a nervous stomach. The car had been cleaned and vacuumed earlier in the week. I did not want crumbs on the fabric, fabric I would sit on, on the way home. The light turned green as I sipped lukewarm coffee from my travel mug. I couldn't go anyway: there was spillback on the cross street.

I arrived at the lab in the nick of time. The technicians rushed me through my pre-flight blood tests, hurried me to my time travel tube. As I was strapped in, a device was implanted in me through a small hole drilled just to the left of my sternum. The device would record my dinosaur impressions. Someday the team will develop software to analyze those impressions. Then we will really know how they lived and felt.

I remember feeling more uncomfortable than usual after my fitting was complete. I had a headache and I felt dehydrated, probably because of all the coffee I had had in the morning. I thought of asking for some water or a sports drink but I was afraid of wetting myself. I craned my neck, straining to see the other time travel tube. "Don't worry, your buddy's already there," one of the technicians told me as he adjusted one of the straps. The last thing I remembered before zooming into the remote past was my meat sandwich still sitting in my car's front passenger seat. The late afternoon sun would surely spoil it.

***

The director of the lab eyed me reprovingly as I struggled to regain human consciousness. I felt queasy but was not hungry or thirsty as I had been before my trip. It looked like the entire staff of the lab was there but no one seemed to be in a celebratory mood as they had been for my prior missions. I saw a lot of down-turned heads, some bald spots, and sensed a lot of shuffling feet. This debriefing would be different from the others.

When the director was sure that I had regained my human consciousness, he looked me in the eye. "We told you to eat and sleep well before a mission," he thundered. "We trusted you." He threw the blood test results in my lap and stormed off. No one said anything.

I asked my supervisor what happened. He told me that I had become a large meat eater, similar to T. Rex. Usually we inhabited smaller dinosaurs, animals that are quick and clever enough to evade large predators. They seemed to be more suited to the lab's intelligence mission. Still, becoming a predator did not seem so unusual. I asked how my buddy performed.

"He was a duckbill, a plant eater. He didn't come back."

About the author: Joseph Carfagno was born in Brooklyn but lives in Connecticut.

5-6 PICKUP STICKS
PETE CARTER

My uncle was an Irishman to his shoes. In traditional fashion, he would sit at the kitchen table drinking beer and telling stories with a glint in his sky blue eyes that always had just a bit of magic in them. His once skinny frame now supported a pregnant gut that hung out over his belt and his hair had been reduced to the faintest wisp on top of his head. He and his wife never had children, although I never knew why. Even when I was young, I always had the feeling he didn't quite know what to do with kids. Whenever my family would visit them, if my siblings or I got too out of hand for my parents to manage, he would offer to send us to the basement of his house and the kids would quiet down right away.

He would stand up from his kitchen chair, the short bowling pin of an Irishman he was, his singular eyebrow stretching across his high forehead and open the cellar door. The old, white, six paneled door was lined with locks. He would click each of them open and swing the door wide with a creak at the end.

"Are ya goona be gud or do ya wanna be sent to the cellar?" he would ask with a smile on his face.

He asked me on a few occasions, when I was bored or tired and stopped listening to my parents.
I could see the old, careworn steps leading down into the darkness. The dust clinging to long gray lumber, with an occasional canned good stuck in makeshift shelving. I always shook my head 'no'.

I was a book-wormish kid with glasses and afraid of the dark unknown and the things that lurked there. Just once, I wanted to say 'Yes' but I never did.

After the years went by, we lost touch with each other. I moved to the other end of the state and started a family. I saw him from time to time at the occasional family get together and he always had a smile and a story. The last time I saw him was at his memorial service.

At his funeral, they talked about his life. I always remembered him drinking a beer and smoking Pall Malls, but there were a great many things he had done that I knew nothing about. He had volunteered for almost every facet of his town's operations, but never in a leadership position. He always opted to be the guy that 'just did the work'. The Priest talked about how he was content to stay in the wings while others paraded across the stage and collected the applause. He helped many people out over the years and given the size of the congregation, the knowing nods and tears so evident in the crowd, people were not going to forget him soon.

I felt very sad then. Not just because of the funeral, but I'd missed a chance to know someone better who was my own flesh and blood.

I saw my aunt at the wake afterwards. She was every bit the antithesis of her husband. She was a tall, Italian woman with a quiet laugh and a giving heart. Her black ringed eyes looked like all the tears had been rung out. Even as she aged, her permed black hair remained frozen in the sixties. I gave her a hug and told her I would miss him.

"He said he wanted you to have this," she said handing me a felt box she had been clutching, "your great-grandfather gave it to him."

"Thank you," I said as I opened it. It was a gold pen set in blue felt.

"There was a letter he had to give you with it, but I have no idea what I did with it. He did say only to use it if you really had to," she said.

I said thank you. She turned and was lost in the sea of friends and relatives.

That was the last time I saw her alive. Her heart was shattered into a million pieces when her husband passed. They only really had each other and when he died, the other half of her died with him. The family tried to bring her back to the land of the living, but she had already made up her mind to meet him out there somewhere and so she left.

A few years later the pen set had made its way into my cherry nightstand along with the gold Movado I got for ten years of service and the sterling silver hip flask my brother gave me at his wedding. I was up late one night in bed, working a crossword puzzle. My wife had just started us on a new diet and I couldn't sleep. Raised by Hippies, she'd always been a real health food nut and was constantly trying new things. With our son in his first year at college, she felt obliged to turn her brunette charm squarely on me. It was one of those high-carb, low fat diets and the food just seemed to roll around my insides refusing to be part of the digestion process.

I was crossing off a clue, when my pencil broke. Being too lazy to get out of bed to get another one, I opened my nightstand drawer and rummaged around until I found the velvet case. I opened it while my wife quietly snored in the bed next to me. Really looking at the pen for the first time, I examined the quill tip and red enameled casing. It seemed like the type of pen you would find on a turn of the century desk. On top of the cylinder was an embossing that looked like a gold eagle. The glass vial, visible only through a slot in the side, looked about half full. I scribbled on a little corner of the newspaper and after a couple of back and forth motions, a red ink line drew on the page.

I violated crossword etiquette by using a pen, but I didn't think the crossword police would be breaking down my door.

I looked at was eight across, 'Actress Barbara St_____,' nine letters. I thought for a moment and wrote Stanwyck. Towards the end of writing, I began to have my doubts. I left one box unfilled. I turned to the back of the paper to see the answer.

I may have forgotten to mention that I am an exceptionally bad crossword player and given any opportunity to read the answer after taking a quick guess, will turn there each time I am stuck.

Turning the paper over, I found the answer and read the name 'Streisand'. While I didn't really think of 'actress' when Barbara Streisand's name came up, I harrumphed and turned back to my work in progress.

The name Stanwyck now fit perfectly.

I did a double take and turned back to the answer. There in the place where Streisand had been just moments ago, read Stanwyck.

I scratched my forehead with the top of the pen and turned back to the crossword. I looked for a big number of blocks and I found it in twelve down.

'The capital of the Ottoman Empire _____,' fourteen letters. I was sure it was Constantinople and turned to the back answer page to make sure. I turned the crossword back over and wrote the word 'Bananas' in the fourteen-word block. I stared at it for a long time and then flipped to the back to see the word Bananas in the answer box. All the other answers weren't quite how I remembered them.

I flipped back to the crossword and there 'Bananas' was fitting perfectly within the box. I looked over at the answer and it said, 'Woody Allen was this in his 1971 movie.' My wife broke into an open mouth snore at that moment and scared the crap out of me.

There are times in your life when you discover something so amazing, revolutionary, so awe-inspiring that you want to wake up the whole neighborhood, scream into everyone's face and phone the ten-o-clock news. Only to discover later, that everyone else already knew or you were completely wrong. My family called me 'Doctor Doolittle' for ten years after I thought I could talk telepathically to the dog and shared that knowledge.

Feeling stupid was something I'd done before. I decided that is was either the raw cauliflower or sourdough bread I had for dinner messing with my mind or it just might be time for me to go to sleep. I turned off my light.

I woke up the next morning and whacked my alarm clock a couple of times before giving up and getting out of bed, showered and went to work. The morning was uneventful; the highlight was finding things on my desk moved around a bit. I moved them back while cursing the night cleaner. I'd brought the pen to work with me and left it in the glove box of my car. The first thing you learn when working in an office is not to leave a pen around.

At lunch, I purchased a lottery ticket at the lobby newsstand for that evening's drawing.

I picked the numbers 7-4-7-4. I worked the rest of day, finished at five and bought the evening edition on the way to the car.

I opened the car door and immediately turned to the second page where the lottery numbers were.

They read 5-4-8-1.

I opened the glove box and took out my pen. I bore down hard on the 5 until it looked sort of 7 like and left the four alone. The red ink came out in fine lines from the narrow quill and I had to repeat the lines a couple of times. The 8 was a bit harder and the 1 was simplicity in itself. I folded the paper and then opened it once again. The numbers in the paper were now in black and read 7-4-7-4.

I had just stuck my hand up the Golden Goose's ass and pulled out an egg. I jumped out of my car and returned to the newsstand where Charlie was just writing the numbers 7-4-7-4 on a grease board. "Hey Charlie," I said, "Looks like I got a winner here." I handed him the ticket.

"Wow, four exact should be a good pay out." He took the ticket and punched it into the system. "It looks like this is worth about 1700 bucks. If you want, you can sign it and I'll take it out of today's lottery money. Good thing too, anything over 2000 and you have to collect it from the lottery." I told him that would be fine, signed the ticket and walked away with a wad of green in my pocket and a ticket for that evening's Super Massive Millions.

I pulled up to my house with dreams rolling around in my head like a pinball machine. I was so preoccupied; I barely noticed the shutters on the house. They were cranberry red when I left this morning and now they were blue. I looked out at the mailbox on the street to make sure it was the right house. On the mailbox was the stupid number four my wife bought at the hardware store. She decided to buy the Roman numeral four, instead of the traditional style. I told her the Roman numeral four looked like the word "ivy", but she refused to listen because she said it was, 'classy'. I was concerned with the mail carrier finding the place, but 'classy' overrules receiving the electric bill every time.

I walked up the stone walkway and into the house. I turned to put my keys on the small table we keep in the entryway and it was on the other side of the hallway.

"Honey!" I called," Did you have the shutters painted?"

My lovely wife of ten years walked in the hallway from the kitchen, she had gained twenty pounds since this morning. Whether you are married or not you can well imagine what would have happened to me if I had remarked anything about it. I held my tongue firmly in cheek and said, "Hey, you look good honey."

"Thanks," she smiled," I think I lost some weight. What were you saying?"

"Nothing important," I said.

Not listening and not paying attention are the two banes of any marriage. She probably told me all about the shutters being painted and moving the table while the Sox were batting in the bottom of the ninth and Big Papi was at the plate. Learning when to keep your mouth shut is something to learn early and often.

"Take a look at this, honey," I said while pulling the chunk of money out of pocket.

"Wow, where did you get that?" she asked.

"The lottery. I think things are going to be easy for us from now on," I said.

"You were gambling," she said.

"Not really, I have to show you this pen from my Uncle," I said.

"You promised me you would never gamble again," she said.

"It's not gambling," I said," I can't lose."

Tears began to well in her eyes, "You've said that before, but it's me that had to bail us out. I'm the one who had to crawl to my father after you lost everything we had on that sure fire tip. You promised."

"It's only the lottery and really I can't lose."

"That's the way it starts off with you. For most normal people it wouldn't be a problem, but you're sick. I not gonna be here if you start this again, not with Joshua in his first year in college. I can't start all the way from the beginning again, I'm not going to have you destroy my life," she cried and left the room.

I sat on my back deck for a drinking a beer thinking about

all those times I had those lame-brained, sure-fire ideas and kicked myself for being so stupid. Here was the one time I did actually have a foolproof method and screwed that up too.

I walked over to the bedroom door, where my wife had barricaded herself in.

"I'm sorry honey. I promise never to gamble, even the lottery, ever again." For as many faults she had, I had twice as many. That was why I loved her I think.

The door opened up a crack, "You really mean that?"

"Yup, whatever I bought today was it. From here on out, it's over."

She opened the door and gave me a hug, "I don't want to lose you."

I had already bought the ticket for tonight's drawing and wouldn't have to buy any more because one was all I needed. If she questioned me, the ticket would have today's date.

She released me and stuck out her hand, where I promptly placed the money.

"This will take care of our hot water heater and the broken central air."

The next morning, still dressed in my shorts, I scrambled down to the end of the driveway and grabbed the morning newspaper. I tucked it securely under my arm, protecting my ticket to easy street and went back into the kitchen. I opened the paper to the second page where the Super Massive Millions number was and changed it to the numbers on my slip. Little bits of sweat dripped off my forehead and splattered on the newsprint. I folded the paper shut, opened it again and there my numbers were in black and white. I did the fist pump and decided to go take a shower and get ready for my last day at work.

I'm not one of those people who would even try to work the next day after winning the lottery, let alone at all after that. I'll be the breeze rushing out to my car you feel when working at your desk. I just wanted to go in to bust my co-workers stones and wish my pinheaded boss my best.

The shower was warm and I remember washing my hair.

I stepped out of the shower and fell straight over. I slammed my head into the vanity, just missing the sink, and stars just like in the cartoons, danced around my head in a Folies Bergere chorus line.

After a few minutes, I pulled myself up to a sitting position using the sink for support. I looked down and saw my left leg was gone just below the knee. After that, my memory was scrambled. I do remember screaming out my wife's name for help and pulling myself up to balance on one foot.

I hopped out of the bathroom in complete shock and saw empty bottles strewn around the living room like dead soldiers on a battlefield. Like a small quiet prayer, I mumbled my wife's name over and over to help me; to try to figure out what had happened. That's when I saw my wife and son's picture on the mantel.

I didn't recognize it, so using the wall for support, I hopped closer.

The picture, dated two years earlier, was gilded in black and had, 'In Memoriam' written on the bottom. That's when I passed out.

I woke up shivering on the carpet. I had been wet and naked when I passed out and the carpet had left wavy marks all over my body making my skin look like a Japanese Zen garden. I struggled to my foot holding the couch and stood wavering. I made my way back to the mantel navigating through the empty nip and whiskey bottles on the floor, my stomach burned as if I swallowed a campfire.

There was a framed article next to the picture on the mantel. It told of a family of three driving on the interstate, when a drunk driver entered the highway going the wrong way. The wife and the boy, a senior in high school, had died instantly while the father, who was still in critical condition, had lost his leg, but was expected to make it.

The drunk driver was a Postal worker.

I dropped the frame to the brickwork and hopped over the couch while a hundred angry Mephistos stabbed the lining of my stomach with pitchforks. I dragged an old, stained afghan around me like a patchwork shroud and dropped to the couch in a lump. I knew I still had the winning ticket somewhere, but that was about it.

I don't know how long I sat on that couch staring at the yellowing wallpaper, but my concentration broke when the front door swung open.

It was an elderly lady armed with a vacuum and mop. I just stared at her as she dropped the cleaning supplies inside the front door and walked over to the couch.

"What the hell are you doing?" she asked.

"I w-was jus-s-t sitting," I said. She had a strong face, graying features and steel blue eyes that could take your measure in five seconds flat. Her hair was curly and cut close to her head.

"Get your damn ass up and get dressed right now. This place is a friggin' shithole again. Do you have any idea what a trashcan is?"

"I-I-I suppose."

"Well supposing ain't doing crap to clean this place." She pointed her thumb to the bedroom. "Dressed, now."

Holding the afghan tight around me, I hopped off the bedroom and found some clothes.

Leaning against my nightstand was a prosthetic leg. After quite a bit of trial and error, I figured out that the strap went around my remaining leg just above the knee. The ankle had a stainless steel hinge on either side.

Getting dressed with only one leg is quite an adventure and I had to roll around on the bed to do it. Do you put a sock on a prosthetic foot? I went back into the bathroom, shaved off a weeks' worth of stubble with an old disposable razor I found and combed my hair. My stomach pain had receded to a constant gnawing.

I shuffled out of the bedroom, using the prosthetic in a shuffling gait and saw that most of the rubble was gone off the floor. I heard the vacuum running down the hall and smelled something cooking in the kitchen.

"Those are your dirty clothes there," she shouted over the jet noise of the vacuum. "Get them to the laundry room before you eat."

I collected the clothing in a pile and after having to return for a sock or two I dropped along the way, got everything down to the laundry room. I was becoming a bit more adept with my new limb, but had a very bad limp. When I came back up the hallway she yelled, "Breakfast is on the table."

I ate my breakfast and for the first time in many hours used my brain. Reality must be like a big bunch of pick-up sticks, each one resting on the other, each stick having others resting upon it and I had pulled one of the sticks from the bottom out when I changed the ticket number, causing the whole stack to settle into new places.

"You're looking better," said the cleaning lady with the booming voice, as she walked into the kitchen.

"I feel better, thanks. Ms. ...?"

"Wow," she said," you are coming out of it. Penny Roberts, formerly of the United States Marine Core."

"Yeah, you seem like a sergeant."

"Sergeant Major in the mechanized division for thirty years. After I lost my husband, I retired and got so damned bored I went out of my mind. I saw this advertisement and thought I would try it for a while."

"When did you lose your husband?"

"Seven years this spring. He was a silly man in some ways. Used to send me yellow daisies with little love notes to where I was stationed. The guys would raze me to no end and he knew it." She looked around the kitchen, "I think I'm done for today."

"Well, I appreciate it. What do I owe you?" I reached for my wallet not knowing if there was a dollar in it.

"Nothing, the church took care of it."

"I still appreciate it."

"I ain't much for religion. I've always thought that it's up to you to grab yourself by your balls and hoist, but I've come to believe that God gives everyone a way out. It's just up to us to figure out which direction to walk."

She rinsed off the dishes in the sink. "Gotta get going, three more houses to do today. Don't forget to put the laundry in the dryer and wash those dishes when you are done."

"Yes, Ma'am. Thanks," I said.

She walked out of the kitchen and collected her

cleaning arsenal. I heard the front door close.

I sat drinking coffee at the kitchen table and wondered if I smoked in this reality. A cigarette would be great right then. I decided against it. Quitting smoking was hard enough once.

There must be a way out of this, I thought. Could I just change the winning number in the newspaper? Pick some random number?

I decided against it because I might screw something up worse. If only I could've remembered what the number was before I changed it, it would be easy

But even if I threw away the ticket now, it wouldn't help. I could change the article on my wife and kid dying, but who knew how badly I would muck it up. Maybe I would kill off half the world in one slip of the pen.

I sat brooding for a long time. I smelled the cold sweat from old alcohol working its way out of my pores. Then it came to me. There was only one person who really knew about this pen and how it worked, my uncle.

I hobbled down the hallway and into my office where I kept some old mementos in the top drawer of my desk. After rummaging around, I found what I was looking for, my uncle's obituary. I stood there a very long time over the news clipping praying to God I wouldn't screw things up.

Using the pen, I scratched out the year he passed and wrote in one twenty-five years from now. I folded the paper and opened it again and the date said exactly what I wrote. Then, the paper started to fade altogether, turned blank and ever so slowly writing appeared filling the void. It became an ad for American Life Insurance

I stood there blankly for a moment. I figured with the date postponed the obituary was a white elephant and couldn't exist, so the newspaper had sold an ad to fill the space.

I thumped down the hallway and found some keys on the side table by the front door. After I opened the door, I saw a white Ford wagon sitting in the driveway. I started the car and the power steering belt squealed in protest as the engine received the mechanical equivalent of Defibrillation. I drove to my uncle's house with a cloud of gray smoke trailing behind me like trapped clouds.

He was sitting on the front porch in a rocking chair when I got there. The sun was angling low in the late August sky making everything that particular shade orange.

"Hey Unc, it's good to see you." I walked to the porch in rhythmic gait.

When I got close he said, "I'm supposing you have the pen?"

"How did you know?"

"After thirty years of havin' that thing, ya start to get a flavor for how it changes tings."

"I need some help."

"I'll do what I can, boy. Sometimes that ting has a mind of its own. Dredge up a chair and take a load off."

I told him the whole story from start to finish.

"Well, tis quite a story. Maybe, not so bad we can't fix it. Just let me tink for a bit."

We sat out there on the porch, rocking away as the sun started to disappear behind the horizon.

"I tink this is the best way to handle this, sonny. Hand me that newspaper you brought with ya, will ya."

I handed him today's paper and I handed him the pen. Where the number for the Super Massive Millions was, he wrote, "Sorry, machine broke", in block lettering. He folded the paper together. When he opened it, written right in the box were those very words.

I felt something I hadn't noticed before. It was as if a wall of fog drifted through me changing the air. Things didn't feel exactly how they were before.

"There, that should do it. Give a call home and see if it did the trick."

I went into the house and used his phone to dial home.

My wife's sweet voice answered.

It was the greatest thing I had ever heard.

"Hi, honey. I just wanted to tell you I stopped by to visit my uncle," my voice was close to breaking.

"Are you O.K.? Junior's back from college and wanted to take us out to dinner if you are up to it."

"That sounds great!" I said with a little too much enthusiasm. "Be home soon. I love you, honey."

"I love you too, dear." She hung up the phone.

I limped back to the porch and told my uncle the good news. He nodded his head and smiled, but I could still see a little sadness in his eyes.

Realizing I had only thought of myself I asked, "Is Auntie here?"

"She passed five years back."

"Can't we just…"

"No, we can't. The pen seems to know when you do something self-serving. Haven't you noticed your leg?" he said.

"Actually in all the excitement, I didn't." I still had a prosthetic leg.

"My Grand pappy won that pen from someone during a card game in Cairo. He had some crazy idea that an Egyptian God named of Thoth, lived inside that thing and hated to be bothered. He said the ink was made from a single drop of blood from a thousand followers, who killed themselves afterward. Anytime he tried to do sometin' that wasn't on the up and up, it blew up in his face. He lost a good lot of things a'fore he figured out the damned thing."

"Why didn't he just throw it away?"

"Aye Boyo, he did. He threw it out many a time and the damned thing just came back. Smashed it to bits he did and found it the next day on his dresser. The only way to be rid of it is to give it to someone."

"Why didn't he?"

"Who do you give it to? Hmmm? Who in the world would you want to have it? I think it's a cross our family has to bear. If I try to bring my love back, I might end up with her coming back a vegetable or paralyzed, you see. Everyone's got to go sometime anyways, just be thankful he only kept your leg when you brought me and your family back."

"Thanks, Unc. I'll leave that thing with you. I've had enough."

"You'll end up with it someday. Just remember to use it as

sparingly as possible and never for yourself. The creator doesn't like it when his weave is messed with. "

I gave him a hug.

"All-righty, you still owes me a fishing trip. I've got all the fishing stuff in the world in my cellar and I could never get you to go down and look at it when you were a kid," he said with a big smile and a wink.

"Deal," I laughed.

As I drove home, I thought about something I had to do tomorrow.

I had to send some yellow daises out.

I just hoped she worked for the same cleaning service.

About the author: Pete Carter lives on Cape Cod where he did most things wrong until he married. You can visit him at his website here http://carterpete.spaces.live.com/

ANOTHER TIME
MARK ROBINSON

"And, can you describe these individuals?"

The eyewitness, sitting across the table, wiped a shaking hand up over his forehead. "They were all wearing bright yellow, hi-vis bomber jackets and rigger boots." Visible beads of fear goose-pimpled in patches beneath his greying stubble and thick, hairy forearms.

"All five of them?" Calm and robot-like; printing everything down that was said to him on a lined A4 notepad.

"Yes; the first one was driving a white transit van with a rolled up copy of the Sun newspaper stuffed in the front windscreen, on the dashboard." Reaching for his complimentary coarse-tasting cup of coffee; the curl of steam burning the insides of the man's mouth with each sip that he wouldn't feel until later on tonight when he was safely tucked up in bed waiting for sleep.

"And, the other four men?" A policeman's direct eyes; chewed biro end hovering above the page, ready.

"They were waiting at the side of the road, near the pub; two of them had carrier bags."
Trying hard to stifle a smirk, the professional policeman continued jotting down the information. "And, these terrorists, Mister Davies; can you tell me anything else about them that you may think is relevant?"

It took at least a minute for the man to speak again; whether he was running through the conversation in his head or trying to find the best way of conveying what was said and what he saw; "I heard one of the men say they were from the future."

All the interview rooms were full so the eyewitness and desk officer were seated in the reception area of the police station; between questions and answering them, the men's eyes were distracted by people traffic and telephones ringing.

"One of the men said this?" The policeman, face turned

to scepticism, voice quiet. Sitting back in his chair; head back, also; mouth wider than it was before.

The eyewitness shook his head; it wobbled above his neck; "Not in so many words." It was unravelling like he knew it would; how it all sounded in his head and out loud where they sat, it was the same dizzy experience as when he watched it all take place in front of him.

"Then, in how many words?"

His credibility, however slight, had all but diminished. From his inside coat pocket, he took out a folded photograph. "How else can you explain this?"

With more physical effort than was required, the policeman leaned forward to take the photo. A reaction was to be expected; it all depended on how open-minded this man was as to what the face might be. "What is this?"

In his own head, the eyewitness who took the photo knew what it was; it was a photograph of the five men and the white transit van. Look a bit closer and anyone would see that the man in the driving seat resembled the man sitting across from the police officer. Look closer still, and the copy of the tabloid newspaper stuffed between the front windscreen and dashboard had tomorrows date on the front page.

"Look; if this is a wind-up, mate." Date emblazed on the bottom of the photo contradicting the one on the newspaper banner.

Reaching into another pocket, he produced a mobile phone; "It's authentic; I've got the originals here."

He gave the policeman a few minutes to view the rest of the gallery before interrupting him. "That can't be me in that photo."

Shaking his head; "Who else could it be? It's been doctored."

The man removed his hat; "Look at my hair; not only is it shorter now but it's a different color!"

The policeman got up; "Don't move." Taking the camera-phone and photo with him. Walking up to a colleague at the desk; "Keep an eye on him will you? Don't let him out of your sight."

Eyes on him; and, because of the man's loud voice, eyes from others sitting in the waiting area around him started watching him.

The authorities in this time had to be told; they needed to know what was going on behind their backs and right under their noses; men disguised as laborers were driving around in white transit van's altering the future. At five, six am these men were standing on street corners; in bus stops; on empty pub car parks waiting for their next assignment. He passed them every morning on his drive in to work; but none that looked like him until two days ago.

As he stood in the queue at the petrol station; there they were standing on the pub car park opposite, waiting to be picked up. If it wasn't for the cash machine next to the window, he wouldn't have seen his doppelganger jump out of his cab parked next to the carwash and react in time to take a photo with his Nokia. Shielding his face as he left the shop, he leapt into his car next to pump five and took another three or four photos. And, as the transit left the forecourt, so did he.

Sipping his hot coffee, staring back at the faces looking back at him, he guessed he was in for a long wait, so decided to take his coat off.

"He knows we're from the future; he's seen the newspaper on the front seat." In agony slumped in the back of the transit, listening to the sounds of broken glass fleck off the front seats and onto the pavement, trying hard to see through the solid darkness at his injured hand whilst listening in to their conversation; what else was he supposed to have done?

"Which one of us does he look like?" Another voice; a strange gravelly lisp that made the man sound like he had a cold and too much saliva in his mouth at once.

Craning hard to hear if he sounded like his look-a-like.

"Me." A weird voice; not the voice he heard in his head or on his voicemail message but the same voice his brother had. Followed by a strong silence.

"What d'you want to do with him?" Another of the men?

"We don't really have a choice now, do we?"

"Mister Davies?" The policeman was obviously more senior to the one he had spoken to earlier; not only was he older, but his handshake was lighter. "Would you please like to follow me?"

One or two of the other faces in the room must have known who this other man was; expressions of panic or shock or pity registered as Mister Davies got up with his coat and followed the policemen through a door that was normally securely locked.

In the policeman's other hand, he held the Nokia and printout that moved as he did, along the corridors and up a flight a stairs. Mister Davies followed, checking doorways and faces he brushed passed; eyeing notice boards and police e-fits and wanted posters and CCTV images; everything would be so different in the future; how were they meant to catch people from another age that looked the same as someone living in this time?

"Through here." They had stopped at the end of a corridor next to an office. "Would you like a coffee, Mister Davies?"

He thought about it and he did.

"Take a seat and I'll be right with you."

The office was fairly high up; below the row of windows he could see the car park below. And, right in the center of the sea, glistening in the sun, was the white transit van; it's occupants looking up. Waiting for their time to strike.

Face-first onto the cracked cold concrete, Mister Davies found his feet and took off toward the light. Behind him, he heard their shouts and doors slam as they got back inside to chase him down.

Bounding the bends, heading down ramps catching level numbers spray-painted along the walls, his reaching footsteps echoing all around him as he neared the exit of the multi-storey car park.

Smashed right hand throbbing with each jagged step, he made it down two levels before he heard the transit engine approach. Everything they had said, he had heard; there were people in this time that would become the living ancestors to a future of powerful men and women; Judges, Police Chiefs, MPs, wealthy financiers; and, their clones, created from another generations genes, were being harvested in one time and sent back to replace the target in another.

Head spinning and body rolling, bouncing through a double door that lead off to the staircase, Mister Davies leaped down two or three steps at once, clutching the banister not looking back.

These terrorists weren't trying to terrify the past but to cause disruptions in the future; without using bombs or hijacking planes, instead they were going back to wreak havoc on a genetic timeline, ripping rifts within a family's dynasty. And, from what they said, it was subtle; nobody burst in with guns annihilating a future great-grandfather of the Prime Minister. Instead, they might infiltrate the future great-grandmother with a clone of herself that couldn't have children, thereby usurping the destined family line and irrevocably altering the future; no offspring, no Prime Minister meant no future law being passed stopping some scientist achieving his goals.

He got it; understood completely the implications of what they were doing but, what about their own paradox? Mister Davies knew a bit about science-fiction; he'd read a few books and watched a few films, so he recognized the fact that by changing the course of events in one time would completely transform the future. Like the butterfly effect, how could these same terrorists keep sending back more clones and change history without destroying themselves or their work? It didn't make sense. Eventually, some small action; some minor change in the space-time continuum would result in these terrorist cells not coming into existence.

Above him, the doors burst open and stampeding footfalls descended down toward him. Another flight of stairs and he would be on ground level. With a clone of his own up there, they either wanted him for something or because he knew about them.

A blue door waited at the foot of the staircase. When he pulled it, he found it was locked. And, when the others found him, he was too late.

"Sorry for keeping you, Mister Davies." The senior officer handed him a coffee in a ceramic mug. "Please take a seat."

Should he tell them they were outside; that he was only doing this because his clone was now inside his home waiting for his wife to return from taking his son to school?

"I've had a look at the photos, Mister Davies. Your statement is also very interesting."

If they locked him up for being crazy, he'd ask that first they checked on his wife and child; before carting him off to the loony bin they take a quick look out the window at the white transit van full of terrorists.

"Did you get a chance to read that copy of the Sun? The very first time I saw a copy of the future, I couldn't even bring myself to pick it up let alone smash through a window just to grab it." The man sitting across from him leant forward with a smile.

"You believe me?" It came out as a question, but after he said it he wasn't sure what the statement was meant to be.

Reaching down to open a desk drawer, the officer laid out a newspaper next to Mister Davies' steaming cup of coffee. Who, confused, leaned forward to pick it up.

"What's it say?" Like a father asking their child to read out the words printed on a present from Santa.

"It's tomorrows Evening Standard."

With a smirk; "We don't all read the Sun, Mister Davies."

Out of his chair and across to the door, where the desk officer he made his statement to earlier stepped inside. "You're with them?" Levelling a finger at the policemen, one at a time. Laughter resounded around him.

"Not quite, Mister Davies; but, we're from the same time, shall we say." Leaving his seat behind the desk and walking up toward the door to meet them. "You're friends out there; we have an understanding; they scratch our back and we, sometimes, scratch theirs. Isn't that right Charlie?"

The desk officer nodded as he moved over to the window and gave the terrorists in the white van a thumbs up.

"What're you gonna do? Lock me up for being crazy?" Trying the locked door handle before completely giving up all hope.

"And, why would we do that?" Hand on his shoulder like a knife through his chest.

"I'm not stupid; there's another me out there; he's got my wife and son. So you don't need me, do you? Just like all the other clones you replace, that's what you do with them; lock them up, say they're all mad and throw away the key."

With both hands on his shoulders, the senior officer looked into Mister Davies' eyes and smiled; "We can't keep replacing you,

Mister Davies; it's no longer cost effective. You see, this isn't the first time you've stumbled onto our little plot."

The strength was leaving his legs; the officer pushed his shoulders back against the door to keep him vertical. "Admittedly, this time was our fault; they should've known you used that petrol station. It's in your file."

He had a file? "Can I see it?"

After another smirk; "Again? You've already seen it. It's just an ordinary police file; I show you, you look through it; you're none the wiser to what we're all about, then you leave. It's a waste of my time and yours."

"How can you be the police? You're clones; terrorists."

Smiling to Officer Charlie across the room, next to the window overlooking the white van; "How do you think the future police deal with these terrorists? Think of us as like the future MI5 or time travelling CIA if that's what helps you to understand." To Officer Charlie; "Send him further ahead, this time; if we send him back again, he'll just get the press involved like he did last time and that's another mess we'll have to sort out."

"What about my wife? My kid?" Screaming as Charlie unlocked the door and forced him out into the corridor.

"Like I've already said, Mister Davies; they weren't yours to begin with." Before he closed the door; "Make sure this replacement does a better job than him."

About the author: Previous writing has appeared in many venues, including Thrillers, Killers and Chillers. He has work coming out in Static Movement, Powder Burn Flash, A Thousand-faces, and Delivered.

OKBOMB
SAM S. KEPFIELD

"We have five hours until the world as we know it ends."

Marine Corps Brigadier General Denny Rivera's face was grim, the voice grimmer. He sat, in full Service Alphas, behind a desk in a windowless office that was completely government issue – desk, chairs, filing cabinets all sturdy metal painted an unblemished and unscratched gray.

"Someone go back and kill Churchill? FDR?" Col. Frank Quinn settled back in his chair, searching in vain for a comfortable position.

"Doctor Kaplan can explain better than I can," Rivera nodded at one of the other men in the office. Nathan Kaplan, Ph.D., was a tall, gangly man of just over thirty, unruly hair barely tamed by a brush, wire-rimmed glasses and a prominent nose balanced by a prominent jaw. He wore a plaid shirt, jeans and sneakers, the uniform of a college professor on a sabbatical, which was an accurate description of his current G14 status.

"It's a discontinuity in the space-time continuum, simply put," Kaplan began in a voice that was surprisingly deep.

"Look, doctor, I'm not a Ph.D. I'm just a dumb jarhead." Albeit one with a degree in psychology and some graduate coursework. "Keep the *Star Trek* stuff to a minimum."

"Someone has gone back and changed history," Kaplan said flatly, and Frank paused. As head of security, it was his job to monitor not just the electrified perimeter of the installation, but also the internal workings of this facility that appeared nowhere in the tons of paper generated by the U.S. Government each year. Frank Quinn's department, two dozen Marines in all, kept a tight lid on the device that sat a couple hundred yards from them inside a large natural cavern.

"Who? And when?" His mind began whirring, trying to recall the past year, the remote sensing and the physical transports –

"We don't know who. Or from where." This came from Helen Moore, Project Pinpoint director. "We don't know from when they went back." The concepts of time travel had outpaced the English language, resulting in tangled syntax.

"But we *do* know to *when*," Kaplan interjected. Rivera's face, Frank saw out of the corner of his eye, grew more glum, saw him put his hands in front of it, rub his eyes vigorously.

Pause for a beat, Frank scrolling all the dates he remembered from American History in college, backwards from September 11, 2001 to November 22, 1963, to July 4, 1776 and the Crucifixion –

"April the nineteenth, nineteen ninety-five." And Frank's world fell out from under him, it had been –

– a day that began like any other, slowly waking from a deep sleep between fresh sheets, warm skin against his chest, arms circling her breasts and waist, soft buttocks against his thighs, shiny auburn hair against his lips, stirring and rousing with sounds in the back of her throat, turn to him and inviting him into her –

"—the file," he heard Rivera say, and felt Kaplan tapping his arm with a sealed manila envelope an inch thick. "It's got all the data in it," Kaplan explained. "If you come by my office, I can show you the remote views we've –"

"I don't know if there'll be time," Rivera cut him off abruptly. Quinn, his head reeling, looked from Kaplan to Rivera to Moore, seeking a solution. He wasn't used to being this knocked for a loop, he was a Marine, damnit, tours in Iraq for both wars, Nigeria and then Venezuela, and he was as disoriented as a recruit fresh off the bus at the recruit depot.

"We believe that the discontinuity in history works as a bubble," Moore explained, brushing black-gray strands of hair from her eyes. "Once the change is made in the flow of time, the changes ripple outward, like in a pond. Or, if you take a three-dimensional view, like a bubble. They proceed at a fixed rate, so many years per hour."

"And when they reach the present. . .?" Quinn asked, tentatively, fearing an answer.

Moore puffed out her cheeks, blew a breath, ran a hand

through graying, frizzy hair. "We don't know. This has never happened before –"

"That we know of," Kaplan began, but Moore waved him off.

"Don't get too metaphysical on us, Nathan, we already have enough to deal with. I'm not going to debate if history's already been changed and we're not aware of it –"

"What happens?" Quinn demanded, his voice tight.

Moore, grabbed by the urgency in his voice, froze, turned and eyed him levelly. "We don't know. I would speculate that it's like being washed over by a wave, that ahead of the wave is what we know, and behind it is the new reality. If you're asking would we know that things had changed, that's beyond answering right now."

Quinn sat and stared at her, and Moore began to fidget under his gaze, but his mind was racing – to be sitting here one instant in this room or in my office or at my lousy empty quarters and the next – *what? waking next to her, sitting beside her on a beach, making love to her, fighting with her, which world would it be? Door Number One? Or Door Number 5,327?*

He looked at Rivera, who coolly returned the look, unemotional, perfect poker face that had won more than a few dollars from Frank's pay, the flat professional look that made clear why Denny Rivera wore two stars on his epaulets while Frank had an eagle. "So I'm here because –" but he already knew the answer.

"We have to stop it," Rivera answered. "Now. The wave, or bubble, is constantly expanding. We discovered it first thing this morning, at 0800. It's now 0900, meaning it's expanded by about five years. By quitting time, everything we know will be gone."

"So you need me to pick someone –" Frank was grasping; he already knew the answer, but had to hear it.

"No. You're going." Rivera motioned to Kaplan and Moore, who rose and left the office. As soon as they shut the door, Quinn waited several beats before letting out a large ragged breath, leaning forward and putting his head in his hands.

"Damnit, Denny –" he broke off as his throat tightened. Rivera sat silently for a moment, then put his elbows on the desk, leaned towards Frank. The Professional was gone, the Buddy surfaced.

"Frank, I'm sorry. I don't want to do this, but when we send someone back, we've got exactly once chance to get it right. No screw-ups, no errors, no missed connections or crossed wires. There's only one person here, available in the next four hours, who can do this."

"Lee or Robbins –"

"Are young. You're sixty-one, same as me. But you're in damned good physical shape." Quinn could still out-p.t. every other member of the security detail and not break a sweat. "You've got combat experience going back to the first Gulf War."

Quinn looked up. "That bad?"

"Could be," Rivera nodded. "We don't know if it's one person or a platoon, though given our limitations I lean towards fewer. And –"

"I know, I know," Frank felt his eyes burning, the inside of his eyelids turning to sandpaper. "I've tried to forget, I don't know if. . ."

"We've been through a lot together," Rivera said softly. Boot camp to Panama to Desert Storm, Frank's brief return to civilian life as a reservist for college and marriage, and afterwards the two young NCOs off to Quantico for officer candidate school, followed by four tours in Iraq dodging IEDs, to Sudan afterward and then Yemen and Myanmar and a half-dozen other trouble spots that required the U.S. Marine Corps' own special touch. Rivera went the tech route, became an administrator and Pentagon rat, Quinn stayed in the field with his troops, his only family. In forty years, the two men had seen a lot together. Rivera was the closest thing to a brother Quinn had.

"I wouldn't do this if I didn't absolutely, completely trust you, believe in you. The psych people are edgy as hell about this, telling me I need to find someone else, that you can't be trusted. I told 'em they're full a shit. You can do it. That is –" Rivera paused. "That is if you agree to it. I'm asking a hell of a lot of you on short notice. I'm not going to order you to do this –"

"I'll do it," Quinn said, his voice husky. *Though I haven't figured out why yet.*

The briefing was quick and concise, held in another cramped office that housed the historical research team. Amid the metal desks and stacks of books and journals sat a desktop computer. Kaplan greeted Quinn warily, and sat back in his cramped space stacked with books and journals.

"I'm told that you have some – knowledge – of this event," Kaplan began delicately. Quinn wondered how much Denny Rivera had told him, then decided he wasn't going to ask or volunteer any information.

"That's right," he replied tersely.

Kaplan waited a beat for more, figured out it wasn't coming, shrugged, and moved ahead with his narrative. The destruction of the Alfred P. Murrah federal building in downtown Oklahoma City on April 19, 1995, had been a crucial turning point in history, though one not appreciated until much later. Kaplan, whose speciality was American history, post-World War II, had made this point for years in several articles and a book. Anti-government groups had sprouted throughout American history – from the Ku Klux Klan to the Christian Identity crowd in the 1940s to the *Posse Comitatus* in the 1980s. They all had a few things in common. They were all self-described "Christians" of the Protestant evangelical stripe, and were implicitly anti-Semitic. Psychologically, they tended towards the paranoid, evidenced by rants against infiltration by foreigners, domination by World Jewry, justifying a world-view which mirrored those of National Socialist Germany.

"Early '95 was really the zenith of the anti-government crowd. Everyone from Newt Gingrich and Rush Limbaugh on down to the camouflage-clad militias," Kaplan explained. "People were openly talking about dismantling large parts of the government – selling the Post Office to UPS, privatizing schools, not even batting an eyelash. Not just the local crazies, but people elected to Congress."

"I remember," Quinn murmured. The earnest, creepy clean-cut types celebrating the Death of the Nanny State that never came, foaming at the mouth over live-item vetos and Robert Mapplethorpe and flag-burning and finally Presidential blowjobs.

"The bombing ended all that. People were on to the anti-government crowd. The militias melted away, their friends in Congress got thrown out, and the former conservatives became government-loving big spenders under George W. Bush. What has happened is that someone stopped McVeigh and Nichols."

"And the result is?" Quinn asked.

"Briefly stated, what you get by 2010 is a totalitarian's dream. Anti-immigration riots, private militias patrolling the border and not afraid to use force and a government that turns the other way. Constant surveillance and spying on American citizens –"

"PATRIOT Act?" Quinn asked. "It happened here, Doctor."

"True. 9/11 still happens, because you have the trigger of the First Gulf War, but the response is completely different. It's too long to give a detailed explanation, but let's say it involves the judicious use of tactical nuclear weapons." Quinn blanched. He'd worn radiation gear in Iraq in '91 and then again in '03, so nuclear conflict was within his experience. But that Americans had used the bomb *again* – what manner of lunatics were running this alternate America? "In the aftermath there's an internment of suspected Arab-Americans on a scale not seen since World War II, packed away without trial or outside contact in prison camps. In America, not Gitmo." Kaplan picked up a file a half-inch thick. "These are some of the images and information we've been able to scan and intercept from our remote viewers. I expect we'll have more by the time you're ready to go." He pushed the file to Quinn. "Take it. Review it on your stay back in 1995."

"Which is how long?"

"We don't know," Kaplan said. "Our scanning, which is not as extensive as it could be, hasn't pinpointed that. We've decided to drop you a week ahead the event."

"Is that enough time?" Quinn asked, heart racing. *A whole week, not just a couple of hours, I could take a small detour, no one would know, or care –*

"Who knows? If it isn't, you're to return to base here and transport back, we'll try it again, go back further." Hating himself, Quinn prayed Kaplan was right.

He was in a small locker room, hanging up his BDUs on hangars, neatly placing his boots in the bottom of the locker, when Rivera entered the room. Frank was naked, but didn't flinch; he and Denny had been in enough squad bay showers with dozens of bare-ass naked Marines to have any sense of modesty. He had a bundle under one arm.

"Got the briefing?" Rivera asked, dropping the bundle on the lone wooden bench.

"Yeah," Quinn replied. "Cheery stuff. Country run by a bunch of Bible-thumping nativists ready to solve the illegal immigration problem by invading Mexico. We'd be real popular down there."

"Jey, whatchu mean `we,' *gringo*?" Rivera said in his Frito Bandito voice. His father had picked vegetables in Arizona, and so had Denny as a boy. Only when he put on his dress blues did people stop calling him a wetback. They both chuckled; Rivera had led Quinn on more than a few tours of Tijuana on liberty. "Seriously, man, you're ready to do this?"

"I am," Quinn said flatly. "I got no choice, after my little chat with Kaplan."

Rivera was silent for a moment. "You've read the protocols for travelers, I presume."

"Hell, Denny, I helped to *write* them." Quinn dropped his jockey shorts, took a towel from the locker. For reasons he barely understood, you went back naked. "Don't you trust me?"

"I do," Rivera said, sitting down. "But... I remember, Frank." Denny had been the first one to call him afterwards, had taken emergency leave from Japan and flown back to Oklahoma, just in time to prevent Frank from doing something rash.

Quinn tucked in the towel, stood, took a deep breath, and faced his oldest friend. "I'm ready. Let's get it over with."

"Yeah," Rivera sighed, then looked Quinn in the eye. "Semper fi, man," he said softly. The Corps' motto had been used to mean anything, depending on the tone of voice and context, from "fuck you, sir" to the closest any of the men would come to expressing love for one another.

Quinn let a faint smile pass his lips. "Yeah. Semper fi, Denny."

A small locker-sized capsule standing upright hooked up to consoles by a spaghetti of wires and cables. The machine's gunmetal gray shone dully in the fluorescent lights hung at the top of the large cavern. The machine and the complex surrounding it – offices, storerooms, living quarters – sat at the bottom of a huge crater created fifteen years ago when the time portal had been discovered. His footsteps were muffled as he walked the distance to the pedestal holding the Temporal Displacement Vehicle, or TDV as it was called, a governmentese nod to an old science fiction time travel novel. Quinn carried Kaplan's file in his hand. Rivera walked beside him. Moore stood beside the TDV, with two of her assistants. They opened the front of the TDV like a clamshell, revealing a small padded chair and a plain interior with a small LED display on the clamshell. They helped Quinn into the TDV. He noticed restraints on the chair.

"The ride on this thing bumpy?" he asked Rivera.

"No worse than a C-130 in a thunderstorm," Rivera said with a ear-to-ear grin, bringing back a memory of a hairy ride over the Atlantic back in '05.

"Yeah, but I don't have a chute here."

Rivera chuckled. "Serious, man. You'll think you were in a Chinook." As they tightened the waist restraint, Quinn looked up at Rivera wordlessly, smiled again as Rivera saluted him smartly.

Silence inside, darkness save for the green LED that showed the date and time. A soft low hum building in volume and intensity, vibrating and building to a bone-rattling, gut-churning rumble –

A second of disorientation falling through space flying up falling down turning inside out, deafness and blindness –

And slowly his senses returned, the rumble fading, churning insides settling, he shook his head clearing out the cobwebs, and focused his eyes on the LED.

April 12, 1995 0812. Four hundred miles east he was awake and preparing to leave the apartment with Kara in his arms, Audrey on her way to work –

A heavy metallic chunk, the front of the TDV unlocked, Quinn pushed the door open and undid the waist restraint. Fluorescent light flooded in, and he looked at his body. He'd hoped that he'd un-age, ridiculously and now, he saw, falsely. There was the faint pink scar across the back of his left hand from a machete back in Panama in '89. Up his forearm, just below the rolled-up shirt cuff, two round pink puckered scars from an IED on the last long haul out of the Green Zone in '09. He felt his right thigh, bumpy scars from a mine in the Philippines in '22.

He got up and exited the TDV. The cavern, looking like a Sean Connery-era Bond set, was emptied. Protocol – No contact with staff downtime. He headed towards the door marked "Exterior Exit," opened it and found himself in a small room, painted white and bare except for a large table at one end. A number of items were on the table, ordered from a message sent from 2031 announcing the arrival of a traveler.

A small black case, opening to reveal a broken-down lightweight sniper rifle, complete with scope and night-vision scope, fifty rounds of 7.62 ammunition. Fifty rounds was overkill, but who knew? A Sam Browne holster with a .45 automatic and six full clips. A black leather wallet containing identification – Oklahoma driver's license, Social Security card, credit cards, all under the name Brian Carruthers. A letter-sized manila envelope, holding $5000 in cash, used bills, Series 1993 or earlier, old green-and white, not the multicolored hologrammed play money used uptime. Jackson, not Reagan, on the twenties. A sealed manila envelope, roughly an inch thick, sealed with red tape and marked TOP SECRET. A set of car keys on a Sooners key fob with #12 enameled on the back.

One more item, a Timex Ironman watch, black plastic, the gray LCD face displaying not the time, but hours minutes and seconds, running down. Now at 168:47:55. Countdown to 9:02 a.m. April 19.

Frank slid the envelope and keys into a pocket, slipped on the holster, pocketed the wallet and watch and picked up the case. A second door led into a garage area lined with 1995-vintage government-issue vehicles. Number twelve turned out to be a white Toyota Camry with Oklahoma tags. Popular car, popular color, perfect if he had to tail someone. A black Crown Vic would be spotted by the paranoid militiamen in a moment; it screamed "government issue."

He unlocked the car with a key, not a touch pad, tossed the case in the back, started the car and backed it out. A door at the front of the garage bay opened automatically, and Frank Quinn drove out into bright sunlight. Into 1995.

Onto a paved apron giving way to gravel that crunched under the tires for a mile until he reached the outer perimeter of the station. No fences blocked it off – too suspicious, a tipoff to any Area 51 conspiracy types that Something Big and Secret was going on in the small metal domes set on the Eastern New Mexico plains. The first travelers back had landed in the middle of the desert, five feet up, and set about hiring contractors to construct the complex, which had taken a year.

Another mile to a paved highway, a half hour to Interstate 40 heading east. He stopped for gas at a truck stop on the eastern outskirts of Amarillo. Filling the tank took sixty seconds, not the ten minutes for battery recharges uptime. A buck and a quarter a gallon, Frank fondly marveled. When the government had mandated electrics in '27, gas had gone for ten bucks a gallon – if it could be had at all. He got change from the twenty, and then dug out another, and indulged in another forgotten luxury.

He walked to the edge of the concrete apron surrounding the truck stop, thumbed the new Bic lighter, put it to the end of the first cigarette he'd smoked in nearly forty years, inhaled deeply, held it. Camels, unfiltered, had been his brand as a mediocre student hanging around pool halls in Milwaukee, skipping high school, barely graduating, and as a Marine. Audrey made him quit, and he had for a time. The FDA ban in '24 had made it permanent. He felt the rush in his head, the delightful dizziness of the first smoke of the day, let it out through his lips slowly. He savored the cigarette, smoking it down to a stub, putting the soft pack in his shirt pocket, and turned back onto the interstate, heading west to a run-down motel a mile back.

He parked the Camry in a row of cars in a strip mall parking lot, walked to the motel, and rented a room for the night with cash, carrying the rifle case inside. He knew he had until two a.m., over twelve hours. A trip to a nearby mall with an Eddie Bauer outlet drained him of another two hundred in cash for shirts and socks and underwear. A trip to an electronics store relieved him of another five hundred for a camera and monitor. He consulted a phone directory, found a military surplus store and laid out another hundred fifty for old-style jungle-print BDUs, another set in black, a set of lightweight boots and a few other accessories. *Damned if I face who knows what in khakis and twill*, he told himself. Back at the motel, he showered, and then slit the manila file with the Ka-Bar knife he had purchased. He lit a cigarette, sat at the desk by the TV and began reading. Not one bit of it was new information to him. He digested the entire file, closed it and went outside to smoke. The sun straddled the horizon, long shadows over the parking lots and strip malls surrounding him, the whirr of interstate traffic. He looked east as he lit up. Two hundred fifty miles that way, straight along I-40 and down, Audrey was coming home from her job, complaining about the traffic on I-35, road construction and dumb Okies making a deadly mix, he was playing with Kara in the yard in front of the small apartment complex, playing catch with a regulation football half as big as she, walking around the block listening to her babble about everything she saw – squirrels and birds and the occasional cat lounging on a porch, wearing her down so she'd go to bed early and give him time alone with Audrey.

He stubbed out the cigarette, went back into the room and went to sleep.

Minus 151:30:45/4.13.95

He awoke at one-thirty, dressed quickly, holstered the gun under his windbreaker and went outside. Quinn found his Camry, sitting alone in the parking lot, and moved it behind the mall. He waited for fifteen minutes, and then he saw it – a ten-year old Pontiac pulling in front of the motel, parking. A tall thin man with a blond crewcut got out, went inside for several minutes, came back out and drove the car around to the side of the motel.

I could do it here, Quinn thought. *So damned simple. Knock on the door, he opens it up, shove my way in, two quick shots to the head and it's over, get out and back* – to what, exactly? A world worse than the one he'd left, chaos and war tearing the country apart, *but would it matter if she was still there* –

The war in his mind immobilized him, and he watched the blond man go into the motel room. And watched for the next eight hours, dozing lightly, until the motel door opened, the blond man exited, got in the Pontiac and drove off. Quinn drove around and parked his car in front of his room, gathered his belongings, left the key on the dresser, and got onto I-40 heading east. The Pontiac wasn't hard to find, and he kept a distance of about a mile. Four hours later, the first towers of downtown Oklahoma City loomed in the hazy distance. The Pontiac turned off at a downtown exit, heading north through the glass and steel valleys, straight north past the limestone federal courthouse, and the target hove into sight, a nine-story concrete box occupying an entire block. The Pontiac slowed, turned to circle the Alfred P. Murrah federal building, passing in front. Frank tailed the Pontiac, and as he passed in front of the building he looked up at the second floor – *Kara napping, chubby arm around Tikky Tat, Mommy taking a break_looking at her*– He tore his eyes from the glass front, caught the Pontiac turn right, and followed it as it meandered around downtown, stopping as McVeigh checked out a parking lot, got back in, and drove off. He followed the Pontiac back to I-35, and north, jogging over to U.S. 77 at Blackwell, going north, headed, Quinn knew, to a storage shed in Herington, Kansas, where he would begin to assemble the bomb components.

Along the way, Quinn kept alert, scanning the flint hills that bracketed the highway, eyed vehicles that passed them, searched the gas stations for snipers. He began sorting out likely scenarios, discarding or filing them mentally. *How would I do it?* He asked.

Time travel, H.G. Wells notwithstanding, wasn't something likely to be invented in a basement or garage. It would take years of research, millions of dollars, sizable support staff (Project Pinpoint was black-budgeted at $15 billion per year, and employed no fewer than 257 individuals). It would necessarily involve a government, which meant bureaucracy, which meant procedural protocols about who went through and who didn't and for what reason. Government involvement also meant security, operational and physical.

So – whoever had gone through had done so at the behest of some governmental entity, had done so through pre-approved procedures, with a set goal in mind to be achieved through a predetermined protocol. This implied that the person or persons – though Pinpoint had never been capable of sending more than one person at a time owing to energy expenditures – would be professionals, not necessarily military, but it would be an advantage.

So, Quinn asked again, *how would I do it? How to carry off what would be essentially a first-degree murder?* He had the ability to literally disappear, but the TDV was in New Mexico, God knew where the other machine was, so that meant avoiding entanglements with law enforcement, meaning no witnesses, *ergo* it wouldn't do to pull it off in broad daylight in public and risk capture. A mine or simple IED by the road? No – as the IRA learned in its war, the damned things were too unpredictable, just as likely to blow up an innocent bystander as the target. And then there was the problem of procuring the materials… No, no roadside bombs. No roadside snipers, either, since it ran the risk of attracting attention, you'd have to know every last little move this guy was going to make, and be able to hit a moving target… For this, you'd get up close and personal. It had to be close-in, handgun or knife, somewhere secluded, no one else around, someplace where the bodies could be disposed of, and any other evidence, like vehicles which, in a few days, would include a Ryder truck not easy to hide. He remembered from the chronology he'd read that there would be a few such opportunities along the way, so he decided to conserve his watchfulness for them.

McVeigh moved explosives from a storage shed in Council Grove to another storage shed in Herington, a trip of twenty miles. He watched as McVeigh drove the Pontiac to Geary Lake, about seven miles south of Junction City off U.S. 77. In five days, he and Nichols would mix the fertilizer and diesel fuel here, and set out for Oklahoma City. Quinn parked the Camry by a picnic table area inside the lake, and waited for an hour. The sun was setting, a soft warm breeze blew from the south.

Minus 108:07:33/4.14.95

Twilight fell, Frank changed into the black BDUs and boots, popped the trunk and assembled the sniper rifle, holstered the .45, hauled out the binoculars he'd bought in Amarillo, and set out for

Geary Lake.

The Pontiac was stalled by the lake, hood up. The skinny blond man was bent over the engine, hands moving. Quinn found a flat spot on a small rise, crept up to the edge, hidden by the tall grass, and watched through binoculars. Eventually, McVeigh gave up, slammed the hood shut, and leaned against the car. By the time night fell and the stars were out, he had crawled into the back seat to sleep. Quinn quietly moved back, around the rise, and came up on the car, stopping in the grass about twenty feet away. He sat in tall grass again, and waited.

The car started up the next day, and it limped north into Junction City. Quinn kept his distance on U.S. 77, and when McVeigh turned into town, Quinn passed him on the interstate, turning off several miles down.

The Dreamland Motel was a '50s era brick spread along I-70. Quinn rented a room for the next five days. It was around the corner from the room McVeigh would rent. He unloaded the car, parked it around back out of sight, and settled in, catching a few hours of sleep. There was little chance of action for the next few hours. McVeigh was going to sell the Pontiac for the yellow '77 Mercury that would become famous in a week. He was going to meet Nichols at the lake, exchange some cash, and then come back here to rent a room.

Around twelve-thirty, Quinn woke from his nap, gathered his rifle and gear, and set out for the lake. He hid the Camry in the brush near the lake entrance, and jogged over to his viewing point from last night, and watched as the Mercury hove into view. A few minutes later, a pickup appeared, and parked by the Mercury. The two men greeted each other warmly, shaking hands. From his vantage point, Quinn could hear snatches of conversation, catching up on each other, talking about current events, and then planning began.

"... about five thousand pounds," he heard McVeigh say, and Nichols replying "big damn bang..." and chuckling. Quinn's lip curled, his stomach churned. "Blasting caps... five minute fuse... thirty-five's the most direct route, quicker...Waco.. payback..." It got to be too much, Quinn realized he was grinding his teeth and his knuckles were white. *So easy, they're both here, two shots clean, no witnesses, this would be an ice cold case, to hell with Time and Space and the Universe, and damn Denny for ordering me into this.* But kill them now, someone else in the movement would pick up the baton and run with it all the way to the Murrah Building. He hung his head, blinking back tears of anger and pain, his heart freezing. Another hour, then they parted, Quinn heaving a sigh of relief, trotting back to the Camry, unscrewing the rifle and putting it back in the case. He drove back to the motel, his hands shaking, heart pounding and the veins in his temples standing out.

Sure enough, McVeigh checked into Room 25 of the Dreamland Motel that afternoon, parking the Mercury in front of the room. The next two days were nerve-wracking for Quinn. His quarry was not fifty feet away, open to interference; Quinn had to prevent it without being spotted or changing history.

And what if I fail? What if some Airborne types in black ninja suits sneak by me and put one between McVeigh's eyes? What happens then? Maybe — maybe — Nichols finds out, calls it all off, goes back to his little mail-order Filipino bride and farts around on weekends in camouflage with crackpots talking about ZOG and black helicopters. The sun comes up on April 20, the Murrah building is still there, and so's Audrey and Kara, but Kaplan's nightmare vision of hell comes true. So what? People lived and loved through the Third Reich, the Soviet era.

He dreamed of red hair and barbed wire and fire and pain all night.

Minus 70:15:34/4.16.95

Easter Sunday. On the road again, heading south on I-35, tailing the yellow Mercury and a blue pickup truck. Quinn hung back a couple of miles, still operating on the assumption that a drive-by style hit was too flashy and too dangerous for any real professional. McVeigh gassed up at a Conoco station on the Oklahoma line, Quinn rushing past him in the Camry, but turning off several miles down and waiting. The two were going to place the yellow Mercury in a lot for the quick getaway after McVeigh lit the fuse. Then, Quinn knew, it would be back to Junction City and the Dreamland and eating take-out Chinese food for the next two days. Frank had parked the Camry in a corner of the parking lot, taking a risk that it would be recognized, but it hadn't been, so he mounted the surveillance camera on the

front headrest, put the monitor in his room, and it worked perfectly.
Minus 44:51:40/4.17.95

It rained all day, and made Quinn's mood worse. He sat in a McDonald's just off I-70, down the road from the motel, staring at the remains of his lunch. Two Big Macs, large fries, and a Coke, something he could never have bought in 2031. After Joe Camel's demise, Ronald McDonald was next, going down under a series of health-food laws passed to combat kids made porky not by trans-fats but by hours at a TV, no activity and chauffered rides to schools. You could still get a Big Mac, but it was – different, somehow. Maybe the special sauce, he thought. He'd have to wait until he got back to the motel for a smoke, though.

McVeigh had been in his room all day, wouldn't move until later in the afternoon to rent the Ryder truck. In the meantime, Quinn had slept in late, made a trip to a military supply store on the main drag, and loitered at the McDonald's.

It was at the supply store that he met his second test of the trip. She was young, short light brown hair, heart-shaped face and elfin nose, big brown eyes, no more than five feet tall and ninety pounds. Far too innocent-looking to be a soldier, but she was, in service alphas, probably in a HQ unit. Caught him looking at boots, and said "take these – they're already shined." Quinn still wore his hair high and tight, Marine-regulation, so she must have assumed he was active duty in civvies, from Fort Riley looking for a spare pair of boots for a junk-on-the-bunk inspection.

"Thanks," he said with a smile. He looked, and they were the right size, eleven and a half.

"That is, if they're for wearing, and not for showing."

"Definitely wearing." Life at Pinpoint was pretty cloistered, and he didn't go much for the spit-and-polish bullshit, focusing on training instead.

"So what unit are you with?" she asked. Quinn momentarily panicked. He hadn't thought to memorize the units based at Fort Riley – the First Armored, sure, but she was going to want regiment, company, and he had no idea about support units, their numbers. He could have bullshitted a civilian. He thought quick, and came to a brilliant solution.

"I'm not. I'm with the Marine recruiting station in Wichita, ran some new recruits to the Kansas City MEPS," acronym for Military Entrance Processing Station, the first stop on the four-year hitch. "Just stretching my legs a bit, since I been up and in a car since zero-three hundred."

Her eyes widened for a second, a teasing smile on her lips. "Really? I wasn't sure how to tell if you were a —"

"Marine? Same as always. Thrown some sand on the wall and see if I hit the beach." An oldie but goodie, sure for a laugh, and sure enough it came. They talked more, about their duty assignments. Brenda Tinker was an E-4, had just re-upped for four years, had an MOS in languages and was taking courses at Kansas State University twenty miles away, had studied Russian but it wasn't in much demand anymore. Frank suggested she take up Farsi. Frank had heard enough tales from the old-timers who had served in 'Nam to be credible about service there, remembered enough from his own experiences in Panama and had gotten an earful from Denny about shitholes like Haiti – just over a year ago to Spec. Tinker, Frank realized with a start – to sound like he'd been there.

At the end of a half an hour, they stood outside the front door, trying to say good-bye but not wanting to, and she asked him if he was busy the rest of the day. "I have the afternoon off," she said. "Maybe we could get lunch, get to know each other," and by that she meant that she wanted Frank, wanted him every way possible, a young bright eager woman attracted to a battle-scarred older man. He could see it, could visualize her body under the alphas, toned and muscled, firm butt and pert breasts, natural, the way it used to be before women thought they had to look like Barbie dolls with shaved pubes and silicon boobs, no tattoos either, only the hard-core gung-ho got those, as Frank's eagle-globe-and-anchor on his left bicep done in a parlor in Yokosuka attested, no pierced navel or nipples or labia. He was tempted to put the mission on hold and screw her brains out and legs off in a proper military fashion... but –

But Frank was here, but also *there*, two hundred miles south and thirty-five years younger and he was married to and in love with an extraordinary girl, was a father, and though he was cleaved in two, as it were, it still felt like cheating. Did the barrier of time and space looped back on itself not make it, if not a crime, at least a moral offense? If they didn't know about it, did it matter? And, quite honestly, in a few days it wouldn't –

"I'm sorry," he said. "My L-T is kind of a prick. He wants me back ASAP so I can contact some recruits." *And if I screw you here, plant my seed between your oh-so-muscled and tanned thighs and it takes, that alters history and you give birth to someone never meant to be – or does it? Maybe me being here was part of history all along, part of what happened – damn Denny for throwing me back here on such short notice, no time to sort out paradoxes that have been tying sci-fi writers in knots for decades.*

Tinker was crestfallen; he saw her eyes dim and her smile deflate. "Oh," she sighed. "Well, I'd love to see you again sometime," she got her screw-me-now look back. "When do you have to go back to KC?"

"Looks like next Thursday, got some more guys heading out. I might have a day off on the weekend."

"Great," she chirped, and took out a small memo pad, wrote down her name, unit number and phone number, tore the sheet off and pressed it into his hand. "Call me. I mean it. I'd love to hear some stories." Her warm hand lingered, squeezed his, and she turned to walk down the street, a very feminine walk, hips swaying as she receded and turned the corner.

At five, he watched the Ryder truck back into the parking lot at the motel. Another piece fell into place.

Minus 27:14:45/4.18.95

The Ryder truck sat in a Pizza Hut parking lot in Herington in the breaking dawn. Quinn had the Camry behind a convenience store, was looking at the truck through binoculars. McVeigh was there, Nichols was a no-show. Giving up, the truck roared to life and lumbered to the storage shed, where McVeigh began loading empty drums, boxes of gel, seventy fifty-pound bags of fertilizer. Nichols arrived halfway through. A heated discussion ensued, McVeigh animatedly pointing at Nichols, raising his voice, gesturing, finally Nichols put up his hands and began loading. As soon as the last three drums of what Quinn knew to be nitromethane were loaded, McVeigh unloaded some items into the shed, and shut the truck.

He watched from his old spot as the two parked the Ryder truck by the lake, and got inside the back. Quinn shut his eyes hard, knowing that they were mixing the fertilizer and gel and fuel, making the bomb.

Quinn had the sniper rifle by his side. A couple of hours into the operation, a truck towing a boat appeared. Quinn brought the rifle up, looked through the scope, waiting for a group of camo-clad Rangers to pile out of the truck and begin firing. It didn't happen. The truck stayed for fifteen minutes, a middle-aged couple going down to the water and eventually going back to the truck and driving off. Quinn kept the rifle up, scope at his eye, sighted on the back of the truck. The two men ripped open bags, poured them in the drums, sloshed diesel fuel into the drums, onto the floor of the truck

Hell, I wouldn't need a good shot, Quinn thought. *Just a match. Blow this whole operation sky-high, take these two mothers out, no questions asked, nice clean and simple, no witnesses, no mess –*

He felt his index finger tightening on the trigger, unconsciously. He hesitated for a moment, then released it and laid the rifle beside him, put his forehead on the ground and squeezed his eyes shut.
Minus 10:31:19/4.18.95

Frank watched as McVeigh pulled the cargo door of the Ryder truck shut behind him. The truck sat on the grass just off the parking lot of a truck stop. A few semis lined the edge of the lot, their engines rumbling. Frank parked the Camry between two of the semis to hide it. He then made his way out onto the tall grass about fifty yards from the truck, rifle in hand. This was another optimum time for an interruption of the historical flow – near midnight in a truck stop along an interstate, no one moving around, good noise cover from the diesels, easy to slip around, pop the door on the Ryder truck, do some quick knife work or drag him out and end it with a bullet –

Motion by the truck. Frank's system went into alert, adrenaline pumping, eyes now acute, movements fluid and quick. Two figures clad in dark clothing, one carrying what looked like a service automatic in the right hand, hunkered down and creeping along the side of the truck. Frank brought up the rifle, quickly, flicked on the night scope, put the crosshairs on the first figure, gently squeezed the trigger and felt the slight recoil and buck as he sent a slug into the cranium of the first figure. Frank watched him convulse and drop, watched as the second figure froze momentarily trying to determine the direction of the shot, which gave him enough time to put the crosshairs on the left chest and squeeze again. A hand flew up, the knees buckled, the second collapsed in a heap.

Frank laid the rifle gently in the grass, crept up to the bodies lying beside the truck. They wore clothing identical to his – black BDUs, boots, gloves, and caps, faces smeared with dark greasepaint. The first was unrecognizable, the face covered in blood. The second –

A scuffing noise by the front of the truck made Frank turn his head, in time to see another figure dart around the side. He got up and followed, plastering himself to the side of the truck in case the third assailant was waiting around the corner with a tire iron or Ka-Bar. He peered around, saw a door on a dark SUV slam shut. He dashed out, too late as the SUV roared to life and sped from the parking lot, tires squealing, the lights coming on as it hit the interstate on-ramp. Quinn slowed to a stop, watched it disappear, heading south – naturally. He headed back to the truck and the two bodies.

Now what? he thought. *I can't leave them here. I can't put them in a dumpster. And if I get pulled over and the county mountie or Smokey Bear hat finds two bodies in my trunk –* He looked at the idling semis, and he had his solution.

Minus 2:15:07/4.19.95

The face on one of the bodies came as a shock, but perhaps Quinn shouldn't have been surprised. He and Denny were close, why should a shift in the space-time continuum change that? He said a small prayer over Denny's body, the got to work.

Stuffing the bodies in the back of the refrigerator truck took only a few minutes, most of it to pick the lock. Quinn loaded them in, quietly shut the door, and retreated to his car, to catch some sleep before waking at 6 a.m. McVeigh, he knew, would be up at seven or so. Quinn went into the convenience shop, bought a cup of coffee, a newspaper and a pack of cigarettes, returned to his car and waited. Promptly at seven, a puff of smoke and coughing growl and the Ryder truck began moving.

It was a straight shot down I-135 to Oklahoma City, just over an hour. Quinn had the radio on, tuned to one of the oldies stations at the top of the dial. He recognized the song at once, and began to sing

Minus 1:00:32/4.19.95

along, as the car sat idling outside. He looked at his watch. "We're going to be late," he shouted to the bedroom at the back of the small apartment.

"I'm coming already," came the reply. Alexandra Quinn turned the corner, loaded down. Diaper bag slung over one shoulder, purse over the other, two-year old in her arms, both of them copper-haired, blue-eyed, same heart-shaped face. Kara, their daughter, was red-eyed and sucking her thumb. "She can't find Tikky Tat."

Frank sighed. Tikky Tat, the stuffed gray-striped plush kitty that he had bought in the hospital gift store the day she was born, was Kara's inseparable other half. "I'll find her," he told Kara, taking her tiny chin in his hand. Kara sniffled once more. "C'mere," he said, taking her, "let's give Mom a break, huh?" Kara put her arms around Frank's neck. Frank carried her to the Ford Escort they had bought three months before, strapped Kara into the car seat, Alex dumped her load into the other half the of the seat, and slid in beside him. Frank put the car in gear, and began the trek from Norman to Oklahoma City.

"Bad this morning?" he asked Alex gently as he sped down the on-ramp to the interstate. "Ugh. The worst so far. That's why Kara's so upset, she hates to see me puking my guts out."

Frank looked at Kara in the rear-view mirror. "Kara, it's okay when Mommy gets sick." He switched to a cheesy Mexican accent. "Uh, yeah, she's just talking to *Raaaaaalllllppphhh*, man." Kara began giggling, then began saying "Mommy talking to *raalllphh, raalllph*."

Alex frowned at him. "Wonderful. Now you've got our

daughter doing Cheech and Chong bits. I see this ending up well."

"Hey, you want her terrified or laughing for the next eight months?" Alex frowned, pulled down the sun visor, began doing her makeup in the mirror. *Another eight months*, Quinn thought, *and there'll be another one. I'll be in Quantico when the baby comes. I wonder if I can get leave for it?*

The ride was uneventful, meaning that he avoided any multi-car pileups. For his part, Frank would have preferred riding on an LAV across the Iraqi desert under fire than deal with the road construction, the sudden bottlenecks and stupidity of other drivers. Alex had to deal with this every day, probably why she needed the neck massages at night. And I'll need more massages after I get back from Quantico, the O-course there is a drizzlin' bitch, at least according to Rivera, who
Minus 1.50:11/4.19.95

was going to be perplexed when he was declared dead, his body found in a freezer truck unloading in Omaha, and knowing the Corps it would take forever to straighten out the paperwork. But it was all Frank could do, get rid of the body that was and wasn't his best friend, thirty-years older than his version here, with a few scars that didn't exist on the Denny he knew in 2031. The Rivera cooling in the truck had been sent here to make sure Frank didn't succeed.

And that was going to be the least of the surprises in store.

The second occurred when, in the wee hours of the morning, he saw a dark-clad figure appear from around the back of the cinderblock building, walk slowly to his car, then lean against it and light a cigarette. Quinn saw it through the night-vision binoculars, couldn't make out any facial features, and lay there pondering what to do. One minute, two, then five, another cigarette and then another for the figure slouched against the Camry. It wasn't random, Quinn decided, and got up, his knees popping as he did so, a crick in his back. He walked to the Camry, and as his boots hit the blacktop the figure turned to him.

"Hey, gringo," he heard Rivera's voice, and stopped.

"You're supposed to be dead," he said.

"Think so?"

"Yeah. Sitting in that reefer truck over yonder," he pointed to the trailer hooked to a blue Kenworth that sat idling at the end of the row of eighteen-wheelers parked along the edge of the blacktop. "Wherever you come from, man, you're uglier'n you are here."

"You ain't exactly Cinderella yourself. Hey, I ain't got all day, so I'm gonna get down to it. Forget hanging around here – no one's gonna hit it on the road. They're gonna try at the target. Not sure how, probably whack the driver before he lights the fuse. So they're laying an ambush down there. Getcher ass down to OKC ASAP."

"What if –"

"No questions, Frank. Can't. Go. Now." They stood there, staring at one another for a moment.

"Fine. Semper fi, man."

"Yeah. Semper fi." Quinn took his keys from his pocket, unlocked the door, and got in. He drove off, leaving Rivera there smoking a cigarette, heading down the dark lonely highway to Oklahoma City. The traffic

Minus 0:25:44/4.19.95

was horrible. There was something about Oklahoma, a confluence of bad roads and the conviction that speed limits were but a mere suggestion, that made a drive on I-35 through the greater Oklahoma City metro area a nightmare. How in God's name Alex managed this was a mystery. Quinn again told her she needed to quit this job and get one in Norman, because she was now an expecting mother again, needed to be more responsible. Alex absentmindedly told him she would.

No breakfast, so Quinn bought Egg McMuffins for everyone at McDonald's, Alex climbing into the back with Kara to prevent a mess. From Norman to Midwest City was fine, a stretch of four-land divided highway that shot through scattered housing and commercial developments. Past Midwest City, though, the going got rough. Three lanes of I-35 turned to one lane, a bottleneck that slowed traffic to a crawl. Hell of it was, the damned cones had been there for weeks and he'd never once seen anyone actually working there.

Kara was babbling to herself, pointing out signs and trucks and laughing, while Alex had finished her makeup and was leaning against the car seat, her eyes closed. It had been a rough night.

At this rate, it was going to take forever to get downtown. He cursed again, swore at himself silently, should have taken Sooner Road, the two-lane road that ran from the east end of Norman nonstop up to I-40, it would have taken him half the time to get to *Minus 00:18.07/4.19.95*

The Murrah Building towered over downtown, a brown concrete and glass box. In its last moments, at 8:44 a.m., it had opened for business and people were filing in and out through the large glass doors in front. Folks needing assistance at the Social Security Office, bureaucrats at the SSA, ATF, DEA, FBI, secretarial staff, all going inside unwittingly to their dooms. Meetings were beginning, jokes made, gossip or talk of favorite TV shows being traded by water coolers or coffee pots.

Quinn had gotten back into the Camry and floored it, going in excess of the speed limits, prepared to deal with any state trooper that pulled him over – but he remembered that it took speed in excess of 90 mph to really get noticed on an Oklahoma highway. He'd hit the north end of the OKC metro area with over a half hour to spare. The Camry barreled down the interstate, weaving in and out of traffic, keeping his eye out for the Crown Vics the state patrol ran and the Chevys that the city cops used. He hit the 6th Street Exit, blew through red lights and stop signs, tires squealing, and parked the Camry in a lot behind the Water Resources Building. The WRB was across the street from the Murrah building, on the northeast corner of Fifth and Harvey, giving him a good view of the scene and any interlopers.

He left the keys in the ignition, checked his watch: 00:09:54. He got out, slammed the door, ran through the parking lot, onto the sidewalk, then ducked back as he saw a lone figure standing on the corner. Quinn peered around the corner, saw a man, clearly a man, dressed in khaki pants and a light coat with a ball cap standing still even though the light was green and the signal said WALK. Standing as if –

As if waiting for someone.

Quinn drew his .45, slid the carriage back and chambered a

round. Taking a deep breath, he turned the corner breaking into a full run, saw the man running full at him, his eyes went not to the face but to the dark blued object in the right hand, now maybe ten feet away. Quinn put his head down, sprinted and threw himself at the oncoming man, felt a bone-jarring impact and a flash of memory back to his high school football days and somewhere in Beirut with shells landing outside the ruined wall he'd used for shelter, his weight and momentum carrying both of them up against the wall of the WRB, felt a nice solid thud and heard the breath rush out of his opponent, with his left hand snatched the weapon – a .45, he noted and gave it no more thought – from the fingers and hurled it backwards, hearing a clatter as the gun struck pavement and bounced but did not fire, pulled the man away from the wall and threw him against it again, driving a left hard into the gut which was hard and toned, he grabbed the front of the coat with his left and with his right brought the .45 up and drew back looking for the first time at his target.

And found his own face looking back at him, in pain from the body-slams, a neatly-trimmed mustache beneath a nose that had been broken at least once more than his own, hair cut short with more gray, an angry purple scar along the side of his jaw.

For a second, ten, neither one moved, just stood frozen mid-grapple staring at one another, brains processing something that couldn't be, like a pink elephant materializing out of thin air into the middle of the intersection.

Quinn2, as Frank dubbed him in his mind, spoke first. "You're here to stop me, right?"

"That's classified," Frank replied cautiously.

"Bullshit. That's a military-issue piece you've got in my face. I'll bet you've got a set of cammies back in the black Crown Vic you drove here."

"They're black, and it's a white Toyota. No more small talk. You're waiting for the same thing I am, a big Ryder truck loaded with a two-ton fertilizer bomb in the back. What's the plan? Pop McVeigh before he lights the fuse then drive the truck off?"

"This isn't some old Bond movie, friend," Quinn 2 said. "I'm not gonna spoil the surprise." His expression grew grimmer. "What

I do has to happen."

"I've seen what comes from it. I prefer my world."

"The U.S. a second-rate power, in hock to the Europeans and Chinese, bogged down in war after war, personal freedom eroding bit by bit —"

"I'll take it over a religious dictatorship —"

"And Alex and Kara dead?"

Frank felt like he'd been gutpunched, Quinn2's question brought all of this home in a moment of blunt, jagged clarity like an ice-pick to the forehead. "That doesn't —"

"Bullshit. It does," Quinn2 was smiling now. "Yeah, they're alive. Alex looks terrific, still. Kara's married, two of her own, she's a biology professor at Minnesota. Danielle —"

"Danielle?"

"Her little sister. Born eight months and five days from today. Dani's in the Air Force, got picked for the astronaut corps five years ago, getting ready for the Jupiter mission. Tell me it doesn't matter, you're lying. You've been doing the same thing I have, watching those two mothers through a sniper scope, just waiting for the right moment to squeeze the trigger, blow their stupid paranoid white trash brains out. Admit it."

Frank was going to deny it, tried, the words didn't come, he stared into Quinn's face, the eyes his own but not. There was something else there, something hard and unyielding born of a hardscrabble existence, the noninvolved stare of those who are constantly watched. But something else, too — a softness, a refuge from the cold surveilled wasteland, a warm hearth in the middle of Siberia.

A revving of a large engine gearing down, Frank turned his head, saw the yellow Ryder truck moving slowly up the street, towards the intersection. It stopped at the light. Behind the wheel, he could see two men, McVeigh and another, shorter, darker, not Nichols —

Quinn felt an impact in his groin, saw stars, loosened his grip, and felt himself flying back, landing hard on the pavement, knocking his head and teetering on the brink of consciousness, saw Quinn2 on top of him, taking the gun from his hand, rising to hurry towards the Murrah building. Running on instinct, he reached out his left, felt it close around a boot, twisted his body and pulled, heard Quinn2 hit the ground, rolled up and over and scrambled to his feet, hitting Quinn2 as he was rising, knocking him to the ground. Quinn2 twisted and turned, delivered a haymaker to the side of his head, producing stars, sending him rolling off and into the gutter. Frank shook his head, again got to his feet as Quinn2 was crawling to the .45 on hands and knees. He jumped, landed pro-wrestling style dead center on Quinn2's back, sent him to the ground, grabbed a handful of hair and found only a skull of bristle-brush, gave it a shove to the pavement, and another and another. His right clamped on the .45 just as Quinn2 rose, threw him off. He landed on his back in the street, grip tightening on the .45 as Quinn2 loomed over him. He thumbed off the safety and brought up the .45, not even aiming the barrel but squeezing the trigger once, twice, thrice, four, watching himself do a deadly jig as the heavy slugs struck home, seeing dimly the puffs of concrete as the slugs went through the body and hit the wall of the WRB. Quinn2 took one step backwards, another, and then collapsed with a look of surprise on his face.

Frank lay there for precious seconds, gathering his wits, shaking his head and clearing it. He slowly rose to his feet, dusted off the gravel and dirt from his BDUs, holstered the gun. The body —

He hoisted Quinn2 over his shoulders in a fireman's carry, jogged to the corner, peered around, saw the back of the truck closed, and twenty yards away McVeigh was running across Fifth. Quinn ran across the street, approached the truck cab, opened the driver's door and hefted Quinn2 inside, depositing the body lying down on the bench seat, slammed the door shut, glanced at his watch. 00:02:37.

Quinn sprinted to the front doors, flung one open, nearly hitting a woman, walked quickly through the lobby, found the staircase. Two at a time, three, he hurled his body upward, felt his heart pounding and sweat beads forming on his forehead. He shoved the metal door open, rushed into the hallway, and stopped halfway down, in front of another door, wooden, with a six-by-six inch window. He pressed his face up against the glass.

Alex stood with her back to him, holding Kara to her,

calming the crying fit Kara threw when Mommy had to go to work, a fit forgotten in ten minutes as she played with the other kids (who would be dead) and seeing Mommy during lunch (not today). He admired Alex, her trim body, the class and poise she oozed, the way she fit into the green dress that matched the coppery cascade of hair to her shoulders, saw her face in Kara's, the smile and the lighting of the eyes (soon to be dead and lifeless) –

Quinn opened the door, went in. One of the attendants looked up, alarm registered on her face as she looked at his face, his disheveled appearance. Kara saw him, looked confused for a moment, but said "Daddy," and Alex turned around, the same confusion but not going away as she squinted at him to make thirty years of gray and lines disappear, and asked "Frank?" Kara giggling and reaching for him, he took both of them in his arms, Kara hugging him and planting kisses on him, Alex's body stiff but yielding to him as she looked up into his eyes seeing recognition as he whispered to her "it'll be all right, honeys," kissed Alex softly

As outside a spark of electricity flared and traveled through wires, a flash and a roar

And nothingness in an instant, then togetherness.

He had muttered some half-hearted disagreement, but had ultimately acquiesced, knowing that he would open the windows when she was asleep.

He needed to hear the surf again, needed to smell the sea.

He knew what he had to do, and felt all the more foolish for it.

Throwing his legs off the bed, he gently left it, resettled the covers around his slumbering wife.

Carefully, quietly, he drew off his night clothes and laid them over the chair near his side of the bed, removed his dark suit, white shirt and tie and clothed himself with them.

Pausing at the door, he thought for a moment about bringing his stovepipe hat, which hung on an overelaborate rack near the door of their room.

"A gentleman does not go out without a hat," he could hear Mary's voice say in his head. "Scandalous."

Scandalous it would be then.

The hat stayed on the rack and he left the room, drawing the door behind him quietly and locking it from the outside.

The hotel corridors were very quiet, with only the slight hissing of the gas lamps to disturb the silence.

He treaded softly, lest he should disturb the sleeping Pinkertons, ensconced in rooms on either side of his own.

Taking the stairs to the lobby, he nodded perfunctorily to the night desk manager, strode past his questioning face to the door, then out into the cool air.

It was about 2:15 a.m., and there were certainly no carriages available at this late hour. Lincoln faced the direction of the ocean, breathed in deeply. The tang of the air, at once both salty and fishy, soothed his pounding headache somewhat.

He would walk there tonight, walk to the ocean and stand a while on its shores again.

Maybe, just maybe he would hear God's voice in the waves, in the wind.

God would tell him what was wrong and how to make it better.

And it would be a different solution than the one offered by his dreams.

The walk was brisk and pleasant. He had the streets to himself the entire way, which gave the trip an almost dreamlike quality. Lincoln was a big believer in dreams. He remembered them, wrote some of them down, regaled his cabinet with retellings of them.

Many thought these retold dreams as thickly spun as some of his other tales from his life in Kentucky and Illinois, but they were just as Lincoln remembered them. They were neither embroidered nor enlarged, but just as they had unfolded in his sleeping mind.

He was laid out in the Capitol, his casket atop a catafalque draped with the colors of the Union. Soldiers guarded his corpse as mourners filed past, thousands of them in a line that stretched outside into the cool, grey spring Washington day.

Or he was a spectator in a large crowd watching a train huff its way slowly down the tracks. A short train, an engine and just a few cars, all draped in black bunting with just a few hints of red, white and blue.

"Whose train is that?" he asked in the dream.

"President Lincoln's," said the young boy standing beside him. "He gave his life to save the Union, and now he belongs to the ages."

Just dreams, they had assured him—Chase, Seward, Stanton—just dreams.

He hadn't given his life.

He hadn't saved the Union.

Dreams. Just dreams.

But they haunted him still, even after it was all done, all over, all lost.

He was still here, disgraced in a sense, while the Union was dead, fractured at the Mason-Dixon line. Two new republics had been birthed to its south; The Confederate States of America and a newly liberated Republic of Texas. Three bickering, disagreeable siblings where once there had been a shining, unique whole.

And he was the midwife.

Still he had the dreams of his honorable death, still the dreams of his sacrifice, still the dreams of leaving behind a Union that was whole, united.

It seemed a punishment of sorts, a torture for no discernible reason.

Wasn't the mere fact that he was still here while the Union was not punishment enough?

No, evidently not.

So, he suffered through the dreams and the headaches.

There was something about the Pacific, though, the warm, mysterious, green-blue waters that stretched from his nation's still intact West Coast all the way to the even more mysterious Orient. Something about it that calmed him, soothed his nerves, stroked away the worry and the pain from his deeply wrinkled brow.

By the time he looked up, he had passed the wharf district and the docks. There were a few more people out here; sailors, stragglers, dock workers overseeing midnight loading or unloading of cargo from the shadowy ships that lay in berth. But no one paid him any attention as he glided by, a tall, thin sliver of a ghost. He was glad he had not brought his trademark hat.

Farther from the docks, the rugged landscape of San Francisco took over again; the craggy hills, deep crevices and ragged trees. He came to a beach of sorts, not the same as he and Mary had visited yesterday morning, but he could see the dark swell of the ocean, could hear it crashing onto the sand, could smell the seaweed and the salt and the distinct fishiness of the cool, moist air.

Walking to the edge of where the waves became an ebb of water, Lincoln paused, facing the ocean, and closed his eyes. He drew in a breath, let it out. With it went a pulse of pain from his head, and he let his shoulders slump a bit, felt some of the tension wash from his weary muscles.

"Lincoln?" came a voice from beside him, and the tension returned in a slam of pressure that raced up his nerves. "Abraham Lincoln?"

The tall man sighed, turned to where the voice had issued from.

"I cannot believe, of all people to come across here on the edge of the United States," the voice continued, and Lincoln noted two things before he even opened his eyes to see who it was.

His voice was loud and clear, stentorian and deep, with an artificial melodiousness to it that sounded as if the person were singing the words to unheard music.

And the words "United States" had been spoken with an edge of clear contempt.

Slowly, Lincoln opened his eyes.

"You have the better of me, sir," Lincoln responded, squinting to make out the figure that stood near him.

A dark figure, all shadows and absences, walked toward him across the beach, limping a bit through the damp sand, favoring his left foot.

The man was shorter by at least half a foot than Lincoln, wirier. A hat topped his head, a casual-looking dark slouch hat, and curls of black hair, nearly ringlets, spilled from beneath it. His face lay in the shadow of the hat, but Lincoln could make out dark eyes, a dark mustache and beard. He could also smell alcohol on him, a sweet, grain reek atop the salt air.

The man made no attempt to shake Lincoln's outstretched hand—a habit from campaigning—just stared at him.

"I know you from somewhere," Lincoln muttered, searching his memory for that face, that voice.

The figure snickered. "I should say so. Mine is probably the most famous face on the continent."

Lincoln could not bring to mind who he was though, and the smaller fellow harrumphed in annoyance. "John W. Booth, sir, pre-eminent star of the stage, wherever that stage may be, in the Confederate States of America, the Republic of Texas or even…the United States of America."

Again, the theatrical emphasis, the derision heaped on those last few syllable. Only now, they made sense. Even before the war was over, even before it was clear who would win, Booth had been a well-known southern sympathizer. Full of whiskey, Booth would tell anyone and everyone what he thought of the Union, Grant and even Lincoln.

"Of course, Mr. Booth," Lincoln said, offering his hand again. This time, the other man sniffed a little, cast a disdainful glance at its owner, then slowly, very slowly, took it in his own, firmly, shook twice, then dropped it.

"I remember seeing you once back in Washington, at… at… " Lincoln rubbed his temples. "Well, you will excuse me. I can't seem to remember. Headaches, you see. They rob me of my sleep."

"Tis nothing, Mr. Lincoln," Booth replied. "I daresay I have tread the boards so many times that I often cannot keep track of all my roles. But at least I was correct in saying that you knew me. I am *assured* of that."

"Yes," Lincoln chuckled. "You were correct."

They stood side by side for a few moments in silence. Lincoln closed his eyes again. The throbbing in his head, which the rhythm of the waves had soothed, was now back, pounding all the more in Booth's presence.

"You know, of course, my feelings for you, for the Union, for the war?"

Lincoln smiled, but did not open his eyes. Yes, he'd had some whiskey; that much was clear.

"Yes, I believe you've made your views generally known."

"And you feel no anger, no hatred, no sense of danger being with me this evening on a dark, out of the way beach all alone?" Booth nearly whispered. "With no Pinkertons in sight?"
Lincoln opened his eyes, turned. "I suppose if you'd wanted to kill me, you'd have had plenty of opportunity when I was president."

Booth sniffed and waved a hand through the air absently.

"Yes, of course, you're right. Absolutely safe now. What need Macbeth kill Duncan if he is no longer king?"

Lincoln, no actor but a keen fan of Shakespeare, replied, "*Murder, though it have no tongue, will speak with most miraculous organ.*"

Booth snorted, actually laid a hand on the taller man's shoulder, squeezed amiably.

"Now, you mix works, my dear ex-president," Booth laughed. "*Hamlet* does not go well with *Macbeth*."

"No?" Lincoln asked as the actor's hand fell away. "Do they not both involve murders?"

"One, sir, involves revenge; the other guilt."

"Are they not different sides of the same coin?"

Booth snorted again, this time lower. He understood.

"I suppose so, sir, yes. I had never looked at the two in contrast before." Booth sketched a brief bow, comically, perhaps even insultingly dramatic.

Lincoln tipped his hatless head, smiled thinly.

"What brings you to San Francisco, Mr. Booth?" Lincoln said, turning back to the dark ocean. "I would have supposed that you'd have eagerly sought those Southern audiences whose views you so championed; to bask, as it were, in their glory."

Booth stiffened beside him.

"It is not as you think, Mr. Ex-President," he said, his voice thinner now, edged. "They have turned on me. Oh not loudly, to be sure, but turned nonetheless."

"How so?" Lincoln asked, his hand absently going to his temple.

"They avoid me, sir. I am no longer booked in the larger cities, asked to the better theatres. I am no longer begged to make an appearance at the best parties and balls. Even the women, the dear southern belles, no longer seek my company, sir. Me, John Wilkes Booth, defender of the Confederacy and the best living actor on the entire continent.

"Why is that? One would think they would be lifting you on their shoulders, filling every seat at your performances."

"No, sir. They avoid me because they wish peace with the United States. They wish a return to those sacred bonds of brotherhood they enjoyed when both countries were one thing and not just brothers. They are embarrassed of me, sir. They wish to forget me and my views.

"No one in the United States, either, wants me anymore. For exactly the same, if stronger, feelings."

Lincoln nodded, massaging his temples and trying to let the crashing of the waves do their magic. But it was as if Booth's presence aggravated his condition.

"So, I was forced to come out West, to play in cattle houses in Texas and bordellos here in California. Have you ever attempted King Lear in front of Mexican barons?"

Booth shook his head ruefully.

"Are you performing here in San Francisco, Mr. Booth?"

Booth sighed. "*You*. Of all people to meet out here on the Pacific, I meet *you*."

Lincoln cleared his throat rather than repeat the question.

"Yes, Yes," Booth answered, impatiently nudging the sand with the tip of his boot. "At The Orpheum. My engagement begins tomorrow and runs until the end of the month."

"What is the piece?"

Booth angrily kicked a clod of sand toward the black wall of the ocean.

"I am reduced to small plays and comedies, doggerels and pantomimes," he replied. "It's become impossible for me to assay a

Shakespeare or a Bacon."

"The piece?"

"*Our American Cousin*," he whispered, his embarrassment emanating from him in waves that were, for a moment, as strong as those of the ocean's.

"As it turns out, I am familiar with that play. It is relatively new, isn't it?" Lincoln asked.

"New? Yes, relatively. Oh, it's a trifle to be sure," Booth said, ignoring or not hearing the compliment Lincoln tried to pay him. "And most come to see Laura Keane, the darling of the stage." Booth's tone was unabashedly jealous, but didn't seem to care.

Lincoln took a deep breath, straightened.

"Will you be performing tomorrow night?" he asked.

"Yes, why?"

"I believe that Mrs. Lincoln and I would like to attend."

Booth's eyes narrowed, and he glared at the president.

"Come to one of my performances? Whatever for? It played for two weeks in Washington several years ago, and you never bothered to come and see it."

"Were you in it then?" Lincoln asked, and a feeling went through him that was unexplainable.

He wanted Booth to say yes, because, for some reason, it would make sense to Lincoln. Something about that play and Booth.

Something about Laura Keane.

Something about these awful headaches.

But Booth shook his head.

"*Our American Cousin?*" he laughed. "I think not. At that time, I was still on top of the world. I wouldn't have gone to *see* it, much less *be in* it. But now, well now my circumstances are somewhat straightened."

Lincoln closed his eyes and Booth's words faded away, washed from his senses on waves of pain.

"I come, then, to see your performance, Mr. Booth," Lincoln said. "I come to see destiny."

Lincoln closed his eyes against the throbbing pain in his

temple.

Beside him, nearly invisible in the dark sea spray, Booth smiled.

"Why, father," Mary clucked at him as she drew on a pair of elbow-length lace gloves. "You seem positively nervous tonight. I have never seen you so excitable. Is something bothering you?"
Lincoln shrugged himself into his long, dark coat, fidgeted with his tie.

"No, no, mother," he said, forcing himself to smile, relax his hands. "Just anxious to step out with my sweetheart on my arm and lose myself in the theatre."

Mary narrowed her dark eyes at him, took his hand in her plump, enlaced hand.

"If you'd rather, we can skip the play and have a private dinner instead," she said, squeezing his large hand and reaching up to stroke his craggy cheek.

Lincoln smiled crookedly. Sometimes she was so lucid, so discerning that it disarmed him, reminded him that the deaths of their children hadn't caused her to completely lose her mind. There was still something of the 20-year-old Mary Todd he had simply wanted to dance with so long ago.

He took her hand cupping his cheek and kissed it gently.

"No, mother, I'm looking forward to going tonight."

"But, *Our American Cousin...* it doesn't seem your type of play. It's not Shakespeare."

He laughed, released her hand and smoothed the lapels of his jacket.

"You make me seem so high-browed, Ms. Todd," he chuckled. "When you know I'm just a rough, homespun country boy. Besides, tonight I wish to laugh."

Mary smiled, a smile that could still light her haunted, hollow features.

"Then, laugh you shall, Mr. Lincoln."

The carriage bounced and jittered down the pockmarked San Francisco streets toward The Orpheum. Lincoln held Mary's hand, stared out the window at the buildings, the people he passed.

Ghosts…all of them, he thought.

Ghosts.

People who had shape and color, but no solidity, no reality. They existed here, but here was not where it was supposed to be, not what it was supposed to be.

He felt it, but didn't know why he felt it, didn't know why these people failed to register on his senses.

The play's the thing, he thought. *The play's the thing.*

For some reason, he believed that a minor farce written by a minor playwright would give him the answers he needed to make sense of what he could not make sense of in any other way.

No, not the play… not the writer.

The actor.

It was John Wilkes Booth.

Somehow he held the key…*was* the key.

Our American Cousin did make him laugh. Ms. Keane was delightful in her role, perhaps challenged all the more by having an actor of Booth's caliber to play off of. Lincoln and Mary laughed, squeezed each other's hands, relaxed a bit in the private balcony the theatre had arranged for them.

Wilkes, cast in the role of the titular cousin, Asa Trenchard, was not quite as believable, though. Here, Wilkes' classical training betrayed him, and Trenchard managed to come off less an entertaining American bumpkin than a bitter, down-on-his-luck Shakespearean actor. Still, the audience forgave him, laughed with him.

Halfway through Act III, Scene 2, though, Booth watched Keane's character flounce off stage.

"Don't know the manners of good society, eh? Well, I guess I know enough to turn you inside out, old gal—you sockdologizing old man-trap," Booth leered after her.

At those words, Lincoln's left hand fluttered to his temple, his right tightened convulsively on Mary's, and he slumped forward in his chair.

The hissing gaslight squeezed down into a narrow funnel of light, and the pain in his head cycled up and up until it became a thin, keening vibration in his skull that carried him into darkness.

He didn't see Mary kneel down to him, cradling his head, didn't hear her call out to those around that the president—*the President!*—was stricken and required assistance.

Didn't see, at the moment his world went black, Booth on stage below, turning to see what had caused the commotion, catching his boot on the floorboard, twisting it roughly, falling to the floor himself.

He awoke in a bed, a thin wedge of hot sunlight squeezing through a gap in the heavy curtains.
Blinking, he tried to figure out where he was, what had happened.

In an instant, he remembered himself seated, a balcony draped in red, white and blue bunting, watching a play, a burst of incandescent pain in his head, falling, falling, darkness.

Had that happened, really *happened*? It was so much like his dreams that he was unsure.

But there was something, something that was different now.

It took him a moment to put his finger on precisely what it was.

His head didn't hurt any more.

The door to the bedroom opened, and it was only then that Lincoln remembered that he was in a hotel room in San Francisco. As this reality settled over him, Mary bustled through the door, nearly elbowing a gentleman aside in her haste.

She fell to her knees beside the bed, the black crinoline of her dress like a chorus of low whispers. Grabbing his hand in hers, now gloveless, she covered it with teary kisses.

"Oh, father, dearest," she wept. "I was so worried... so worried lest you leave me here all alone."

Momentarily irritated, Lincoln let it pass, reached down to gently stroke his wife's hair.

"Mary, dear," he said, finding his voice. "I am well now, whatever happened. It has passed."

The man Mary had elbowed past cleared his throat.

"I am Dr. Samuel Mudd, sir," he said, in a curiously flat voice. "I am the house doctor and oversaw your treatment last night and this morning."

"Ahh, doctor," Lincoln said, sitting up in bed. "Thank you for your care, but I feel well enough now. You say it is morning?"

"Oh, father," Mary, almost forgotten, snuffled. "You fell insensible last night at the play. We brought you here, and here you have passed the night unconscious until this very minute."

"Morning," he repeated. "What time?"

The doctor fished a pocket watch out of his waistcoat.

"Seven twenty-two... no... twenty three," he responded. Lincoln rubbed his forehead, more out of habit than any other reason, as there was now no hint of any pain, not even a ghost.

"You have a guest, Mr. Lincoln," Mudd said, slipping the watch back into his waistcoat.

Lincoln saw Mary flash the doctor an annoyed look, as if she had—and probably had—warned the doctor about mentioning this.

"A vistor? At this hour? Who?"

"Mr. Booth," Mary sniffed. "The actor from last night's play."

Mudd snapped his bag closed. "He injured his ankle right after you collapsed. I asked to take a look at it, but he waved me off."

Mary sniffed. "I asked him to leave several times, but he would not. He's been in the parlor all night."

Lincoln raised his eyebrow. "All night? Well, we must let him in, mother, mustn't we? If he was concerned enough to wait all night...."

Mary frowned, but said nothing. Instead she rose, smoothed her skirt and went to the door. The doctor lifted his bag and followed her.

Lincoln heard a few sharp, muffled words, then Mary flounced back into the room.

"Mr. Booth," she said, turning her head aside in disapproval.

Booth lurched into the room, a dark and rumpled presence, but a presence nonetheless. Lincoln rose up in the bed and offered his hand, noticing how Booth favored his left foot.

Doffing his slouch hat, Booth stepped toward the bed and took Lincoln's hand.

"I hope my presence is no inconvenience, sir," he said, the Southerner in his blood taking over. "I had wanted to ensure that you were recovering from your collapse last night."

"Of course," Lincoln said, smoothing his bed clothes. "And thank you for your concern. I hope I didn't ruin the performance for everyone."

Booth raised an eyebrow. "Ruin *that* play? It was ruined when word was first penned to page."

Lincoln began to demur, but Booth stopped him. "If it isn't too bold of me, did the doctor say what it was?"

"Oh, exhaustion. Nervousness. Stress. Take your pick. I see, though, that you have suffered some injury of your own since last I saw you."

Booth frowned, not as if annoyed that Lincoln had noticed, but rather more in confusion. Then, he remembered.

"Ah, the ankle," he said, looking down at it. "Yes, well, in my attempt to see what was happening in the balcony, I twisted my ankle a bit. Nothing more."

"I had noticed the other evening that you seemed to be favoring that very foot."

Booth smiled, but it was transparent and theatrical.

"Why, yes, interesting you should notice. This ankle has been bothering me for quite some time, really. The twist last night seems to have aggravated it."

"You should have had the doctor attend to it while he was here."

Booth waved a hand dramatically through the air. "It is nothing."

Lincoln considered this for a moment in silence, then turned to Mary.

"Mother, would you mind leaving us for a moment?"

Mary turned a blank face to her husband, blinked several times.

"I have some private words for Mr. Booth."

Mary pursed her lips and a slight flush came to her face.

"Very well," she said, flashing a distinctly unfriendly look at the actor before leaving the room and drawing the door shut behind her.

Lincoln rubbed at his head. There was a slight, just a slight pulse of pain in his temple now, but growing, cycling up.

"You've had that pain in your ankle for a while, haven't you," he said, not opening his eyes, his voice quiet.

There was a pause of a few seconds.

"Yes, I have.

Lincoln nodded.

"As have I this infernal headache," he answered. "And your ankle, its pain trebles when I am near, doesn't it?"

"Yes."

Lincoln nodded, let his long arms rest at his sides. He looked up at Booth, who stared at him with wide, dark eyes.

"As my pain does when you are near."

"What are you suggesting, Mr. Lincoln?"

"*Suggesting*," Lincoln laughed, drawing himself up on his bed. "I scarcely know. But let me ask you, Mr. Booth. Do things feel right in your life? Do things feel…as they should be?"

Booth walked to the room's window, drew the heavy curtains apart. The day was overcast, and a cold, grey rain fell outside.

"No. They do not. Nothing has seemed right since…since…"

"Since the war was lost."

"Won, you mean."

"Yes, of course."

"No. It seems off-kilter, like the whole world has taken the wrong path, except… "

"Us two.

Booth turned from the window with a curious look. Lincoln's comment had been a statement, not a question.

"Us two?" he whispered. "But how can that be? I've had dreams…nightmares."

"I, too, have had my share of nightmares," Lincoln responded.

Booth laughed. "I would dare say, Mr. Lincoln, that my nightmares are *not* shared by you. You shall have to take my word on this."

Lincoln considered this for a moment as Booth turned back to the window.

"I would not be too sure, Mr. Booth. Somehow you and I, your nightmares and mine, are tied together in this."

"Not to be rude, to be sure, but you and I share nothing," Booth said, turned back to Lincoln. "You stand for everything I hate. Or should I say *stood?* We share nothing, sir.

"Nothing," he repeated.

"Were it not for the nightmares, the strange pains that seem to amplify in each other's presence, I would agree with you," Lincoln said. "But faced with this, there is something. I don't know what it is, but I feel it. And I believe that you feel it, too."

Lincoln waited for this to sink in, then pressed on.

"Something has gone wrong, something involving the two of us," he explained. "And because of it, things are not right."

Booth shook his head.

"Madness," he sneered. "I thought you mad during your presidency, but this...this is *extraordinary.*"

"There's something about the play, too...something that ties us together."

Booth burst out laughing, but Lincoln heard the laughter float on a stronger wave of anger and bitterness...and fear. His laughter was thick with fear, and Lincoln recoiled from the force of it.

"The play?" Booth hissed. "*Our American Cousin?* That piece of tripe? That somehow ties us together, eh? The former president of the United States of America and the man who wanted to..."

Booth trailed off, his hands flexing and unflexing at this side, the color draining from his cheeks.

"Are you alright?" Lincoln asked.

"Stay away," Booth said, placing his hat back atop his head. "Stay away from the theatre, from *me.* You ruined my performance last night, and I can't afford that. I can't lose this role."

"I can't stay away," Lincoln said. "This must be put right. We have to figure out how... ."

"There is no 'how!'" Booth shouted. "No 'why!' Leave it be, sir. I pray you, leave it be. You have no idea of what you are meddling with, what you're questioning. *What you want.*

"Let things be as they are."

Booth took hold of the doorknob, twisted it.

"I cannot," Lincoln said.

"You *must*. Don't come back to the theatre."

Booth drew the door open.

"Mr. Booth, there is something I have learned from my years of enjoying the theatre," Lincoln said.

Booth half turned, the door partially open. Through it, Lincoln could see his wife, eyes wide at the shouting.

"Yes?"

"It is that, in every performance, though lines are forgotten or otherwise altered, though the actors miss their cues or stand in the wrong places, or one actor is replaced by another, the play proceeds apace, always to the same end."

Booth stiffened, went through the door, closed it behind him.

"Always to the same end."

After Booth left, Lincoln rose and dressed, slowly at first, but then realizing that he felt reasonably well, he quickened his pace. Though Mary voiced her concern, they took an early lunch in the hotel's dining room, and Lincoln felt his appetite was large for the first time in years.

When they were finished with lunch, Lincoln and Mary walked, arm in arm, along the streets of San Francisco. Lincoln, ordinarily not a shopper, indulged Mary and went with her into an endless procession of shops. She purchased a new dress, a parasol, several pairs of gloves, and an expensive pair of kid leather shoes. For his part, he allowed her to pick out the material for a new suit for him, as well as a new stovepipe hat and a simple walking stick.

They returned to the hotel, unloaded their purchases, and took dinner in the dining room. Over dinner, Lincoln told Mary that he had a surprise for her.

Two tickets to see *Our American Cousin* at The Orpheum.

Dubious, she agreed to go because he told her a simple thing. He had to see the end of the play.

They went that night, and the next, and the next. The following night, confused and concerned, Mary begged off, telling her husband that she had a headache and didn't feel well. She had hoped that he would stay with her, reading from the Bible or Shakespeare, as she did some needlepoint. She was cross when he didn't offer to do so, just quickly kissed her forehead and told her not to stay up too late.

He took a carriage to the theatre, bought a single ticket, and watched from the main floor this time.

Lincoln didn't think that Booth noticed him in the audience any of these times.

But Booth did notice, each and every time.

And it began to weigh heavily on him.

Tuesday evening, and the performance seemed a bit off to Lincoln. Of course, unlike other members of the audience, he'd already seen the play eight times. Tonight, though unnoticed by his fellow patrons, Laura Keene's performance seemed superficial and bored, and her lethargy affected how much energy the other actors exerted.

Except Booth.

His performance seemed sharp and electric, his body as taut as a piece of rope pulled in two directions. The audience, at first unsure of the ferocity he threw into his performance as the American hayseed Asa Trechard, eventually settled down and matched his vehemence with exaggerated laughter.

"Mr. Trenchard, you will please recollect you are addressing my daughter, and in my presence," said Mrs. Mountchessington. "Yes, I'm offering her my heart and hand just as she wants them... with nothing in 'em," Booth's Trenchard said.

Laughter, even Lincoln chuckled a bit.

But the laughter died fitfully as the audience recovered, saw that the play had stalled, with Booth staring out into the audience.

"August, dear, to your..." Mrs. Mountchessington continued.

"*You*," Booth whispered, and the actress playing Mrs. Mountchessington paused and blinked furiously as she tried to figure out exactly whom Booth was addressing.

But Lincoln knew.

They locked eyes, Booth leaning down a little to get a straight line of sight.

"*You... again*," he repeated, this time a bit louder.

The audience looked around, tried to find the object of Booth's frustration.

As heads turned, they, too, found Lincoln, sitting ramrod straight in his chair, looking directly back at Booth.

"You!" Booth roared. "I warned you, I *begged* you not to come here anymore. But you won't listen, will you? You persist in coming here each evening and driving me mad! You have no idea, sir... none! No idea what you ask of me!"

Sighing, Lincoln rose from his seat, smoothed his jacket, bowed slightly to Booth, then excused himself as he left the row, departed the theatre.

"Lincoln!" Booth shouted after him. "Lincoln! Don't come back. Don't come back to this damned theatre anymore. Leave me be! *Leave it be!*"

The tall, somber figure continued up the aisle and out the doors, never turning back, never answering the actor raving from the stage.

"This play will not go on to the same end!" he screamed as the door closed behind Lincoln.

After that evening's performance, Lincoln returned to the hotel and was able to slip into bed without awakening Mary.

Booth slumped in his dressing room for two hours after the play ended, taking off his makeup in a desultory fashion, a bottle of whiskey and a half-filled tumbler at his elbow. People didn't knock this evening, to invite him to parties, to catch a late dinner, to have a few drinks. But Booth didn't miss them at all.

As the owner came to close the theatre, Booth donned his jacket and slouch hat, grabbed the bottle and left his dressing room, pushing past the man with a muttered "Good evening." He burst out the rear door of the theatre into a dark alley.

A man leaning up against the building held the reins of a horse. When he saw Booth, he straightened, tugged at the reins to liven the animal.

Booth snatched the reins from the man, muttered a "Thanks" and tossed him a coin.

Jumping into the saddle, he gave the horse's side a quick kick, spurred it out onto the main street.

A brief ride along mostly dirt streets brought him to the saloon he was looking for, a run down and unsavory place he'd found his first night in San Francisco. It was far enough from the theatre and disreputable enough for few there to recognize him, pay him any attention.

He made his way through the throng of people to a deserted table near the rear of the place. There, he took a long pull directly from his bottle, plunked it onto the table, eyed it suspiciously,.

A woman came and asked him what he wanted, eyeing the bottle herself, but saying nothing. He asked for another bottle of the same and a glass. And then he asked to be left alone. She laughed at that, but went away, coming back with the single bottle and the single glass. In the time since she'd left, he'd drained the first bottle. He pushed it across the table, and she took it with a rueful smile.

Uncorking the second bottle, he splashed some into the glass, sighed, drained it. He waved off the advances of one of the establishment's paid ladies, a patron who recognized him from earlier performances and a drunkard who was looking for donations to continue the evening's work.

Glass after glass, the second bottle of whiskey went into him. Rather than calming his mind or, better yet, rendering him senseless, though, the alcohol seemed to fuel the flames that already burned inside him.

The bar, the life around him faded into the background, and the dreams, the infernal dreams came forward into sharp focus.

If Lincoln only knew, he would surely stop coming to the performances, surely stop harassing Booth with his presence.

But, he feared, even the knowledge of Booth's dreams would not keep Lincoln away. Even the outburst he'd had tonight would not keep him away.

Because there was something, just as Lincoln said, something that drew the two together, though Booth found the idea repellant and somehow discomfiting.

But there was something, and it plagued his mind, plagued his dreams.

Because he, too, had dreams.

They were unpleasant, murderous, streaked with blood, slopped with it.

At the end, the blood was his. Shot. To die in a barn.

Always to the same end.

It was the "always" that dogged him, frustrated him, scared him.

Because Lincoln could not possibly know, in the way Booth knew, what that end was.

"Father," Mary said, quietly drawing an evening glove up her plump forearm. "Must we see that play again tonight?"

Lincoln sat on a small divan near the foot of the bed, drawing on his boots.

"The play amuses me," he said, a little more crossly than he'd intended. "There have been so few amusements in our life as of late."

"But you've seen it a dozen times already."

Lincoln pulled the cuffs of his dark trousers down over the tops of his boots, wiped absently at a scuff.

"It makes me laugh, mother."

Mary came to him, placed a hand on his shoulder.

"But you don't laugh," she said. "I watch you, father. You don't even smile."

Lincoln lifted his face to hers and sighed, deeply.

"I may not be the smartest or loveliest woman you know, but I know you better than anyone. This play doesn't amuse you at all. There's something else. I don't know what, but I know that much. And it frightens me," Mary said.

Lincoln sighed again. "Yes, there is something. That much I admit. But what it is, I don't know quite yet."

"Your dreams?"

Lincoln nodded, silently and solemnly. She'd heard him cry out in the middle of the night, eyes wide, hands clenched; awaken with his bedclothes soaked with sweat.

"Oh, Abraham," she said, burying her face in the tangle of hair on the top of his head. "You are keeping something from me… *something bad.* I just know it. I feel it. I feel that you're going to leave me alone."

Lincoln stiffened at this, but gently pushed her away so that he could stand, enfold her in his arms.

"Mother," he breathed. "The only one who can take me from you is God. And despite what he may feel, my feelings on the subject should be quite clear to you."

He lifted her head to look up at him, kissed her cheek.

She relaxed a little, managed a blush.

"Well, they had better be," she said, in a mock-scolding tone of voice. "My father will not appreciate you leading me on for so long if your feelings for me aren't clear."

Lincoln smiled, an open and uncomplicated smile. "Well, I would be foolish to disregard the anger of your father, even though long dead."

He kissed her again, and they drew apart, smiled at each other.

Lincoln offered his arm, and she took it. They left their hotel room, arm in arm, and made their way down to the waiting carriage.

In the lobby, they glided through the early evening crowd, some eyes on them as they always were, accessing, judging, hating, feeling pity or disregard. Lincoln simply ignored them, and Mary did her best to hold her head up and focus on what was immediately before her.

"President Lincoln!" came a shout from nearby.

Instinctually, Lincoln jerked as he heard his name, quickened his already lengthy pace.

"Sir!" came the voice again, and two people nearly dashed before him to cut him off.

"Major Rathbone," said Lincoln, relaxing and squeezing Mary's hand as he recognized the man.

Rathbone was dressed in his military uniform, his dark hair and mustache gleaming. On his arm, a beautiful, fashionably dressed woman looked upon the Lincolns with bright, wide eyes.

Lincoln shook the officer's outstretched hand gratefully. Rathbone bowed to Mary as Lincoln took the other woman's hand and gently shook it.

"Is it still *Miss* Harris?" he asked with a slight smile. "Really, major, how long will you make this beautiful young woman wait?"

Miss Harris' smiled beamed, and she turned to look at her date.

"Not much longer to be sure, Mr. President," he answered.

Lincoln shushed him gently. "Best to leave that title where I left it, back in Washington. Besides, what are you doing all the way out here?"

"You shall always be a president, sir, to me," he said. Then, Rathbone looked around, turned back to Lincoln. "I am taking a brief respite from planning."

Lincoln's eyebrows raised, but he said nothing.

"It is not over, sir," Rathbone whispered. "President Greeley has made it quietly known, after all, that he does not believe the Union can survive much longer without the South restored. Plans are afoot... ."

"Major, major," Lincoln chided, brushing the air with a hand. "Surely this is neither the time nor the place to discuss this. And surely I am not the person to discuss it with."

"I only meant, sir," the young man said, blushing extravagantly.

"We were just leaving to take in *Our American Cousin* at the theatre," Lincoln said. "We would be delighted if you joined us, right, mother?"

"Excellent, sir!" Rathbone said. "We, too, were on our way there, having tickets for tonight's performance!"

"But we couldn't possibly intrude," Miss Harris protested.

Mary, facing an uneasy evening with her husband's mysteries, agreed wholeheartedly with this arrangement. She took the young woman's hand in hers and smiled.

"We will not hear of it," Mary said. "Of course you shall join us in our box. Two additional chairs will be no imposition at all. Besides, while the gentlemen watch the play, we can discuss how best to speed up Major Rathbone's request for your hand."

Mary drew Miss Harris near, where they began speaking and laughing almost immediately.

Lincoln looked at Rathbone, shrugged, and the party made its way to the carriage.

The carriage pulled to a sharp stop at the front of The Orpheum, and the driver hopped down, put a step out, drew the door open and helped the women out.

Lincoln stepped out of the carriage last, unfolding his lanky form onto the dirt street and placing his hat atop his head.

He breathed in the cool, night air, took Mary's arm and proceeded up the steps to the theatre's entrance. As they mounted the steps, Lincoln saw the playbill posted outside the doors; the same playbill he'd seen countless times.

But this time, not the same.

"They've replaced Booth," he said, to no one in particular.

"Good," Mary sniffed. "Horrid man."

Lincoln allowed himself to be drawn past the sign and into the theatre's lobby.

As Mary spoke with an usher about being escorted to the balcony, Lincoln saw the theatre's owner walking across the lobby.

"Sir," Lincoln said to his passing form. "The playbill outside? Booth. Is he no longer performing?"

The owner jerked once at Lincoln's voice, then stared at him harshly.

"Mr. Lincoln," the man snapped. "I would have thought you of all people would know exactly why Mr. Booth is no longer appearing here, after the ruckus the night before. I had to let him go. His understudy, Mr. Harry Hawk, will play the part until the run ends, sir."

The man pursed his thin lips, looked as if he might say something else, then walked away through he crowd.

Mary was tugging at his arm, looking at him curiously as he turned back to his group.

Outside, John Wilkes Booth sat on a rickety wooden bench in front of the theatre. His brooding, black eyes watched as Lincoln and his guests stepped out of the carriage.

He watched them ascend the steps, saw Lincoln stop as he noticed the playbill with Hawk's name replacing his own.

As Lincoln went inside, Booth took another deep draw from the silver flask he held. Capping it, he slipped it inside his vest, stood, and walked quickly down the alley to the back of the theatre.

His hand went to his coat pocket, touched the cold metal that lay there like an affirmation that this wasn't a dream… not yet.

Lincoln noticed the difference in the atmosphere as soon as the play began. Hawk's portrayal of Asa Trenchard was broader, lighter, more comic and less florid than Booth's. More deft and confident, and less as if the character were a slight or an unfairness thrust upon the actor.

But there was more.

Booth's absence made the play itself, not just the character of Asa, more fluid and contagiously funny. Though he'd seen it a dozen times thus far, Lincoln found himself laughing more than he could remember at any other performance. He remembered that this was a comedy; something that hadn't really struck him before.

Mary, too, could feel it, Lincoln sensed. Her grasp on his hand was lighter, less stressed than usual, and she paid more attention to the play than to him, smiling whenever she did glance over at him.

Major Rathbone and Miss Harris, too, seemed to be enjoying the play, and Lincoln relaxed in his chair.

He realized that his headache was gone, gone for the first time in weeks.

Sighing, he squeezed Mary's hand, smiled at her.

Behind him, there was a grating sound, as wood upon wood, and the door burst open.

Lincoln did not notice. He had leaned forward in his chair, looked down upon the smiling faces of the audience.

A figure entered the box, and Major Rathbone turned to see who it was, started to stand.

Booth pulled the pistol from his pocket and aimed it directly at the back of Lincoln's head.

He pulled the trigger, and Lincoln slumped forward.

The rest was a blur.

The noise of the gun, though rather small, caused everyone, even those on stage to look up.   For a single, fierce moment, Booth was glad he'd ruined Hawk's line, as Lincoln had ruined it for Booth.

Then, Rathbone was upon him, but Booth slashed at him with a knife held in his other hand.

He set his foot on the edge of the box, looked down to the stage, leapt.

The other actors scattered.

His ankle, the one that had been giving him trouble now for the last several years, snapped beneath his weight.

Collapsing to one knee, he wobbled, produced the pistol, brought it to his own head.

"*Sic semper ludius!*" he shouted.

For a moment, he stared out at the audience as they tried to comprehend what had happened, what he meant.

"*Not to the same end,*" he whispered to himself.

The pistol spoke the last line.

In another place, another time, nearby but not too much so, Lincoln lay diagonally across a narrow, rickety bed. His coat and boots had been removed. His injured head propped carefully atop a pillow onto which his life had ebbed out over the last several hours.

His breathing, which had slowly risen and ebbed throughout the night, finally paused.

One last whistling inhalation, one last rattling exhalation.

Then silence.

The group of men that has crowded near his bed throughout the night stood on in silence, their own breathing stopped.

Then one, a man with a long beard who eyes were red-rimmed behind his glasses, stepped forward, placed his hand gently on the dead man's shoulder.

He saved the Union. Now he belongs to the ages."

And somewhere near, but not too near, another man raced away on horseback, a broken ankle jammed into a stirrup, toward an end in a burning barn.

About the author: Sam S. Kepfield's work has appeared in various publications.

CAROUSEL – A SHORT STORY
TERENCE KUCH

An alarm sounds. Robert Morgan, Ph.D., jumps from its suddenness; its loudness clatters against his quiet thoughts. Carousel number three starts up with lurches and rattles. Luggage from Flight 760 begins to pour and bump onto the moving belt as passengers subtly jostle for position near the carousel's disgorging mouth. Morgan's old brown Samsonite does not immediately spew forth.

A dog, in its carrier, has been placed beside the carousel. Morgan considers the dog. He doesn't have one; hadn't had since he was a boy. Perhaps he would have one now if he'd ever married or had a child.

Married? He remembers one or two young women who'd liked him, when he might have married. Like Josephine. Yes, Josie was a fine young person. And the other one, her friend, what was her name? Ruth, he thought. Yes, that's it. Ruth showed some interest. Perhaps he might have — he tastes, in his mind, thoughts of Josie and Ruth.

He waits. The belt stops. Sounds of motors outside on the tarmac. The belt starts up again. More bags appear, pushing and shoving those that arrived before, dropping on them like clumsy birds of prey. Bags are wrestled off the belt by adjacent arms. Still nothing for Morgan.

One by one, passengers reunite with their luggage, jerking them off the moving belt, sometimes colliding with other passengers; you shouldn't have been standing so close to me. Me? I was here first. And so on, none of it aloud.

Eventually, only a new-looking red suitcase, and the dog, and Morgan, are left circling the carousel or standing beside it, orbiting slowly or watching impatiently. The dog shows a face of resignation, as if to say that Morgan will have to do if Master fails to appear.

Morgan looks at his watch. 4:31 pm. It can't be that late, can it? He shakes his watch as if to punish it. Still 4:31 pm. He is undecided between waiting longer and reporting the Samsonite missing. But first, he feels the need to urinate, perhaps more. He has never been very good at understanding what his body wants. He glances around the claim area, spots the proper icon, enters the proper room, picks out a stall, devolves authority to Morgan-body to do what it has to, while Morgan-mind mulls what his recent trip to Marseilles hadn't accomplished, how he is still a failure as a physicist, even if now a well-traveled international failure with jet lag to prove it. 4:36. His watch is still obeying the law of springs and sprockets, hands going round and round endlessly until something breaks.

He thinks about his trip to France: the inattentive seminar, his failure to convince them how close we in 'Ourworld' are to the alternate universe he calls 'Altworld'; breathe and it breathes, too, a favorite example of his. His listeners were barely polite, filed out afterwards without a smile or a nod.

Here in Austin he has no grants, few students, no U.T. colleagues hinting they'd like to be 'et al's on his next paper. No citations in the literature except a few 'see also's, which everyone knows means 'don't bother to see also.' Maybe next time. But in the middle of his middle age, Morgan knows that now or never has turned to never.

His attention comes back to the present with a jolt. Something strange, some odd sensation, as if the world has nudged him sideways. Oh, well, he thinks. Too many drinks on the flight, and jet lag too. Or he might be getting sick. Those escargot —. But this doesn't feel like the first dizziness of stomach flu; more like the world itself has dizzied.

Morgan exits the men's room and returns to the carousel. The dog is gone; its owner must have come for it. The red suitcase is still going round and round. Where is that damn Samsonite, anyway? Probably missed the connecting flight at JFK. Oh, well, the airline will deliver it later. Nothing important anyway, only lecture notes and dirty clothes.

Another few bags are retrieved. Finally, Morgan is left alone with the large red bag. Around and around. He is dizzy again. He wishes the belt would reverse, help him unwind his mind. He decides to wait another ten minutes, then give up and go to the taxi stand.

Trying to take his mind off his troubles, Morgan recalls the flight attendant he'd met on the plane; he headed for the cramped toilet, she coming from it. He'd shifted his body to his right, she to her own right. They jiggled around back to back with tiny steps like porcupines afraid of each other's quills.

In the toilet compartment, he'd imagined her there not two minutes before, the scent of her perfume, the smell of her skin still in the air, her fluids filtering through various pipes. He felt a surge of sensuality for the woman. What was her name? — Nancy? At least it was 'Nancy' on her name tag.

Morgan awakes from his reverie to find a woman running up to him, kissing him on the cheek.

"I'm really sorry I'm late!" she says, breathlessly, "but the traffic on 71, you know, and then I couldn't find—." She stops short, seeing his consternation. "What's wrong, Bob?"

"Ah, ah, nothing, I guess," he stammers. She seems slightly familiar, as if he'd known a younger version of her a long time ago.

"Poor dear, you must have had a miserable flight, and with a transfer at JFK, too, just the worst place!" She looks around. "Why haven't you picked up your bag?"

"It isn't here yet." He couldn't bring himself to say "Who are you?"

"Certainly it is! Right there." Ruth points at the red bag.

"But mine is brown! My old brown Samsonite!"

"Not hardly! I bought you that big red one for your trip, so it would stand out — you know how bad your eyes are these days. And that old brown suitcase of yours was on its last rollers." She laughs at her own joke.

He examines the tag — it's his name, all right, in his handwriting, and the claim-check number matches his stub. I must really be having problems, Morgan thinks, if I can't remember this woman who obviously knows me. Maybe that flu, or the foie gras, or the dizzy spell in the men's room—.

Dutifully, he tugs the red suitcase off the belt and follows the woman out the airport door, across two service lanes, into the garage.

He lags back so he won't walk right by whatever car she is headed for. He is desperately wondering how to figure out her name, and how she came to know him well enough to buy him a red suitcase and give him a ride.

She pauses by a Peugeot, opens the trunk, gets in the driver's seat. He puts the suitcase in the trunk, sits in the rider's seat. She exits the airport, merges onto freeway traffic.

On the way, all she wants to hear is about his trip, where he stayed, if his hotel room had a bidet ("they all have those, from what I hear!") what he ate, if the French really don't understand a word of English or just pretend they don't, and so on.

Finally, a lucky break. The woman's cell phone rings. She glances away from traffic, looks at the phone number, obviously doesn't recognize it. "Hello, this is Ruth Morgan," she says, guardedly, then "Oh hi, Marge, you must be calling from work. I took today off for Sally's party and to pick up Bob at the airport." Morgan gains no useful information from the ensuing 20-minute conversation, except that her ring finger, gripped to the wheel, bears a gold band. That, and her last name, leads Morgan to the obvious conclusion.

By the time the car turns onto Ladera Norte, it's obvious they are going home. His home on North Cat Mountain, where he lives alone and doesn't vacuum enough or get the dishes very clean.

They pull up the steep driveway, enter the house. It's his house, all right, but there are differences. The furniture is new, expensive. The front yard is a lot neater. Not as much exterior paint has flaked off. And there is a new addition in back, a sunroom.

Morgan stands around while Ruth chatters on about the doings of the neighborhood in the five days he's been gone: Little Dicky Larsen sprained his ankle on something; the Millers put their house up for sale; Old Man Kline got loose again and wandered around the park scaring the children.

At a momentary break in her monologue, Morgan confesses to Ruth that he is feeling disoriented. Must be jet lag, or bad air in the plane, or haut cuisine, or whatever. She is sympathetic, tells him to rest.

***

The next morning he drives to the university, half afraid they'll never have heard of him. But no, the Physics Department receptionist smiles and asks how his trip went, winks and says "oo la la," not expecting an answer. Al Smithson waves at him through a glass door. A couple of TA's pretend to be busy.

But something is different. Where his office had been — should be — there's a new name on the door, "Rosalind Gross, Ph.D.," a name he doesn't recognize. He is dismayed. He turns to leave, but then sees his name on a different door: "Robert Morgan, Ph.D." Not his office, is it? But it must be. He enters. There are all his old books, his mementos. His office. But this is not his office. It's larger. With a table, now, beside the desk, and four chairs instead of two.

He logs on the computer and reviews his class schedule. For today, anyway, no changes. His 10 o'clock will meet in the usual room. I'm just a little woozy, he thinks; I'll be all right in a day or two. He goes to class, gives the planned lecture. The students seem more attentive than usual, even ask a few questions.

The rest of the day goes reassuringly. He encounters Rosalind Gross, pretends to know her. She is oddly deferential, not the treatment he is used to from faculty members.

At five o'clock he returns to his office, reassured that everything is fine. Couldn't imagine how he could have forgotten Ruth, or Rosalind, or the exact location of his office. But there are more surprises in that last hour of the day: he's acquired an admin, an eager young man named Edgar, a stack of business cards referring to him as "Associate Chair, Physics," and several requests from students who want him to be their thesis advisor. No student with anything higher than a C-minus average has ever asked that privilege before.

"I'm going to see a doctor," he tells himself. He uses the same words to a surprised Edgar as he leaves, and to Ruth as he enters his almost-accustomed house. She sympathizes. Later, she takes him to bed, lets him make love to her, curls up and goes to sleep.

The next day he visits the university infirmary and obtains a referral to a reputable (it is said) psychiatrist, and an appointment for that very afternoon. The sooth-sayer says sooth-ful things. Morgan feels better. Yes, he really does. Even the feeling of dizziness is disappearing. He is married. Has been for a long time. Must have been, for a long time.

Gradually, he figures out where he and Ruth met, years ago. How foolish he's been, not remembering how well they'd got along from the start, how it entered his head, after strong hints from Ruth, that they should marry. How could he have forgotten that? After all, she'd bought him a new red suitcase only last month, hadn't she? And there it had been, going round and round and round on the carousel. And no one else had claimed it. Everything is all right except him; but he will recover, he is confident. He tells himself he will recover.

***

The world is a better place, now, for Robert Morgan, Ph.D. and Associate Chair, Physics. Gradually, his memory returns. He begins to fill in details of his past life, checks them with Ruth and with friends at the university (subtly, of course), makes corrections to his memories as needed, regrets their sometime lapses.

Ruth has a little surprise party for him to celebrate the 'monthaversary' of his 'recovery.' He wonders how he could ever have been so foolish as to doubt his life with her. Ourworld / Altworld was now only a foolish fancy. But if there really is an Altworld, and he's in it, that's all right; life is better here. He sees the psychiatrist several more times. Notes are scribbled. Ah-hmms and uh-hahs are said. The feeling of being separated from his own life almost leaves him.

Time passes, several years. His theories? That there is an 'Altworld,' and only one Altworld, at that? Well, he gave up on that 'loony' theory long ago, didn't he? No one recalls that he was once considered 'on the fringe'; 'not reputable.' He has recovered nicely, and is now respected. Highly respected. In a way, it was the Altworld theory that made his name — not the theory itself, but the new mathematical approach he developed to try to prove that Altworld exists; he's won several major awards for that. No one remembers, now, the eccentric, unverifiable theory the math was designed to support.

He decides that he is happy. Even if this world is not real. But surely it is real. — Isn't it? What is 'real' but experience, anyway? And it simply can't be that he is right and everyone else wrong. That is called 'madness.' So he decides that his life is real, the world is real. Whatever 'real' means; but that's for the philosophy department to haggle about, not for him. This must be his life. Things must have always been this way. Consistent. Predictable.

More years pass. Morgan is satisfied. Even the humdrum seems magical compared with his old nightmare of delusion. The psychiatrist, whom he seldom sees any more, is delighted with his progress. Morgan will be retiring in a few more years. Perhaps he will collect postage stamps or keep bees.

***

But then — disturbing things happen that only he thinks are odd. For example: Edgar the admin is gone, and 'Elissa' is in his place. No one remembers Edgar. Elissa has been there for more years than anyone can remember. She knows where everything is filed. She is famous for going on and on about her grandchildren.

Another example: Bob and Ruth have a daughter named Caroline. She lives on the Coast and plans to visit them to show off her new husband. Why has the existence of a daughter never come up in conversation before? Now, Ruth can speak of nothing else, and how much she would like to be a grandmother. She says she'll have to straighten up the old bedroom upstairs, the room that hasn't been touched since Caroline went off to college. Morgan stays awake until 2 a.m. that night, sneaks upstairs. Yes, there's a young woman's room, complete with music posters and sports banners — but why had he never —? Wasn't that a laundry room yesterday?

Greatly troubled, Morgan visits the psychiatrist again, this time without telling Ruth. He receives a prescription. He suspects it's a placebo. Morgan is not pleased.

More of the world changes retroactively. By now, there are altogether too many examples to bear relating. So far, they have been harmless, perhaps even pleasing. But over the following month, Morgan's world starts going seriously wrong.

Item: He had written a paper for *Physical Review Letters* that was at first called "an exciting conceptual breakthrough," and acquired several et als and other hangers-on, distinguished scientists all. But then, a critical article appeared. His department head now calls the paper "stupid." The university shamefacedly and regretfully retracts his paper.

Item: Morgan has lost two chairs from his office, and the table.

Item: He is informed of a space crunch in the departmental offices, so could he please just make himself comfortable somewhere in the undergraduate library?

Item: His old office is now occupied by Rosalind Gross, Ph.D., the new Associate Chair, Physics.

Item: Ruth mentions that Caroline died at age four. Everyone was devastated. A flower fund was established in her name.

The changes become more frequent and disorienting, threatening. Radically different news stories are in the papers day by day; no one recognizes any contradiction. Terrorist plots are discovered; several bombs are set off, one as near as Houston; but the next day everything appears to be fine, nothing has happened. Countries 35 and 36 join the nuclear club. The military draft is reinstated. The Canadian border is sealed. Electricity goes off at the university at disconcerting and unpredictable times. Diplomats are evacuated by helicopter from third-world cities.

Morgan is desperate, panicked. He tells the psychiatrist what he is experiencing. The psychiatrist is puzzled, doesn't see a problem. It occurs to Morgan, suddenly, that he might really be in some other universe —Altworld. Perhaps his theories were right all along. Could that be? And this world, whether it is 'Altworld' or not, is unstable, becoming incoherent, breaking up. How could this be happening? He remembers seeing a photograph of two galaxies colliding. Are two Altworlds colliding? But in his theory, the one he repudiated but is now again beginning to believe, that's impossible: there is Ourworld, and there is Altworld. That's it. No more, no room for another. He is afraid that Altworld will be destroyed like a dream, like it never was, with all those in it, including him.

What should he do, now that he thinks he understands what's happening? What *can* he do? Could he return to Ourworld? How? He dusts off his old notebooks, works the math again, tries to understand when and how he was ported to Altworld. He thinks back. Of course, it was at the airport. He goes over everything that happened: the carousel, the dog, the red suitcase. No clues.

But then he remembers that he visited the men's room, had an odd dizzy feeling while waiting for his brown Samsonite. Something must have occurred at that particular time and place where he happened to be. It wasn't drinks or French food; something happened, right there, that thrust him into Altworld.

He studies, refines his theory. Altworld had irrupted into Ourworld, dragged him back with it. What could disrupt the boundary between worlds? Searching through the physics library, he happens to stumble on an intriguing fact: 'solar maximum,' the peak of the eleven-year cycle of solar flare activity, occurred in late October, eleven years ago. Unusually for a flare, it had caused strong geomagnetically induced currents that had been detected underground on a line from San Luis Potosí, Mexico, to Tulsa, Oklahoma. Morgan found a world globe, traced the line. It intersected Austin, Texas, exactly.

But how could he have been affected? He'd been sitting on a ring of porcelain, a relatively non-conducting material. He tried to think back. He called the time into mind over and over.

There it was. When he began feeling dizzy, disoriented, his hand had been on the flush lever. Connected by iron and steel into the earth, into those magnetic currents!

After days of intense study, he concludes that if he returns to the airport at exactly the same day and time, exactly eleven years after the previous solar maximum, the earth's rotation and orbit will have brought that exact spot precisely in line with the flare, and there is a chance he might be ported back to Ourworld. A long shot, because solar flares seldom happen exactly on schedule, but he'll take it. He

will have to be in the men's room, because that's where he was when
the disorientation came to him five years earlier. There was no way of
knowing how narrow or broad the effect was, so he will need to place
himself there, even in the same stall. What if it's occupied?

Meanwhile, Altworld continues to lose coherence:

Item: A nuclear device explodes in eastern Montana. No
group claims responsibility. The government vows to retaliate against
someone, somewhere, soon. The minority party spreads rumors that
the administration is rolling dice to select the nation we will strike.

Item: Eight million people attempt to leave Greater Chicago
at the same time, in advance of the approaching radioactive cloud.

***

Morgan doesn't remember exactly when he returned from
France. It was definitely in late October, eleven years ago. He consults
his computer, prowls through his paper calendar. He knows the
hour: it was 4:31 pm when he looked at his watch with annoyance.
That must have been about two minutes before he entered the men's
room, and five more until——. He remembers the day within a few
days, but not exactly. Casually, he asks Ruth if she recalls when he
returned.

She thinks for a minute. "Of course, Bob! I was on my way
from Sally's birthday party; so that must have been ——" she pauses.
"Sally's birthday is October 23rd, so that's when it was." She smiles.
"Thanks for reminding me, Bob; I'll have to give her a happy birthday
call."

Today, he thinks, today! Morgan's watch reads 3:58 pm.
Thirty-eight minutes. Barely time! Or if he misses, he will have to
wait eleven more years— and the way things are going, even a month
may be too late. He grabs at the car keys, misses, has them in his hand
this time, rushes out of the house. "Where are you going, Bob?"
Ruth calls after him. He doesn't answer.

He gets in the Peugeot, rams it into gear, takes off down
the hill. His thoughts are a jumble: Be careful; being stopped for
speeding would make me too late; slow would make me too late;

thirty-one minutes left; eye out for the troopers, but this is Texas —
everybody speeds.

He takes the ramp from Far West onto Mopac but in front
of him police have stopped all traffic; they seem to be checking for
bombs. He waits, fuming and desperate. Twenty-eight minutes.

Waiting, nothing to do but dwell on his predicament. But then
the thought comes to him: has time been ticking away in Ourworld all
those years? If it has, how is his life turning out when he's not there
to direct it? Perhaps he died sometime in those years? Or would he reenter Ourworld at the exact instant he left? His theory is inconclusive
as to that point; the mathematics could support either alternative.

The policeman pokes around the Peugeot, gestures Morgan
on. Thirteen minutes left. Because of the traffic stop behind him,
the road ahead is now almost deserted. Figuring all the cops are back
at the checkpoint he steps on the gas, pushes it to 90. He makes the
wide turn off Mopac and heads east, tires screaming.

Chaos continues to build in Altworld. The car radio announces
an incoherent alert in some angry color. Far underneath Morgan
there is a deep, rolling sound. The road shakes, cracks. Eight minutes.
Finally he sees the terminal in the distance. He takes the airport off-
ramp. Three and a half minutes. He zooms around the approach road
trying to remember which door is closest to the carousels, thinks he
remembers. Two and a half minutes.

He's there. He slams the Peugeot to a stop in front of an
entrance, bumping the curb savagely, jumps out of the car. Behind
him, he hears a security guard yelling. Morgan ignores the sound, runs
through the doors into the terminal, finds himself, greatly relieved,
at the baggage claim. One minute. He sees the men's room. He
runs through a tour-group with a muttered 'sorry.' The tour-guide's
umbrella clatters to the floor.

The men's room is blocked off for cleaning. A yellow 'piso
mojado, cerrado' plastic sign is propped up in his way. He kicks it
aside, enters. A woman is cleaning. She protests. He dashes into a
stall, locks himself in.

The woman is making a fuss outside the stall door, in
Spanish. Thirty seconds. Then it occurs to Morgan to wonder which

stall he was in before. He tries to think. He doesn't remember. The Spanish grows louder, more shrill. Too late to switch stalls, even if he remembers which one is right. Three to one against him. It is now exactly 4:26 pm. He places his hand on the flush lever. If this isn't the right stall, it may all be over. For a moment, nothing; but then the feeling returns, the queasy feeling of slipping sideways.

The cleaning woman's angry voice fades. Morgan becomes dizzy, mops his forehead. Has he succeeded? He can't immediately tell what has happened, which 'when' he is in, which 'now' this is.

Hopeful but worried, he steps out of the stall, leaves the men's room. The cleaning woman is not there; the 'cerrado' sign is nowhere in sight. Good omens. He approaches carousel three. It seems about the same. Have there been changes? He doesn't know — perhaps.

Most of the luggage has already been claimed. And the red suitcase — yes, it's here, but surely this time it's someone else's, not his. —Or is it?

The dog is beside the carousel, exactly as before. It looks at Morgan, barks softly, paws the netting of its carrier. This must be Ourworld, he thinks. He is vastly relieved, even though in Ourworld he's not the famous physicist he was in Altworld, won't be Associate Chair, Physics, won't have such a nice house, won't have a wife.

His brown suitcase isn't on the carousel belt. But it wasn't there before, either. He turns toward the exit door, thinking that his car has surely been towed by now — but no, the Peugeot was in Altworld. In Ourworld, he expected to catch a taxi, and so — now he will! A few years late, but right on time! A smile spreads across his face.

He is now halfway to the terminal door. He sees a woman hurrying in his direction. For an instant he is afraid it is Ruth, that he hasn't escaped from Altworld after all. But then he sees it isn't Ruth.

She is smiling at him, waving. He glances around. There is no one nearby. She is blond, pretty. He knows her. No, he doesn't. Then he remembers: it's Nancy, the flight attendant, the woman he wanted to have sex with eleven years ago, or was it just 20 minutes ago?

"I'm really sorry I'm late!" she says, after giving him a quick kiss on the cheek, "the traffic on 71, you know, and all those rumors about a war coming. And now I'm parked illegally out front, I'm afraid." She stops short, seeing his consternation. "What's wrong, Bob?" And then she looks beyond him, at the belt. "What about Rusty?" she says with a slight cry of alarm. "You're not leaving him behind, are you?" She goes to the carousel, picks up the carrier. She turns, smiles at him. Together they leave the terminal, get into an idling car, drive away.

Rusty, released from its carrier, licks Morgan's hand and stares into his eyes. Morgan realizes that he isn't back in Ourworld, but he isn't still in the Altworld he knew; the spin of the cosmic carousel has put him in — it must be — a different Altworld.

Far overhead, he sees contrails. In the sky there is a sudden brilliant flash. For a very few seconds, there is silence.

About the author: Terrence Kuch is a consultant, avid hiker, and world traveler. His publications and acceptances are many.

TSAURUS-90
KYLE HEMMINGS

Under the dining room table, Nick all of ten Sun-god years old, peered into the egg-shaped crystal, sturdy and small enough to fit into his hand. It was given to him by his grandmother, before the stroke left her babbling and lazy-eyed...before she passed beyond the gleaming fields of Oberon. Inside the egg, a woman with wings sat upon a white horse. Her name was Phaetha, and she pledged her love to a knight wielding a magic sword. In that world, there was no darkness; only a prism of multi-colored lights playing off each other.

There, he was known as Tsaurus-90 and was hailed as defender of the Oberon Castles; the knight who would defeat the stegosaurus Oomphs and mastodons, keep the triceratops scavengers at bay. His eyes veered away from the crystal egg, and he listened to the strange sounds his mother and father made, themselves victims of virtual Oomph viral-attacks. His parents were distant refractory pieces.

His mother's voice weighed heavy with concern.

"John, he's still having problems in school."

"I don't know what else to do," said his father. "He's been tested for everything, even schizophrenia."

His mother's voice grew lower. "The doctor suggested autism. The lack of eye contact... the obsession with that egg..."

"And?"

Nick could hear the anger begin to rise in his father's voice.

"He's being picked on at school. The teacher called again."

"He's my son!" screamed his mother. "There's nothing wrong with him! He'll grow out of it!"   Nick listened to the sounds of their fighting. One word stood out. Autism. In Oberon it meant a form of invincibility to a knight of the Tsaurus Order.

**

In high school, Nick took his crystal egg everywhere and kept it hidden in his jacket as a reminder that he was one of the last Knights of Oberon, the defenders of its jasper, pyrite, and ruby-zoisite forests. Sometimes, the teacher would turn from the black board and cast a penetrating gaze into Nick's face. "Are you with us, Nick?"

The class would laugh and someone would fire a spitball against Nick's head.

The school was full of Oomph Replicates. They'd do anything, Nick thought, to find out where Phaetha, the Princess of Light, was. They'd hurt her and hold her prisoner. They would make the world dark.

The Oomph Replicates constantly bullied and humiliated Nick. They would call him names like 'faggot,' or 'loser.' They said he had Frankenstein eyes and asked if he was still a virgin.

And to that Nick always replied, "I am pure of heart."

On the school grounds, they would tackle Nick and rub dirt in his face or stuff grass down his throat. Nick thought: No matter what they do, I must protect Oberon. I must not reveal where Phaetha roams.

One day, a new student was introduced to the class. Her name, she said was Phoedre, and her parents just moved to the county. She said she couldn't wait to make new friends. Phoedre turned to look at Nick, and her smile lingered. Nick returned her stare, and he jerked in his seat. Her hair was long, the color of ebony, and there was a humble beauty about her face.

At home, that evening, Nick pressed his eyes against the crystal egg. Phaetha's face loomed larger. Her voice was soft, distant, yet clear.

"Tsaurus," she said, "I need to be rescued. "Lord Stegosaurus has ordered my capture. You are the last Tsaurus-90. Only you can save me from darkness."

Her face disappeared.

His mother called him down for dinner.

***

During recess and at lunch time, Nick felt Phoedre stalking him in the hallways, on the grounds, her eyes always upon him.

One day, outside, Phoedre walked up to him. "You're so quiet in class," she said. She smiled at him. There was a queer change of color to her eyes, one that reflected the ruby color of Oberon forest squirrels.

She reached for his hand. Hers felt like air.

Her voice took on the gentle intonations of Phaetha.

"Do not be afraid of the Replicates. You must stand tall. Keep your chin up. No matter what they do. Remember. You are a Tsaurus-90."

She dissolved right in front of him. Nick's hand kept reaching out.

Just then two Replicates interrupted and one said, "Hey, fruitcake. Talking to yourself again?" The other kept pushing Nick towards the brick wall of the school.

"Who you talking to, fruitcake?"

Nick began to shake, and, sensing this attack was ordered by Lord Stegosaurus, he reached for the crystal egg and held it up high.

He stuttered, "D-don't make me smash this! If I do, it will end your w-world."

The two Replicates looked at each other. They both wore varsity jackets. One had a pants leg rolled up.

"Hey, what you got there, fruit? A grenade?"

He looked back at his companion. They both chuckled.

"Don't make me do it," said Nick.

The ugliest Replicate wrestled with Nick's arm and bent it backward. Nick cringed and screamed. He threw Nick to the ground and began to hit him repeatedly. Nick covered his head and felt blood oozing from his nose. He was having trouble breathing. Their voices sounded distant.

"What the hell is this," laughed one, "a little magic egg to see your ugly face?" They laughed, snatched the egg from Nick and smashed it to the ground, where it shattered into a thousand pieces. Nick stopped breathing. The world turned black.

***

Slowly, the darkness cleared. Nick stood at the edge of a cliff overlooking a blue transparent sea. He held hands with Phaetha.

She turned to him. "Don't be afraid. After all, you are a Tsaurus-90. The only one."
Nick held out his magic sword and they jumped. It felt as if he was flying forever.

***

In Oberon, Tsaurus-90 and Phaetha rode on the same horse. Above them, the sky was a glass dome. Tsaurus studied the stegosaurus and Oomph Replicates around them, now frozen, locked in glass dome prisons.
"They'll never attack again," said Phaetha.
"This world is so beautiful," said Tsaurus-90. "It was well worth fighting for."
"It's the only one," said Phaetha, and they rode into the many jeweled forest, ruled by the grandmother of Tsaurus-90-Queen Phoedre.

About the author: Kyle Hemmings works and lives in New Jersey. His stories, poems, and artwork have been featured in online journals such as Abyss and Apex, Niteblade, The Horror Zine and others.

JUST PRESS ERASE
JOHN X. GREY

"Wow," Patrol Officer Ronald Woods shook his head in amazement at the strange twist of fate he and his partner Charlie Kaufmann had just witnessed, "you're lucky to be standing after that collision, Sir."

Jaime Rapidez sat down on the curb staring across the city street at the twisted remains of his Red Porsche against the Metro Transit Authority's #22 Bus's left side, the larger vehicle having swerved to avoid another car zipping out of the parking garage exit it now blocked. He was still shaken from the accident of mere minutes ago, but something about this outcome seemed wrong inside the young executive's mind. Jaime had left his tower office half-an-hour early to avoid the late afternoon traffic and get home early.

The bus swerved into my lane before I could - no, wait. I don't remember swerving in time or being thrown clear of the car at braking speed.

"Do you feel like giving me some information now?" The light-brown Woods addressed this man seated before him with deference, due to the obvious value of the sports car and Rapidez's tailored blue three-piece suit. "I mean you must've slowed down enough at the last second so the asphalt didn't give you a burn or even broken bones from rolling clear. Also, if another car had been passing in the opposite lane, you might've been road kill instead."

"Yeah," Jaime nodded after a few more breaths, "I can think clearly again. I'm just shaken after the excitement is all. It's cool."

The patrolman took down his relevant information for the accident report, as Kaufmann spoke with the bus driver and put out an APB on the black Pontiac responsible for this mishap. Jaime Eduardo Rapidez was a vice-president at Outer Groove Records in charge of new talent, after he had a brief successful career as Latino Hip Hop artist *Suave Sexo,* and graduating valedictorian of his high school and college classes before that fame. The 30-year-old man possessed the ice-blue eyes, jet-black hair and good looks of a male model, despite his parents seeming at least above-average in terms of its inexplicability. He was still married to an exotic-looking ex-bikini model (from some obscure Rust Belt small town) in her mid-20s also blessed with physical beauty even after birthing their two daughters (she was now two months along with what the ultrasound told was their son-to-be).

"Hey, yeah," Woods snapped his fingers holding the pen, pausing in writing out the accident report upon recognizing the man standing to face him now, "I remember you singing that *Viva Rico Gigante* song when I was still in college - that was one tight groove."

"Thanks," Jaime shrugged as he straightened the blue suit jacket, "but I figured out that a life on the road performing would ruin any marriage, so I parlayed my mojo into producing, and the rest is history."

Woods cleared his throat as if in semi-embarrassment, then informed Mr. Rapidez: "I'll need you to sign off on this report, Sir, if you don't mind."

Yeah, right, Jaime realized this was different from his first car accident report at 17, having never been required to sign anything then, *he just wants my autograph. I don't mind, long as it doesn't end up on eBay or used in ID theft scams.*

"Thank you," Woods nodded at reading the 'autograph,' then offered, "the paramedics want to look you over once for any hidden injuries before we get you a ride home. Your family has been notified of the accident, and Mrs. Rapidez is on her way I understand."

Thank God, Jaime followed the policeman over to the waiting ambulance, where a few bus patrons were being treated for minor injuries, *no camera phones around to get photos for the Enquirer or Star - 'former hip-hop singer in near-fatal car crash miraculously survives.'*

Since turning 30, Jaime has been looking at himself more in the mirror, not to see the rather handsome man reflected there, but wondering what he had done to deserve all the perfection in his life thus far. Each time he greeted himself on a reflected surface in private, the successful man often recalled more discrepancies in his past like the one just survived, moments where this successful person should have failed, or crashed and burned on occasion, but did not.

I should've been crushed against the dash and steering wheel, but instead my seat belt chose that moment to snap open and the door popped open at the first impact.

Before that happened, he felt things slow down and reverse, but it seemed unreal.

One EMT said the Jaws of Life were needed to free someone in my scrape, and I should've been killed on impact.

Jaime Rapidez accepted his relieved wife Katie's hugs and kisses, before they departed the accident scene, watching the wrecker taking the man's totaled Porsche away to some scrap yard for recycling.

"Stacey and Heather are both waiting at home." The stunning brown-haired, green-eyed Katie Rapidez explained as Jaime admired her tan mini dress while she drove the red Escalade.

"What did you tell them," Jaime fixed his black hair without using a mirror, "after the cops called to let you know I'd been in a crash?"

Katie was more careful driving through the midtown streets than any time since Jaime had met her, both mindful from the Porsche's crushed body that he might have died today.

"I told them that 'daddy' was involved in a little accident, but that he was okay. I'm grateful for that part."

"Is Olga staying with them?"

"No," Katie took her sunglasses from the sun visor to conceal tears (thankful the waterproof blue mascara was living up to the manufacturer's advertisement); "I called your parents to watch them until we got back. Your father almost wouldn't come, working on something important in the basement again."

Jaime briefly chuckled before realizing Katie's annoyance at his reaction.

"Sorry, Babe, but it's just that Dad was always busy down there when I was growing up with something in his spare hours. We never spent that much time together, but whenever we did as father and son, those were the happiest days of my life."

Katie was puzzled by that admission, and even Jaime found himself searching his memories as if they were two separate sets of thought images that did not match or blend well.

I remember playing catch with Dad, getting swimming lessons from him, help with building a birdhouse or soapbox racer. Yet he always had something else to do in his workshop.

Jamie then realized those memories were at odds with the Old Man working downstairs alone, never allowing wife or son there and always cleaning that space himself.

"Well," Katie seemed relaxed when they reached the highway leading to the Rapidez's home outside the city, touching an abdomen still not showing the 'bun in her oven' yet, "I hope you'll spend more time raising our son than that man did with you. Y'know, your Mom told me how you always seemed to think he was wonderful, more than seemed to be deserved for an absentee parent in a boy's life."

Why am I confused? Was it the accident? My past feels too perfect, as if everything has gone my way. Do successful people always feel that way after achieving dreams?

"I always try to make time for you and the girls, and will still after our son is born."

***

Jaime and Katie greeted their daughters and said goodbye to his parents after visiting for a few minutes. His wife then gave the girls their baths, even if four-year-old Stacey felt too grown to need 'Mommy's' help. After arranging himself a leased car for the next weeks' commute to the record company, Jaime wandered to the peruse family's scrapbook and memories albums. These included boxes with home movies of the couple's wedding, their two daughters' births, and other treasured captured moments of the Rapidez family.

I don't know what I'm looking for here, Jaime flipped through the photos, but nothing seemed out of place or missing there, except that he saw a few images there seeming different from those he remembered, *except something which seems wrong now.*

The first items that did seemed 'wrong' were photos from a family picnic when he was 10 in the state park fifty miles north of the city. He recognized his mother's handwriting labeling the color snapshots' borders, but could not remember the particular outing with both parents.

I also recall being an only child all my life, but also having my two younger sisters when reminiscing before. Jaime could now find no record or image of those siblings; memories once clear as today's earlier car accident. *I had another accident like that. I went cruising with some buddies and wrapped Dad's Chevy around a lamp post near the river front park.*

Recalling how a paramedic on the scene said he should have died then also, not being buckled up behind the wheel but removed from inside belted in the seat.

No, wait, the glass cut me from a tree branch breaking the driver's side window, but I didn't have a scratch and missed the tree when we skidded.

The confused young executive was watching the home movies on the DVR machine, his Dad having recently transferred the old video tape recordings to this format, when Katie finished with getting their children into bed and appeared in the basement's den.

"He really did a good job copying those," the 3-months pregnant lady sat beside her man in a short pink bathrobe, untying his tie as Jaime had only removed the suit's coat and vest since their return from the accident scene, "whatever I think of his failings in parenting, Hon."

Jaime helped her set the tie aside on the green sofa, as they snuggled closer and watched their dream wedding from five years ago at the small chapel she had attended since childhood, Katie's mother and father appearing content their youngest of three daughters had found a good prospect for her future beyond modeling swimsuits.

"Katie," he asked with some hesitation, "do you ever get the feeling that our life together here has been 'too' perfect?"

"What the fu-," she caught herself swearing, "is this because of your accident?"

Jaime sighed as the younger Katie in an off-the-shoulder white wedding gown tossed the red rose bouquet (caught by her best friend Lynn Westmore) on the 32" screen they were watching, shaking his head before he explained further.

"No, I've been thinking about details of my life more since the last birthday, and I think some things from the past don't fit. I was my high school class' valedictorian, a perfect student athlete and the talented amateur in theater and singing. Then I was the best in my college class and got discovered by the talent agency before I even graduated there. It just seems as if my life's been too good."

Humoring her troubled husband, Katie rubbed his shirt collar and dismissed the concerns by changing their subject.

"I'm going to bed, and you've got auditions to supervise tomorrow. If you want some fun, the obstetrician said we could still do it until I get to five months. I'll be waiting."

She doesn't believe me. She doesn't understand. I shouldn't have expected it.

Katie was always kind and giving, putting her career aside to have their children, but never a deep thinker he often realized.

My children's mother isn't stupid, but she was a B- student before modeling school.

Jaime dressed for bed and indulged his wife in gentle intercourse with her on top, then played 'spoons' before she drifted to sleep, but the man could not relax even after mild physical activity. He sat up from their bed two sleepless hours later; realizing he must ask the one man that always seemed to have all the necessary answers.

Dad - I'll go see him. I know it's late, but - he always understood me - I think.

***

Jaime took Katie's Escalade after throwing on a tan work shirt, blue jeans and sneakers over his red-striped boxer shorts, and half-an-hour later rang his parents' doorbell in their suburban neighborhood until Benito Rapidez answered the door with one confused expression.

"Jaime, what brings you here," the old man finished tying a gray bathrobe over the red floral pajamas, glancing at a glow-in-the-dark clock behind him in the living room, "and so late, Son? Is something wrong? Are Katie and the girls okay?"

Jaime now realized the bizarre timing and purpose for his visit, hesitating to answer the man rubbing sleep matter from blue-gray eyes.

"Sorry about that, Dad, but it's just, after realizing some things today, I need to
talk."

"All right," the man grumbled as he welcomed Jaime back into the place he last lived a dozen years earlier, "we'll get any problems off your chest, but downstairs in my den. I wouldn't want to disturb your mother talking around here."

That's weird. It's always been his private work space.

Jaime also recalled Rosalia Rapidez had been a sound sleeper since he was born, and the two men had talked in the living room before a few late nights while she slept.

"Are you sure, Dad? You never let me go down there before."

I assumed he kept dirty magazines there. Some friends had fathers hiding things like in such places. I never could pick the lock or get a key for the workshop to find out.

"It's okay, Jaime," Benito scratched his mottled scalp beneath thinning black-gray hair as he led their way toward the basement, "I knew you've been curious about it all your life."

The staircase beyond a hallway door seemed normal in turning at right angles and stopping at small landings, before the two men reached a den-like area where Jaime now remembered having been a few times when his parents were out together. Beyond a wood-paneled sanctum with its couch, TV and home bar area, there was the reinforced metal door centered in the basement's one inner partition wall. Benito Rapidez took a key from beneath the DVR machine on a shelf below the TV in its stand, opening the forbidden metal door with casual familiarity.

What have I gotten myself into? Why is he showing me this now?

"I knew you brought your buddies down here when I was away," the older man confessed as his fuzzy blue slippers scraped across the crude concrete floor beyond the door, "but as long as you boys didn't get into my liquor, I was cool about any trespassing."

"Dad," Jaime almost gasped after his father pulled a cord a few feet inside this darkened room and revealed blue-gray painted walls with few windows (containing thick privacy opaque glass) and the various electronic devices on work tables, a wheeled swivel black leather chair awaited them in this room's center. The overhead fluorescent lights hummed as Jaime now recognized some of the machines were visual editing devices for film work. In one corner, a large locked safe stood out from the room's many electronic devices.

"Welcome to my workshop, Son. This is where my life's greatest magic happens, and you are the first person I've allowed to ever see it. Not even your mother knows exactly what it is I do down here, respecting my privacy."

"Is this where and how you edited those home movies for Katie and me?" Jaime examined the more familiar boxes around him. "How could you afford sophisticated equipment?"

Benito shrugged as he retrieved a cigar box and cigarette lighter from one shelf above the TV, lighting one stogie and puffing it to life beginning his tale.

"I came to America with dreams, an inventive mind and skilled hands, but little else. Most people saw me as a greasy smelly Spic, but I learned English fast and soon had a repair business in this neighborhood that prospered." The man set in the room's one chair, then rolled it toward one row of disc burning machines. "I tinkered with the most advanced electronics from all the home entertainment machines at the shop, met and married your mother, a cleaning lady for some rich houses in the surrounding counties. We loved each other, but neither of us were models for the successful American dream in terms of appearance. After Rosalia and I learned she could not have children, I vowed to remedy that problem somehow."

What in God's name does he mean? Am I adopted or something?

Jaime stood in front of the locked safe now, sensing on some instinctive level that it was the one item here with secrets, aside from his father, as the older man continued.

"I worked with unconventional power sources and altered electronics to forget we couldn't afford fertility treatments, and your mother resisted adoption. Then I had a great revelation, after almost being electrocuted working here one night. I acquired unusual components from sources I can't divulge to anyone, setting to work on my great project."

Jaime faced his father, seeing the man was cool and collected, not raving while saying things making little sense to him.

"I created an editing system to change and perfect life. I learned how to alter aspects of living beings, 'making' Rosalie pregnant as the first experiment, and tinkered more after that."

"What the hell do you mean?" Jaime circled Benito's seat, seeing nothing special about this electronic laboratory on its face. "You said Mom couldn't have children? But somehow she got pregnant after you made a technical breakthrough down here with editing machines?"

"I could create new life and modify its outcomes here. I know it sounds loco, but that's how we had you, Son." Benito placed the lighter down at the chair's left arm and moved to activate smaller video monitors tied in with some of his video equipment on the tables and shelves. "I also discovered I could 'edit' lives created with the computer simulations having parameters input to a visual representation. I made you, Jaime, where no life before had been possible in a childless barren woman."

This is whacked out. My old man's going crazy. He's got that disease - dementia or maybe Alzheimer's.

"You can't create life on a computer and then alter reality to make things happen."

Benito patted his son's back twice, blowing a smoke ring out of smiling pride.

"But I did, right here. Of course, I had sex with your mother so she'd believe it was a miracle from God when the pregnancy began. Then I did it twice more, but decided the later conceptions had been a mistake after some years watching our other kids growing up."

Jaime felt memory fragments of two young girls at the fleeting edges of consciousness, as his father mentioned 'other' children. He snapped his fingers in struggling to remember their names, sitting down in Benito Rapidez's chair.

"Maria and Juana - I had sisters. Why can't I find any picture of them in my family albums, attending my wedding, or in old childhood photos? It's almost as if -"

Benito flicked ashes from his cigar into a glass ashtray near the TV on an end
table.

"As if they never existed. It wasn't an easy decision on my part, Jaime. All my gear was eating up our extra income, but I persuaded your mother it was back taxes and wages for my employees at the shop. We couldn't afford to raise three children and give them everything I wanted for my offspring, so I 'edited' them both out of our lives. I had to do it."

Jaime leaned forward in the chair and placed his head in both hands for a few seconds, not wanting to believe anything the older man was claiming.

"You can't play God. No one should have such power."

"He has allowed me to do this, or at least never stopped my experiments so far."

Jaime shot from the chair and paced toward the metal door hiding this private 'laboratory,' then asked his overconfident father: "What else have you done in this basement, Dad? What other ways did you play God with my life or memories? I want answers, even if they sound crazy by any rational standard!"

Benito sighed and returned to the chair, before making a suggestion for his son.

"Go in the next room, get the rolling desk chair in the den, and bring it here. I sense you'll want to be seated for the rest of the incredible story I tell you. I can see it's going to be a long night."

Jaime felt disconnected from everything as he complied with his father's request, carrying the tan rolling swivel chair with small armrests from the den's small battered desk. He sat a few feet from the older man. The next hour would prove shocking and revealing, but the son was scarcely prepared for the rest of Benito Rapidez's incredible tale.

***

"My whole life - everything I've accomplished from my first day in kindergarten, you sat here in this room and manipulated reality to make it easier."

Jaime still could not fully accept the story after Benito was finished. The man had changed his son's life at key points to eliminate disappointments and defeats, making Jaime Rapidez into the fortunate child he had often been across three decades.

"But I also didn't want you to get a swelled head and sense of invincibility from all that good luck," the older man finished his second cigar and walked to the ashtray for snuffing the butt, "so I gave you occasional tragedy, especially after entering a rebellious teenage phase. The sports contest losses, the car wreck the summer after your junior year, and the high school sweetheart committing suicide because of her depressing home life. I'd never let you be hurt physically, but provided certain emotional pains and brushes with death to mature my boy for the future, and it worked. Look how you've turned out since then."

Jaime felt numbed as his father's words evoked more memories, before he asked additional questions about this perfect life.

"So, I succeeded at whatever I tried - my music major in college, the hip hop singing career, a rebounding creative career in the music business. I romance the pretty model after we meet at a

Hawaiian Tropic contest, more serious than all my flirtations with the ladies since high school. Katie and I click and want the same things together. We marry, have our beautiful daughters, and an unborn son on the way now."

"It's grand, Jaime," Benito sat again, "I gave you many wonderful things."

"But it's all fake," he groaned and smacked the right fist into the left palm, before vaulting from the smaller desk chair, "none of this should've happened, not even my birth."

Sighing as he rubbed his wrinkled eyelids, Benito Rapidez shook his head before continuing their conversation.

"I thought you had developed the emotional maturity as a responsible businessman to handle the truth. I viewed your search through the albums and DVDs tonight for answers to memories that didn't match inside."

"Why did I realize this? Is something happening to end my phony reality?"

"The editing process is not always smooth and unnoticeable," Benito confessed as he grabbed himself another cigar from the box, "sometimes an erasure leaves afterimage patterns, such as the fleeting memories you kept after I made the changes. I did it all for the best."

"My little girls, my wife and son to be, are all a sham," Jaime then noticed the locked safe one more time, "I never deserved anything."

"I created Stacey and Heather to compensate for the removal of your sisters, Jaime," Benito stood by his son's side, before the younger man noticed two keys in his father's right robe pocket and slipped them from there before the older man returned to the executive's chair, "but made the births two years apart, instead of the fraternal twins like Maria and Juana, so you wouldn't recall two erased siblings when having daughters."

"If you're the creator of my life," Jaime stuck the two brass keys beneath his left leg in sitting before Benito noticed he had taken them, "why is Katie pregnant again? We were unsure having another child was for the best, and now she can't wait to give birth again."

"I wanted you to have a son, Jaime," Benito paused, lighting the cigar to life, "so he could go out in the world and do more than you had. He's going to be the apple of your eye, trust me on that point."

I've got to find out what he's hiding in that safe.

"You have it all figured out, Dad. I'll be the son you can be proud of, and the baby will be the grandson you'll dote on in old age."

"I couldn't change my own life or Rosalia's circumstances, but wanted to give a child the best possible future, and just used different methods to accomplish it."

Jaime sprang from the chair; both keys clenched in the right hand and tried each on the safe's locking mechanism, finding that the second key (not used at the door) opened it.

"Stay out of there, Son! NO, don't touch -"

Jaime grabbed the pile of media discs and a large black three-ring binder folder beneath them on the safe's bottom shelf, shoving Benito aside to the concrete floor when he grabbed for those materials and to close the iron box's door.

"What the hell? My name's stenciled across the binder - 'Jamie Eduardo
Rapidez.'"

And these CDs, DVDs, or whatever the discs are - they're labeled with dates and key words on each one's individual contents.

"Jaime, son, please - I've tried to explain why this was necessary. Don't do anything rash that we'll both regret."

Jaime Rapidez laughed as he carried the media to sit at the chair, and then read through the binder's meticulous notes on his lifetime's existence and each change Benito made.

"Please, Son," the older man grunted in standing again unaided, while Jaime kept an eye on the man he had called 'father,' "I could adjust the recordings I'm making tonight, so you never have any reason to doubt your life and future again."

Jaime then realized that some of the recording devices were running now, having not noticed their red and green lights and readouts in the almost two hours since his arrival.

"You'll just keep playing god with my life to the end, right Old Man?" The executive then dropped the discs in their jewel cases and stepped on each one, including 'Jaime's Wedding,' 'Stacey's birth' and 'Heather's birth.' "I won't let you get away with it anymore, so help me God!"

Jaime hurled the folder at the operating recording machine across the room; snatched away his father's lighter from the floor and used it to burn the binder's pages, with Benito fighting him for it too late to prevent that destruction. Jaime suddenly felt cold all over and stumbled backwards, releasing the burning folio as Benito tossed it in a wastebasket and retrieved the wall-mounted fire extinguisher too late to prevent any loss.

"Dad," Jaime slumped into the executive chair, clinging to its armrests to keep from sliding out, "I'm sorry. I just wanted to be a normal per-"

Benito shed a few tears, watching the handsome young man he had loved so much fade away with the unfinished sentence, and regretfully surveyed damaged electronic items.

"If I'd realized how strongly Jaime felt, I could've told him to just press 'erase' on the master recorder."

About the author: Currently between jobs and still stuck in his Southern Ohio hometown striving for a writing career, John X. Grey is the more marketable and memorable pen name of Edwin R. Haney, published during 2009 with one sci-fi/horror and one fantasy story credit

LOCOMOTIVE MAN AND PHOLUS MACHINE
LAWRENCE BARKER

The ground fell away a few paces before Nikolai Mikhailovitch Tebenkov's running feet. Nikolai stopped. He shivered as he stared into the steep valley. Vines, violet in color and seeming more at home in a Brazilian jungle than in the Alaskan wilderness, carpeted its floor. A sickly sweet smell rose, as though unseen funeral flowers curtained the valley. The gorge emitted a sense of *wrongness,* as though a pile of steam engine parts had spontaneously assembled themselves into a human form and walked.

The war whoops of his Tlingit Indian pursuers reminded him of his peril. Nikolai's slender fingers drifted to his small percussion boxlock pistol, better suited to concealing inside a tunic than for defending oneself from savages. After frightening a bear away from his dried salmon cache, only one bullet remained. The Tlingits had surprised him moments later, intending to take the pelts that his long and lonely labors had yielded. Thoughts of using his last bullet on their leader, Fox in Den, had darted through Nikolai's mind. But considering how the Tlingits treated Russian captives, Nikolai had decided to save his last bullet for himself. He had run, feet pounding the Kolushan Forest's mossy floor.

More Tlingit cries sounded from the forest behind him. Nikolai's hands became fists. Nikolai did not care if his father, fat old Mikhail Dimitrivitch, condemned as inadequate Nikolai's every accomplishment. Only last year, Nikolai had obtained the single finest otter pelt that the Russian America company had ever seen. But when he brought the fur to the New Archangel fort, the old man had dared to accuse Nikolai of claiming another's catch as his own! Nikolai, Mikhail Dimitrivitch had said, could never have done something so impressive! Nikolai snarled. No matter if Mikhail Dimitrivitch wanted to drive him to suicidal despair, Nikolai wanted to live. Nikolai launched into the valley, landing with a bone-jarring impact.

He expected Tlingit lances to rain down. Instead, the Indians stopped at the valley's edge. Although their language remained a mystery, he understood their now-wary tone. Fox in Den's voice rang out in an order. The Indians fell silent and retreated.

Nikolai wrapped himself in his coat. The lush vegetation had made him suspect that hidden hot springs warmed the valley. Instead, the valley's raking chill reminded him more of a Siberian autumn than an Alaskan spring. He rose, pale blue eyes squinting. Tlingits, armed with lances and daggers, charged unafraid into Russian muskets. But the Indians avoided this valley. Nikolai ran his fingers through his shaggy blond hair. A wise man would avoid whatever so frightened the Tlingits.

He had taken a few steps toward exiting when a unfamiliar fur-bearing animal appeared. Wolf-hound sized, it combined the hooded face of an elephant seal with the lambent orange eyes of a horned owl. Nikolai might have been mistaken about its six legs or its three-toed paws, two toes forward and one backwards, parrot-fashion. Although uncertain about the creature's legs, Nikolai was certain about the blue-black fur. It made sea otter fur, the richest known to the Russian Alaska Company, seem a moth-eaten mountain hare's pelt in comparison.

Demanding and difficult old Mikhail Dimitrivitch would rejoice at such a fur. He would do so even if the fat old man's disgraced and despised older brother, Gleb Dimitrivitch, presented it! Nikolai raised his pistol and took aim at the trunknose. "Devil's Grandmother take me," he whispered as he thought better of shooting. Bears and savages stalked the countryside between here and New Archangel. He might need that last bullet.

The trunknose emitted a hoot, simultaneously high and low, as though two sets of vocal chords filled its throat. Its rigid tail shot up. The animal vanished into the undergrowth.

Nikolai holstered his pistol. He might not have the mechanical skills of Gleb Dimitrivitch. Uncle Gleb, exiled over a foolish flirtation with the notion of releasing the serfs, had even built a marvelous iron steamship, impervious to cannons. That ship might have given the Tsar the Black Sea, had Uncle Gleb not espoused such questionable politics, and had a storm not sunk the newly-completed ship. But even without tools, Nikolai could make a trap. Had he not set snares in his boyhood?

Nikolai found the trunknose's trail and a nearby stiff pseudo-sapling. He set about constructing a spring snare, the best trap when one has no bait. Less than half-way through, a dozen trunknoses emerged from the undergrowth, surrounding him. Nikolai blinked. As he had thought, the trunknoses truly had six stubby limbs.

The largest, a one-eyed specimen, stood up, supporting itself on its four front limbs. One-eye waved the hind two limbs in a signal. Its compatriots responded with ascending and descending hoots, sounding fiercer than ten Tlingit war bands. As a mass, the animals advanced, bodies pressed against the ground. Their short tails vibrated like those of the rattling snakes of the Americans' portion of the continent. Orange spheres covered with sharp spines, looking like the spiked weapons of medieval knights, sprouted from their mouths. The creatures' flowery reek grew stronger as they approached.

Nikolai's hand brushed his pistol. He shook his head. One shot would do little. He had battled fierce Yakut warriors in Russia; he would not sell his life cheaply here. Nikolai uprooted the false sapling. It could serve as a weapon of sorts.

A clanking and hissing, like a train engine heaving up a steep grade, echoed from behind Nikolai. Vegetation snapped, as though crushed beneath the massive weight of Sviagotor, the steppes' fabled giant. Acrid coal smoke filled the air.

One-eye chirped. The trunknoses retracted their spiky weapons. Their tails stopped rattling. As one, they turned and ran.

Nikolai turned to see what had saved him. His jaw dropped. Behind him stood a locomotive man of riveted iron, fourteen feet tall and with smoke emerging from its back. An array of polished lenses on the front and sides of the giant's head were the only features on its bullet-shaped head. The right arm ended in a great four-fingered claw while the left ended in a hook. Carriage-sized metal plates served the giant as feet. A sealed hatch covered its chest.

"What are you?" Nikolai whispered, his thumb and first two

fingers instinctively forming the Orthodox sign of the cross.

Gears turned within the locomotive man's chest. The hatch creaked open. Inside, contorted into a position that it scarce seemed possible that one so aged to assume, sat a feeble, gray-bearded man. About him lay a marvelous array of knobs, dials, and gauges.

"Uncle Gleb," Nikolai whispered, recognizing a man he had not seen in years. "What? How?" he sputtered.

Gleb Dimitrivitch surveyed the surrounding vegetation, as though scouting for an immanent attack. Seemingly satisfied, he flipped a switch. The locomotive man stooped. Its right arm curved into a cradle. "Climb aboard," Uncle Gleb answered. "They will return soon, armed. Possibly even the larger ones, far more dangerous than those you have seen, will join them."

"But…" All attempts to articulate the thoughts roiling Nikolai's mind failed.

"Only room for one inside." Uncle Gleb motioned Nikolai forward. "I will explain when we are safer."

Nikolai climbed onto the giant's arm. The hatch swung shut. The locomotive man turned and strode out of the valley.

Soon, the locomotive man reached a wooden palisade, smaller than New Archangel but more precisely built. Outside the wooden stockade stood a machine, similar to the locomotive man but smaller and more resembling centaur than man. Before Nikolai could comprehend this wonder, the locomotive man set Nikolai down amid a grove of sighing hemlocks. Again, the chest swung open. This time, Uncle Gleb scrambled down a hemp ladder. Feet on solid ground, he brushed the soot from his quilted jacket. "Welcome to Kiev East," Uncle Gleb said, gesturing at the palisade.

"Kiev East?" Nikolai wondered what had caused his uncle to bestow such a name. Irony, or did he really think his dwelling rivaled that grand city?

"Come inside. My servants have prepared a samovar," Uncle Gleb responded. "I buy tea from American ships. True, the Tsar has forbidden such trade, but the Tsar's Secret Police are far away." His face brightened. "I have cakes as well, although sweetened with spruce tip. Making alcohol to fuel the Talos Machine's more delicate mechanisms has exhausted my supply of sugar," he said, gesturing toward the locomotive man, "but spruce tips substitute nicely for sweetener."

"Talos Machine?" Nikolai asked. "You mean the locomotive man?"

Uncle Gleb's lip's curled. "I chose the name 'Talos' in honor of the bronze giant of classical myth. I suppose 'Locomotive Man' is descriptive, if not as poetic." He turned and, using a cleverly wrought series of pulleys and levers suited to his frail build, opened the fort's heavy gates. "Come," he commanded. "Here in Kiev East, I have stoked a spark of civilization amidst the wilderness. Now, that light will be shared."

Bewildered, Nikolai followed Uncle Gleb. The gates slammed behind them, and Uncle Gleb lead him into the log house. Within was something as marvelous as the Locomotive Man. Uncle Gleb's 'servants' were clockwork mechanisms with workings far beyond Nikolai's understanding. The gears and shafts meshed so that they not only fired the samovar but, when it grew hot, poured tea into waiting cups! And, beyond that, another series of cleverly wrought gears brought a bow to the strings of a violin, playing the sentimental melody *Along the Petersburg Road*.

Nikolai, following Uncle Gleb's lead, ate and drank, the cakes tasting strangely but pleasantly of evergreens. Nikolai smiled. Uncle Gleb had not exaggerated when he named his comfortable home. It exceeded New Archangel as much as Moscow stands above a nomad's rude hut!

"You have many questions," Uncle Gleb said, disconnecting the violin machine. He seated himself on a divan of antlers, padded with American cotton. "The least important is, 'why is Gleb Dimitrivitch not in Kamchatka, where the Tsar exiled him?'"

Nikolai nodded. "You were ordered to repair the Karymsky Lake bridge."

Uncle Gleb looked indignant. "Should I have buried myself in that dull land, redesigning a dull bridge for dull people?" He made a scoffing sound. "No! I caught a freighter across the Bering and made my home in these wilds. Here, I perfected the Talos Machine, or, as you say, the Locomotive Man. The device had occupied my mind since university days, but I had never had the time to complete it." Uncle Gleb glanced upward. "When I left Kamchatka, I had no notion that God would, through wrecks of British and American steamers, provide me with mechanical parts. Nor that He would let me finish my Locomotive Man precisely when it was needed." He sat quietly, as though preparing the next words. "And now, He has sent me a good right hand."

"Meaning what?" Nikolai shifted uncomfortably in his seat. His almost invisibly blond eyebrows knitted together.

"I mean that I heard the Tlingits. Since they avoid the Loathsome Gorge, where I found you, I knew they chased some poor unfortunate. I came to help, never realizing that I would rescue my own flesh."

"That does not explain what you meant by 'good right hand.'" Nikolai took another drink. The tea's flavor and the warmth had vanished, leaving a cool, insipid presence on his tongue.

"Did you think the animals that I saved you from were New World weasels?" He laughed at his own feeble joke. "No weasels. Rather, they are the spawn of the Moonmother."

"Moonmother?" Nikolai confusion grew by the moment.

"She fell from the sky in a rounded bower woven of purplish vines. That bower bounced and bounced until it came to rest in the vale that I have named 'the Loathsome Gorge'."

"This bower originated on the moon?" Nikolai had forgotten what astronomy he might have once known, but he was fairly certain that his teachers said that the moon was an airless void. Uncle Gleb shrugged. "She is neither demon nor does she originate from this world. Since no sphere is closer, the moon is where she must have begun."

Nikolai pursed his lips. Had Uncle Gleb's exile driven him even madder than he had been when he wanted to free the serfs?

Uncle Gleb leaned forward. "At first, the Moonmother was alone. Then she began to breed, like an ant colony's queen. Even worse, she began to convert the valley into an amethyst outpost of hell. I tried to reason with her." He looked dejected. "Her only response was to show me, speaking in her own fashion, her intentions."

"Which were?" Nikolai was uncertain if humoring a madman was better than objecting to insanity.

"To spread her domain." Uncle Gleb settled back. "I then realized the Locomotive Man's grand purpose: to prevent the Moonmother from remodeling this land into an image of her Lunar home." Uncle Gleb's gaze fell to his feet. "I could only contain, not defeat, her. The Locomotive Man's coal reserve only allow brief periods of operation. If I modified it to carry more, it would lose too much maneuverability. I built the Pholus Machine, named for the most elegant of the centaurs, to follow and keep feeding coal into the Locomotive Man."

"The Pholus Machine? The four legged device outside?"

Uncle Gleb nodded. "It is none other. But I could not operate the Pholus and Talos Machines simultaneously, and I never succeeded at automating Pholus." He looked back up. His face brightened. "But now the Tebenkovs, together, will defend the Tsar's lands! No matter how large a form the Moonmother might have taken!"

Nikolai stood up, pushing the tea and cakes aside. "You want me to operate your device while your Locomotive Man fights some giant trunknose?"

"Trunknose," Uncle Gleb echoed. "That is as good a name as any for the Moonmother's spawn. While she is more than a larger version of her progeny, your words are essentially correct."

"This is insane!" The words burst forth unbidden.

"Sleep upon these matters." Uncle Gleb smiled. "Tomorrow, I will educate you in operating the Pholus."

Uncle Gleb lead Nikolai to a guest bedroom with a surprisingly comfortable mattress of dried moss atop a bed of birch limbs. Nikolai did not sleep. Instead, he waited until Uncle Gleb grew quiet. Of course he appreciated Uncle Gleb's help. But gratitude did not equal joining the old man in his madness.

Nikolai, leaving a note of apology, took some of Uncle Gleb's dried salmon and berries. He felt certain he could operate Uncle Gleb's gate. After some fumbling, Nikolai stood outside the palisade. The clear sky might make the night colder, but they provided a half moon to illuminate his way.

Nikolai started toward New Archangel. He stopped, thinking of how Mikhail Dimitrivitch would scorn a son who returned empty-handed. No matter what he had thought earlier, a trunknose pelt to shield him from his father's disdain was worth his last bullet. Mikhail Dimitrivitch would not dare say that the bearer of such a rare fur had accomplished nothing! Nikolai turned toward what Uncle Gleb had called the Loathsome Gorge.

Soon, he reached the valley. He breathed deeply, steeling himself against its floral reek. He heard the chittering of approaching trunknoses. This could be the perfect opportunity for an ambush! Nikolai melted into the forest.

Three trunknoses emerged from the valley. Two crept close to the ground, front limbs providing their locomotion. Their back limbs struggled to carry a heavy orb of purplish vines. The third stood erect on its two hind limbs, rattling its tail. Although the features were beyond Nikolai's reading, there was no mistaking a serf-master's mien.

The serf-trunknoses wedged the orb among a fallen spruce's roots. The serf-master continually berated them in its simultaneous bass-treble voice, sometimes cuffing them with its free paws. At last the orb was in place. From behind a rock, the trunknoses watched with an air of expectancy.

The orb emitted a mosquitoish whine. The ground trembled. Nikolai sensed motion about the orb, suggesting that almost invisible, slender, dark threads, shot out and writhed into the soil. The orb deflated like a rubber balloon. Violet vines sprouted from the soil, from the dead spruce, even from the rocks. They grew with a horrifying rapidity, radiating a freezing aura. After only a few moments, what had been clean wilderness became an extension of the rank valley.

The two serfs rattled their tails in what seemed to be pride of their accomplishments. The serf-master cuffed its charges. Nikolai saw no reason, but what serf-master ever needed one? Then the three slipped back into the valley.

Nikolai locked his hands. The trunknoses, as Uncle Gleb had

said, really did extend their domain. True, they acted slowly. Only a few tens of square yards had been gained. But many iotas of lost land added up. And what if they spread faster?

Could he rush to New Archangel and return with troops? No. New Archangel's governor would have even less reason to believe him than he had had to believe Uncle Gleb. Uncle Gleb's machines were the only hope.

Nikolai turned back toward Kiev East.

When he returned, Uncle Gleb waited for him.

"I... I..." Nikolai stuttered.

"You thought me deranged," Uncle Gleb replied. "You needed to see for yourself how the Moonmother's stain spreads."

Nikolai shook his head, trying to deny his planned desertion.

"Your reaction was expected," Uncle Gleb soothed. He produced a bottle and two glasses, inlaid with the insignia of some British steamer. "We will empty my last bottle of vodka. Tomorrow, we will begin your training."

The next four weeks were the hardest in Nikolai's life. Little by little, he learned to operate the Pholus Machine, discovering how to function inside without striking his head against the controls. He learned to feed coal into the Locomotive Man's back. He learned to steer the Pholus Machine guided only by the faint images from the machine's camera obscura. And Nikolai witnessed the old man's nightly forays against the trunknoses, driving them back and smashing their viney orbs.

One Sunday morning that came far too soon for Nikolai's taste, they stood at the edge of the Loathsome Gorge. "You have always struck at night before, except for my first day here," Nikolai observed, glancing up at the cloud-shrouded sky. "What makes this time different?"

Uncle Gleb, hands on the Locomotive Man's rope ladder, flashed a cryptic smile. "Because this day we oppose the Moonmother herself, and not merely her spawn. Daylight weakens her. We shall need every advantage."

Nikolai let those words soak in. He filled his lungs with the cool, clean, spruce and hemlock scented air. This was his last chance to reconsider.

"I remind you," Uncle Gleb continued. "The trunknoses are dangerous. More dangerous still is the Moonmother." He shook his head. "She does not appear as you might expect."

Nikolai frowned. "What does she look like? You have never told me."

"Just don't forget the signals we worked out," Uncle Gleb answered. Without another word, he climbed into the Locomotive Man and sealed the chest

Nikolai took his place in the Pholus Machine. The Locomotive Man lumbered forward on two legs, while the Pholus Machine followed on four. Into the valley they went, clearing a path through the rank purple vines.

In moments, the trunknoses beset the lumbering giants, some armed with bludgeons of violet vegetation, but most only with their own claws. Until then, Nikolai had harbored a shred of doubt about the trunknoses being as dangerous as Uncle Gleb had warned. The trunknoses' vicious behavior made that doubt evaporate. And, as the battle progressed, so vanished his questions about Uncle Gleb's ability to direct the Locomotive Man in battle. As long as Nikolai fed the Locomotive Man coal, Uncle Gleb kept the hooked left arm swinging, skewering trunknoses as the clawed right hand grasped others and threw them beneath the Locomotive Man's crushing feet.

The battle lasted what seemed like days, but could, at best, have been an hour or so. Then the Locomotive Man's arms raised above its head, the signal that they had almost reached the Moonmother.

Nikolai braced himself, ready for anything. Something large moved within the tangled vines. A gray-black mass, as tall as the Locomotive Man and surrounded with pulsing boneless limbs, emerged. Was this walking rotten potato, this orange-eyed slug-mountain, the Moonmother? The thought that, possibly, it both was and was not made Nikolai squirm.

The slug-mountain emitted a cry of challenge. Its eerie wail traveled from something so low that Nikolai more felt than heard it to something so high that it vanished from Nikolai's hearing. Its staring round eyes contracted to pinpoints. The slug-mountain charged. The Locomotive Man, hook drawn back to land the killing blow, countercharged.

Three of the slug-mountain's limbs wrapped around the Locomotive Man's legs, stopping the metal giant. The Locomotive Man's hooked arm descended, severing a limb. It lay on the ground, writing and spurting a thick orange fluid. Even though it claimed a limb, the counter-attack came too late. The slug-mountain's many limbs struck the Locomotive Man's chest. The chest plate sprung open. One writhing arm extracted Uncle Gleb. It flattened him against the great, gray-black mass. Uncle Gleb gave one pained scream. Other limbs joined the first. They contracted about Uncle Gleb and then dropped him.

Nikolai needed no attending physician to tell him that Uncle Gleb was dead. In his brief instant of freezing in place, dozens of trunknoses, sized more like horses than wolf-hounds, charged. Some descended on the Locomotive Man, ripping parts from it and discarding them. Most threw themselves against the Pholus Machine. The Pholus Machine's right front and the left rear legs crumpled. The Pholus Machine collapsed, crushing trunknoses beneath it. Other trunknoses, seemingly unconcerned with their fellows, attacked the Pholus Machine's access port. In moments, the orange eyes and drooping snout of an enormous trunknose were only inches from Nikolai's face.

Nikolai reached for a lever, loosened in the machine's fall, to use as a club. Before he could, trunknose claws encircled him. Nikolai closed his eyes. He whispered a prayer to St. Barbara the Great Martyr. Instead of the anticipated sensation of claws ripping him to cat meat, he felt himself lifted, carried a short distance, and placed on the ground. Nikolai, rising to his feet, opened his eyes.

He stood a few feet before the slug-mountain. Its great glaring eyes stared down at Nikolai's coal-smudged form, holding no emotion that Nikolai could read. Nikolai glanced about, looking for a weapon that he could use against the hulking monster. He saw nothing. "Do your worst," he snarled, intending to die bravely.

The slug-mountain split open. A shape, standing slightly smaller than Nikolai, writhed its way out. Nikolai stood dumbfounded. Before him, unashamed of her nudity, stood the most beautiful woman Nikolai had ever seen. Her dark hair hung in ringlets about her pale shoulders. Her face and breasts surpasses those of any model that had ever served any sculptor in the Tsar's court. The only thing marring her otherwise perfect exquisiteness was her extra pair of arms, mounted below her rib cage. Even that, Nikolai decided, could be termed more an eccentricity than a mark against her.

Nikolai glanced about him. The trunknoses had bowed before her, worshipping her as a goddess. "The Moonmother?" he whispered in awe, realizing that she had controlled the slug-mountain as he himself had controlled the Pholus Machine.

Instead of answering, she leapt for him. Her four hands wrapped about his head.

Images flooded his mind. The origin of the Moonmother, for such she must surely be, was so lost in antiquity that she herself failed to recall it. She remembered only ages of sailing an infinite sea of blackness, dotted with unblinking stars. She recalled riding a great sphere, woven of a material of which Nikolai could not conceive.

Images of that sphere bouncing onto a frozen purple swamp ruled by trunknoses flashed into his mind. He felt her joy in finding the trunknoses, believing they could serve her purposes, purposes he still did not understand. He shared her disappointment when she realized that the trunknoses were worthy solely of serving as templates for slaves! He experienced her sadness as she again set sail in her strange vessel, and her renewed joy as she bounced onto this green and fertile land.

Then she removed her hands. Her index finger pressed against his temple. Other thoughts, different in texture, flooded his mind. With them, came complete understanding of her needs.

He experienced the thoughts that had passed through the Moonmother when she had considered Uncle Gleb for her purposes. She had rejected him as too old, too frail. He lived through her thoughts of Fox in Den. The Tlingit chief was strong but too tradition bound to accept the changes that the Moonmother would bring. He, too, was unacceptable.

A fiery sensation filled Nikolai as he realized that the Moonmother evaluated him. He was young and strong. He could adapt, as he had when he had learned to operate the Pholus Machine.

In short, the Moonmother thought that Nikolai was the perfect mate with which to couple, so their progeny could be the soldiers of her kingdom-to-be. He did not understand why she needed a mate, when she had produced her trunknose slaves on her own, but he was somehow aware that she did.

New sensations ripped Nikolai from his questions. He not only saw, but felt in his hands – in his entire being – the grandeur could be his. He would rule with her, a Tsar greater than any who had ever lived. He could ascend to a position of glory only slightly below her own.

And, best of all, he would rub his ascension in blubbery old Mikhail Dimitrivitch's face. Nothing Nikolai had ever done was good enough? How dare a little fur trader, sitting in his little log fort, pass judgment on the consort of a divinity?

She stepped back. She smiled at him. Her features were exquisite, as an angel's might be inhumanly beautiful.

Nikolai's hands trembled. True, she was Uncle Gleb's killer. True, she incited him to rebellion against God and Tsar, the greatest of wrongdoings. Those counted against her. But the cold and the flowery scent that so bothered him were extensions of the trunknoses. She would, at his word, extinguish them. And she offered him wealth and wonder surpassing imagination. This woman, if that was the word for her, offered him something far beyond what he could ever achieve on his own.

What he could ever achieve on his own...

Nikolai, mind still linked to hers, felt the pain that the light of the alien sun caused her. Even through the iron-gray clouds, it weakened her, just as Uncle Gleb had said.

Nikolai's jaw set. The Devil's Grandmother take Mikhail Dimitrivitch. Here was something that he, and no one else, could accomplish.

Mind fixed on that fact, Nikolai Mikhailovitch pulled the pistol from his tunic. He shoved its barrel against the Moonmother's temple, and squeezed the trigger.

Her mouth flew open in a circle of surprise. She crumpled.

Her six limbs jerked. Then she lay still.

A noise like three earthquakes sounded from behind Nikolai. He turned. All about him, purple vegetation withered. The trunknoses, as one, used their claws to gut themselves, dying with their leader as Japanese warriors were said to do. In moments, self-slain trunknoses and dying vines filled the Loathsome Gorge.

Nikolai turned to the Moonmother. "These lands are the Tsar's, now and forever," he snarled. Maybe the words were true and maybe they weren't. But saying them made him feel better.

He glanced at Uncle Gleb's body. Nikolai would bury the old man in Kiev East, the kingdom he had built for himself. Then he would begin the long trek back to New Archangel.

And if, on arrival, fat old Mikhail Dimitrivitch said that Nikolai had accomplished nothing, then Nikolai Mikhailovitch Tebenkov would punch his father directly in the old man's over-stuffed, self-important, dominating gut.

About the author: Lawrence lives outside Atlanta, Georgia, with his wife Pam, and numerous quadripeds. In addition to writing, Lawrence plays old-time banjo. Lawrence›s work has been published in a variety of venues. Lawrence is the winner of the 2007 James award for his short story, Cyrus Felbs Blues, a tale of a space alien vampire in 1950›s rural Georgia.

TIME CIRCLE
LAWRENCE R. DAGSTINE

"The Interdimensional Portal Pad is broke," said Dr. Clive Hoffman sadly.

"You mean we're trapped in another time and place again," said Ves Barton.

"What do you expect from something as tiny as a calculator? For the moment we can't create a portal between dimensions so I can get you home." He pressed a few buttons on the small miraculous device. "The wormhole manipulator must be stuck, as well as the keypad's numeric changer. Otherwise, it blew a circuit."

Barton shook his head. "I thought you were a genius."

Clive parted a half-smile. "Sometimes. But even geniuses have their—"

"I know," Barton interrupted him. "They have their *moments*. You are erratic indeed, Dr. Hoffman. I've never come across one like yourself before, and I highly doubt I ever will again."

Clive grinned. "Well, since you put it like that." A moment of rethinking. "The great traveler of other dimensions and time periods do have their faults."

"Uh-huh." Barton nodded. "You belong in a mental institution, not time."

***

The lost adventurer, Dr. Clive Hoffman, and his dissatisfied interdimensional traveling companion, Vestibule Barton—Ves, for short—did it *again*. The correct data coordinates submitted into the handheld portal pad for Northwood, England 1897, had been logged wrong, causing the internal continuelizer's circuit to blow. Sparks were emitted from the device—an obvious blunder on Hoffman's part, but his purported inventive mind and chronometer were not really of any help either. The two were not sent to Northwood 1897, but helplessly transferred and shorted by the last portal jumping to another place in time; this time it was further back, and to a different European country. The gateways were once again *misguided*....

As Clive went through his gadget-filled pockets, he found something; it was of the utmost importance. Another device which at least told him the year and date. It was March 17th 1826, and from the look of things, the two must have jumped to Scandinavia. That much was certain. Probably Norway, and during a time when minister of fisherman was the most reputable profession.

They landed on a beach where remnants of leftover antimatter and molecular transferent solvents stained the sands a deep red. The icy waters surrounding the shoreline reflected what was left of the time portal's blueish-gray dazzle...up until the minute the continuum, the streams and strains of time itself, disappeared.

Clive dusted himself off, and helped Ves out of a sandpit. They took in a deep breath of air and glanced around: grass, a strange body of water, followed by a big lighthouse up the beach, and hundreds of foreign-made fishing boats, docked at a few wooden piers. The crashing of the waves was mildly unsettling. Norway was a wonderful country, but unfamiliar to them or any of their preceding excursions; unexpected was more like it. Clive produced an electronic watchlike reader out of his Victorian-styled velvet coat pocket. The tall graying man of temporal defiance was full of many gadgets, but it was the portal pad which mattered most in order to punch in the numbers and create the necessary wormholes.

"Where are we?" asked Ves bewilderedly. His hair was full of sand; he ran his fingers through it, loosening some of the grains that stuck to the roots.

"The year is 1826," Clive said, a smile adorning his face, "and I think this time we've landed in luck." He put his arm around Barton's shoulder.

"Yeah, Clive, but I have a midterm paper due in 1997. You need to get back to 1897 in order to bring me back to my own time period. That chronometer seems to be off again, as usual, everything you've told me misinterpreted, and as for the continuelizer on your portal pad—*poof*." There was a hint of sarcasm in the teen's voice.

"Stop bickering, Ves. You know I'm trying everything in my power to get you back home. Once I'm able to get back to 1897, I can build a machine—and please, no H.G. Wells jokes—that'll allow us to control the portals' destination points. So I can't do anything for the moment, not without the temporal time-distorter. And that's hidden away in my Northwood laboratory."

"Then tell me 'oh great traveler', how did we land in luck?"

"My dear Barton," Clive said, pinching his cheek. "We've either landed in luck or pure coincidence. You see, a few miles from here is the University of Oslo, and a very extraordinary man dwells there. A thinker. In the meantime, let's tread up to that lighthouse. We'll freeze standing here. Norway is a cold place at night."

Ves stopped and picked up a few smooth-surfaced limestones from the beach floor, tucking them in his satchel. The youngster was a bit of a rock collector back in his own time period. "A thinker?" he said, smiling. "You mean like those weird-looking chronologist fellas from the 31st Century?"

"Sort of, but we were up to our necks there," Clive answered. "You remember, I see, and which also means you remember everything I taught you. But this time if my knowledge of history serves me right, we might be able to get back home." A moment of silence, as the time traveler scratched his chin. "Ves, ever hear of <u>Niels</u> <u>Henrik</u> *Abel*?"

Barton shook his head.

"I didn't think so. Abel was one of history's most notable mathematicians. He made a remarkable series of contributions that weren't recognized in his lifetime. He's known for his work with integral equations—mathematical expressions that are used to compute the area beneath a curve. He also investigated the numerical field of elliptic functions. An ellipse is an oval with special properties. That leads to quantum-theory, the indivisible amount of energy necessary for the wormholes that bend dimensions within the time-continuum itself."

"You sure know your physics, Clive. But what does this Abel's equations have to do with controlling a time portal? Or you getting back to 1897 so you can bring *me* home?"

"It has a lot to do with it! Ellipses are oval, and so are the portals. The special properties are circles. Time circles, rotating so fast that a new wormhole emerges whenever and wherever. It would be the gateway we're looking for, and work in a forwarding fashion. A much slower process of time travel, but swimming our way through the continuum, the years would pass us by until we reached 1897."

"I understand now," Ves said, snapping his fingers. "Using Abel's math skills, you'll use what's left of the continuelizer's energy, but on the chronometer. Then, if I'm right, you'll turn these elliptic functions into a wormhole. The chronometer will be a substitute for the portal pad, restabilize time fluctuation and finally work clockwise, but at a slower pace where we get it right. We're stuck for the moment, but eventually we'll reach 1897, and that's our bus stop!"

"Very good," Clive said with a grin. "I knew you'd comprehend it. All we need to do is get some of Abel's blueprints. History tells that he often carries a journal, a book of sorts, with him. He documents all his work in it. What's left of the pad, or at least the remaining continuelizer's energy, can record from it and reuse each function in temporal reality when the time is right. The chronometer says sixteen hours until the next portal attempt, so we might as well get a good night's sleep."

"Do you think there's a main road to Oslo?" Ves asked him.

"I'll check from the top of the lighthouse. If there is, we'll follow it at sunup."

***

They both slept in the tower that night. By sunrise, they left for the university along a dirt path. A farmer offered them a ride on his horse-drawn carriage, as he was heading to the Scandinavian Capital anyway to sell grains, barley, vegetables, and many different kinds of fruits to support his family.

For many miles, moving east, the two time travelers not only rested their legs on back of a cart filled with plush wheat and rye, but further discussed the history of Abel. A man with such talent, to die so young; perhaps this was the reason why he was never fully recognized. He was only twenty-six at the time of his death. It happened in 1829, and he had succumbed to tuberculosis—almost a decade after his father's death. Everyone at the University, including admiring professors and teachers, who contributed to his upkeep from their salaries knew of his infectious disease. But that didn't matter. It was overlooked. Especially by <u>Bernt</u> <u>Holmboe</u>. As Holmboe's prize pupil grew, so did his mathematical skills. Holmboe would go on to publish his works in 1839, opening new doors in the world of math. For Dr. Clive Hoffman and Vestibule Barton, the world of wormholes. Abel had attended the University of Oslo for four years. He traveled, but returned often—to teach or to lecture. Most of his free time was spent writing papers on mathematics, and it wasn't until he met August Crelle, a German engineer, that he started a journal.

That academic record would be necessary for Clive's portal.

The grain and fruit-filled carriage reached Oslo before noon. Ves thanked the farmer repeatedly, though the ride had been a slow one. The farmer shrugged his shoulders as he couldn't understand or speak English, but it was obvious through facial gesture that he had helped the two foreigners immensely.

The University lay down a thin cobblestone street, with a large fountain and a marble arch towering over the entrance. Large cathedral bells rang out, signaling the noon lunch crowd. Seagulls and pigeons fought over stale bread in the plaza, thrown away from the neighboring bread shop. The fountain decorated the plaza, trickling water from its basin, a place where students could sit and eat. A smaller, granite arch surrounded a garden behind it, filled with lush plants, bulbous roses, and loose swans. "We're finally here," Clive said, removing the chronometer from his coat pocket; though it was a futuristic device, like the portal pad, it looked like a gold pocket watch. Not your ordinary timepiece. A little standard in design; yet so advanced and full of so much potential.

"How long have we got?" Ves asked him, concerning the next portal attempt.

Clive looked at the chronometer in grim silence. "Two hours," he replied. "It's amazing how time flies."

"That doesn't leave us much. Not only do we have to find this

'Abel', but scan the notes in his journal. Without them, the portal's return is meaningless."

"You worry too much, Ves. Typical of 20ᵗʰ Century Americans. Try and be an interdimensional traveler for as long as I have. Time has no distinction. Think of the places I've been, and on such short notice. I've escaped World War One tanks and bombs through a portal that lasted mere seconds. I've been pursued by nasty pirates, nabbing their dubloons, and jumping portal within minutes of having my throat cut. I've even outstretched the battle axes of formidable brigandines. Two hours is enough time. I don't need to make Abel's acquaintance. We just have to sneak in his room, borrow the journal, and bring it back when we're through so as not to cause a crack in the ordinance of time."

"You make it sound so easy. Besides, I thought you'd want to meet Abel. You couldn't stop talking about him in the carriage."

"You're starting to be an annoying companion," Clive said. "Come. Let's go to college."

***

Niels Henrik Abel put his papers away for the day. He removed his pince-nez glasses, taking a cloth from his back pocket and mopped his forehead. It was long and hard work, but he'd finished his latest mathematical equations. There were a few books left scattered by the door which he hadn't even had the time to at least thumb through and make cliff notes: *Formulas, Functions, and Graphs, and Evariste Galois' Modern Algebra Notes.* They were to be taken with him to Paris, for the French Mathematician's Convention; and his journal too, which had a critical paper inside for presentation at France's Academy of Sciences.

Abel struggled through the night on it, hoping when he arrived the professors responsible for evaluating his work on elliptic functions wouldn't ignore it. It was the funding that counted, and lucky for him the University headmasters allowed a home-away-from-home for much of his study, and his chambers untouched. This was his life, and he practically lived out of his school office when not teaching.

He cleaned off his desk, which was littered with papers—mathematical essays and jottings, an indispensable tool—for the students he taught. Two bookcases in the far corner held the mathematician's teaching devices; if it wasn't the wrought-iron abacus with crystal beads, then it was the wood-carved apple with the special curves, or the Jesus figurine or the glass-bottled ship.

Yes, these were his tools.

Abel's toy collection always defined shapes, functions, and involved equations or deduction problems; they have special *properties* surrounding their structures, he often remarked. This was the most important part of his lesson, using peculiar objects or gadgets as a mathematical example.

Someone knocked at his door. It was a student, not much younger than him.

"Hold on," he said, wiping his ink-sodden hands across his clean shirt. It was unusual being sought after this time of the afternoon.

"Mr. Abel?" The student shook hands with him and was invited in.

The mathematician was extremely busy, getting ready for his trip, but if there was one thing he was known for, it was his politeness and refusal to turn away the aspiring young mathematical mind of tomorrow; and the young man happened to be one who had studied most of his work and appeared at one too many lectures.

They conversed in Norwegian, boasting news for several minutes. Interesting news indeed, it seemed, as Abel would have a little competition at the convention. August Crelle, the engineer and math expert, would be attending. Still nothing to worry about. Crelle was friendly with Abel and his work—even compensated him in the past.

They spoke a mixture of Norse and English. "Vidunderlig," Abel said, and the word had meant wonderful. "So Crelle *will* be at the Academy of Sciences. Please, tell me, how did you hear of this?"

"I overheard two tourists," the student answered, "back in the main hall. And it was like... like they *knew* Mr. Crelle personally.

Call me crazy. I need help with a math problem though, sir. One in patterns and principles."

"Is that it?" Abel laughed, looking down at the student's workbook. "Consider the following question, youngster: does there exist a number with such a property that the result of adding it to three is the same result as subtracting it from fifteen or less? The amount in asking is a number which satisfies an open sentence. Now consider the open sentence, because it may be converted into a true statement."

"But how?" the student asked.

"By replacing each occurrence of the variable **x**," Abel said in reply, "but with the numeral six. It may be converted into a false statement by replacing each and every occurrence of the variable **x**, with the numeral two. Because of the property behind it, each pair of numbers *satisfies* the open sentence. The generalization is called the commutative principle for addition. Understand?" He then handed the student Galois' book on algebra notes. "Here," he then said, fixing the youngster's ascot. "You'll need this more than me. It contains just about everything you need to know concerning patterns and principles."

The student was overjoyed. "Thank you, Mr. Abel!"

"Don't mention it. Return it when you're through. And study hard!"

Abel had explained it bluntly. It was no wonder students and professors alike looked up to him, relying on his knowledge. He was an admirable genius, as Clive had made him out to be. Concepts of modern algebra were useful in his branch of mathematics. He gained a considerable reputation in European math and circles, and several attempts were made to find him a professorship.

The aspiring student smiled and thanked him again. "This means a lot, Abel," he said. "I really appreciate it!"

"Any time," the mathematician said. "Your future is bright, my pupil. If I can help towards it, then I feel I have done my job. Come, I'll walk you back to class."

He escorted the student out, closing the door behind him.

***

Abel was gone from his room for some time, allowing Hoffman and Barton to sneak in unannounced. They were there for one reason, and one reason only. To find the journal and scan the mathematical equations within it.

"It's definitely here," Clive said, closing the door lightly. He was holding what still remained functional of the continuelizer, now hooked up to the chronometer.

"Nobody's here," Ves whispered. "How can you be sure he left the journal?"

"You may not know this, Ves, but the leftovers to the continuelizer have a tiny scanner. Sort of like my time reader." He held it up for his companion to see. "It's this microscopic beacon on the end, makes it a tracking device. It can home in on scrolls, written documents, and books as well."

"We've wasted almost a half-hour already, asking for directions!"

"There's never enough time, is there?" Clive shook his head. "Ah, you must be talking about that guidance counselor. What a talkative nuisance she was."

"It's because of her we got lost in the mezzanine," Ves said, browsing through the titles on the bookshelves in the far corner. "Clive, this is hopeless! Abel's book could be any place. This school has so many offices and classes. For all we know, the library might have it."

"Then we'll go library hunting," Clive said, checking Abel's desk drawers. "It's not like we'll have to resort to that, but my instincts never failed me before so why should it now?"

"I know your locater works. *You're* the one with the loose nuts and bolts."

"Rather harsh words, Ves. Why not trust me for once?"

"I'm sorry, Clive. I... I shouldn't have jumped at you like that. I forget. You're the inventor, I'm the assistant. Still, there's no journal and I've practically looked everywhere. The only things I've shuffled through were strange trinkets with odd shapes and books on geometry, linear equations, and the importance of variables. Nothing on elliptic functions. Are you sure it looks like a diary?"

"It's shaped like one," Clive remarked, "but it has a sketchbook-type interior." He looked around some more. "Probably onionskin for this time and era. Ah, this is an odd book,"—which he picked up with interest—"untitled and has absolutely nothing to do with arithmetic or algebra. It's about Samuel Adams. The man was one of the firebrands of the American Revolution, combining great ideals with the element of shrewd politics and helping change America from a British colony into an independent nation. He died in 1803. Not too long ago. You'd never know it's his memoirs—a half-translated copy, of course." A most inappropriate book for a Norwegian mathematician to own. "Perhaps I can find a better home for it. Put it in your satchel, Ves, along with your rock collection."

"You've got to be kidding me!" Ves exclaimed. "We're keeping it? That book is not going to help us any."

"Never turn your back on an interesting piece of literature. Besides, that very book you're holding has no place in this period. We're helping reassess the fabric of time by bringing it back with us."

Ves shook his head and rolled his eyes. "Whatever, Clive," he murmured half-aloud, opening his satchel and tucking the book inside. "Whatever you say, boss!" The boy did not want to dwell on subjects having little or no consequence. But as he tied the handle to his satchel, he inadvertently trod forward and tripped over a different kind of book. It was lying in the middle of the floor, concealed by a heap of crumpled paper.

It was Abel's journal.

"No wonder we couldn't find it," Ves then said. "This math expert desperately needs a maid."

Clive rushed over and picked it up. It was blue and perfect bound, the initials N.H.A. engraved on the cover. "Superb!" Clive was overjoyed. "Abel's equations of elliptic functions should be on pages 295-320. I'll start winding up the scanner to blueprint copy mode."

Ves shook his head. "Imagine that. This stupid book helped me find that one. Well, what are you waiting for? Use the continuelizer!"

"That's just what I'm going to do, Barton. I'll slowly scan each page, making a record of the basic figures necessary for our perfect portal. Then all the equations will be added together, retrieved by one memory bank: the chronometer's power-stabilizer, which the scanning energy of the continuelizer has been hooked up to." He twisted a dial on the gold pocket watch, with the reader and beacon hooked on top, across one line and one page at a time. It recorded everything. "When we get to portal jump again, I'll reface its structure by aiming a secular beam into newly-formed circles. In other words, the math figures will create the wormhole for us."

He spoke too soon.

The door slid open and Abel entered. He looked about haggardly. "Goodness! What is the meaning of this? Who are you?" he asked, confused and unknowing if the trespassers were thieves, trying to steal his mathematical notes, or scholars in strange-looking garments seeking advice.

"Clive, what's he saying?" Ves ran behind Hoffman's coattail frantically. Clive dropped the journal and continuelizer as well, in nervous reaction of being caught in the act. And he was, but he strove to be cheerful.

"Neither of us will be able to understand him," he said quietly. "He's speaking Norwegian."

"What are you doing here?" Abel asked again, clenching his hands together; it seemed he was growing angrier by the moment.

"I think he's got the wrong impression about us," Clive muttered. "It's always the historical types who get a bad rep. I'll try and communicate with him. Maybe clear things up." Clive rushed forward with an open hand and introduced himself. "I am Dr. Clive Hoffman, English inventor and historian of time. It is an honor to make your acquaintance, Mr. Abel. And this is Vestibule Barton, from America, a pupil and traveling assistant of mine."

Barton smiled. "Ves, for short," he said. "I'm from Boston, Mass."

"Ah, yes," the mathematician mumbled. "England? Boston? Are you scholars, by any chance?" By now he was no longer talking in his native tongue.

"Yes, we are," Clive answered. "I see you speak English rather well."

"It's like a second language to me. I also speak Danish and some French, too. But that doesn't matter. I want to know how you got in here. And what were you doing with my journal?"

"*Ahem!*" Clive cleared his throat. "Oh, nothing horrible really. My pupil and I were just going to copy some of your notes for a very critical purpose."

"Liar! Thieves!" Abel shouted. "You probably work for Karl Jacobi. That man will do anything to get my notes!"

"No we don't!" Ves said, in defense of himself and Clive. "We don't even know who August Crelle is." A moment of silence, and then a mistaken: "*Whoops!*"

"Nice job, Ves." Clive patted him on the shoulder. "Do us both a favor and put your foot in your mouth."

"Enough of this," Abel finally said. "If you're both visiting scholars then prove it, otherwise I will be forced to get school security."

Ves tugged on Hoffman's coattail. "What now, Clive?"

"Then I will," Clive said, smiling. "You want proof that I am an historian? Ah, so be it… then it is history and the elements of time I shall serve you." He began to pace back and forth; Ves looked on, remaining silent as a mouse. "You, my fellow, are Niels Henrik Abel, are you not? You were born on August 5th 1802, in a straw shack on the island of Finnoy, near the port of Stavanger. You were the son of the hapless, impoverished minister-type, and a terrible student till the age of fifteen." A moment of silence, as Abel couldn't believe what he was hearing. "By age fifteen your school had hired Bernt Holmboe," Clive went on, "a very strict math teacher. He became your instructor, and you his pupil. He recognized your talent; he even encouraged you. You soon surpassed him. Now others look up to *your* brilliance, and learn from it. Is that enough scholarly proof?"

Abel's face was not only one of sufficiency but that of reverence. "But how did you know all this? Have you… have you followed me my whole life?"

"We come from the future," Clive said. "You wanted proof.

There you have it. We're scholars, just visiting... but at the same time trapped you might say."

"That doesn't prove you're scholars," Abel said. "Still, you... you just explained my childhood to me." He shook his head. "My experiences and my memories."

"You better show him what's what, Clive," Ves said. "He still looks confused."

"I suppose you're right, Mr. Abel. It is hard to fathom. I'll tell you everything if you at least take the time to listen and believe."

"All right. I'll listen. But do make it quick, as I have a convention to attend in Paris tomorrow."

"Can you accept time or interdimensional travel as a possibility?" Clive asked, creeping closer. "Using such a possibility from a mathematical perspective?"

Abel gave no reply at first; his mind was cluttered and he suddenly flew off on one of his tangents. "No," he finally said. "There's no such thing as time travel."

"Oh, but there is, Mr. Abel," Clive said, "and the future is where we originate. I come from 1897, and my companion here comes from 1997. I'm what you'd call a chronologist. Not just an inventor. As for time, it is constant and involves math such as yours, but history is only temporary."

"You want me to accept this? That mathematically time is a continuous factor and that history is but temporary? Nonsense! How does math play a vital role?"

"Math is the foundation for everything in the universe," Clive said, "including matter and antimatter. That's why I needed to scan your journal. Your papers on elliptic functions were not only a major breakthrough but required. For the time-being we're stranded in 1826, and we don't have much time left because we've got a portal to catch. An oval-shaped portal called a wormhole, rotating so fast that a series of time circles are created. Basically, a gateway to the future. Without your mathematical knowledge, and my scientific gadgets, my assistant and I are lost."

"Lost? Preposterous," Abel said. "You don't want to scan my notes. You want to steal them—for glory!"

"Not so!" Ves said, once again in defense of what he felt was an attack on both himself and Clive's legitimacy of the matter.

"Like your elliptic functions, the portal's ovals are *also* elliptic," Clive said. "It then in turn creates circles around the boundaries, through rotation and function. How do I make you a believer, Mr. Abel? The special properties are *circles*."

"Wait a minute," the mathematician then said. "What you just said about how the special properties are circles. Not even Karl Jacobi knew that. Those answers were merely theories inside my head, which I had considered for some time. And they were never part of my notes. I kept it strictly confidential; up in my noggin." He narrowed his eyes at the two, actually beginning to believe them. "An ellipse's special property may very well be a circle, but in a rotative state; that's just one of the functions. I never revealed it to other professors, because I did not want to be discredited by August Crelle in the event I was wrong. So I decided to leave it out of my journal purposely. How could you know this?"

Clive picked the journal up and put it flat on the mathematician's desk. "We'll help you finish your notes," he said humbly, "if you help us get home."

A moment of forethought. "Well, you are rather strange indeed. But you have made a believer out of me, Dr. Hoffman. If my notes can help you get home, then you have my permission to use them. In linear terms, one day I'd like to learn the boundaries of these gateways or portals as you call them."

"Matter transference," Clive explained. "Taking a solid object, human, animal or insect, table or chair, to another point in time. Antimatter is what's leftover as the portal closes but as a liquefied solvent which can coexist here."

Abel's mouth was agape; he was more or less fascinated.

And then, Ves interrupted by saying, "What's that irreparable noise?"

"The continuelizer," Clive said. "Our portal attempt is here, and the red signal says it's coming from the University's roof. Come, both of you. We must hurry!"

The notes were scanned hastily and they were out the office, up the stairs, the roof door forced open, and finally upon the moment they'd been waiting for.

"It's starting to materialize," Clive said, aiming the chronometer forward.

Abel was awestruck. "I... I can't believe it. My math helped formulate this?"

"You did it," Ves cried out, laughing excitedly. "We can go home now!"

A wormhole opened before them... the familiar blueish-gray dazzle as always.

"They were formed by circles," Abel muttered. "No, ellipses. Nonetheless, my eyes are playing tricks on me." The time travelers insisted he come with them, not only to bid them off, but witness firsthand his life's work take shape and form.

"One more thing," Clive said, "you must never tell anyone about this or of our existence, as it could affect the time-continuum. It must *always* remain a secret."

"Yes, of course," Abel said agreeably. "I don't even think the professors would believe me. They'd call me crazy."

Clive agreed. "That they would." He shook hands with him, as Ves sprinted to the portal and jumped in first. "And don't forget about the special properties, Mr. Abel. You have pages 321-330 to finish up on yourself. You will be remembered, and highly regarded for this journal, in time to come." He handed it back to him.

"Goodbye, Dr. Hoffman," the mathematician said.

"Goodbye."

Clive now entered the portal himself. The blueish-gray dazzle surrounded his very being, transferring his body, mind and soul to another point in time. And he had hoped that this time it would be Northwood, England, 1897.

The wormhole disappeared two minutes later.

Abel considered what he had just seen, wishing them luck. The theory behind time travel would never leave his thoughts, even twenty-four hours later when the convention was to take place. He would fail to win the recognition he deserved in his lifetime, *especially* at the convention by prominent French math professors; it would be the competition between himself and a young German math expert who went by the name Karl Jacobi. That would be the beginning of his downfall. You see, Karl Jacobi was also investigating the field of elliptic functions. Shortly after, Abel's life would turn upside-down, coming home jobless, with debts, no upkeep, and no prospects. Just a man and his journal. He'd get sicker, and as a man torn apart from the inside, he would reach his grave in less than three years. But there would be a familiar saying engraved on his tombstone...

Math is the foundation for everything.

About the author: Lawrence Dagstine is a freelance writer whose byline has appeared in *hundreds* of print magazines and webzines viewed all over the globe.

JOHN WILKES BOOTH
R.H. REESE

April 14th, 1865—10:00 P.M.

In Baptist Alley behind Ford's Theatre, John Wilkes Booth handed the reins of his horse to Joseph Burroughs, a handyman employed by the theatre's owner. He then entered the rear of the theatre and took the passageway beneath the stage to a door on the opposite side of the building that led back outside. From there he walked up the narrow walkway to the side entrance of the Star Saloon. He went in and ordered a whiskey.

After finishing his drink, Booth walked out of the saloon onto 10th Street, turned right, and walked north for a dozen paces until he was directly in front of the theatre. He casually walked through the main entrance into the lobby, turned left, climbed the curved stairs to the second floor balcony, and circled behind the audience to a white door above stage right.

Behind that door was a small vestibule that led to the unguarded presidential box.

Inside the vestibule he took the small pine board he had previously hidden there and wedged it between the door and the wall — effectively preventing anyone else from entering. He then peered into the President's box through a small hole in the door.

Directly in front of him sat President Lincoln in a red rocking chair. To his right was Mary Todd Lincoln, then Clara Harris, and finally, on a small sofa, Major Henry Rathbone. Major Rathbone and Miss Harris had eagerly accepted the invitation to accompany the President when General Grant withdrew at the last moment.

Booth waited for some laughter to fill the theater and then walked through the door, puts his .44 caliber derringer to the back of Lincoln's head, and pulled the trigger. A dull explosion drove the lead ball deep into the President's brain.

Major Rathbone instantly hurled himself through the smoke

at the assassin. Booth dropped his small, single-shot pistol and slashed at the Major with a large bowie knife — inflicting a deep wound on the Major's left arm.

Booth then climbed over the railing and jumped to the stage below. However, one of his spurs caught on a flag draped on the front of the box, causing him to land off balance and break a bone in his left leg. Not deterred by the pain, he faced the audience and shouted: "*Sic semper tyrannis!*"

Before anyone in the audience understood what was happening, he limped across the stage, exited the back door, mounted his waiting horse, and disappeared into the night.

April 15ᵗʰ, 1865—3:30 A.M.

Several hours earlier the stricken President had been taken across 10ᵗʰ Street to Petersen's Boardinghouse to draw his last breath. Several hundred people remained outside on the unpaved, gas lit street hoping for some word of the President's condition.

Slowly, one man in the crowd, wearing the well-tailored uniform of a Union army captain, backed away from the group and slipped unnoticed into the lobby of the now deserted theatre.
He hurriedly retraced Booth's path into the vestibule, picked up the board that Booth had used to block the door, examined it briefly, and put it back on the floor.

After peering through the hole in the door, he entered the President's box and carefully studied the scene.

He moved behind Lincoln's rocking chair and caressed its red velvet. Then, after first glancing nervously to his left and right, he carefully lowered himself onto its plush cushion.

After just a few seconds he sprung to his feet and stood with his hands on the box's railing whilst surveying the gas lit stage, orchestra pit, and empty chairs in the audience. After taking in the scene completely, he ran his hands over the draping flags until he found the small tear from Booth's spur.
He then stood against the wall and put his finger into a barely visible hole near the ceiling.

With a pocketknife he scraped around the hole until a piece

of plaster about four inches long fell into his hands. He placed the plaster on the railing, reached into the hole, and pulled out a small video camera.

He took a quick look around as he slipped the camera under his tunic and into his waistband. He then pushed the piece of plaster back into the wall.

After adjusting his tunic, the "Union army captain" lowered himself from the railing and dropped onto the stage. After taking a last look at the theatre, he walked to the rear of stage left, exited onto Baptist Alley, and disappeared into the night.

December 22nd, 2012—Late Evening

The HD screen on the wall was filled with rank after rank of blue-clad soldiers with fixed bayonets marching up a broad, dusty avenue. Following the infantry were scores of canvas-topped wagons, dozens of horse-drawn artillery pieces with caissons, more infantry, long streams of cavalry, and then more infantry coming on by the thousands.

The unpaved avenue was lined by thousands of cheering spectators. Many of the viewers were sheltering themselves from the noonday sun with umbrellas or by standing in the shade of trees or under the awnings of nearby buildings.

The colors were vivid, especially the white clouds drifting above the green trees in the radiant blue sky. Dramatically, at the far end of the avenue, the distinctive dome of the U.S. Capitol was clearly visible as the screen went blank.

Standing to the right of the screen was a young man about twenty with long dark hair and wearing the uniform of a Union army captain.

The only other man in the room was seated on a red leather couch directly in front of the screen. He was much older, tall and slender, and had gray hair down to his shoulders.

"Well, you've always put yourself up to be such an authority on the Civil War, so what do you think of what you jus' saw?" asked the young man.

The old man looked away from the screen and said: "I suppose what you've just shown me was meant to be General Grant's victory parade up Pennsylvania Avenue following Lee's surrender. I also saw, in that first segment, what I could only describe as a poor, B-movie-style re-enactment of Lincoln's assassination.

"So, I give the assassination an F, but the parade up Pennsylvania Avenue was damn good. In fact, I've never seen any other footage of its kind so well done. There aren't many people, even out in Hollywood, who could have staged that so well. It was flawless; for one thing, not a single extra gave it away by staring into the camera. Where'd you come by it?"

"Prepare yourself for a shock," the young man said. "What you saw was not some kind of re-creation by re-enactors or some of that computer-generated shit, but footage that was shot live, on location, as it actually happened."

"Oh please, just how gullible do you think I am? Thomas Edison didn't even invent the motion picture camera for another thirty years."

The young man quickly lost his temper: "What's the matter, can't you believe your own damn eyes? Have you had your nose in those damn books of yours for so long that you don't recognize the real thing when it's staring you right in the face? Could I've faked Grant's whole army?"

"Calm down, there's no need to get so upset," said the old man nervously. "I know that we've talked of visiting the past and meeting with some of the great men of history, but get a hold of yourself. Dreams are one thing; reality is another.

"And did you really expect me to take one look at that footage and just accept your story? Extraordinary claims demand extraordinary evidence. I'd need to see a lot more evidence, unimpeachable evidence, before I'd swallow that one."

"Oh, so you want unimpeachable evidence? I almost forgot, that reminds me of somethin' else I'd like to show you—this way, in my study."

As they walked towards the study, the old man sensed the lingering anger in his young host and, feeling uneasy, made a conciliatory gesture: "But I will say this, your technique, whatever it is, will make a fortune for you in Hollywood. In fact, in a few years, you could own Hollywood."

Inside the dimly lit study they found a disheveled man in his mid-twenties reclining on a couch with his left leg up on a stool. A look of recognition swept across the old man's face.

"Allow me to introduce you to Mr. John..." began the young man.

The old man cut him off: "No need for an introduction. I've seen that face in a hundred photographs and would recognize it anywhere. I'm so glad to meet you Mr. Booth; I've *always* wanted to talk with you."

About the author: A graduate of Moravian College in Bethlehem, PA. he is presently employed as a deputy sheriff and lives by the Delaware River in penn.

WHY KILL OSWALD?
R.H. REESE

Dallas, Texas; November 22, 1963:

A feeling of excitement fills the air at the Texas Schoolbook Depository this cool Friday morning; President John F. Kennedy's motorcade is scheduled to pass directly in front of the depository in less than an hour. As if on cue, the sun has just broken through some dark clouds that had threatened rain, and it seems that a beautiful day lay ahead.

It is exactly 11:45 A.M., and a tall, slim man with graying hair and wearing a bright red jacket walks through the main entrance to the depository. He walks over to a group of book-handlers discussing the President's visit and calmly asks where he can find Mr. Lee Harvey Oswald. One of the men, Buell Frazier, who had given Oswald a ride to work this morning, points over to the lunch room where Lee can be seen dropping a coin in the Dr. Pepper machine.

The stranger turns and walks into the lunchroom and approaches Oswald. Oswald, always one to keep to himself, turns from the stranger and starts to leave the room.

Without a word, or a moment's hesitation, the stranger pulls a small crowbar from his belt and brings it down on Oswald's head with a loud smack. Oswald drops to the floor like a rag doll, a pool of blood forming around his head. Then, as if to be sure of what he has done, the assailant smashes the heavy metal bar down onto Oswald's shattered skull a second and third time.

From the time the stranger entered the building, to the thump of Oswald's body hitting the floor, not sixty seconds passed. But the execution, and that's what it was, was witnessed by at least six employees. But each of these men is too stunned by the horrific sight to even think of moving to help the victim —that is until a woman's scream filled the building. Then, their trance-like state shattered, the men rush to the entrance of the lunchroom to prevent the killer from escaping.

There is another scream, then shouting. "Call the cops."

"Grab that nut." "Get an ambulance." But no one in the group in front of the lunchroom is anxious to take on a homicidal maniac with a steel bar. The man in the red jacket seems strangely tranquil.

He slowly bends down, wipes the blood off the crowbar with Oswald's own shirt, and then gently sets the murder weapon on the lunch table. He walks to a corner of the room and stands there, almost as if waiting for a slightly overdue bus.

Within minutes a police car shows up, followed seconds later by an ambulance. Dallas Police Officer J.D. Tippit takes the killer into custody without a struggle.

Oswald's lifeless body is rushed to Parkland Hospital where he is declared dead on arrival.

The President's motorcade passes through Dealy Plaza without incident.

Dallas Police Headquarters, 12:30 P.M.

Detectives Elmer Boyd and Richard Simms (Homicide/ Robbery) are standing outside the small interrogation room on the third floor. Inside the room, the suspect from the Schoolbook Depository is securely handcuffed and shackled to a chair. Captain John Fritz, the Homicide Chief, is explaining the case to them.

"Here's what we've got from Officer Tippit's initial report, mainly from the victim's co-workers. This psycho walked into the schoolbook warehouse over on Dealy Plaza just before noon, took a crowbar and buried it in the skull of this guy named, uh... let me see, Oswald, Lee Oswald.

"No question that we've got the right man; a half-dozen witnesses saw the whole thing. This guy did it, and then just waited around to be picked up — like he hadn't a care in the world.

"The victim was an ex-marine married to a woman living over in Irving with a friend. Apparently he and the wife didn't get on that well; he was living in a room on Beckly Street, although he did visit her on weekends. Also, they had two small girls, what a shame.

"He kept pretty much to himself and didn't seem to have any friends — or enemies for that matter. Nobody at the depository recalls seeing the killer before or can connect him with the victim, but then Oswald had only worked there a few weeks.

"We got what we need for a conviction: witnesses and the murder weapon. But a motive and a confession would be nice. Try to find a connection between these two men — there's got to be some connection."

The Interrogation:

In accordance with departmental policy, the suspect is informed that he has the right to have an attorney present during questioning. The suspect waives this right.

It's agreed that Simms would play the "good cop," and Boyd the "bad cop."

The suspect had no identification in his possession when taken into custody, so the first item on the agenda is to establish who he is.

"What's your name?" Simms asks in as friendly a manner as he can muster.

"Winston Smith," he answers.

"Your address?"

"None."

"Social Security Number?"

"I don't have one."

"Got a library card or any kind of identification?"

"No."

"Well, where are you staying?"

"Nowhere, I just arrived in town."

"From where?"

No answer.

Boyd, "the bad cop," cuts in. "Listen, you son of a bitch, you just smashed in the skull of some poor guy who never did you, or anybody else, any harm in his whole life. And you left a widow and two small girls without a father. Now go on being a smart-ass with us, and you just might find yourself falling down those backstairs; it happens every once in a while around here, no matter how careful we try to be!

"And just keep in mind that we got a shitload of witnesses that saw you smash that guy's head in, and we got your bloody fingerprints on the crowbar, and you have his blood on your damn shirt. The way I see it, the noose is already around your damn neck, so do yourself a favor and don't piss me off."

"Easy Elmer, this guy has been through a lot, and I'm sure he's really upset and probably not thinking too clearly, so give him a chance to get himself together, OK?

"But, what my partner says is true. You're in pretty hot water, so why don't you do yourself a favor by telling us exactly what got you into this situation? You seem like an intelligent man; you must have had a reason for what you did."

"I don't think there's much point in saying anything; you wouldn't believe my story anyway," the suspect says.

"Try us, we just want you to help us get this thing settled; I'm sure you had a reason for what you did, right? Had you met the victim before this morning?"

No answer.

"Look, we're going to find all this out sooner or later, so just save us all a lot of trouble and tell us exactly what led up to this. How about a cup of coffee?"

"Coffee? Real Coffee?"

"Well, Boyd made it, so it's almost real."

"Yes, I would like some coffee, thank you."

"Cream or sugar?"

"Yes, cream and sugar. I haven't had real coffee in years."

"OK, go on, you were going to tell us why you killed Oswald."

"What?"

"Why kill Oswald?" Simms asks.

The suspect takes a swallow of his coffee and seems totally relaxed and reconciled to the situation.

"Oswald was going to kill your President."

"What?"

"Oswald was going to kill President Kennedy as he passed through Dealy Plaza."

"And how did you come to know this?"

"I just knew."

"How did you know?"

"I'm a historian," he says matter-of-factly.

"What's that got to do with it?"

"I know from my study of history all the details of the assassination of President Kennedy and its effects on the course of world events."

"Oh, I get it," Boyd says. "You're claiming to be from the future, and you think that this story will get you off with some kind of bullshit-insanity defense."

"The first part of what you said is true, and I guess it doesn't matter what I say or do now. So, do you want to hear my story or not?"

"Yeah, keep talking, we're listening."

"I had to. I *had* to kill Oswald, and here's why: After the murder of your President Kennedy, America underwent a shift in its attitude. It wasn't something anybody could quite put their finger on at the time, but the effects were significant, if subtle, over the years ahead.

"It took time, but slowly that sense of trust, fair play, and optimism that had distinguished Americans, trickled away to be replaced by greed, suspicion and fear. As you would put it, everything went downhill, and it all began with that assassination.
"And the more America lost faith in itself, the more it sought to reform the world. And the more it sought to shape the world around it, the more enemies it made abroad —while the decline at home accelerated."
"OK, this story is getting good, but how does it end?"

"It ends with a catastrophic American military defeat in East Asia, the collapse of the greatest economy in the world, and the fragmentation of a once great nation into hundreds of feuding political, racial, religious, national, and economic factions. It ends with the death of what was once called the 'American Dream.'"

"I bet that made the rest of the world happy," Boyd says.

"Yes, for a while it did, until the rest of the world realized how interdependent the globe had become. The catastrophe that destroyed your society created a worldwide ripple effect that, in a few frantic months, drew the rest of the world down into that same chaos.

"When I left, what you call the future; there were just a few isolated pockets of high civilization left in the world. I, and a few others, decided that something had to be done. We gathered the few remaining scientists and technicians into a team that built the transporter that would enable someone to travel backwards in time and change the course of history."

"And that someone was you? You were the one chosen to save the world, right?" Boyd asks.

"Of course," Smith replies. "Who else? I was the one that isolated the fulcrum of history; the one point in the past that if changed would create a `butterfly effect' that would replace the crippled world of the future with something better."

"So, you think you succeeded?" Boyd asks.

"Yes," Smith replies

"How do you know?"

"Because I'm still here, obvious isn't it?"

"No, it's not obvious."

"Do you know why I didn't try to escape after the killing? Because after I completed the mission, I was to be instantly drawn back to 2078 A.D., and when I wasn't, I knew that the team and the transporter no longer existed. They no longer existed because their future had been replaced by a new world. They sacrificed their very existence for that brave new world. The mission *was* a success."

Then Simms asks an obvious question, "Well, if your future doesn't exist, how come you're still here, shouldn't you have never existed — just like your friends in the future?"

"No," Smith replies. "I was out of the temporal loop when the changes occurred and therefore unaffected. Obvious, isn't it?"

At that moment, a light crackle of electricity fills the

interrogation room, and the suspect, Winston Smith, is drawn into the future.

Reykjavik, Department of Iceland; 2099 A.D.

"Well, what do we have here?"

"Winston Smith, time-hacker, pulled him back from 136 years ago."

"Anything else?"

"Yeah, he caused the death a man named Lee Harvey Oswald in a city called Dallas.

"Let's get started."

"How do you do Mr. Smith? I'm Dr. Brian Williams, and this is my associate Dr. Sarah Goodwill."

"You're doctors?"

"Of course, you've just been pulled through 136 years in less than a second, you're lucky to be alive."

"Thanks, I think."

"No need for thanks, it's part of our job to examine those in need of assistance. How did you manage to slip that far back into the past? Don't you know that it's very dangerous traveling in time? Another few minutes and a temporal vortex would have crushed you."

"What's the year?"

"2099, of course."

"I'm not about to be punished for violating any laws or regulations, or whim of some local authority, am I?"

"No, Mr. Smith, the global authorities don't `punish' anyone, just tell us what happened, so we can better judge what help you may need."

"OK, here's the whole story...."

The Diagnosis

"What do you think Sarah?"

"I believe him."

"Me too," says Dr. Williams. "After all, our scan did indicate that he was definitely from this era."

"But, Dr. Williams, I do find it somewhat far-fetched that one man could cause the drastic changes in the time-flow that he claims; it goes against all the best scientific predictions our scientists have made."

"True, but the fact that he even *desires* change makes him dangerous. Tell him that you're escorting him to his new living quarters, and then guide him into a disposal unit and see that his body is *totally* reduced to ash."

"Of course, but what if what he said is true, what if we actually are a product of his tampering with the time-flow?"

"All the more reason to get rid of him. Would you like to give him a chance to change things again? To change everything into a world where you and I do not even exist?"

"I see your point, Dr. Williams."

"Besides, nothing ever happens up here, and this case could be the big break that puts a gold star on my sleeve — and a transfer off this iceberg to the Capitol! Also, keep in mind, that when I do end up in the Capitol, I will need a loyal assistant to watch my back, and that's you."

"Thank you, sir!"

About the author: A graduate of Moravian College in Bethlehem, PA. he is presently employed as a deputy sheriff and lives by the Delaware River in penn.

THE GOSPEL
JO THOMAS

"Brother Ysambard de la Pierre, of the order of Saint Dominic, of the convent of Saint James of Rouen."

Hearing his name called, Ysambard stepped forward to take his place as witness before Guillaume Bouillé and the gathered advisors. He took some comfort in how austere his black garb would look to these brightly clothed men but he could not forget that they had much more power than he. Their power had called him back to this great, draughty hall that had witnessed the condemnation of Jeanne almost twenty years ago. Dipping into a small bowl, he pushed back the hood of his black <u>cappa</u>.

"My Lords."

The stern face of Bouillé looked down on him, "Brother Ysambard."

The tone was firm and resolute; despite the nature of the inquiry that it found itself party to. Rouen had only recently won back by the French King and the might of the English King was still evident. Neither Bouillé nor his master would not wish to stir up the hornets' nest by finding against the English nobles who had devised the original trial. Nor would they want to find against the men of the Holy Church who had worked with their enemy. This inquiry would not clear the name of Jeanne d'Arc, despite the claims that had been made. Bouillé had no doubt been picked because of his ability to deal with such difficulties delicately. Unfortunately, even the slight motions that Bouillé would make might disturb findings that the Holy Church must object to.

"Was the trial of Jeanne d'Arc fair?"

Ysambard thought back to his younger days, when he had served as a confessor to the captured Jeanne. The girl had been gentle and devout, committed to the Faith. She had not deserved the treatment that the Bishop of Beauvais had dealt her. She had had more piety than that false Bishop.

His gaze caught upon Ladvenu waiting his turn to be called forth as a witness to the Inquiry, his brother in both Order and duty. Ysambard knew that Ladvenu believed in Jeanne in a way that was unseemly, elevating her even beyond sainthood. There was a gospel, a life of the Maid of God, that the other maintained held salvation for the world. The thought of it, the secret writing that collected the remembrances of many, filled Ysambard with horror. He had no doubt that the good Jeanne would have felt similarly. The gospel was a heresy, and Ysambard knew what such heresy could cost. But nor could he bring himself to betray a brother in Christ.

"On one occasion, I, with many others, admonished and besought Jeanne to submit to the Church. To which she replied that she would willingly submit to the Holy Father, requesting to be taken before him, and to be no more submitted to the judgment of her enemies. And when, at this time, I counseled her to submit to the Council of Bâle, Jeanne asked what a General Council was."

For all her apparent gifts as a leader of men, she had been little more than a country mouse. Her knowledge of the Church that she followed so devotedly was limited, having only been educated by her parents and the village curate. Ysambard shrugged, putting aside the remembered vulnerability. It was not how the French wanted to see their Maid of God.

"I answered her that it was an assembly of the whole Holy Church and of the Faith, and that in this Council there were some of her side as well as of the English side. Having heard and understood this, she began to cry, "Oh! if in that place there are any of our side, I am quite willing to give myself up and to submit to the Council of Bâle." And immediately, in great rage and indignation, the Bishop of Beauvais began to call out: "Hold your tongue, in the devil's name!" and told the Notary he was to be careful to make no note of the submission she had made to the General Council of Bâle. On account of these things and many others, the English and their officers threatened me terribly, so that, had I not kept silence, they would have thrown me into the Seine."

There was a murmur from the advisors and Bouillé nodded as if the question had been answered. Perhaps it had, for the speech had shown Ysambard's failed attempts to protect and to guide the girl.

Bouillé leant forward, "And the Maid's return to a man's dress?"

A key point, the alleged heresy that had seen Jeanne condemned. But the Church had no laws against women wearing men's clothing in the case of necessity. Ysambard bowed his head, ashamed of how the men of the Church had stooped so low so that they could remove an enemy of the English King.

"After she had recanted and abjured, I and many others were present when Jeanne excused herself for having dressed again as a man, saying and affirming publicly, that the English had done her great wrong and violence, when she was wearing a woman's dress; and, in truth, I saw her weeping, her face covered with tears, disfigured and outraged in such sort that I was full of pity and compassion."

Tears gathered in his eyes even as he thought about it, remembering the moment. Where Ladvenu remembered Jeanne d'Arc as the austere if gracious warrior, her weaker moments a sign of her humanity and her worthiness, Ysambard would always think of her as Jhenette —the child that she had described being in Domrémy. To him, her moments of frailty were the frightened girl showing through the chinks in the armour of resolve that she had taken up so that she could fulfil what she saw as her destiny. It was unfortunate that so many of their brothers seemed to prefer Ladvenu's version. They were attracted to his gospel, and his worthy heroine, by the flavour of the fairy tales that Ladvenu used to embroider Jeanne's story and make his lessons more appetising. Ysambard simply thought it wrong to lie and to use such peasant imagery, hiding the true person behind the romance of the Maid.

The voice of Bouillé rang out again, 'So Jeanne's relapse was caused by the English who guarded her?'

Ysambard sighed at the thought of the little Jeannette that he had never known and replied, 'When Jeanne was proclaimed an obstinate and relapsed heretic, she replied publicly before all who were present: "If you, my Lords of the Church, had placed and kept me in your prisons, perchance I should not have been in this way."

The advisors murmured again and one lent towards Bouillé,

perhaps with the question that next came from the man's lips, "What was the Lord Bishop's response to this?"

After the conclusion and end of this session and trial, the Lord Bishop of Beauvais said to the English who were waiting outside: "Farewell! Be of good cheer: it is done." Such difficult, subtle, and crafty questions were asked of and propounded to poor Jeanne, that the great clerics and learned people present would have found it hard to reply; and at these questions many of those present murmured.'

It had been difficult for the Bishop of Beauvais to trap the young woman, for Jeanne had been wily and had shown more intelligence than had been expected but eventually the Lord Bishop had won. He had destroyed a young woman who once desired to improve the world around her, rather than suffer this world and wait for the next as the Holy Church taught. Yet she had been the most devout person that Ysambard had ever met. Jeanne had been a strange and complex character. Ladvenu's simplified gospel did her no justice.

"Did you or others comment on the fairness of the trial?"

Unwilling to state outright that the trial had been a farce or to openly admit to his own cowardice, Ysambard found himself once more describing a single moment that illustrated his thoughts, "I was there myself with the Bishop of Avranches, an aged and good ecclesiastic, who, like the others, had been requested and prayed to give his opinion on this case. For this, the Bishop summoned me before him, and asked me what Saint Thomas said touching submission to the Church. I sent the decision of Saint Thomas in writing to the Bishop: "In doubtful things, touching the Faith, recourse should always be had to the Pope or a General Council."

Ysambard paused, unwilling to go on. Each word he spoke seemed to confirm his own cowardice and inability to prevent the death of an innocent.

"And the Bishop of Avranches' response?"

He held his breath for a moment before replying, "The good Bishop was of this opinion, and seemed to be far from content with the deliberations that had been made on this subject. His deliberation was not put into writing: it was left out, with bad intent."

Jeanne should have been taken before the Pope. Perhaps then she would have had a fair trial, if the Bishop of Beauvais had permitted her such access. Ysambard had advised her to request it so many times, but it had been a lost cause. Her trial had been orchestrated by the English. Perhaps they had been scared that her abilities truly come from God and that her existence condemned them all to Hell for fighting against the rightful King of France. Or perhaps they were simply too angered by her success in leading the French army.

"When was Jeanne sentenced?"

"After Jeanne had confessed and partaken of the Sacrament of the Altar, sentence was given against her, and she was declared heretic and excommunicate."

"By whose authority was the Maid executed?"

By the authority of a Bishop who had promised his English friends much, but Ysambard could not, dare not, say it.

"I saw and clearly perceived, because I was there all the time, helping at the whole deduction and conclusion of the Case, that the secular Judge did not condemn her, either to death or to burning. She was, entirely without judgment or conclusion of the Judge, delivered into the hands of the executioner and burnt, it being said to the executioner, simply and without other sentence: 'Do thy duty.'"

"The Maid died well, then?"

It was an unusual question, and softly spoken by Bouillé with a hint of satisfaction to his tone. The French King had not intervened, had not ransomed or freed the woman who had aided him in the war for his crown, but his servant apparently found some satisfaction in Jeanne's nobility. It would not be well to speak of the girl's fear, then.

"Jeanne had, at the end, so great contrition and such beautiful penitence that it was a thing to be admired, saying such pitiful, devout, and Catholic words, that those who saw her in great numbers wept, and that the Cardinal of England and many other English were forced to weep and to feel compassion."

Ysambard could not bring himself to speak of one certain Englishman. He had not spoken of that Englishman to anyone since that day almost twenty-nine years gone. To speak of how that man professed to have seen the dove of Jeanne's soul fly free up from her burnt body would bring questions that he did not wish to answer, in case he must tell of his own vision. He had not even told Ladvenu, despite knowing that the other had seen it as well. Even now, the thought of that great, fearsome Angel towering over the market place sent a tremor through him that he could barely conceal. The great, booming voice echoed in his memory.

I am Michael, the first-born of God. I am the Lord of the Host and the Father of all Men. I bring you this message.

Ysambard blinked away the memory of the fiery, winged being speaking things that were against the Bible. He must finish telling of Jeanne's death.

"As I was near her at the end, the poor woman besought and humbly begged me to go into the Church nearby and bring her the Cross, to hold it upright on high before her eyes until the moment of death, so that the Cross on which God was hanging might be in life continually before her eyes."

Ysambard concentrated on the thought of Jeanne's devoutness, but he could barely contain the Angel Michael's remembered message as it rolled through his mind like the tolling of the convent bells. It was a message that had been intended to be heard by all mankind. Perhaps that was what had driven Ladvenu to write his heresy.

Since the birth of Man, God has twice sent my brother Gabriel with the message of peace. Twice you have killed him. I also have twice walked among you. Twice you have killed me. Your brother Raguel has saved you once from God's judgement of the wicked. It will not be so again. I would rather kill my children than see you continue in your ways or bend yourselves to the will of those who oppose God.

The silence of his mind that followed the ominous speech was broken by Bouillé speaking in an annoyed tone as if repeating himself, 'And then, Brother Ysambard?'

"Being in the flames, she ceased not to call in a loud voice the Holy Name of Jesus, imploring and invoking without ceasing the aid of the Saints in Paradise; again, what is more, in giving up the ghost and bending her head, she uttered the Name of Jesus as a sign that she was fervent in the Faith of God, just as we read of Saint Ignatius and of many other Martyrs."

In his gospel, Ladvenu seemed unaware of the difference between Jeanne's quest and the message that the freed Michael had declared as he had sprung from the spent body. While Ysambard was left to wonder, unsure about how much of Jeanne had been Michael, of how much the saintly warrior had misinterpreted the soldierly Angel's intentions. She had claimed to be guided by the Angel Michael; she had never claimed that she was the same being. Nor had she ever spoken words that had resembled the message of the Angel.

Ysambard thought of Jeanne's firm belief in God and her conviction that Charles, the seventh of that name, was King of France by God's order. Was something in her confusing God's fight against His enemies with the French King's fight against his own? Had the clear sight of the Angel been blinded by the flesh, confused by the mortal world that the heavenly soul had found itself in? Whatever the truth, there could not be two like her in his lifetime, and perhaps in a hundred lifetimes. For Michael had only made mention of three Angels walking among humans. Such a sight would never come again, for which he was grateful. The thoughts that the Angel had left behind Ysambard with were alien and dangerous.

'Immediately after the execution, the executioner came to me and to my companion, Brother Martel Ladvenu, stricken and moved with a marvelous repentance and terrible contrition, quite desperate and fearing never to obtain pardon and indulgence from God for what he had done to this holy woman. The executioner said that, notwithstanding the oil, the sulfur, and the charcoal which he had applied to the entrails and heart of the said Jeanne, he been able to burn them up, at which he was much astonished, as a most evident miracle.'

In the hall, the wonder of the executioner's alleged vision brought a murmur of noise from the gathered advisors. It was a story that the executioner had no doubt made up. Perhaps he had been influenced by the same force that had inflicted visions on so many that were present, like that Englishman. Ladvenu had collected the more detailed of them for his gospel, using them as proof that following Jeanne-Michael in devotion to God would lead to such ascensions for everyone. None of the witnesses had seen the Angel as Ysambard had, as Ladvenu claimed to have in his gospel. Not one had heard a great voice. Or it had not been reported in the gospel, at least.

Bouillé stayed silent for a while before giving a dismissal, "You may be seated, Brother Ysambard."

Ysambard bowed once more before turning away, grateful that Bouillé had either not heard of the many visions or that he chose to ignore the rumours of them. The distressed brother lifted his hood to cover his head once more as he returned to his place amongst the witnesses, and in doing so he brushed against the waiting Ladvenu. He did not acknowledge the brief touch, too lost in his own thoughts and prayers that the other would not speak of his beliefs. This was neither the time nor the place to reveal them.

It is always the time and the place, brother.

Grateful that his hood hid his face from the men around him, Ysambard took his seat in silence.

"Brother Martel Ladvenu, of the Order of Saint Dominic, and of the Convent of Saint James at Rouen."

What had just happened? Like the vision he had seen those years ago, Ladvenu had not spoken, his lips had not moved, but his voice —firm but forgiving —had sounded in Ysambard's head. He darted a look towards the other and saw that Ladvenu's face was calm as he removed his hood. But his bow was turned slightly away from Bouillé, who frowned in annoyance. Ysambard looked in the direction that Ladvenu had bowed and barely held back his gasp. How had he not noticed the bright light that the two figures cast as they stood behind the gathered advisors?

"Was the trial of Jeanne d'Arc fair?"

The great wings of the two figures brushed against the ceiling of the hall. One was clearly the remembered Michael, with sword and scales at his side. The one beside him was slightly smaller, the light it cast a little dimmer and not as far reaching. Ysambard wondered if it was Gabriel or the Raguel mentioned in the message.

"Many of those who appeared in the Court did so more from love of the English and the favor they bore them than on account of true zeal for justice and the Catholic Faith."

A murmur ran through the advisors that Ladvenu allowed to take its course before continuing, "In the extreme prejudice of Messire Pierre Caushon, Bishop of Beauvais, there were, I assert, two proofs of ill-feeling: the first, when the Bishop, acting as Judge, commanded Jeanne to be kept in the secular prison and in the hands of her mortal enemies. Although he might easily have had her detained and guarded in an ecclesiastical prison, yet he allowed her to be tormented and cruelly treated in a secular prison,' Ladvenu took an audible breath, "Moreover, at the first session or meeting, the Bishop aforesaid asked and required the opinion of all present, as to whether it was more suitable to detain her in the secular ward or in the prisons of the Church. It was decided more correct that she be kept in ecclesiastical prisons; but this the Bishop said he would not do for fear of displeasing the English."

The murmur returned and an advisor leant forward to Bouillé, who held up a hand to block the man and the noise, 'Continue.'

"The second proof was that when the Bishop and others declared her heretic, she relapsed and returned to her evil deeds. In prison she had resumed a man's dress. The Bishop met the Earl of Warwick and a great many other English, to whom he said, laughing, loud and clear: 'Farewell! farewell! it is done; be of good cheer'."

It was clear from the way that he had bowed in their direction that Ladvenu saw these angels. Indeed, it almost seemed as if he was talking to them, though the words that came from his mouth were for the Inquiry. There was something about his expression and about the faces of the two Angels, although they seemed blurred by the light that came from them.

"Was Jeanne's relapse caused by the English who guarded her?"

The witness remained apparently confident. There was no strain on his features or in his stance. He was committed to whatever path he had chosen to follow, "The Maid revealed to me that, after her abjuration and recantation, she was violently treated in the prison, molested, beaten, and ill-used; and that an English lord had insulted her. She also said, publicly, that on this account she had resumed a man's dress."

It was a resolve that Ysambard did not like. He prayed that Bouillé would not ask Ladvenu to clarify the statement he had made after Jeanne's execution, when Ladvenu had not been able to prevent his conviction that the Maid had been an Angel from leaving his mouth. To do so would bring his gospel to the attention of the Inquiry. Once such knowledge was widespread, Ladvenu would doubtlessly be put on trial for heresy himself. He would be unable to deny it, even if he wanted to, and a death at the stake would surely follow. Others that he had been known to talk with would face the same fate.

"By whose authority was the Maid executed?"

"When she had been finally preached to in the Old Market-Place and abandoned to the secular authority, although the secular Judges were seated on the platform, in no way was she condemned by any of these Judges; but, without being condemned, she was forced by two sergeants to come down from the platform and was taken by the said sergeants to the place where she was to be burned, and by them delivered into the hands of the executioner."

Ladvenu paused then continued with steel in his voice, "A short time after, one called Georges Folenfant was apprehended on account of the Faith and for the crime of heresy, and was in the same way handed over to the secular justice. In this case, the Judges sent me to the Bailley of Rouen to warn him that the said Georges should not be treated as was the Maid, who, without final sentence or definite judgment, had been burned in the fire."

But the other's ability to commune with the two Angels showed the truth of his beliefs. How many holy men where gathered here? How many of them saw the Angels? They would all think Ysambard mad if he pointed to the figures and proclaimed their presence. He watched the Angels, full of wonder but unable to show it, fearing the blind men that surrounded him.

"And the executioner?"

If Ladvenu had known that the Angels watched all this time, then perhaps his own thoughts were not as simplistic as his gospel. If that was so, then the fairy stories were only the first step on a path towards God's Grace. Their simplicity was nothing more than a way of making their message acceptable while hiding the more alien ideas from the Church. But devotion to God did not matter if it was not in the manner that the Holy Church approved of. Once Ladvenu's new doctrine became known, he and all who supported him would pay.

"The executioner, about four hours after the burning, said that he had never been so afraid in executing any criminal as in the burning of the Maid, and for many reasons: first, for her great fame and renown; secondly, for the cruel manner of fastening her to the stake for the English had caused a high scaffold to be made of plaster, and he could not well or easily hasten matters nor reach her, at which he was much vexed and had great compassion for the cruel manner in which she was put to death."

Perhaps Ladvenu was right that all men could ascend, that they could learn to become Angels. He and Ysambard had been taught that death was not an end to life and they had taught others so in their turn. But how many of them truly believed it? How many would open their arms to death? How many would invite it in the hope that they would cast half the light of even the weakest Angel? Did Ladvenu do this in search of his own glory? Did he do this thinking he would be granted wings of his own?

"And the death of the Maid?"

It seemed to Ysambard that the second Angel turned towards him and smiled. He felt strangely comforted.

"I can testify to her great and admirable contrition, repentance, and continual confession, calling always on the Name of Jesus, and devoutly invoking the Saints in Paradise, as also Brother Ysambard has already deposed, who was with her to the end, and confirmed her in the way of salvation."

There seemed to be a flicker in the Angels' light, a touch of two Angelic hands, a shared smile, and Ladvenu's frame relaxed. Ysambard knew that the Angels had communicated something to the man being questioned.

Ladvenu took a deep breath that could be heard clearly and said the words that Ysambard had been dreading, "eanne's soul was freed. Jeanne was the Angel Michael."

The first, the voice of Michael himself rolled through Ysambard's mind.

A laugh followed and another voice, weaker but still much stronger than Ladvenu's rebuke, replied, *No, Father, the second.*

Indeed, the great voice boomed out like bells once more, *It is easy to forget that you were born, not created, Raguel.*

There was a ripple of gentle laughter and Ysambard found himself aching to be acknowledged by the owner of such a joyful voice, *You forget nothing.*

True, but you did not live a full life as these did. You were not the same, Michael's response held an answering feeling of amusement and affection.

Ysambard closed his eyes for a moment, feeling tears gathering; tears for Ladvenu whose life would soon end, tears for Jeanne who never knew herself for what she truly was and who had died as Jesus had so that all men might be free. With his eyes closed, he felt them leave and opened his eyes, expecting to find the hall grey without their light.

But the light remained, for Brother Ladvenu's face cast with the same glow and Ysambard could only feel pity for the blind men about him, even as they captured the new Angel that was among them. They thought to kill Ladvenu but they would in truth be setting him free.

About the author: Published in Hub, Crossed Genre, Twisted Tongue, Neon Beam and others, Jo Thomas is also an amateur photographer, a poor fencer and a worse blacksmith. She lives in the UK with her dog, Finn.

CAMERA LUCIDA
KEN HEAD

Data made holy
hologram seasons
wired lives

There are cameras everywhere by then,
millions of them, each keeping its eye
fully focused on a street-scene somewhere,
car parks, shopping malls, late-night lap-dance bars
with sleazy reps. Minute by minute,
they keep on working, triumphs of function
and intelligent design, forever
recording new data, transmitting it
to secret archives where finely calibrated
smart machines evaluate its worth.
Accurate to a tee, they watch that last long
winter bear-hug the life out of a dying world.

In darkened rooms
ghosts watch old movies

BERG
SEAN MONAGHAN

The Zodiac dropped two feet into the icy water and Tony realised that it must have been a different tide. He started looking for the iceberg and saw it off to port, maybe two miles away.

"There," he said, pointing and Geoff started up the outboard, moving them across the glassy surface.

Tony scanned the horizon for lights but couldn't see anything. She must still be a long way off. They had plenty of time. Geoff moved them up and Tony put a piton into the ice, and then tied the boat up. They looked it over and decided the best place to put the explosives. Geoff got out the hot drill and they clambered up with crampons and ropes. They had to get into the heart of the berg and it took twenty-five minutes longer to drill the hole than Tony had expected. He saw the running lights on the horizon. She would arrive very soon.

"She's coming," Geoff said. His breath left a wispy trail. Like Tony he was dressed in full Arctic thermals.

Tony checked his watch. 11.21pm. Lots of time. He dropped the thin explosive pack down and tamped the lead to the detonator, hooked in the radio receiver and switched it on.

"She's getting close," Geoff said.

Tony looked and saw that the ship was perhaps a mile away. He smiled to himself as they made their way back to the boat, keeping their crampons away from the inflatable sides. Geoff backed them off and Tony realised that it would be close.

"Stop here," he said. The ship was perhaps five hundred yards away now, already turning.

"Come on," Geoff said.

Tony pressed the button. Nothing happened.

"Do it."

"I did it already." Tony pushed the button again and again. The ship was nearly on the berg.

"Too late," Geoff said. "Leave it."

The ship was beginning to make its gradual arc around the berg, moving slowly south of them. Tony was transfixed. It was extraordinary to watch this event occurring just yards away from his eyes. He'd seen it so many times in various movies, and reconstructions. He read about it so much he could have written a dissertation. Yet the experience was something entirely different. He felt his throat clench.

The percussive sound of the hull striking the berg gave him such a start that he dropped the transmitter.

The explosion rocked them back and Tony had to grab Geoff to stop him falling from the Zodiac. When he looked again the ship was already head down, sinking fast. It was supposed to take nearly three hours. It shouldn't be going so rapidly. The explosives, intended to break the berg up into relatively harmless flows, must have blasted a hole in the hull and the sinking was taking moments.

They bucked in the waves as the wash from the explosion hit them. The propellers were up, the bridge already underwater. Tony remembered the Lusitania, torpedoed, taking only minutes to go down.

There was screaming and in just a few minutes the ship was gone.

"Holy crap," Geoff said.

Tony stared at the still shivering water, listened to the screaming of the people who'd been thrown clear, freezing to death.

Geoff started the engine again.

"What are you doing?" Tony said.

"Picking them up. Wasn't that the idea? Save their lives. We've surely screwed that up, so let's do something."

"How many do you think there are? Fifty, sixty? Most of them were in bed."

They pulled twenty live ones from the water and got them to the Carpathia.

And that gave Tony an idea for their next try.

Geoff didn't like that any better than the explosives, but at least it gave them a chance to get there early and stop their other selves placing the package.

A week later they dropped back into the water a couple of hours earlier. They pitoned a buoy to the iceberg with a message to themselves not to blow it up, that everything was under control, then they sprinted for the Californian.

Once aboard, in period costume they sat next to the wireless room and created their own CQD distress message. The captain started the ship moving towards the iceberg, further away than the 1912 estimate, but closer than the 1992 vindication.

"What's he doing?" Tony said nearly two hours later as they watched from the Zodiac.

The Californian had arrived before Titanic and was slowly turning. The berg rested close by.

"He's wondering about the distress call," Geoff said. "This is the position, but there's no wreckage, no boats."

Titanic had crested the horizon and Tony realised that the Californian was dark, all the cabin lights out as the crew slept, just her small running lights showing.

"Lost amongst the stars," Geoff said.

Tony thought he was doing poetry, but then he saw the problem. "They must see her," he said. "They must."

The Titanic was bearing down on the now stationary Californian. Lord had heaved to for the night again, unwilling to move into the ice field in the darkness. The Titanic lookouts hadn't seen the berg, but surely they would see the other vessel. Surely. The big ship had a massive head of steam up. Looking for a record time. It swept past the Zodiac like a black curtain.

"This," Geoff said, "is just one screw up from the beginning."

Titanic cut the tiny Californian in half. The split little ship heeled over and began going down. The Titanic, slowed somewhat, still smacked hard, bow first, into the berg.

Tony noticed that their buoy was gone and saw the other Tony, and the other Geoff, silhouetted, arms upraised in disbelief.

And then Titanic began going down too. Her hull must have been cracked by the impact. Both impacts. Tony kept hoping that the watertight doors would work, but she just kept sinking. Faster.

"Any better ideas?" Geoff asked, as Titanic's took on a list that was preventing half the lifeboats getting away.

"Maybe," Tony said. He had to put this right. "Something much more simple."

"Well, count me out."

"You'll like this, though."

And of course Geoff did come.

They pitoned in another buoy, with instructions for the first team to leave their buoy, and *not* to call the Californian.

"Okay," Geoff said when they'd backed off. "You still want me to circle the berg?"

"That's the plan. The lookouts were searching for breaking water, but there never was any because the sea was totally flat. That's why they saw the berg so late the other time." Tony waved to himself in the other Zodiacs as they went around.

"Yeah, well, if this doesn't work, neither of us get born, right?"

Both other sets of doppelgangers had got the idea and soon all three Zodiacs were circling, creating wakes that left breaking waves on the face of the berg.

Tony smiled. "It doesn't bear thinking about. My head spins with the paradoxes."

About the author: You can find John at his website: www. venusvulture.com

FUTURE ECHOES
ANDREW MALES

Deep down I probably knew what I'd find, but it was still a shock to enter the bathroom and see myself dying on the floor. Five minutes ago, my mind had been raging with my spiralling anguish and self-hate, leading me down to the darkest of places. I had just been about to make one of the last decisions of my life when I had heard my own voice upstairs: "Don't do it. Don't take the easy way out." An echo from the future, and one that I had now caught up with.

As I looked down, I saw the stained carpet all around him, with messy crimson trails over my favourite pair of jeans. The sink was streaked in red, like the shave from hell. Slumped against the bath, head bowed, he gradually became aware of my presence and turned his face towards me. This was no reflection; this was me looking back at me, his sad glazed glance meeting my incredulous stare.

"I didn't know if you would hear me," he said, a tired, slight smile appearing on his face.

All I could do was nod.

"I mean it," he said, voice fading, "please, don't take the easy way out."

I looked around the room, uneasy at this unnatural sight before me. The razor blade, the suicide note atop the toilet seat – these had been *my* thoughts just moments ago. I realised I was an observer of a scene in which *I* should have been the participant. I looked at his stricken state. The thought of calling an ambulance rushed through me, but an explanation simply didn't exist and the consequences of saving this alternative me were too complicated to fathom. Soon, however, this became irrelevant. The shallow breathing stopped, the stains became lighter, and as I saw the last glimpse of regret in his eyes, he vanished.

* * *

The ceiling was a good audience. I didn't ask how it had acquired the strange yellow stains that adorned most of the area above the bed, and it didn't ask me about Beth. It probably knew as much about her as I did now, which wasn't much if I were honest. I had chosen this hotel at random from the many that had flashed by me on my long journey to nowhere this morning. Anything to escape from the surreal memories of yesterday.

I talked through her last moments in great detail, but the mostly-white expanse above didn't cry with me, waiting patiently for me to continue. We hadn't been seeing each other long, and even though she was so clingy that I had been contemplating ending the relationship, she didn't deserve what happened to her. But then, I didn't deserve what might have happened to me, had I not acted quickly. I recalled the night out, the drinks, the argument that I now knew every word of. The image of her car flipping as I took the corner too fast, shaking us around like lottery balls before the car finally coming to rest down the embankment. She had borne the brunt of it and had died within minutes.

I longed to open the mini bar and devour all I could find, but the thought of tasting alcohol again made me dry-retch. I tried to justify what I had done – it *was* an accident after all – and she had been dead when I made the switch. Her car; her fluffy keyring; her life over. My pleas went unheeded as the ceiling looked on, judging me. Luckily, the inept police had fallen for my lies and quick-thinking and didn't have to hear my excuses.

Tonight's confessions hadn't given me an appetite, so I decided to skip dinner; the football was on soon anyway. Hopefully a good World Cup qualification win would cheer me up. I reached over towards the remote control, but before I got there I heard the unmistakable voice of John Motson, "Oh yes! England has surely snatched it in the eighty-eighth minute!" The TV sat silent, innocent, not even a red standby light for show. No radio, or even noise next door. The alarm clock showed in bright red digits that it was a full fifteen minutes to kick off. I sank back in the bed and sighed. Sometimes hearing the future was beneficial, but mostly its random nature in timing, content and how far ahead you heard made it useless. This time, it was annoying; yesterday, it had been life-changing. I had heard myself before, experiencing the déjà vu feeling when I said the same words in the present, laughing, knowing that I'd just communicated back to the past at that very moment. Yes, it screwed with your head just thinking about it.

I sat and contemplated what I'd just heard. Maybe it wasn't this match, maybe it was the next one, or even later... then I realized that this was our last qualifier, our last match for a few months. Based on experience, the odds were I'd just heard the end of tonight's match. Cheers, Motty. The mini bar was calling me. The bile started to rise again.

* * *

It had been a week since I'd seen myself die, but stepping back through the door made it feel like it'd just happened. I put my bag down and sat on the second stair up. The Travelodge had seemed a good idea, but it hadn't brought much respite, and had just seemed to stall things. What did I think it would do? Fix everything? Suddenly make Beth walk through the door again? Turn me into a normal person? Fat chance. I'd killed her, and thanks to my other self I was going to have to live with it.

I went upstairs, but upon reaching the landing I froze, glancing at the closed door at the end. I knew that this time there would be nothing unusual contained within, but the images of that strange encounter still haunted me, so I made my way downstairs again. The stereo was my next destination, and I chose carefully. No-one could be heard above this CD cranked up, not even Motty. I sat on the sofa and let the lyrics go right through me.

The track ended softly, and silence filled the room again. I closed my eyes and the only sound came from the blood rushing in my ears.

"OK, it was me."

I sat upright and quickly scanned the room. Did I just say that out loud? Here, now? My heart started to thump. I was pretty sure I hadn't said anything, which meant only one alternative.

I rose and walked into the kitchen to make some coffee, anything mundane to counter this madness. I was overcome with a deep worry that I knew the exact meaning of what I'd said. But *when* would I say it, though, and why here? I considered leaving the house, but I knew that I would have to come back sometime, and this voice could be from way into the future. The kettle glowed its vibrant blue, the minute's wait giving me more time to think. Mission complete, the kettle clicked off while the water continued to thrash around inside for a few seconds more, like demons trapped in a watery hell. Silence followed. I strained my ears to see if I could hear any sirens, but nothing. Picking up my coffee, I stepped towards the door as the room erupted in noise.

"Jesus!" The scalding liquid cascaded onto my hand. "Every bloody time," I grabbed a tea towel and cleared up the mess. When I looked up again, Beth's brother was in front of me.

"Good CD this. That bonus track at the end always gets me too."

I stepped back. "How did...? What are you doing here, Mark?"

"Have a good little trip did you? Enjoy a nice, relaxing, care-free break?"

I backed off further as his tall presence loomed in the doorway. "Yes. No. Well, it wasn't a break, not really. More of a ...I don't know. Just had to get away, you know."

Mark nodded, looking away. "To try and forget what you did, I take it?" His eyes had flicked back to me, now on the edge.

The singer prepared for the chorus.

"It was an accident, I -"

"It weren't no accident, was it!" Mark said as he rushed towards me, grabbing me by the throat and pushing me back. I decided not to struggle.

"You were the one who was driving, not Beth, and we both know it."

Spittle flew across my face.

"You lied. You lied to the police like the pathetic drivel you are and you got away with it." He shoved my neck, banging my head against the wall. Through watery eyes I saw his disgust as he seemingly contemplated his next move. Heavy guitar rocked the walls. I should've expected this, I thought. Maybe I wanted this; we had to clash sometime so it may as well be now. He reached round his back and pulled out a gun.

Mark went to the stereo and turned the volume up, gun continually trained on me. He returned, grabbing me by my arm and throwing me to the floor. He knelt down and placed his face millimetres from my ear.

"Say it!"

"A-accident." With my face squashed against the cold, wooden living room floor, it was all I could say between sobs.

"But you were driving, you're the one who took Beth away from us! Nineteen years old – that's all she was. Nineteen, you cowardly bastard."

Glancing sideways, I could see the crazed look etched all over his face. I could smell the stale smoke from his breath being exhaled rapidly in my face. What good would the truth bring him? What would happen to me if it came out? It was an accident. I don't deserve the misery of prison just for one stupid misdemeanour.

"We had both been drinking."

"And?"

"And…nothing. You know the rest. You know – "

"I know you're a lying son of a bitch!" he said picking me up and throwing me across the room onto the chair.

The final chorus began to thunder out.

"Last chance! The next words you utter had better be what I *know* is the truth!"

I knew at that precise moment that it didn't matter. Beth had told me a few stories about Mark, and by the look on his face I was quite sure that he was going to kill me, whatever I said. He just wanted to be sure; to be set free. Maybe I did owe him that. Maybe I was getting what I deserved. I thought back to my confessional future words I'd heard earlier. It was an accident, after all. The lyrics now finished, all that was left was the crescendo before the end. The future was now, and it was my turn to echo back.

"When you hear this, run!"

Mark looked at me with bemusement at my outburst to - as it appeared to him - no-one. It did nothing to stop him, however, as he fired his weapon in a rush of hatred. Pain seared through my body. My final words had torn up the script. I hoped that the saved had become the saviour. As life sunk slowly out of my body, I silently apologised to the Mark in the other timeline; he may have got justice here, but I would have my freedom there.

About the author: Andrew lives in south-east England and has spent the last year running a marathon, seeing the Northern Lights, getting lost in Tokyo, riding a horse in Australia and fitting in a bit of writing when he can.

MYSTERY HOUSE
KRISTIN AUNE

A house full of mystery and wonder! Wonder beyond your deepest imagination. This was what Rhea had been hearing from the neighbors as she investigated houses that were creepy, weird, and out of the ordinary. This one house played music late at night even when nobody had lived in there for centuries. Some children were dared to stay in the house overnight a few days ago and they never came back out. Rhea was a paranormal investigator, a proud one at best. She never let down a case, no matter how crazy it seemed to be. This one however, was the most extraordinary house she ever heard of. Since this was supposed to be a magical house she wouldn't need all of her gizmos for ghost hunting, no, she was going to have to find out all by herself.

As she entered the house she felt a shiver going down her spine, but she still continued onward. No sense in running away now! She had a job to do. The inside was much different from the outside. Outside it was a small rundown house, nothing pleasant about it. While the inside was enormous and beautiful! Rhea felt like she had just stepped into a mansion. As she walked across the lobby room she looked up and saw a magnificent chandelier. It seemed to be floating all on its own. No chain attached to it whatsoever and all of the candles on it were lit.

She took a look in the next room, she sighed; it was just a normal looking, ancient library. Everything was dusty, some books seemed out of place, and small tables had lamps that looked like they were before her own time. She gazed at the bookcase and noticed that a few books were missing. Rhea figured that the original owners of this place took them when they moved. She shrugged; she was a little disappointed about this room and went on to the next one. As she left, the books behind her started to move on their own and organized themselves while filling the empty spaces.

The next room was the kitchen. The kitchen was spotless! No

dust, no spider webs, and not even dead mice! Her eyes widened as the dishes seemed to be cleaning themselves. How was this possible? She had to find out. If only she could contact the owners who once lived here. She was about to leave the room and explore other areas of the house but before she could, she tripped on a broomstick. She fell on the ground and moaned.

"Well, that's just perfect." She muttered. "The house is trying to kill me." She half joked. Before she got up, she checked to make sure there were no broken bones. Nothing was out of place so she continued exploring on.

The family room was more bizarre than the kitchen! Dusters were cleaning pictures all by themselves; they fell down and stopped moving when she entered the room. The fireplace remained lit. There were ghosts, she couldn't believe it! But there they were, sitting on the chairs reading books from the library. One ghost looked up at her.

"You shouldn't be here." It said. "Leave now before it's too late."

"What are you talking about?" Rhea asked. But the ghosts were already gone. "That was weird." She ignored its warning. She wanted to find out more about this house of wonders.

She decided to go upstairs and see what other fascinations awaited her. A hallway appeared before her with doors on each side. She entered the door on her left. It was a bedroom, the only things that remained in the bedroom was the bed itself with no blankets, just a mattress, and a window with worn out curtains. She noticed a letter on the bed and decided to read it. It was old, but she could make a few words.

Leave, now. Don't. Come. Back. No. Escape. Forever. Trapped. Was all that she could read. Did that mean that if she didn't leave the house soon she would stay in here forever? Or was this just something to scare her off? It seemed pretty real though, so she decided not to stay here any longer and leave. She came back to the hallway but the doors were gone and a winding hallway appeared before her. She screamed. How was she supposed to get out now? She ran in the direction she came from, but the hallway seemed to never end! She kept running and running, until she felt something touch her hand.

"Trust us." A voice spoke out loud. She stopped running, calmed down and closed her eyes. She opened them again and found that she was in front of the house again. She shivered and left. She never wanted to go back in there again.

The magical house still remained a mystery. Nobody was able to discover anything about its origins or what happened to the missing children. On the night of a full moon, it disappeared and never returned.

About the author: Kristin Aune likes to read in her spare time. On weekends she likes to hang out at her cabin.

NO TIME LIKE THE PRESENT
IAIN PATTISON

The blast blew me half way across the office. Cart-wheeling through the air, I hit the filing cabinets hard and fell groaning to the floor as a blizzard of glass rained down on me.

Dazed and bleeding I crawled under my desk frantically seeking some sort of safety. My ears throbbed from the booming shock wave and the banshee scream of the security alarm.

What the hell had happened? I shook myself, trying to make my brain kick back into action. There'd been an explosion, but where? How?

My cell phone rang and I snatched it from where it lay dented and battered in the rubble.

It was Frank Peters, my deputy. "It's the particle accelerator lab," he told me, voice tight with excitement and fear. "Most of the block is gone; leveled. The proton exciter is a pile of twisted scrap and the rest is burning wreckage. It's a bloody shambles, Jack. "

My heart sank. There were nine scientists in there at any one time, manning the silvery doughnut-shaped atom smasher.

"Any word on casualties?" I asked, dreading the answer. "How many are hurt?"

I could hear Frank swallow hard. "No-one got out alive," he said softly, "they're all dead. Everyone is dead."

I fought the urge to throw up.

"Okay," I told him, "call a priority one alert. Until we know what's going on, I want the entire base evacuated. I'm on my way. Don't let anyone near the blast site until I get there."

Staggering outside, I headed for my car. Thoughts of sabotage attacks and sneak terrorist bombings flashed across my mind, but I knew our security was too good for that.

No, this had to be the terrible accident I'd been dreading since our boffins announced they were intending to recreate the conditions that existed at the very beginnings of the universe. For months they'd been colliding supercharged positrons and electrons at astonishing speeds.

"We're dying to learn what the Big Bang was like," they'd excitedly told the world's scientific community.

Well, it looked like they'd got their wish.

Frowning, I sped across the outer perimeter towards the main section of the base. I could imagine that night's news when journalists got word of the blast and the TV crews turned up. It was going to be a circus.

As head of security at The Institute I'd warned the base commander about the dangers of the experiments weeks earlier. The equipment was too powerful and unstable; too dangerous. But he hadn't listened.

"It's not a security matter," he'd said. "I appreciate your input, Jack, but I think we'll leave health and safety concerns to the experts, don't you? Dr. Jennings and his team know what they're doing."
The fool. How wrong he'd been, how stupidly negligently wrong. With those scientists killed it had become a whooping great security matter.

I felt anger surge through me. Jerking the wheel over, I spun the car round the corner, up to the gatehouse at the entrance to the research wing. The soldiers on guard looked dazed, clutching their rifles with whitened knuckles.

I'd never really bothered to look at them before but it struck me just how young they seemed. They barely looked old enough to have enlisted, never mind be put guarding one of the country's most sensitive research establishments.

Another thought hit me as I drove through the huge chain-link gates. Hadn't the concrete guard bunker just been repainted? It had been sparkling white the last time I'd seen it. Now, it seemed dull and shabby - as though it hadn't seen a lick of paint in years.

It was odd, but I shrugged it off. It must be a result of the blast damage.

Frank was waiting for me, his car parked beside the convoy of fire trucks and ambulances. He'd taken me at my word. No-one had been allowed anywhere near the devastated laboratories.

"You look like shit," he said, motioning to the cuts and bruises on my face.

"I've been better," I conceded.

"All non-essential personnel have been evacuated, as you requested but I've paged Dr Mitchells," Frank said. "I thought we might need him. They're helicoptering him in."

I nodded. It was a smart move. Mitchells was one of The Institute's top scientists - a typical mad professor, but a good man to have around in a crisis.

"Are we absolutely sure that no-one's left alive?"" I asked. There was no sense putting the emergency crews at risk unnecessarily.

"No chance of survivors," Frank replied bleakly. "No-one could have lived through the blast. It ripped the lab buildings clean off their foundations…"

I glanced through the fence to where a quarter of an acre of flattened destruction smoldered sadly. It was impossible to believe that just minutes before this had been a complex of concrete, toughened glass and re-enforced steel. The place had been leveled as though a squadron of B52 bombers had used it for target practice.

The whacking noise of the base helicopter announced Doctor Mitchells' arrival. Ducking below the spinning rotors he came running over at a crouch.

"My God," he said when he saw the scene. "It's unbelievable! I've never seen anything like it."

"Total destruction," I agreed. "The force must have been incredible. What would have caused an explosion that big?"

Mitchells frowned, grey eyebrows puckering. "They must have been running the accelerator at full pelt. It's a dangerous procedure at the best of times." He shrugged. "But if they reversed the polarity on the Celeron discharger at the same time …"

He mimed an explosion.

I turned to Frank.

"You look like shit," he said, motioning to the cuts and bruises on my face.

"I've been better," I conceded.

My stomach spasmed as I felt reality take a sideways step.

"Didn't you just say that to me?" I asked, hoping that it was just one of those silly moments of déjà vu.

"Did I say what?" Frank asked, puzzled, and looked up to the helicopter coming in to land nearby. Dr. Mitchells jumped out and was running towards us, crouched under the spinning rotor blades.

I did a double take. It wasn't possible. He was here already. I'd spoken to him. I spun to where he'd been standing just a second before. The space was empty!

"My God," he said as he surveyed the scene. "It's unbelievab-"

I cut across him. "Doc, something weird is going on here. I don't understand it but I think we've got big trouble..."

***

I couldn't blame Doctor Mitchells for thinking I was losing my marbles. He had no memory of talking to me about Celeron dischargers and particle accelerators. As far as he was concerned he'd just arrived.

"There are two possibilities," he said, his face darkening. "You were more badly injured in the explosion than you think. You may have a bad concussion or ..."

"Or?" I prompted anxiously.

"Or the explosion had somehow damaged the fabric of space and time."

I hoped it was the first option. A bump on the head I could cope with. Having the universe doing crazy things was too scary to contemplate.

I thought about the way the guard-house bunker had reverted to its pre-decoration drabness and a chill ran through me.

"It seems that time is hiccupping backwards and forwards," Mitchells observed when I told him about the suspiciously young guards.

His face suddenly filled with fear. "Use the rocket launcher," he screamed. "It's our only hope..."

What! I looked at him as though he was mad. What rocket launcher? What was he babbling on about?

"There are two possibilities," he remarked, face darkening. "You were more badly injured in the explosion than you th- "

I grabbed him. "Doc," I yelled. "We're stuck in some sort of time loop. We need to get away from here."

Dragging him away, I glanced over my shoulder. Where the labs had been was now a green field with a sign announcing the planned construction of a complex of research buildings. The completion date said: October 1996!

**

"You look like shit," Frank told me, motioning to the cuts and bruises on my face.

I ignored him, concentrating on getting us all away from the blast site. If we could just get into the car and off the base's research wing we might be able to raise the alarm, to warn the authorities. I didn't know what they'd be able to do about a time rift but that was their problem.

I almost wept as I stared at my car. The gleaming new Lexus was gone. In its place stood a model-T Ford!

"It appears the effects are gaining momentum," Doc Mitchells said, half to himself. "This is serious. If it's not stopped there's no telling what will happen. Time could collapse in on itself."

Closing my eyes I cursed those egghead idiots who'd thought they could just muck about with malevolently charged sub-atomic molecules. God knows what catastrophe they'd set in motion!

Roughly bundling Frank and the Doc on to the model-T, I cranked it up and we were off towards the gatehouse. The bunker shell was flickering like a mirage, old and grey, then dazzling white. As we sped past I could see the guards. In one instant they were toddlers crawling around the ground, the next grey-haired, wizened old men!

I was too busy staring at them to see the horse blocking the road. I hit the brakes and swung the wheel over hard. We skidded to a halt, half in a ditch. The gun was an antique, but it looked deadly enough.

"Stand fast and deliver," the highwayman shouted.

He fired and a small metal ball imbedded in the dashboard as Doc Mitchells said: "It seems that time is hiccupping backwards and forwards …"

The masked figure went for a second pistol - and pointed it straight at my head. I yelled just as reality shifted sideways again and we found ourselves standing back at the explosion site. I looked down at my watch. The hands were spinning backwards.

This was getting too damn crazy!

Frank's face drained of all color. "What the hell is that?" he shouted, pointing. I followed the line of his arm and realized our troubles were just beginning.

***

It danced madly across the blast site, bobbing up and down like a kid's balloon. It was difficult at first to tell what it was, but as it came nearer I could see that it was some sort of tornado, a spinning, churning, roaring vortex.

It was sucking in matter, objects twisting and elongating as they streamed into it. Everything in its path was being stretched and devoured, whisked away to God knows where.

"It's an inter-dimensional rip in the fabric of space," Mitchells whispered, awed. "The explosion must have caused a breach. It's distorting time, tearing the continuum apart."

I didn't know what he meant but I knew it was bad, as bad as it gets.

"Can we stop it?" I asked, unable to take my eyes off the screaming hateful whirlpool that was tugging and chewing at reality.

"I don't know," he replied. "This is beyond my expertise. This is unknown outside of the wildest speculations of theoretical quantum physics. Your guess is as good as mine."

I grimaced. So much for science.

Frank grabbed my arm. "Look," he said excitedly, "an explosion caused this thing. Maybe another explosion can stop it."

"Yes!" Mitchells agreed. "It's possible. The force of a second blast might seal the rift."

I did some quick thinking. The Institute was Pentagon-funded so there were all sorts of explosives on site - but what to use, and how much?

The vortex lurched towards us, sucking down a length of metal fencing in one noisy gulp.

Then I remembered the Doc's earlier outburst. He'd yelled about using a rocket launcher. It hadn't made sense then but now it made all the sense in the world.

It took ten minutes to locate the hefty weapon in the arms store and break it out of its secured housing. By the time I'd sprinted back with it, the vortex was twice as big, the air around it crackling with electricity as cars flew through the air and disappeared into its ravenous jaws.

I looked pleadingly into Doc Mitchells' eyes.

"Are you sure this is going to work?" I asked softly.

"No," he replied. "But it's the only option we've got."

He warned that the missile must explode just as it entered the lip of the tornado. If it worked, we'd shut the inter-dimensional door. There was no margin for error and no chance for a practice shot.

"Ah well, no time to lose," I muttered sardonically and shoved the rocket into the firing tube.

The vortex was a moving target and I struggled to get a lock on it. I asked myself questions I couldn't answer. What if I failed, would the rift grow larger and larger until it swallowed up everything on the planet?

I lost concentration for an instant because the next I knew it was upon us. I felt my body being pulled, sucked, twisted.

The Doc's face suddenly filled with fear. "Use the rocket launcher," he screamed. "It's our only hope…"

I didn't need telling a third time. I took aim at the screeching circle of destruction, gulped and fired …

***

The agonizing roar seemed loud enough to shatter my

eardrums. It felt like someone trying to scoop out my brains with a spoon.

The shock wave hit us a millisecond later, lifting us clear off the ground, sending us sprawling. We landed painfully on the concrete several feet away, giving me a whole new set of bruises to add to my growing collection.

"Look," Frank yelled, pointing towards the vortex. "Something's happening. It's changing."

He was right. As we gazed in amazement, the whirlpool shuddered and slowed its spin. It was rotating at only a fraction of its speed - and it was shrinking!

"The second blast is pulling the ripped edges together," Doc Mitchells hissed over the noise. "It's working!"

I sighed in relief, but I knew we weren't out of the woods yet. The vortex was still remorselessly sucking in objects, still distorting the space and time around it. Things could still go terribly wrong....

The whirlpool grew smaller and smaller, the furious bellowing roar diminishing rapidly.

"Keep going," Frank urged it, fist clenched. "Just a little bit more."

A tree flew over our heads towards the spinning circle, then suddenly dropped like a stone as the vortex snapped shut.

I don't know which frightened me more - the giant oak crashing to the ground just inches away, or the sight of the vortex folding in on itself and disappearing with an electric whip-crack.

"We've done it," Mitchells yelped, jumping up and down. "We've closed the fissure."

I was about to smile, but something wiped it from my face.

"My God," I gasped as I looked across at the devastation that had been the physics labs. Something was happening... something *really* weird!

Chunks of wreckage were leaping off the ground and sticking together, as they went in a blink of an eye from blackened debris to colorful painted fragments of wood. Whole sections of building were magically gluing together like an invisible giant's construction set.

All around the site, smoldering rubble transformed itself as tongues of flame unlicked the damaged framework of the buildings. Glass shards flew at high speed, a snowstorm of tiny pieces colliding and coalescing into whole unblemished sheets.

Time was running backwards! The explosion was un-doing itself, repairing the damage!

"I don't believe this," I muttered, shaking my head. "It just isn't possible."

Over at the guardhouse bunker, the concrete shell was growing whiter by the instant, as though an unseen giant had picked up a brush and begun slapping on paint.

"Time is reverting to its pre-blast state," Mitchells told me, his voice now low in awe. "It'll be as though the explosion never happened."

This was madness, but I was ecstatic. If there had been no accident then the scientists weren't dead! No-one had been harmed!

I hugged myself with glee as time sprung back to its previous course. It was like watching a video tape wind backwards, the labs reassembling in a mesmerizing aerial ballet.

"I don't know what we're going to tell people," I observed. "No-one's going to believe us." I pointed down at the stolen missile launcher. "And I think I might have some awkward explaining to do."

Mitchells patted me reassuringly on my arm. "It'll be okay," he promised. "I'll tell them that you were sealing up a rip in the fabric of the universe."

Frank grinned. "Yeah, don't worry, Jack. We'll explain it was an emergency sewing job ... a stitch in time that saved nine!"

About the author: Iain Pattison is a full-time author, creative writing tutor and competition judge. His short stories have been widely published in Britain and the US and broadcast on BBC Radio 4. His book *Cracking The Short Story Market* (Writers Bureau Books) is a best seller. www.iainpattison.com

SCATTERBRANE
WILLIAM WOOD

Kincaid stumbled on the sidewalk, but stopped himself from falling by planting his shoulder into a brick wall to his right. The disorientation brought on by the transition was fading and his senses were beginning to process the environmental data evolution had intended. Temperature and pressure, light and sound, odors and—

He coughed hard.

—oh, yeah. Pain.

The gnawing cold in his gut was subsiding quickly, as it always did. In no time, he'd be right as rain.

In no time. He smiled and wiped away the spittle from the corners of his mouth with the cuff of his overcoat. Looking up into the harsh noonday sun, he sighed.

Summer this time. A scorcher by the feel of it.

The road in stretched left and right, bracketed by storefronts. The signs were mostly neon, but that didn't narrow it down much. Neither did the parking meters along both sides, except they only took nickels and dimes. And the cars looked old, but he'd never been good with that sort of thing.

A teenage boy in jeans and a t-shirt strolled by, quickening his pace after glancing Kincaid's way.

I must look like crap, thought Kincaid. "Hey, kid, what year is it?"

The kid turned his head to avoid eye contact and moved even faster down the street.

Yeah, that's the way to do it, moron, Kincaid chastised himself. *How long have you been doing this now? Oh, yeah. Who knows?*

There was no one else on the street. No newspaper boxes or phone booths. No traffic. Kincaid mopped beads of sweat from his forehead.

A muffled clatter of dishes came from behind and he turned to see a middle-aged woman looking back at him through a plate glass window. She wore a pink button-up shirt with a wide white collar, an apron, and a little hat. She flashed him a smile he was almost sure was sincere. The oddness clinging to him that had scared off the teen, didn't seem to faze her. But she was a waitress, after all.

He looked up. The sign over the door announced simply, MANKO'S. Righting himself, Kincaid straightened the wrinkles from his overcoat with a sharp downward tug and stepped into the fluorescent lights of the greasy spoon.

The interior was all chrome and stainless steel-trimmed Formica with padded stools placed evenly along the counter and rows of booths running along the windows and walls. Elvis sang about love from a jukebox in the corner and Kincaid wondered if the King were still here, not that it mattered.

The 1960s in some rinky-dink little town in Middle America, maybe, but that didn't feel quite right either.

"What'll it be, sugar," asked the waitress. She wasn't as young as he'd thought when he'd first seen her from the street. The glare on the window had had a year shaving effect on her face that the mirror behind the counter did not have on his own ugly mug. Gray hair that needed cutting and deep wrinkles across his forehead that needed forgetting looked back at him.

The waitress interposed herself between him and the mirror, leaning in close, eyebrows raised, trying to get his attention. She reeked of cigarettes and too much perfume. *Charlie* by Revlon, if his memory served. Funny how well he remembered scents from his childhood, but so little else. Yeah, that was the funny part of all this.

He shook his head to clear it, a corner of his mouth turning up in a wry smile. "Sorry. I'm afraid I've forgotten most of my manners over the… years."

"Haven't we all, hun? So, what's it gonna be?" She smiled, taking up a pen and an order pad from the countertop, striking the timeless stance of the only-just-barely patient waitress. Her nametag, pinned low on cleavage a few boxes of Twinkies too big for her blouse, read Betty.

Besides himself, she and one guy sitting at the bar with his back to the door were the only people in the place. His stomach cramped and he winced, reminded of winter and the place *between*. He didn't want to yet. Not until he knew he was going to be around more than a few minutes. He had trouble keeping food down if he ate to close to a transition, coming in *or* going out. And arriving in a new place and time puking his guts out never made for easy greetings with the locals.

"Fine," said Betty. She produced a coffee cup, filled it from a steaming pot, and slid the cup across the counter toward him. "For while you think about it. And take off that coat, would ya? You must be burning up in that thing."

Kincaid grabbed the lapels of his coat and looked down at himself. He should relax a little. And the coffee smelled great. The thought of something warm in his stomach was too much to resist.

He watched as Betty disappeared through two swinging doors into the kitchen. He placed his coat on a stool beside the other man and sat on the next stool himself. Taking sips from the mug, he felt his shoulders slump and the tightness in his neck eased several orders of magnitude. He'd not realized how tense he was until he'd begun to relax.

"Just passing through?" asked the other man.

Kincaid looked up from the shimmering black liquid in his cup. "Yeah, you could say that."

The other man was in his twenties, dressed in slacks and a button-up shirt. Kincaid was taken aback by the man's icy blue stare. He'd seen those eyes before but in a much older face. "What brings you to Waynesburg, Mister...?"

"Kincaid," he supplied automatically. Waynesburg? Who had he known from a Waynesburg?

"I'm Latimer," he said, nodding and smiling for the first time, as if the mere exchange of names somehow set all well with the world again.

Latimer? Kincaid sputtered, coffee dribbling down his unshaven chin. "Doctor Joe Latimer?"

The young man's smile evaporated into a look of surprise and suspicion. "Joe, yes, but I'm not a doctor yet. Do you know me?"

Kincaid placed his coffee cup on the counter with an unsteady hand. The transitions had always kept him close to home, close to family and friends even. A connection was almost always apparent if he dug enough, although some had been in times and places he not been able to figure out in the duration of his visit, which varied wildly from minutes to days. Truth was, in many visits lately, he'd not even tried. But if this was Joe Latimer—*the* Joe Latimer—this might be his only chance. Kincaid knew he was not a young man anymore, subjectively speaking. Sooner or later, he was going to die.

"Doctor—I mean, Joe... look, I don't really know how to say this but—"

"Spit it out, old timer," said Joe.

Kincaid smiled. "You're about twenty-five or so?"

Latimer nodded.

"And studying physics?"

Latimer brow furrowed and he leaned back crossing his arms. Taking a slow sip from his own coffee, he nodded.

"Now here's the crazy part." Kincaid took a long slow breath. "Forty years from now or so, you'll have a student and you will propose some pretty radical ideas about the way the branes are stacked—"

"Branes?"

"Parallel dimensions. Alternate realities—anyway, forty years after that, the student will build a machine—a time machine based on those theories. That student will get ripped out of time, sent bouncing along unable to return to the primary timeline—"

"Whoa, whoa, whoa." Latimer laughed. "So, eighty years from now some poor sap is going to build a *time machine* and get himself lost in time?"

Kincaid nodded.

"You?"

"Yes."

"Okay, buddy," said Latimer, standing and placing a few bills next to his coffee cup. "I've really got to get back to my parents' house. They're giving me a ride back to school tonight and—"

"Doctor Latimer, I'm still aging—subjectively—if I don't figure out something soon, I'm going to die bouncing from one place, from one time, to another."

Latimer's shoulders slumped and he stepped closer to Kincaid, placing a hand on his arm. "Your theories. Maybe…" Kincaid racked his brain, his memories, for any inspiration. He might never meet up with this man again, in any time period. But what could he do, now? He was hardly more than a kid.

A buzz came from his pocket and Kincaid growled in anger. "No, not now!"

"What's that?"

"A detector that lets me know when a transition's coming." He dug in his pocket and placed the slick, black slab on the counter. Swiping his finger across the glassy face of the device, he silenced the buzz. With a few more strokes of his finger, a three dimensional graph sprang into the air above the device. Waves of dots swirled, coalescing into a pulsing red spike.

Latimer stood transfixed on the floating display before flopping down onto the stool again. "You're… serious."

With a heavy sigh, Kincaid nodded and placed the device back in his pocket. "It's too late now, anyway."

The young man stared into future student's aging eyes as if unable to believe his own. Kincaid watched his future professor's expression shift through multiple emotions, settling on resolve. "But now I can do this. I can figure a way to help you. Forty years is a long time to work out what went wrong. I can—"

"You can't." Kincaid stood and pulled on his coat. The next transition might be the dead of winter. He never knew.

"Sure I can. I know the basic problem—"

It was Kincaid's turn to place a consoling hand on the younger man. "Turns out time doesn't work that way, Doc. Your theory was always that whenever a time traveler arrived in a new time, a new branch would form. A complete new timeline would form in addition to the original. Where there was one before, there would be two. The original and the one created by whatever changes the traveler influenced. You could never truly go home again since you'd be on a new stream, but you could live out your days in the new one."

Latimer's face was a study in confusion and ideas still too

big for his growing intellect. "So… your problem is that you keep bouncing from one to the next? Never settling down?"

Kincaid shook his head. "If only. As near as I can figure after… years of jumping, is that there is only the primary timeline. The only thing we do by traveling is fray that timeline."

"Fray?"

"Yeah. The primary timeline continues, but now a strand is formed that sticks out a little like a piece of string."

"And the traveler—you—are trapped on the strings?"

"Exactly."

The kitchen doors swung open and Betty bustled toward them, adjusting her blouse for maximum cleavage.

Latimer met Kincaid's gaze. "So what happens when you get to the end of the fray you're trapped on?"

"Hey, fellas!" Betty leaned over the counter, flashing her smile and smacking the point of her yellow Bic pen to an order pad. "You two haaaave time for a… nother cup…of…"

Kincaid's mouth twisted into a grimace and he fought down the urge to scream as he had so many times before. Beside him his old college professor—who wasn't even old yet—was frozen still, a wisp of steam from fresh coffee hanging in the air near his face.

Numbing cold radiated from his stomach as if he'd swallowed a cup full of ice cubes, whole.

"No, Betty. I really don't."

About the author: William Wood lives and writes in Virginia's beautiful Shenandoah Valley from an old farmhouse turned backwards to the road. You can visit him at http://writebrane.blogspot.com/

BIRTHDAY
GREGORY MILLER

He could trace his motivation back to a single memory. All the years of work and toil; of diligent research and public ridicule; of failure, despair, more failure, and, finally, after half a *century*—

Success.

Seventy-six years old to the day, hair white, skin pale, eyes rheumy, David Halburn sat back in his swivel chair and looked at what stood before him.

A time machine.

"Thomas Wolfe, eat your heart out," he murmured through dry lips. "I'm going home again."

***

"Mommy, what's that man looking at?"

David's sixth birthday party breathed magic. Outside, the world grew green and smelled of warm earth, flowers, and bees. Sunshine fell through white curtains, heating the yellow carpet, illuminating chubby faces of kindergarten friends. His house, huge in mystery and secure in safety, blazed with banners, streamers, balloons and confetti. In the center of the living room, a great birthday cake with "E.T." carefully drawn on the top in icing awaited inevitable destruction. Chocolate ice cream sat cooling in the freezer. Wrapped presents, bulky in ways that promised Transformers and GI Joes, Star Wars figures and He-Men, rose up on the coffee table like an offering, a celebration, a reward for being born.

In the hallway, children played "Pin the Tail on the Donkey." In the den, an ATARI 2600 blipped to the tunes of "Pitfall" and "Tron." In the living room, his father, quick to laugh and easy with life, detached his thumb with causal aplomb, then wiggled it to applause. And sitting on a chair while his mother tied his shoe, David stared through the open bay window and wondered aloud about the strange man in the street.

His mother, still girlish in early womanhood, looked where he was pointing and smiled. "It's just an old man," she said. "He's probably thinking about all the fun we're having in here."

The old man stood in the street, staring at the house, an odd expression on his face. David looked again. Their eyes met.

"He looks sad," he said.

"Maybe he's remembering what it was like to be young like you," his mother said, turning back to the offending shoelace. "Maybe he doesn't have anybody, and seeing your party makes him think back on happier times."

"Will I ever be old like that?" David asked.

His mother leaned forward and kissed his cheek.

"Not for a very, very long time," she said. But that wasn't the same as "never," and David knew it.

Then the call came to light the candles on the cake, and for a long, long time—many years—his sorrow was forgotten.

***

But time, whatever else one may say about it, is dependably punctual. Years passed as surely as clockwork, taking with them seasons, family, friends, and any feelings of security he had once possessed. True, it gave as well as took; wisdom, perspective, knowledge, maturity, and love all found their way into his life when he wasn't looking, and all were welcomed. Yet loss, that feeling of watching sand run through your fingers all the faster as you try to stop it, became first a dim background distraction, then an annoyance… and then, finally, an obsession.

Favorite places changed. Favorite people grew old and passed away. Summer faded against a background of work in windowless rooms. Winter, no longer a wonderland, became a battleground for deep-freeze wars with cracked carburetors and icy roads.

And then…

Then…

David's father called his apartment, voice quavering, heavy

with the news that his mother was riddled with cancer.

"This isn't supposed to happen," David told her as she lay in her hospital bed and tried to smile. "You're not supposed to die."

"Funny, I thought the same thing!" she said softly. Her laughter became a long series of wracking coughs before trailing off.

"Grandma Rose and Grandpa Ted, Aunt Emily and Uncle James. My rabbit, Flopsy. My dog. Two dozen pets and half a dozen relatives. Five friends. All of them gone, each loss a chip with a chisel, a tap with a hammer. I'm being worn down by death, Mom. And you—"

"Me," she repeated.

"A great sledgehammer blow that will shatter me to pieces." Tears rolled freely down his cheeks.

"David."

He shook his head.

"David, look at me."

He raises his red eyes, and only then did he remember that long-ago birthday party so deeply buried beneath other memories.

"This is the way of the world," said his mother, her voice drifting up into the room from a far-away place. "It's natural. A mother isn't supposed to outlive her son. Time rolls around and the great game continues, but with other players, each possessing a part of those who came before. You live in me, I live in you."

"It's damned unfair, Mom," he said. "Everyone says it's the way of things. I don't care. It doesn't make the loss any easier."

"You don't have a choice," she murmured, strength fading away. "*That* makes it easier."

We'll see, he thought, even as he nodded and tried to smile. *We'll see*.

***

The time machine wasn't, of course, a constant project. He tinkered with it now and then, here and there, but always it was in the back of his mind, a comfort, tantalizing, a bright spot to stave off despair. He married, had children of his own, and watched them grow. He didn't worry as his hair turned gray, didn't pine away as his little girl married, didn't flinch in the face of clocks.

Once it's done, I can see it all again whenever I want. The thought sustained him through long years and short, bad years and good.

Unlike Jay Gatsby, he had no illusions about repeating the past. Childhood was gone. The years behind were more numerous than the years ahead. But to be able to chat with his grandfather, pet his old dog, see his children young again, watch his mother laugh—*that* was the great desire, the burning hope. He was fervently convinced that loss was responsible for old age, more than anything else. To skip back and forth, skimming the surface of time like a rock across a still, clear pool—it would be a retirement gift fit for the gods, a chance at peace such as he had not known in a long, long time.

Now, a palsied hand caressed the cool metal skin of the device, finally finished. Gently, two brittle legs stepped into the machine's small chamber.

David closed his eyes, smelling the oiled gears, taking stock of a million choices.

After long moments, silent save for the tick of his watch, he brushed his hands across a series of buttons, pulled a lever, twisted a dial, and, eyes still closed, held on tight.

***

1994, he thought, looking out. *A good year.*

More than anything, he wanted to see his mother. She wouldn't recognize him, of course, and he wouldn't say anything to even remotely suggest who he was.

On his sixteenth birthday, the teenaged David had been in Florida visiting friends over Spring Break. His father would be at work. His mother?

Home.

He stepped out of the machine, which had materialized in an empty lot at the top of his old street.

A man with car trouble, that's who he was. Could he use the

phone? And she would say yes, and he would be inside his childhood home again—once more part of the world he had left behind, if only for a moment. During that moment he would breathe in the ambiance of living memories, feel the near-silent hum of youth reborn.

He whistled as he walked down the street, past the old, familiar houses that would eventually be demolished to make way for a new bypass, past the trees that smelled, for one glorious week a year, of apple blossoms that carpeted the street and paved the sidewalk with delicate white petals.

I remember when they were cut up by the construction men and uprooted by the bulldozers, he thought.

He breathed in, smiled, exhaled, and continued on.

His house, when it came into view, shocked him. It was far, far smaller than he remembered. Yet it felt familiar, like an old pair of shoes not worn in years that still retained the contours of his feet. It felt familiar, and that meant comfort. It was *right*.

But what *wasn't* right were the cars in the driveway. And the E.T. balloons tied to the mailbox. And the children who laughed and played beyond the open front door.

No one is supposed to be here but Mom, he thought. *Not in 1994.*

He stopped, lost in thought.

Which means... which means...

This isn't *1994.*

One inadvertent jerk of a finger, one wrong number. He should have paid closer attention.

Twenty feet away, his sixth birthday party was in full swing.

Just a quick glimpse, he thought, still planning on making that phone call. *Yes, a broken-down car, that'll do.*

His eyes, slightly glazed, focused again.

His mother sat framed in the great bay window, tying the shoe of a small boy he almost recognized.

"Mom!" he screamed, heart pounding. All thoughts of concealing his identity were instantly forgotten. There she was, young and healthy and smiling and full of life. "Mom, it's me!" he called out.

But all that issued up from his throat was a whisper.

I want my mother, he thought, and took a heavy step forward.

The child he almost recognized turned and caught sight of him.

"Mommy, what's that man looking at?"

His breath caught in his throat.

No, he thought numbly.

"He looks sad," the little boy said.

"Maybe he's remembering what it was like to be young like you," David's mother responded. "Maybe he doesn't have anybody, and seeing your party makes him think back on happier times."

"Will I ever be old like that?" little David asked.

His mother leaned forward and kissed his cheek.

"Not for a very, very long time," she said.

The offending shoelace now firmly tied and double-knotted, David and his mother rejoined the party. In the background, a dim shadow, his father placed candles on the cake, whistling cheerfully.

Outside, in a sunlight that didn't seem as warm or as bright as he had once remembered, David turned, smiling faintly, and walked slowly back up the street toward a time that was his own.

He missed it very much.

About the author: Gregory Miller's stories have appeared in over two dozen national publications. His first collection, *Scaring the Crows: 21 Tales for Noon or Midnight*, was published in 2009 by StoneGarden.net Publishing, and has garnered positive attention from such luminary authors as Piers Anthony, Brad Strickland, and Ray Bradbury, who recently wrote, "Gregory Miller is a fresh new talent with a great future."

Lightning Source UK Ltd.
Milton Keynes UK
30 September 2010

160589UK00001B/47/P